Twisted Lies

GHOST TOWN TRILOGY
BOOK THREE

VM RHEAULT

Brock

The moment I picked up Olivia's friend from the airport, I knew my life would never be the same, but like the characters in a sad music video, I've been unlucky in love.

Agatha is beautiful, compassionate, and kind, and she understands my creative eccentricities in a way my ex-wife never did.

I try to resist, but I fall desperately in love. I want to ask her to stay, but Eddie's been snooping into Derrick's past and what he finds out won't be good for me. Derrick may be dead and buried, but his secrets aren't . . . and neither are mine.

Once the truth is exposed, I'll never see Agatha again and Shep and Eddie won't want anything to do with me. My money can buy a lot of things, but it can't buy forgiveness and that's the one thing I need most of all.

Agatha

Brock's a locked box and I want the key. He says he won't like what I find, but I'm not worried about that. The pain in his eyes and his broken heart tell me all I need to know.

The longer I visit Liv and Sheppard, the more entangled I get, and I want nothing more than to stay in California and build a life on my terms.

But there are things I'm running away from, and they'll catch up with me.

Nothing in my life has been mine, but because of my twisted lies, Brock won't be either.

He's one of the most famous rockstars in the world, and when I finally tell him the truth, I'll walk away and never look back.

And I know, without a doubt, he'll let me go.

Chapter One

Brock

"Can you pick up Agatha from the airport?"

I look away from Scout's big brown eyes to Olivia who's standing just inside the living room. Since Clarissa and Mason moved into Eddie's house, I've been spending more time at Shep and Olivia's. They're just as new to the relationship thing, but lying on their couch with Scout on top of me doesn't seem as intrusive as plopping my ass at Eddie's. He wouldn't mind if I lurked, but hanging out here is different somehow—at least, Olivia hasn't complained about feeding me like a stray pup looking for a forever home.

"Right now?" I ask reluctantly. It's a small thing she's asking for, but I don't want to entertain an old lady I have nothing in common with, which I know will be my job considering I have nothing else to do.

I have plenty *to do*: articles and music to write, movies to watch and dissect for plot holes. My head is exploding with ideas and lyrics, blog topics and quarter notes, and I push them all back like I always do, a constant pressure behind my eyes.

"Her flight lands in an hour, and I have to sit in on an unexpected conference call with Gina. I would ask her to order a car, but that doesn't seem very hospitable, especially since I kind of forced her to visit." Olivia lifts a corner of her mouth in sympathy, apologizing for inconveniencing me.

I push back a sigh. "Yeah, sure. It's no problem."

"Thanks. I'll grab her flight information and text her you'll be picking her up. You can bring Scout, if you want. I hate to break up your date."

"Funny." I nudge the Golden Retriever off my chest, and she jumps down and heads immediately to the patio door. Olivia doesn't ask me to let her out, but I do and follow her onto the sand.

The wind is warm, the waves brushing the shore. The endless expanse of blue is a metaphor for the melancholy I feel inside. Deep, dark parts unexplored and untouched by another human. Too menacing for anyone to try to reach.

Scout rests a paw on my thigh and whines.

"Yeah, I know. Come on."

Olivia's waiting with a piece of paper held loosely in her hand. "Her flight lands at 1:19. Terminal 4, Gate 42B, Baggage T4A, whatever that means. Will you be able to find it?"

"Yeah, sure." Traffic around there is a bitch, but it's nothing I'm not used to.

"Thanks." Her phone chimes, and she glances at it. "I better go. Gina's wondering where I am. I'll be back by the time you drop her off. I really appreciate it."

"Where's Shep?" I ask, and under the question is, *Why can't he do this?*

"He's at a therapy appointment, or I would have asked him to go."

Heat crawls up my neck. I thought he was in the den

working out a song. I've been bothering Olivia all morning and didn't know.

She squeezes my arm. "I like having you here."

"Right," I mutter. "Come on, Scout. You can help me look for the old ba—girl."

Scout yips, happy to be invited along, and I hurry out the door. It's one thing to bum a couch off Shep, another to be in Olivia's way. I need to get used to sitting at my house by myself, even if I can't stand my own company.

It's almost an hour from Shep's to the airport, and I'll be cutting it close if her flight lands on time. I don't drive around much—from my place to Shep's and back again—and I try to appreciate the sun and fresh air. I keep the top down, and Scout sits in the passenger seat, a grin on her face. It's difficult to stay low around the dog, and I rub her neck. I hope Agatha doesn't mind the top down, but if the wind messes up her old lady curls, I can put it up. Maybe she'll sleep on the way to Shep's, and I won't have to say anything to her.

Vehicles fill the streets around the airport, and I keep a close eye on the exit signs. I haven't been to LAX in a while—when we went on tour, we didn't fly commercial.

A crowd's gathered on the sidewalk outside the terminal's baggage claim, weary travelers who want to finally reach their destinations. Dirty buses clog the road, and their engines cloud the air with toxic fumes. There's just enough space, and I'm able to park at the curb. I turn my hazards on and hope one of the buses picking up passengers to carry them to the car rental offices doesn't sideswipe it.

I scan the people waiting, searching for an older woman. "Where is she, Scout?"

Scout props her front paws on the passenger side door, panting in excitement.

A woman with long, greyish-white hair pushed away from

her face with a headband steps from the baggage claim area, dragging a large suitcase behind her. A gigantic purse hangs from her shoulder. Wearing a navy blue blazer, matching skirt, and sensible shoes, she definitely looks like a literary agent, and I slide from behind the wheel to help her load her luggage into the car.

"Agatha Sterling?" I ask, reaching for her suitcase. "I'm Brock Farris. Olivia asked me to pick you up."

She frowns. "Get away from me."

I step backward, bumping into someone who impatiently elbows me in the side. "I'm sorry. I can put your luggage into the trunk of my car."

"I'm not going anywhere with you. Fuck off," she says in a tone that does not go along with her kind, grandmotherly appearance.

My patience thins. "Olivia asked me to drive you to their house. If you don't want to ride with me, please text her and tell her you'll order a car."

"I have a ride. My grandson is picking me up. I might be old, but I'm not senile yet, young man, and you are not him."

"Scout!" a clear, feminine voice exclaims behind me, and I jerk my gaze toward my car. A slim, *young*, black-haired woman is hugging Olivia's dog, her face pressed into Scout's snout.

Confused, I ask the older woman, "You're not Agatha Sterling?"

She glances over my shoulder to the woman hugging Scout. "I am not." She narrows her eyes. "You know what you are for assuming."

I've been called an ass many times in my life. "I do. I'm sorry for bothering you."

She scoffs. "Perhaps open your mind."

"Yes, ma'am," I say, but I haven't had an open mind for

years. I keep it locked up, otherwise all my demons will come out to play.

Tentatively, I approach the woman rubbing the area between Scout's eyes. I know how much she loves it—I do it too. "Agatha Sterling?"

"That's me," she says, turning her body fully toward me.

Her scent drifts in the air, sugar and maybe a hint of chocolate, and I grasp her hand. "I'm Brock Farris. Olivia sent me to pick you up."

"It's nice to meet you. Olivia's told me a lot about everyone," she says, trying to pull her hand away.

"Oh, sorry. Ah, these yours?" I release her and gesture to two silver suitcases sitting behind us.

"Yes, thanks."

I store them in the trunk while Agatha stands uncertainly by the car. Scout's in her seat, and I point to the back. Scout whines but does what she's told, and I open the door for Agatha. She slides in and nudges off her heels. I think she mutters, "Fuck," but that sounds unladylike and maybe I misheard.

She reclines the seat, covering her eyes with an arm, and I sit behind the wheel and carefully meld into traffic.

"You wouldn't happen to have a drink, would you?" she asks, not looking at me.

"What? Are you an alcoholic?" I sound like I'm teasing, but if she's got a booze problem, Olivia didn't tell us.

She lifts her arm just enough to glare at me. "No. You can drink on the plane. I don't like flying, and I'm a bit nauseated."

"You're not going to throw up, are you? If you have to, can you do it over the side and not in my car?"

"You're a real gentleman. I'm not going to puke."

Chuckling, I wait until I'm at a stoplight and feel around

under my seat. I pull out a flask and toss it into her lap. "Have at it."

"Jesus Christ on a bicycle," she says, but she unscrews the cap and takes a long swig. She sighs and wiggles in the seat, her dress's hem inching up a lean thigh.

"Better?"

"Definitely." She lifts an eyebrow. "Maybe I should be asking you if you're the alcoholic. Not everyone keeps a flask under their seat."

"Just like a drink now and then," I say, tearing my gaze away from her leg.

"Right." She sips again and screws the cap on.

She doesn't give it back.

I shake my head.

Scout pokes her head over Agatha's shoulder, and Agatha gives her another kiss. "I missed you, baby," she says, and Scout licks her cheek.

"Are you staying for a while?"

She closes her eyes and melts into the seat, the booze doing its job. "For a couple of weeks. Sometimes you just need to get away, you know?"

"Yeah. You're lucky you have a place to go."

Agatha opens her eyes into slits and shifts, sitting on a hip, her cheek pressed into the back of her seat. Her hair is an inky black, her eyes a sparkling blue, and her skin is clear, a light bronze, as if she spends time outside sunbathing. A scarf is tied into her hair, and the ends flutter past her shoulders. The pink is the same shade as her dress, the neckline showing off a hint of cleavage. I check her left hand still wrapped around the flask. She's not wearing a ring, but that doesn't mean she's not taken. "Aren't you part of Ghost Town?" she asks, "or am I wrong?"

"I am," I say, easily passing a car not going fast enough for my taste.

"Then you should have plenty of places to go."

"No one to go with. You're visiting a friend."

"A friend who moved half a country away to marry a rock-star and pop out his babies," she says, but she doesn't sound bitter.

"You miss her."

She sighs and unscrews the flask's cap. "Yeah."

We don't talk after that, the traffic too loud to hold a comfortable conversation. Agatha closes her eyes, hopefully in fatigue rather than motion sickness, and the breeze teases her hair. I want to brush it out of her face, but it wouldn't do any good. She hugs the flask to her breasts, and her skirt slides farther up her legs.

Maybe keeping her company while Olivia works won't be so bad.

"You know how to play poker?" We're nearing Shep's house, and I slow down.

She rubs her eyes and grins. "You got money to lose?"

"Sure."

It's all I've got.

Chapter Two

Agatha

Brock's nice, but not everyone keeps booze in their car. There's a story there, and I'll dig it out. I am my mother's daughter, for all the good and bad that entails. It was amusing watching him try to herd an old lady into his car. I get that a lot, and I wasn't offended. My mother thought she was being traditional, naming me after her grandmother. My name doesn't even have a good nickname to go with it. I hate "Aggs" and "Aggie" so don't call me that unless you want me to punch you. "Hey, A" is just as nasty. It's Agatha or nothing, and it's a mouthful. But sometimes, late at night, when I've had enough to drink and a man whispers it across his pillow, it sounds pretty, turning the harsh syllables into something more.

Then the booze wears off and he goes home.

Brock parks behind a black and white two-stall garage. I recognize it from the pictures Olivia texted me. Reluctantly, I offer him the flask.

He pushes it back at me. "You better keep it. Shep doesn't have alcohol in his house."

"Oh. Right. Liv told me about that." I shove it into my purse. "Thanks."

"Tell me when you need a refill. I'll smuggle you some more."

"You have no idea how much I appreciate that." I meet his gaze, and the pain in his eyes surprises me. I didn't get a good look at him at the airport or on the drive here. Now there's nothing but the birds flying overhead, Scout's panting, and the clicking of his cooling engine. "Do you have a headache?"

"I always have a headache. Come on. I'll grab your bags."

"Thank you." He doesn't wait for me to ask him anything else, and he's popping the trunk and pulling my suitcases out of the back before I can unlatch my seatbelt and put on my heels.

Scout hurries ahead of us, and Brock opens the door between the garage stalls. He's tall compared to my five-foot, four-inch frame. I'm about the same height as Liv, and I always understood when she would sigh over how safe Michael made her feel. I, too, have always dated men much taller than I am, but it isn't his height or his weight, or how much scruff he keeps on his jaw. It's his hands, and the truth they tell when he touches you. It's the words he whispers in your ear that you want with your whole heart to believe.

Brock leads me up a short set of stairs and opens a door revealing a hallway of blonde hardwood. He sets my suitcases on the floor and gestures me to follow him. Scout dashes inside, and she's gulping water from a bowl near a set of sliding glass doors by the time we step into a large kitchen. Liv and Sheppard are standing next to a breakfast bar, and my jaw drops. "Oh, my God, look at you!" It comes out in a cheesy whine, but I can't stop it. "Aren't you California dreamin'." Her hair is lighter than it was in Minnesota, and she's put on weight that she needed. I hurry to her and give her a tight hug.

Even she didn't know how worried I was about her the past

three years, or how I pushed her to take this job to help her see there was more to life than grieving.

I haven't seen her since the day I drove her to the airport. I was too busy with a crumbling book deal when she and Sheppard flew to Minnesota to be at her mom's wedding ceremony and to put her house on the market. She spent as much time as she could with her sister, and the night before they flew out she called and made me promise to visit, heartbroken we couldn't see each other before she moved to California for good.

"The color's a little lighter," she says self-consciously, fluffing her hair. "Gina's hair stylist went overboard with the highlights."

"It looks great. You look amazing. I'm so happy for you, Liv. And you," I say, turning to Sheppard. "I don't have to kill you and throw you off a pier after all."

"No, no, there's been plenty of that," he says, giving me a hug. "Don't need an encore."

"Shit. I am so sorry." Liv's kept me up to date on the things that have happened. I've read some fucked up memoirs, but what's been going on here beats all of them.

"Don't worry about it. How was your flight?" he asks, and I step out of his embrace.

"Good. Kind of. I need a glass of water and to lie down for a bit. You know." It would be nice if they could show me where I'm going to sleep, and we could save the catching up for later. I want to change out of my dress and heels and breathe. I'm not a good traveler, and Liv understands, having travel anxiety. I don't have anxiety, only a severe dislike of flying, but I wasn't going to pass up a chance to see Liv and escape some of my own problems, not to mention my mother, and I tolerated the long, stressful day.

Liv winces. "Actually, something came up. Sheppard's

mom and brother planned a spur-of-the-moment visit and want to stay with us. I'm so sorry."

I'm disappointed, but that's not such terrible news. Sheppard, and now Liv, have a ton of money, and the accommodations will be five-star. I'll have to rent a vehicle as soon as possible; I don't want to depend on anyone for rides.

I wave it off. "That's fine. I'm sure there are plenty of hotels around here."

"You don't have to do that, you can stay with me," Brock says, leaning against a counter with three stools underneath it.

He gave us space to have our mini-reunion, and I turn in surprise. Happy to see Liv again, I almost forgot about him. "Oh, but I shouldn't. I don't want to be in your way."

"It will be easier getting booze to you," he says, and a corner of his mouth tilts upward.

"Well. That's convenient." It will be. I wasn't sure how staying in a dry house would work for me.

"That's great," Liv says, not at all perturbed by our exchange. Maybe she can smell the whiskey on my breath. "I didn't invite you out to stay alone in a hotel." She looks around me to Brock. "Why don't you take her back to your place, she can get settled in, and we'll meet up for dinner? Sheppard's mom and brother should be here by then and we'll make a party out of it."

"Sounds good," Brock says, pushing away from the counter.

I hug Olivia again; I missed her so much. "This was such a good thing," I whisper in her ear.

She leans away with tears in her eyes. "It's hard to let go."

"Yeah, it is. I'll see you later."

I follow Brock, my suitcases once again clutched in his hands, out to the driveway.

It *is* hard to let go. Especially if the person you're running from won't let you leave.

"You live here all alone?"

Brock's house is huge, two sprawling stories and more grass than a city park.

"It's considerably smaller than what I used to live in when I was married," he says, opening his door and climbing out, tired, maybe, after spending two hours on the road to pick me up. He pops the trunk and yanks my suitcases out of the back. It's better Sheppard's family is arriving on the same day I flew into LA. Once I unpack, I want to stay put until I fly home.

The front is grey brick and glass, with two white pillars supporting an overhang and flanking the front door. There are trees and shrubs everywhere. He leads me up the sidewalk and opens the entrance, letting me in ahead of him into a spacious foyer. A skylight sparkles sunshine onto the tile, and I look around with interest. I live in a two bedroom apartment in downtown Minneapolis. While I make decent money selling books, there's no way I could ever afford something like this—even adjusted for the cost of living.

"What's it like, having money?" I trail my fingers over a painting's frame that looks expensive.

"Doesn't matter how much you have if you can't buy what you want."

"You mean women. I'm sure there are plenty who would want to be with you for what you have."

I've experienced that, a time or two. Men who wanted to be with me because of what I do. They thought my job gave them respect and social status in creative circles. In the literary world, my success is prestigious and they would boast who my clients are and the book deals I've done, but it never lasts long.

Not when they peel back the layers and realize all I really do is read manuscripts, do market research, find books to fit a niche, and go to bed early because I have a headache from sitting in front of a computer for twelve hours a day.

"I mean this," he says, setting my suitcases onto the floor. He yanks me against his hard body, a hand to my lower back, and grazes his fingers across my cheek. "When you feel a pull that won't let you go. When you crave someone with all your heart, and she reciprocates. When she sits in your lap and snuggles into you like there's nowhere else she'd rather be than in your arms. When, if you lost every penny you have, she wouldn't care because she's not with you for that. That's what you can't buy."

His forehead is wrinkled with the headache he hasn't shaken, his brown eyes shadowed. His beard is tinted red and it's turning grey, but he doesn't look old, only distinguished in the way men do when they age. The sunshine brings out the red in his hair, shorter on one side than the other. If he wore a plaid flannel shirt instead of his Aerosmith t-shirt, he'd look like a burly lumberjack, not a guitar player for the most famous rock band in the world.

I could be scared of him, this close, a man I've only known for a couple of hours, but I'm not. He's hurting too much on his own to hurt me. "How long have you been divorced?"

"Too long but not long enough. I'll show you a couple of bedrooms and you can choose. My daughters each have one, but they never stay here."

"You have kids."

"Two girls, Lexi and Layla. People think they're twins, but they were born twelve months apart. They're fifteen and sixteen now and not interested in hanging out with their old man."

He tries to pass it off, but I can hear how much it hurts. "What did your wife think about that?" It couldn't have been easy having kids back to back.

"Lexi was delivered by cesarean. After the doctor pulled her out, he tied Brianna's tubes. That's how she felt about that."

We use a wide winding staircase to the second floor, and at the end of the hallway, Brock pushes a door open. I step into a bedroom decorated with a queen canopied bed and mahogany furniture. Sheer curtains that match the bed's canopy frame a large window that looks over his backyard. A pool glimmers in the sun and a firepit built into the ground sits off to the side surrounded by gorgeous grey brick and comfortable-looking furniture. "I'm sorry. You wanted more kids."

"I wanted the choice to have more kids. She took that away from me, but it wouldn't have mattered. The kids I have now don't want anything to do with me. I doubt having more would have made a difference. What about you? Do you have kids?"

I rest my hand against the window picturing a family playing in the pool, steaks on the grill. How idyllic and nothing I came out here for. "No. I'm not the maternal type."

"Might change your mind when you meet Mason. Will this bedroom be okay, or do you want to see another?"

"This is fine. Thank you. Who's Mason?"

"Eddie and Clarissa's son. He just turned eleven months old. Cute little kid. Breaks your heart when he cries."

"Right. Liv mentioned them, but it's difficult to keep track of everyone. Having faces to go with the names will help."

"I don't know if you'll meet them tonight, but you will eventually. I'll let you unpack then." He pauses. "I'm sorry about downstairs. You have no reason to trust me, but I won't hurt you."

"I know. Just keep me stocked with booze and we'll be

fine." I smile, try to joke, but I'm tired too, and just want to use the bathroom, take a few more sips of the whiskey he already gave me, and lie down.

"That's easy enough. I'll give you a tour before we head back to Shep's. You're free to go anywhere you want. I've been told I'm . . . eccentric. If you hear something odd, don't worry about it."

"Odd like sacrificing goats in your backyard odd?"

He laughs. "No. Not being able to sleep at night odd. If you hear me moving around, just ignore it. We'll leave about six. You have a couple of hours."

"Thanks."

He closes the door and I sink onto the bed, relieved I can turn myself off. I've never minded meeting people. It's what you do when you're an agent, what you do when you go to bookfair after bookfair, meet editor after editor, talk to author after author, in person and on the phone. Meeting Brock wasn't a big deal—I haven't met many people as famous as he is, but I've met my share of celebrities, Liv among them, though she would disagree. I'll meet more people tonight, by the sounds of it, and a couple of hours to myself to recharge is what I need right now.

I drag my purse onto the bed and gratefully pull out Brock's flask. It's good whiskey and I sip, letting the booze trail a comforting burn down my throat. My cell rings, and I pull that out too, my heart hitching when I see who's calling. My number one reason for this trip to LA was visiting Liv and spending time with my best friend. Number two was this man, and I reluctantly answer.

"Graham. What do you want?"

"Agatha, please tell me you didn't mean what you said."

"Of course I meant it or I wouldn't have said it."

"I miss you. It's only been a day and I miss you." His voice is low, sad, and sincere. He honestly believes what he's saying, and that was always the problem between us. His lies weren't lies because in his mind they were the truth.

"I'm sorry. I'll be back in two weeks. I need this. Don't ruin it."

"If I do, it's only because I can't stop calling. I need to hear your voice."

I cap the flask and lie back onto a fluffy pillow. I can't fight the smile that finds its way onto my mouth. I used to live for these conversations, when he'd sit in the station's parking lot and use the burner phone he hides in his glovebox to keep his phone calls to me a secret. I convinced myself it was romantic, our forbidden love.

"We weren't working. You know that. Let me move on."

"No. We'll have it out when you get back. I know I've broken promises. Let me fix them."

There's no way he can. "I'll let you know my flight information. You can pick me up and that's it. You're hurting me."

"I'll stop. I love you."

"Goodbye, Graham."

"Say it back," he pleads.

I disconnect. I can't say it back.

I stopped loving him, even if it feels like only minutes ago.

"Are you ready to go, or would you rather stay here? I can beg off for you if you're jet-lagged." Brock leans against my door-frame, his arms crossed over his chest. He changed into a different pair of jeans and a denim button-down shirt.

I dozed, pushing back tears and misery that didn't let me fall completely asleep. I wish Graham wouldn't have called. I hate myself for liking he's thinking about me. "No, I'll go." I sit up and rub my eyes. I don't want to cry in front of Brock. "Should I change?" I'm still wearing the dress I wore on the plane.

"Olivia and Shep aren't fussy," he says. "Do you have shorts and a shirt? That's all you need. I don't know if we'll set up a fire on the beach, but if we do, no point in getting a dress sandy."

"She's pretty settled, isn't she?"

Brock tilts his head, agreeing with me. "Did you want her not to be?"

"No. You didn't see her after Michael passed away. I'm happy she's found what she needed here."

"But?"

I slide off the bed and lift one of my suitcases onto it. They both hold the same thing; it doesn't matter which one I choose. "There's no but," I say, unzipping the top and flipping it open. "I would be a shitty friend."

"There's always a but. But you wish she wouldn't have found her place so far away. But you wish she would have more time for FaceTime calls. But you wish it would be easier to travel to see her, because flying sucks and I can see it doesn't agree with you. You don't have to take away what she found for there to be a but."

I pull a pair of denim shorts and a white button-down blouse out of my suitcase. I hold them up. "Okay?"

"Yeah."

"Can you undo my zipper?" I turn my back to him.

His fingers graze my neck as he grapples with the little piece of plastic, and he yanks the zipper down. Cool air hits my skin and goosebumps travel over my body. "How did you dress yourself this morning if you need help? Do you have a room-mate? A boyfriend? You're not married."

I laugh. "No, not married. No roommate, either. I would just prefer if you didn't watch me contort like a circus freak." I shimmy out of my dress, leaving it in a puddle at the foot of the bed, and yank on my shorts. I seriously don't care he's standing there. If we use his pool, my bra and panties don't cover any less than my bikini will.

I tie my white shirt into a knot at my belly, leaving a sliver of skin exposed, and flip the scarf that was in my hair onto the floor with my dress. Standing in front of a dresser that has an attached mirror, I gather my hair into a bun and fasten it with an elastic I kept around my wrist. Rolling up the sleeves of my shirt to my elbows is the last of it. I could reapply my makeup but I don't bother.

Brock hasn't moved.

"What? Are you going to get weird on me now? I don't have anything you haven't seen before. You're a rockstar. I'm sure you've seen your share of T & A."

"Just enjoying the view, angel. Come on. I'll show you where everything is."

"And booze," I remind him, digging a pair of white sandals out of my suitcase.

"Yes. And booze. My bar and my wine cellar."

I brighten considerably. "You have a wine cellar?"

He pushes back a smile. "You act like you don't have alcohol in Minnesota."

"Look," I say, brushing past him to step into the hall, "life is hard."

"Yeah, it is." He hooks an arm around my neck. "Yeah, it is."

Since we're already here, we start on the top floor. He doesn't open the doors that belong to his daughters, keeping their memories locked away. I don't know when they visited last, and I don't ask. It's obviously a sore spot, and if I have a chance to talk to his ex-wife, I will. How much he hurts breaks my heart, and I barely know the guy.

There are more guest bedrooms, but I don't regret the one I chose. It's only for two weeks, and I doubt I'll spend much time there other than to try and sleep. The bed is comfortable and that's all I care about, but he didn't need to warn me about his nightly activities. Chances are I'll be awake to hear them.

"Where's your room?"

He shrugs and we backtrack down the hall. He opens a door to what I thought was a closet tucked into the corner and steps inside.

The suite is enormous. A huge king four-poster bed sits between two windows that create the entire back wall. The en suite bathroom is as large as my entire bedroom at home. The bathtub is the size of a hot tub. Maybe it is. The shower stall is huge, the sides made of clear glass. Nothing will hide you if you shower here.

"This is a beautiful room." I look out the window and see the same view I saw from mine. Our bedrooms are across the hall from each other. Maybe that's why he didn't show me his. He didn't want to scare me.

"It doesn't see much action."

I don't think he means sex. I smile sympathetically, but he's already retreating and misses it.

Downstairs is beautiful, too. His living room is gigantic and looks over the yard the size of the entire block my apartment building sits on. The pool shimmers, the grass a brilliant green. The picture of the family spending an afternoon outdoors isn't far from my thoughts, a day I don't think Brock has ever had in this house.

Attached to the room is another living room or den, maybe. I don't know what people call their rooms here. It's definitely not a family room. Sunroom? Except, thick curtains cover all the windows and the only furniture in the entire space is a couch and a gleaming piano. "Is this where you write music?" The piano calls to me, and I sit on the bench. The instrument shines, and I would bet my career it's perfectly tuned. I place my fingers where I think they would go.

"Do you play?"

"No. Your parents have to nurture that part of you, don't they? When you're small. My mother didn't care if I could play the piano. She had my whole life mapped out since the day I was born, and music wasn't a part of it."

"What about your dad?" he asks, sitting next to me.

I lightly press a key, and the note hangs in the air. "I don't have one. I mean, obviously. But my mother wanted a baby and went to a sperm bank. She knew exactly what she wanted and browsed in a catalogue for the perfect donor. She shopped for me like a pair of heels."

"If she loves you, that's all that matters."

"Yeah," I say to stop talking about it. "Your parents supported you?"

"Yeah. My mother described me as a strobe light. Flashing and fast, too bright. I could play any piece set in front of me by the time I was ten years old. My mind was always speeding in a hundred different directions at once. I couldn't sit still. The high school counselor encouraged me to go into the military. She said the rigid schedule would do me good, but I said no. I wanted to stay with my friends."

His arm brushes mine, and I turn my head. He's inches

away and it would be nothing to lean just a little and press my lips against his. "That turned out to be a good choice."

"That, angel, depends on who you ask. Come on."

He shows me a library with a sleek computer, fireplace, and shelves upon shelves of books. The room is so cozy I would love to sit and read manuscripts in it. With a cup of coffee, it wouldn't even feel like work.

The wine cellar isn't a cellar, but an entire room. He pulls a bottle of red off the shelf. "We'll bring this with us. Shep's mom is a lush."

I bark out a surprised laugh. "You're joking."

"Nope. If you like to drink, stick with her. She plays a wicked hand of poker too, if you weren't kidding you can play."

"I can, but I don't have a very good poker face."

He grips my chin between his thumb and forefinger. "You have a very pretty face."

"Thanks. Not so great for poker though. I can't lie."

"Sometimes that's a good thing."

He leads me into another room, and I suck in a breath. "A theatre."

"Well, we posh people call it a viewing room. I get all the movies before they come out. I used to write reviews for the *Los Angeles Times*."

"Used to? Why did you stop?"

"Bri didn't like the time it took away from her. So I quit."

I flop onto a couch equipped with beverage holders and prop my feet up on another couch in front of me. This is how to watch a movie. "Why didn't you start it up again after you divorced?"

"It's difficult to do things alone. When no one supports you."

I understand that. Before Graham, the only person I had to

tell of a lucrative book deal was my mom and all she would say is, "Do it again."

The soft leather is supple under my butt and I wiggle. "It doesn't sound like she supported you," I point out. "When you're a creative, sometimes the only person you do things for is yourself, married or not. I see it over and over again with authors I represent. They want outside validation, but until I offer to sign them or sell their book, there's no one. If you let her make you quit so easily, maybe you didn't like it. Can we watch movies in here?"

"That's what the room is for," he says wryly.

"Cool. How about *Jaws?*" I get up and join him at the door. We need to leave or we'll be late.

"Sure. I've got all four."

"Awesome. Tomorrow?"

He laughs. "All of them? In one day?"

"Why not?"

"No reason. I thought you were here to see Olivia."

"I will. I mean, I am. She has work. I do, too. I brought a couple of proposals to look at."

"Between shark killing sprees."

"You do what you gotta do."

I hold the wine on the way to Sheppard's, appreciating the view more than I did before. I've been to California a couple of times, for business, never for pleasure, and I want to enjoy my time here. I'm steadier, if not a little jet-lagged, my body's time clock two hours later. Maybe I'll actually get some sleep tonight. Before I get out of the car, I check my phone. Graham texted me. *I miss you.* That's it. A simple I miss you. I used to fall for it, the minimalist phrase stark and romantic. Now I realize sometimes it's all he has time for before having to hide his phone. Nothing meaningful. Nothing heartfelt. Just *I miss you.* Right.

I shove my phone into my purse. Brock's waiting for me by the car's front bumper, and I force a smile.

"Everything okay?"

"Yeah. People, you know?"

"That I do."

With a hand resting between my shoulder blades, Brock leads me into the house.

Chapter Three

Brock

"I need to talk to you," Eddie says, meeting us at the door. "Hi," he says to Agatha and then to me, "right now."

"I'll meet up with you later," I say, nudging Agatha toward the kitchen. Olivia's there with Clarissa and Abby looking over papers that no doubt have something to do with EmpowerHer, Inc. Shep's sitting at the kitchen table with his mom and brother, bouncing Mason on his knee. It's a lot Eddie trusts Shep with Mason after his display at Dalt's.

Dalt and Melody are missing, but I didn't think they'd be invited. I'm due to drive up to his house and check in. It's the only way I'll see them now.

Agatha frowns and lingers, her fingers brushing my arm, but Olivia gestures her over. "Okay," she says reluctantly.

"Who's that? Where's Agatha?" Eddie asks, jerking his head toward the patio. "Scout. Let's go outside."

Scout lifts her head in hope. She doesn't like crowds, and she bounds to her feet, eager to hit the beach.

"Hi, Mrs. Carpenter," I say, leaning over Shep's mom's

shoulder and kissing her weathered cheek. I haven't seen her for years, and her presence makes me miss my own mother with a sharp jab of longing I haven't felt in a long time. I spent a lot of time at Shep's when we were kids. My mom's chocolate chip cookies were better than hers, but I never told her that. "I found you a drinking buddy, and I brought your favorite red."

Shep laughs. "Don't encourage her."

"He very much needs to encourage me. I'm on vacation. Thank you for thinking of me, dear." She looks at me, her eyes twinkling, happy to be with her two boys again.

"It's emotional support, and she's right. She's on vacation. It's nice to see you, Tony." I offer my hand. He liked listening to us jam at Dalt's, and at the beginning, he would be the only person in the audience.

Eddie's waiting impatiently by the door, and he slides it open when I'm done.

Scout bolts out of the kitchen and onto the patio, her claws searching for purchase against the wood in her excitement.

Eddie and I follow but at a slower pace. "That *is* Agatha."

"Oh. I pictured . . ." He smiles in self-deprecation. "She's pretty. She's staying at your place since Eunice and Tony are here?"

"Yeah. I said I wouldn't mind."

"If it bothers you, she can stay with us."

"I already warned her I don't sleep. We'll give it a few days. She's here for two weeks." I don't want to sound like her sleeping at Eddie's would be a big deal, but I already like the idea of hanging out with her. She'll fill some of my time.

"Just let me know. Clarissa and Abby have been busy decorating and replacing the furniture at the house. You'll have to come by and check it out."

"Yeah, I will. I suppose we'll be doing a lot of this kind of thing," I say, gesturing toward Shep's house. "He looks good."

"He doesn't know everything." His voice is tense, and his jaw is set.

"Why do I feel like I don't, either?"

"You don't."

"Does anyone know everything?"

Eddie shakes his head.

"Great. We'll need a Venn diagram to sort through all the shit."

"You're not wrong." He picks up a stick half buried in the sand and throws it, and Scout happily runs after it. "I didn't want to tell you this in front of Shep. When Clarissa and I broke up for that minute, Abby blamed the band."

"It *was* the band. You didn't want Shep to know you were in love with her. I'm sorry Clarissa had to leave for you to understand Shep's approval isn't everything."

"Yeah, well, it was just history repeating itself. Do you remember that garden party? It was at Arnold Griffin's house. The girls were five or so."

Scout runs back to us and offers me the stick, dropping it on the sand in front of my feet. I bend over, pick it up, and whip it as hard as I can. "That was a long time ago, and we went to a lot of those things. Why?"

"He had the huge topiary shapes in his yard," he says, trying to jog my memory. "It was a month before Shelly filed for divorce."

I shake my head. That was about the time Shep and Melody married, and it was one party after the next. "Sorry."

"Doesn't matter, but that night, Derrick raped Shelly."

I stare over the water. Ten years ago, the girls had just turned five and six, a week apart. We always celebrated their birthdays together, and that year was no exception. We'd thrown them a huge party, complete with pony rides and a gigantic bounce house in the shape of a pink and purple castle. Things were already over between Bri and me, and looking back, I'm not sure how we lasted another three years. "Shit. I'm sorry. She didn't tell you."

He sighs. "No. She didn't want to break up the band."

"We can't know that it would have."

"It would have. If Shep wouldn't have kicked him out, I would have left. Either way, we wouldn't have been the same. I loved her. There was nothing I wouldn't have done for her and Abby."

Scout drops the stick in front of him and paws at his thigh. She always knows when someone is hurting.

He rubs the fur along her neck and throws the stick again. She runs after it, enjoying the game.

"Shelly didn't let me see Abby after the divorce because she was keeping her away from Derrick. Since he's no longer a threat, she told Abby she could visit me again—whenever she wanted. She's living with us through the school year. I missed her so much." His voice cracks.

I know how much he missed his daughter and hated Shelly for keeping her from him. Now that he knows the truth, he can let the past go. I'm happy for him, but I understand what Agatha's feeling with Olivia here in LA. Her buts don't take away from Olivia's happiness and my buts won't take away from Eddie's, but it's difficult to stay in one place when others are moving on without you.

"Because Shelly and Bri are friends, I thought maybe Bri was doing the same. It would be worth talking to her."

Shelly wouldn't have told anyone what happened. Not even my ex-wife. Secrets never stay secrets in Hollywood. I'm not calling Brianna a snitch—things just have a way of getting out. Shelly must have come clean with Abby so Abby would understand why she wasn't allowed to see her dad, but if Shelly was smart, and I know she is, no one but Shelly, Abby, and Derrick knew what happened that night.

"Sure. Thanks. Let's head back."

"Come on, Scout," Eddie calls, and the dog bounds over the beach, sand spraying under her paws.

Olivia took Mason's place in Shep's lap, and he hugs her close while they talk to his mom and brother. I haven't seen him this happy since Ghost Town was at the height of our fame and he and Melody were newlyweds. This is a quiet kind of joy, Shep sitting at the table with family who had drifted away, a woman who's content to walk the beach with her fiancé and dog. Shep found something different with Olivia, and at a time in his life when he needed it.

Agatha's holding Mason, the little boy perched on her hip. Her hair is out of its bun, Mason's hand twisted in the glossy black strands. She's talking to Clarissa and drinking a glass of wine, but she looks tired. I'll check in with her later. There's plenty of time for things like this and we can leave early if the evening gets to be too much.

"Can we have a quick meeting?" Shep murmurs, suddenly at my side.

I'm surprised he'd want to do business during a family function, but I say, "Sure." It must be something important if he's willing to let it pull him away from his mom and brother.

I trade a glance with Eddie, and he purses his lips. Okay. It's not about Ghost Town. If he doesn't want to talk about the band, there's only one other thing it could be.

Fuck.

We follow Shep into his hidden den and he closes the faux wall. The sounds of the party fade, the room soundproof, and I take my place at his piano like I always do when we have a sit-down. The notes are like cool water over my scorched skin, and the melody I made up for Eddie's song flows through my fingers. I like it, and I like more Shep told Eddie to sing it. The three of us getting equal time will be different and adds to the pressure behind my eyes. I haven't written any material for the new album, and my voice is rusty.

The keys are smooth under my fingertips, the notes pure. I could let the music drown me; it's so tempting to let it sweep me away. It would be fitting to let what I've lived for kill me.

The guys let me finish, and Shep says over the last note, "They let Sharyn go." He sinks onto the coffee table.

Eddie clenches his jaw.

Shep doesn't know Derrick raped Shelly, but what Derrick did to Clarissa should be enough for Shep to renounce their friendship. When we were on the beach, I should have asked Eddie if Shep at least knows that. Eddie can't expect Shep to see his side of things if he doesn't have all the information.

"What were they trying to charge her with?" I ask before Eddie explodes.

"Prostitution and concealment of a crime. She admitted she found women for Derrick, but the DA's office doesn't have what they need to arrest her unless some of the women she found for him to abuse come forward and say Sharyn paid them off to keep quiet." He glances at Eddie. "Clarissa said she's willing to give a statement, but that won't be enough. Derrick's dead. This is about Sharyn, not what Derrick did to Clarissa while he was alive."

My heart slams and my fingers shake against the keys.

This is not good for me.

I have a date tomorrow night, and I forgot all about it with Agatha staying at the house. Sharyn sets me up weeks in advance. I have my evenings scheduled until Christmas.

"Sharyn won't serve any time if they try to move forward with only a prostitution charge. Her attorney will get her off with a slap on the wrist and a fine. I wanted her in jail for covering up Derrick's shit, but the woman I know who could give a statement worth any weight is too scared." Eddie's angry.

Shep spreads his hands. "Then we might just have to take what we can get. If she has other clients, maybe she keeps a paper trail, but unless the cops have enough evidence for a warrant to search her house, it won't matter."

"I'll talk to Clarissa. If she can promise her friend she'll have her legal representation paid for if she needs it and protection from any retaliation Sharyn may dish out, she might go along with it. If not, maybe we can find other women who would be willing. I don't know. He did this for years, Shep. With her help. Someone should pay for that."

It's on the tip of Shep's tongue to say Derrick did pay for that, with his life, and God, I hope he shuts the hell up. Derrick's fall has little to do with this.

"He can't do it anymore," I say quietly. "Maybe you need to leave it there."

Eddie whips around and glares, but I meet his stare. We've been friends for a long time, and we're closer to each other than other members of the band. I will always have his back, but after it comes out that I've used Sharyn's "services" so to speak, I don't think he'll always have mine.

To my surprise, he says, "You're right. I have Clarissa and Abby's in my life again. I'll never have to protect Mason from that son of a bitch. Let Sharyn sell her ugly jewelry in that swanky store she paid for with Derrick's money. I don't care, but if there is ever a chance for me to expose what she's done, I *will* take it."

"That's fair," Shep says, rubbing at his scruff, "but we can't do anything about it now. What do you say to a jam session tomorrow? We gotta get going on this album. I want to wrap it up. Liv will feel better. She's skittish, and so am I. I want to marry her."

"Then do it. Your mom and brother are here. Agatha's here. Fly her mom and sister out, and get it done," I say, liking the idea. If the cops dig up more shit, Shep will be in a better place if he and Olivia are legal.

Shep tries to tamp back a grin and fails. "I like it, but I don't know if she will. I'll talk to her. But for now, practice, and you don't have anything yet?" he asks me.

My headache grows, icepicks ramming at my brain. "No. Not yet."

"Get to it. We've got two that will be good enough, but we need more. Let's meet up tomorrow for a bit."

"I can't. I'm busy."

Eddie frowns. "Doing what?"

"Agatha and I are having a *Jaws* marathon." I leave out what I'll be doing after we're done watching eight hours of sharks mauling people.

Eddie laughs. "Is that a euphemism of some kind?"

"I don't know what you do with Clarissa in bed, but that doesn't describe what I do in mine." I laugh to smooth over some of the sting. Eddie will always be touchy about Clarissa and how Derrick treated her when they were married.

"Of course it doesn't. When was the last time you had a woman in your bed? Maybe I should warn Agatha you're starving. It's closer than you think, buddy."

Shep shakes his head. "Okay, enough. If you're hungry, we're eating dinner soon. But get on writing something. Both of you. I figure three each and one we do together. Then we call it quits and move on."

Move on to what? I want to ask, but Shep and Eddie are already walking toward the door. Shep pushes it open and laughter fills the silence.

Out of sorts like I usually am these days, I sit on the beach rather than try to glue a smile onto my face for Shep's family.

Scout lays next to me, and I test feelings, run emotions through my head I can put onto paper that won't make me sound like a complete jackass. I have nothing to write about but how lonely I am and I don't know what, or who, can fill that need. I want the things I told Agatha about earlier this afternoon, but neither of the women I pay to spend time with have flipped a switch. I want fire and passion; I want what all the love songs are about. But under it, I just want a woman who can love me despite what a fucking trainwreck I am.

I don't move from the beach until Agatha stumbles onto the sand, her face pale. "Can we go?" she asks, her voice paper thin.

I'm not sure what happened in there, but without asking, I tuck her under my arm and drive her home.

Chapter Four

Agatha

"Agatha, this is Clarissa, Eddie's fiancée, and his daughter, Abby. Abby and Clarissa, Agatha, my literary agent and good friend."

Olivia introduces me to a little blonde and a teenager who isn't any taller. Clarissa's eyes are such a light blue they look grey, and her hair is wavy, like Olivia's. She's beautiful, her features petite and perfect. She's the epitome of a California girl, and I'm instantly jealous.

"It's nice to meet both of you. I've heard a lot about you," I say, doing the feminine hand-hold instead of a brisk shake I'm used to giving clients and editors at book conventions.

"Same. I envy you," Clarissa says wistfully.

"You do? I can't imagine what for." Not when she's gorgeous and is going to marry Eddie Conrad, drummer for the hottest rock band practically ever.

"Your job. It sounds so cool, doesn't it, Abby? Selling books people all over the world will read."

Abby wrinkles her nose. "Not really. I like animals. Do you work with any animals?"

"Nope. The closest I've come to that is when I sold a coffee table book about dogs. I don't have any pets. I don't have time to take care of them." Whenever I needed a pet fix, I visited Liv and Scout. When Liv was mourning, I stopped by every day to check on both of them.

"Clarissa's working with us to launch EmpowerHer, Inc, and we were going over a few things. I was hoping you could tell her the best formatting and publishing classes to take. We're going to print our own handbooks," Liv steps in smoothly.

Hmmm. Liv's a life coach, and from what she's told me, Clarissa used to manage a bar and doesn't have a college education. Maybe there are some self-esteem issues Liv's trying to waylay.

"Being an agent can be lucrative, but it can be a huge pain in the ass, as well. I can suggest some software to look into, if you're interested. Right now?"

"No, we have plenty of time for that," Liv says. "This is supposed to be a party."

Clarissa forces a smile that looks more like a grimace. "That would be great. Daytime is best—I'm training in a few girls to run the bar I used to manage and I'm busy from late afternoon until about ten in the evening every night. I need to go to the bathroom before Sheppard gets tired of holding Mason. I'll be right back." She excuses herself and dashes off. Abby follows her and flops onto the couch in the living room, pulling out her phone from the back pocket of her jeans. I empathize with her. My mother used to drag me to grown-up functions, too, and I always felt bored and out of place.

"I'm so sorry about the bedroom situation. Sheppard was thrilled Eunice and Tony wanted to drive down, and he didn't want to put them off," Olivia says when we're alone.

I set the bottle of wine on the counter, and my mouth waters. I'm not an alcoholic, but I never turn down something that can make me feel better. Even if it's only for a little bit. "It's fine. Brock's house is crazy. Have you seen it? He has his own movie theatre."

"No, I haven't yet. Sheppard and I went to Eddie and Clarissa's a couple of weeks ago, but I've been so busy with the book, my blog, and EmpowerHer, Inc, that we haven't done much else." She sounds a bit frazzled.

I lean in and hug her. "Breathe. You know how happy I am for you, don't you? When you called and told me you were flying back to Minnesota, my heart broke into a million pieces."

"When I thought Sheppard and I were done, the only thing that kept me going was knowing you would be there for me. Since the moment I met you to discuss my proposal, I've considered you my best friend." She pauses. "I'm pregnant."

I brush a piece of hair away from her face, needing to touch her in some way to offer support. "Why do you sound scared?"

She shrugs and flicks Sheppard a glance. He's happy talking to his mom and brother, a baby sitting in his lap I assume is Mason, a tire pressure gauge of all things clutched in his fist, drooling. "I wanted to be married. I don't want to tell my mother until we are, but things are crazy."

"Oh. Sheppard doesn't know."

She shakes her head.

"Then you need to talk to him. Tell him you're going to have his baby and want to be married first. Call your mom—her new husband can marry you. How romantic twill that be?"

"Do you think so?" Tension pulls at her eyes.

I hate seeing her this way. "Sheppard would fly to the moon and pull it out of the sky for you, Liv. Why are you acting like giving him what he wants is a bad thing? You're wearing a huge rock and you're going to give him a baby. Tell him tonight, when you finish making love and you're lying in his arms. It's what those moments are for. Michael didn't use them. He wasted those precious seconds. Don't do the same."

She drags in a breath. "You're right. Let's open this. I mean, I can open it, and you can have a glass. I'll introduce you to Sheppard's mom and brother. Are you sure you don't mind staying at Brock's? I hated the idea of them staying at a hotel. It's been years since Sheppard's seen them, and when they asked, he was so relieved they wanted to spend time with him."

"It's no trouble, none at all. Don't think about it anymore."

Clarissa hurries out of the bathroom and lifts Mason out of Sheppard's lap. He's disappointed but doesn't complain. Liv shouldn't have any doubts that Sheppard will want their baby.

Liv uncorks the wine bottle and slides two stemless wine-glasses onto the counter. She fills them each half way. "I'm going to sit with Sheppard for a bit. Will you be okay?"

"She'll be fine," Clarissa says, approaching us. "I want to pick her brain before Abby gets too bored and wants to go home."

"After the day I've had, I feel like a truck ran me over, but I'll do my best." I sip my wine and set the glass onto the counter just in time to have Mason fling himself from Clarissa's arms into mine.

"Yikes." Unaccustomed to holding children, I'm lucky I didn't drop him.

"Sorry about that. He likes people. And hair."

Somehow, his little fingers find my elastic and loosens my bun. I help him the rest of the way and shake it out. He laughs, tangling his fingers in it.

"You don't have to worry about him being a boob or leg man. He'll be all about the hair." I flinch. The kid's got a grip.

"He'll be like his daddy, then," she says, blushing.

Graham liked my hair too, asking me to pin it up into

elegant twists to expose my neck. Then he would kiss me, leaving behind little love bites I'd have to cover with concealer. I brush it off. I don't want to think about him. I left my phone in my purse and dropped it near the door. I don't want to check any messages or email. I want to enjoy my time away.

Clarissa and I talk about publishing while I bounce Mason on my hip. Liv delivered Sheppard's mother her wine and curled up in his lap. She's content, smiling at something Sheppard's brother said.

Brock, Eddie, and Scout come into the house from the beach, and Brock glances my way. He and Eddie must have spoken about something serious. Eddie's face is set, his eyes stormy, his lips stiff.

"What do you think they talked about?" I murmur.

Shep nudges Liv off his lap, and he joins Eddie and Brock. They walk past Abby and disappear around a corner.

"Probably Derrick. Do you know about him?" Clarissa asks, stealing my wineglass and adding more from the bottle that's already close to empty. She sips.

"Yeah. Liv told me a few things. I'm sorry. I've never been in an abusive relationship."

Not physical.

"Eddie saved me. He loves me and loved Mason even when he thought he was Derrick's. I'm lucky."

I squeeze her arm. "You and Liv."

"What about you?"

"Oh," I say, waving her off. "I just went through kind of a nasty breakup, and he's not taking it well. My vacation was good timing, and it will give him a chance to cool off. We weren't going anywhere—I just admitted it first."

"You're brave to leave like that. It's hard to be alone."

I reach for my wineglass that looks very comfortable in Clarissa's hand. "That's not what I heard about you."

She lifts her chin. "Eddie hid us because he was afraid of what Sheppard would think. I won't live like I'm a piece of trash. I told him if he wasn't proud to be with me, he didn't deserve me."

Graham hid me too. Dark corners in bars, hotel rooms reserved under a different name. "I understand that."

"There were other reasons he didn't want to say anything. Leaving forced him to tell me what they were. He was scared I couldn't love him after I knew, but I only loved him more."

"That's usually the way things work. The more you know, the more you love."

A lovely blonde woman knocks on the sliding glass door and lets herself in. For God's sake, is every woman I'm going to meet a gorgeous blonde?

Her eyes land on me. "You're Agatha Sterling."

I'm taken aback to say the least. "I am. And you are?"

Liv bounces from her seat. "This is Gina Baker, Jeffrey Morgan's fiancée."

"Oh, right. Liv's told me a lot about you. She's working with you on a documentary."

Gina strides across the kitchen, passing Sheppard's mom and brother without giving them a glance or even a slight smile, her eyes locked in on me. "She is. And you would be perfect to help me finish it off. I put the whole project on hold to create EmpowerHer, Inc with Olivia, but I need to complete it quickly if I want to enter it into the awards track next year. You have just what I need."

Blood pounds in my ears, and I grip Mason. I know exactly what she wants to talk to me about. "I would prefer to not."

Gina smiles sympathetically. "Please, let me at least talk to you about it. You don't have to commit to anything."

Clarissa frowns. "What is she talking about?"

"Something I really, really want to forget," I mutter, passing Mason to her. "I'll give you five minutes."

"Thank you. You won't regret it."

I meet Liv's eyes. "I already do."

Gina leads me across Sheppard's living room, lifting a hand at Abby, and we settle in a corner made of floor-to-ceiling windows. The ocean is a beautiful view, but it doesn't calm my nerves. We sit on a couch, and I drag a pillow into my lap. She tucks her legs under her and opens her mouth to speak, but Sheppard, Brock, and Eddie step out of a hidden room in the rear of the living room. Brock doesn't look any better than he did after talking to Eddie, and he lets himself out onto the beach. I'm not the only one going through a tough time, but knowing that doesn't boost my spirits.

"What has Olivia told you about my documentary?" she starts.

I know plenty about Gina's documentary. She's been filming women who have failed in their careers in some way but were able to bounce back. I can only imagine how tough talking about something like that was for Liv. She blamed herself for Michael's death, and it wasn't until I convinced her to come here and she worked with Sheppard did she understand it wasn't her fault.

"Enough I don't want to participate. What happened to me could happen to anyone."

She leans toward me, her face shining with earnest. "But see, that's *why* I want you in on this project. Things like that *can* happen to anyone, and if you're a role model and can help women understand that, you're doing so much good."

I get where she's coming from. I really do, but that was a

very difficult time for me. My whole career, my entire professional reputation as an agent, was called into question because of a mistake I made that wasn't even a mistake when I made it.

"What would you say to a woman who's going through what you did?" she prompts when I don't respond.

I think about that for a while. What would I say to a woman, maybe someone like Clarissa, who wants to know how to fight back? "That there's light at the end of the tunnel? That having someone in your corner can be the difference between coming back stronger than ever and not coming back at all?"

"Who did you have in your corner, Agatha?"

"No one. I had no one." That shoves Liv into a bad spot, but she was mourning Michael. She didn't have time for my bullshit. That doesn't give Graham any credit, either, but our relationship isn't for public consumption and I can't talk about it in a documentary that hundreds of thousands of people will watch.

"Then it's even more impressive, and more *imperative* that we work together." Gina squeezes my arm. "Think about it. Run it by Olivia and ask her what she thinks."

Against my better judgment, I say, "Fine. But I've tried to put it behind me. Your documentary will keep it front and center."

She smiles. "Maybe for a little while, but what you do with that will be up to you."

"Yeah, and I've already dealt with it. I'll get a hold of you through Liv. It was nice to meet you." I try to sound friendly, but my tone suggests it was anything but nice. I stagger to my feet and find Liv in the kitchen. She's checking on a gigantic tray of lasagna I couldn't eat without throwing up. "I need to go. I'm tired and it's been a really long day."

"Are you feeling all right?" she asks, closing the oven's door.

"No, I'm not, but a shower and some sleep will help a lot."

"I understand. I'm not great with traveling, either. Where's Brock?" She scans the kitchen.

"I saw him go out to the beach. He looked upset after talking to Sheppard and Eddie, and I don't think he'll mind I want to go."

"What do you want to do tomorrow? We can go shopping or have a picnic on the beach. Eddie and Clarissa said we're welcome at their place to swim if we want. Their pool is gorgeous. You can lie out in the sun all day."

"Ummm. Brock and I are going to watch *Jaws*." Not that I don't want to see Liv, but a day to relax before I start filling my hours with people will be nice.

"You should have plenty of time. I can pick you up."

"Ah. No. All of them."

She blinks. "All of them. How many are there?"

I force a grin. "Four."

She opens her mouth to say something, then presses her lips together. She sucks in a breath, but stops. "Okay. Text me when you're not . . . busy."

I have no idea what's going through her head, but that's nothing I can add to my plate right now. Hugging her, I say, "I'm happy for you. I'm going to be an honorary aunt. Tell Sheppard tonight."

"I will."

I say hello and goodbye to Sheppard's family, goodbye to Eddie, Clarissa, and Abby, and gently kiss Mason's cheek with a thank you for not ripping all the hair out of my head. I trudge through the sand, tired and sad, maybe homesick too, but I don't know why because no one is waiting for me to go home except my mother and only because my vacation is a huge inconvenience to her. "Can we leave?" I ask Brock.

He's hunched over, his arms looped around his knees, staring into the horizon. He looks up at me and nods. He wraps his arm around my shoulders, and just for a second, I lean on him.

"Are you hungry? Did you eat something?" he asks, letting us into the house. I dozed in the car, and my stomach churns.

"I had some wine and that's it, but I don't think I could eat. I need a shower and some sleep. It's eight here but ten inside my body and past my bedtime."

There's a hint of concern in his eyes, and he reaches toward me then drops his hand. "If you need anything, just ask."

"Thanks." I hurry up the stairs and into my room. Brock didn't specifically say I could use the bathroom attached to it, but I don't see why I can't. I start the shower in the pretty white and light blue room, the bulbs over the sink a soft glow. While the water runs, I dig for my nightgown and a fresh pair of panties.

I feel tremendously better after a hot shower, and I stood under the spray for longer than necessary. I towel my hair dry and drink a gallon of water using a plastic cup sitting on the sink. There's a hamper in the corner, and I toss my towel into it. Brushing out my hair, I try not to look in the mirror. My skin is pasty and dark shadows rest under my eyes. I should pop a sleeping pill and see if I can't get in a few good hours of sleep. I dig the pill bottle out of my suitcase, but holding the little blue tablet in my hand, I decide not to. Maybe tomorrow night, if the stress of traveling and the time change doesn't help me fall asleep tonight.

I move my suitcase off the bed and settle under the comforter with a couple of proposals. My mother was extremely upset I cashed in some vacation time, though I earned two weeks off after selling a famous makeup artist's how-to book in a fantastic deal. She might even have forbidden me to go if I had wanted to visit anyone but Liv. She admires Liv—and miracle of miracles, actually felt sorry for her when Michael passed away—but I think she admired what Sheppard did for her career more than anything Liv has ever done for herself. That's Mom. Exploitation at its best.

In the middle of a sentence, my eyes drift shut, and I dream of bananas.

I roll over, paper crinkling under me. Bananas. Why am I dreaming about bananas?

My eyes flicker open, and I reach for my cell. Graham texted me last night right before I fell asleep. I didn't see it, but that's not what I'm looking for now. The time. What time is it? A little after three in the morning.

Bananas.

I inhale. Not bananas. Banana bread.

I slide out of bed and tug on the robe that matches my nightgown. I peer into the hallway, but no one is there. Faintly, I hear a piano, but the notes aren't pretty and light. They're hard and sharp, full of pain and anger. Leaning against the wall, I stumble down the stairs, not fully awake.

There's a high-pitched beeping, and I shuffle into the kitchen. The oven's on, and the timer's shrieking, unhappy being ignored. I turn it off and open the oven's door. Two beautiful loaves of banana bread are positioned exactly on the middle rack. I open a couple of drawers but don't find oven mitts and using a hand towel instead, pull them out, using another towel in place of potholders or a cooling rack.

The sink's a disaster, dirty measuring cups and bowls. I turn off the oven and wash everything, the heavy notes full of pain and fury rattling my bones. I should let him be.

I should, but I don't. I dry my hands and follow the music into his sunroom.

Brock's hunched over the keys, his head bowed.

Slowly, I approach him, and when I reach him, cover one of his hands with mine. "Stop."

"I can't get it. I can't make it sound right," he mumbles.

"You need a break."

His hand trembles under mine.

"Pour me a drink and show me your pool."

Without a word, he slides from the bench. He doesn't look back to see if I follow, but I'm there when he pours two high balls of whiskey at the bar. I like them, rimmed with gold, golden leaves circling the glass. What my grandmother would use to entertain guests.

The air is hot and sticky, and the lights in the pool shine. The water shimmers. It broke my heart the day I learned pool water isn't that blue, that the walls and bottom are painted that way. I was ten or so, I think, when I found out, and ever since then swimming has never been the same.

We sit at the edge and I dip my feet in. "It's warm."

"Heated," he says, his voice low and rough.

I lift the glass to my lips and laugh. "Right."

He sips then swears. "Shit. I have something in the oven."

Resting a hand on his thigh, I say, "I rescued them. Can I have some for breakfast?"

He relaxes. "Sure. I'm sorry if I woke you up."

"It's good." I tuck my nightgown between my legs and kick. A heated pool. After *Jaws*, maybe I'll go swimming.

"Brianna hated it."

"Banana bread?"

"That I baked it in the middle of the night."

I lift a corner of my mouth and meet his eyes. "Don't you need rotten bananas for that?"

He chuckles. "I bought a bunch a week ago and forgot I had them."

"Right."

"You didn't look happy at Shep's."

I lift a shoulder. "You didn't either."

"There are a lot of things we're keeping from him. About Derrick, mostly. A lot of balls in the air. Some of them are mine, some of them are Eddie's. They're all going to fall, and none of them are going to bounce."

"Liv's pregnant. That will perk him up."

"Yeah, it will. You want to meet Melody and Dalt while you're here?"

"Why not? I'd like to meet the man who started this whole thing."

"Now it's your turn."

I sip. It's very good booze, but I shouldn't have expected less from a rockstar. "Gina Baker wants me to be in her documentary."

"Isn't she doing something on people who have fucked up?"

"Yep. Yep, she is."

"What did you fuck up?"

I nudge his arm. "What did you?"

He grimaces. "Can we not go there?"

"Absolutely."

We sit until the sky turns pink, sipping on our drinks, kicking our feet. Tension drains out of him. The birds start singing, and he slumps in fatigue.

"Let's go to bed."

"Together?" He stands and offers me a hand. I grasp it, and he pulls me up.

He's not talking about sex, maybe wanting to prolong the quiet we felt sitting, not speaking.

Peace.

"Why not?"

There isn't any anticipation; we don't hurry upstairs. We

place our empty glasses on the bar, and slowly, deliberately, giving me every chance to change my mind, he leads me up the staircase and down the hall. He pushes the door to his bedroom open and lies on the bed. I didn't notice before, but this room, too, has blackout curtains attached to the windows. He lowers them, and we're in complete darkness.

I crawl onto the bed with him, settle between his legs, and rest my cheek against his chest.

And just like that, I'm out cold.

Chapter Five

Brock

I wake up hard and with something on top of me. "Scout," I murmur. Did I fall asleep on Shep and Olivia's couch? Without opening my eyes, I pat my hands against what's weighing me down. I feel hair, not fur.

She speaks. "Coffee."

I force my eyes open and grab my cell. "Holy shit."

"Hmmm?"

I actually got some sleep last night. I can't remember the last time I laid in this bed and slept. The early morning comes back in bits and pieces. The banana bread I got into my head I just had to have right at that second. Remembering Shep told me to get on writing a song and the frantic attempt I made until my desperation turned into fear I will never be able to write anything worth putting on a Ghost Town album.

Agatha found me, not a moment too soon. I was close to ripping my piano to nothing but kindling.

The drink by the pool.

The calm.

And when I suggested we sleep together, she didn't bat an eye. Simply crawled into bed with me and fell asleep.

She wiggles, and I swallow back a groan. She's going to feel how hard I am, and I hope she understands it's natural and I can't help it.

"What time is it?" she mumbles, her breath seeping through my t-shirt and warming my skin.

"Noon."

"Christ." She sits up, to my relief and my cock's regret. He liked having her pressed up against him, and I did too. "I haven't slept that hard without a sleeping pill for years."

I can't see her, the blackout curtains doing their job too well. I fumble for the remote control sitting on my nightstand and raise one a couple of inches.

The sunlight streams in and my heart damn near stops.

Agatha blinks against the light, the shoulder of her robe sliding down the sun-kissed skin of her arm. She's rubbing her eyes, her hair a sexy halo around her head.

Jesus Christ, she's beautiful.

I'm tenting, and I sit up, hoping to hide it.

"It's been a while for me, too, but I don't take pills. I just suffer. We better get moving if you want to fit in all four movies today. Are you sure about that?"

"Yeah. I need today to shake off yesterday. You were right when you said traveling doesn't agree with me. If I couldn't stay for a full two weeks, I wouldn't have bothered. I'm going to shower, and you promised me banana bread for breakfast."

"Thanks for not letting them bake into bricks." Too caught up with shitty lyrics, I'd completely forgotten they were in the oven.

"You're welcome. I'll meet you downstairs." She glides elegantly off the bed, her robe billowing behind her as she dashes into the hallway to her room.

"Fuck. Get it together," I mutter. "She's not going to want you when your own wife wanted nothing to do with you. Jesus."

I shower and get myself off, dreaming about sliding into her, the sexy sounds she would make. I don't need much to blow, and it's better than having sex with the women Sharyn sets me up with. I met with a few before finding two I clicked with. I'm seeing one tonight, and I'll need to contact Sharyn. I don't know what I'm going to say. Put off my dates with Polly and Anne until Agatha goes home? It's more than physical intimacy I pay for, and I don't know what I would do if I stopped completely. I need something. I need someone, and I won't apologize. Even if I have to pay for it. I'm not an asshole like Derrick, and I have never once mistreated either of them. It would have solved a lot of problems if I could have just fallen in love with one, but I didn't and I won't settle. I know what falling in love feels like, and I want that again.

I probably won't keep it once she finds out I was paying cocktail waitresses in North Hollywood to listen to me cry about how hard it is to be a rockstar, but one can always hope, right?

Yeah, right.

I finish my shower and dry off, dress in jeans and a t-shirt. I don't want Agatha to think I'm going to try anything sitting in the dark with her for eight hours. Fuck. I hope she doesn't need too long between movies, or I won't be on time.

She's downstairs leaning against the kitchen island wearing black leggings that stop just below her knees and a sloppy grey sweatshirt, the worn-out neckline slipping over her shoulder. She's sipping coffee out of one of my Ghost Town mugs. My entire house is a souvenir shop, and she can take that and a few t-shirts with her when she goes home.

I clear my throat. "I'm glad you didn't wait for me. Did you find everything okay?"

"Yeah. Took me a second to find coffee grounds. I don't keep them in the fridge. You need more milk. Yours is almost gone."

"I can put in a food order, or if you don't mind going shopping, we have a Whole Foods I like snooping around in."

"You grocery shop? Don't adoring fans mob you the second you step inside?"

"They don't care about me. Not when they can watch Jennifer Garner choose breakfast cereal."

"Right."

"You don't sound impressed. You don't care if she likes Special K?"

"*I* like Special K. The kind with the chocolate pieces in it. Maybe we can go tomorrow?"

That sounds too domesticated for me, but I offered to let her stay here, and along with room, there's board. I stifle a sigh. "That sounds good."

"Cool."

"You still want banana bread?"

"Yes. If it tastes as good as it smelled last night, I'll be happy. Do you like to bake?"

"I like to bake and cook. When you're not at Shep's, I can cook for you."

"You mean when *we're* not at Sheppard and Liv's."

I cut thick slabs of the banana bread, plate them, and warm them in the microwave. "What do you mean, we? Do you want butter on it?"

"Of course I do. Slather it on."

Between us, we demolish half the first loaf.

"Come on, we can watch and eat."

"Nothing like a little blood to go along with breakfast," she says, holding her plate, a fork, and her coffee mug. "I mean we. Aren't you supposed to be working on an album?"

"You heard my poor attempt last night."

"You've written songs before."

"I've been in better places in my life before."

A leather reclining loveseat sits in the front of the room flanked by two recliners, and four couches are positioned behind those on an elevated floor. Off to the side, there are more recliners. I told my decorator I didn't need all the furniture, it was just me living here and would only be just me, but because I gave her the freedom to do what she wanted, she outfitted the space properly. The screen fits the entire wall, and a fireplace complete with a mantel and firewood stacked on the hearth is built into the wall adjacent to the screen. It works, but it's August. There's no need for a fire now.

"Do you mean if you're happy you write better songs?" She sits on the right side of the loveseat like a little kid—crisscross applesauce.

The loveseat is directly in the middle of the screen and I like sitting there best, something in my head needing to be exactly in the center, but I fidget. I don't want to sit next to her unless she wants me to sit next to her. Fuck. I'm overthinking this. I choose a recliner to her left.

"Don't you want to sit in the middle? I slept on you last night. I don't care if you sit here."

"Are you sure?"

Ignoring me, she sets her coffee cup on a tray and digs into her bread.

I move next to her, her knee brushing my thigh, and set my mug near hers. "To answer your question, no, I don't need to be happy to write decent songs, but mentally, I'm not in a good place to write at all." I use the remote and flick on the screen. I own every movie known to man, and I use the search bar to find

Jaws. The third one is in 3-D, and I have glasses around here somewhere.

"What do you do about that?" She sips her coffee and peers at me over the rim.

"What do you do?" I start the movie.

She turns toward the screen. "Things I shouldn't."

"Then, angel, we're on the same page."

We take breaks between movies to go to the bathroom. For dinner, we fix tuna salad sandwiches and munch on chips. She's not fussy or complicated, reclining and enjoying the movies. She hides her face against my arm during some of the gorier parts, and I laugh when she squeals. She wasn't pulling my chain; she really wanted to watch these. For a second, I thought she was fucking with me.

"What day is it?" she jokes when we stumble out of the viewing room after the last movie.

I chuckle. It isn't often I lose a whole day watching movies, but this was all right. No phone calls or emails, no texts. Eight hours of sharks eating people gave my overactive mind something to do. I want to hang out with her, but I don't want her to think I don't have a life either, and it's almost a relief to say, "I have somewhere I need to be. Will you be okay alone?"

"Yeah. You don't need to babysit me. I have work and I should check my phone. Liv wanted to get together today but I put her off. She'll want to meet up tomorrow and probably called to ask what time we can get together."

"Okay. I'll write my number down and leave it in the kitchen, and if you need anything, text. Because you haven't been in the house long. If you can't find something."

"I'll be fine. Have a good time."

She flutters her fingers at me and trots up the stairs to her room.

After scribbling my number on a notepad stuck to the fridge, I find my keys and I'm on the road a minute later. Eddie and Clarissa's house has a few lights on. Mason will be asleep, but it's too early for anyone else to be in bed. It used to be I had no problem stopping by, letting myself in, and helping myself to a beer, hoping for an afternoon of Madden on his PlayStation.

Those days don't have to be gone, but they are, for now. Clarissa's had it rough, and I understand Eddie wanting, needing, to spend as much time with her as possible. With Abby back in his life, he's got everything he could want, and I'm happy for him.

It was different when Shep hooked up with Olivia. Shep and Dalt were always closer, Derrick too. Shep hiding after his death didn't carve a hole in my life the way Eddie's relationship with Clarissa does.

The night's balmy, the sky pink and blue with sunset and light pollution. I know this drive by memory; I've traveled the streets once or twice a week for a few years now. After Brianna divorced me, I gave up finding anyone, but it's human to need someone. Even if it's manufactured. I didn't know Sharyn was setting Derrick up until one afternoon not long after my divorce was finalized he caught me in the parking lot of the recording studio in the middle of an anxiety attack. "You need to get fucking laid," he said in that unkind way that snuck up on us.

I didn't need to get laid, but I said, "Fuck. It's not so easy finding something like that."

He smirked. "It is for me. Sharyn sets me up with tail. Let her help you."

"Sharyn?" I asked, confused. All I knew of his younger

sister was she liked to pretend to design jewelry and sell it in her store for exorbitant prices.

"She's got connections to some girls in North Hollywood. Pay them well, and they'll keep their mouths shut. Call her."

I did, and that began my weekly "dates."

Sharyn reserves a suite in a hotel chain that's decent. The hallways are carpeted with dark green, pink, and beige, the walls painted cream, sconces lighting my way. I use the elevator to the seventh floor and the room's located at the end of the hall.

Polly's already there; she keeps a keycard. She's standing by the window, looking over the city, and she turns my way when I open the door. "Hi, Brock," she says, tucking her hair behind her ears. Stones glint at her earlobes.

"Hey. How are you?" I kick off my shoes and head to the minibar like I normally do, but I stop. I don't want to drink here. Maybe if Agatha's still up when I get back, we can sit by the pool again. I liked it.

"Oh, fine. There's been talk about Shotgun Sally's and the Guitar Pick. Someone bought them and gave 'em to a waitress who used to work at Sally's. Isn't that crazy?" She sounds wistful.

"I know." I don't have anything to do with EmpowerHer, Inc, but Eddie's talked about buying the bars for a woman Derrick abused. Clarissa's training her and the waitresses, teaching them how to manage a bar at night while they attend college classes during the day. It's a lot of work. I know what it's like to go to school, have a side hustle, and punch in for cash. It was a few years before Ghost Town brought in enough to replace the day job I needed to help my mom and dad.

I sit on the bed, and she pads over to me. She crawls over the bedspread and snuggles into my side. I don't always want sex. Polly understands that it's not primarily what I come here for.

"If you work there, you get to go to school," she whispers, her lips grazing my neck.

Rubbing her back, I ask, "Do you still work at Teddy's?" I realize why she brought it up. The women who work at Shotgun Sally's and the Guitar Pick must feel like they won the lottery, while the waitresses who work at other bars in the area look on, sick with missed opportunities.

"Yeah. It's okay. The manager's not a creep, and that counts for a lot."

I lean against the pillows propped against the headboard, and she follows me, resting her upper body on my chest.

She's pretty, light brown hair, amber eyes. She's always tired, and I think that's why she became my favorite. More often than not, after a couple of hours of conversation, she'd fall asleep, trusting me. I'd sit and watch over her until morning.

"What would you do if you could go to school?"

She jerks a shoulder. "Doesn't matter."

I rub my thumb over her cheek. "Humor me."

"I want to be a family law attorney."

"Yeah?"

"Yeah. Kids never get a say when their parents are being assholes. I would help kids like that."

"Were you one of those kids?" I don't know much about her childhood.

"Maybe. My mom tried to sue my dad for child support. He won, and we were broke until I started working. It wasn't bad. She did her best." She laughs, but there's no happiness in it.

"What's stopping you from going?"

"Money. I help her and grandma with bills. We live together. We only have one car, and Mom uses that for her job.

I ride the bus to Teddy's and to meet you. No tuition money, but I could get grants and stuff. I looked into it and I qualify, but I don't have a ride to campus and I work all the overtime I can. When I'm not there, I'm here with you." She wiggles up my chest and brushes her lips over mine. "Are you in the mood for a little? I wouldn't mind."

I turn my head and nudge her shoulder. "No, sweetheart, not tonight. You and the other girls feel left out."

She sighs and scoots away. I pay her more when we have sex.

"When the news started its way around, a lot of us cried. Lilah, a friend who works with me at Teddy's, wants to be a teacher. She went into the bathroom and bawled her eyes out—she could barely work her shift. We thought it was unfair, but that's life. Not all of us want to go to college. Not smart enough or whatever, but the girls who do, it was hard to hear it." Forcing a smile, she says, "Did you come here to talk about that?"

"No. In fact, I won't be able to meet you next week. I have a houseguest and can't get away."

"That's too bad. Will you be okay?" She rubs at my beard.

"Yeah. This wasn't a permanent thing."

"Needing someone is always permanent."

Brushing my hand over her hair, I say, "That's true. Do you have a boyfriend? Someone you love?"

"No. Don't have time for it. I double-dip with you." She rests her head on my chest like Agatha did last night.

"I'm sorry."

"Why?" she asks without looking at me. "You're a nice guy. Some of the girls I know who do this on the side, they tangle with the not-so-nice guys. Like your buddy, Derrick."

He hasn't been my buddy for a long time, but I let it go. "I'm still using you."

"You don't hurt me, Brock."

"Yeah, sweetheart, I do. Even if it doesn't feel like it." I've been with Polly for half an hour, and in the back of my mind I've wondered what Agatha's doing. Did she go to bed? Is she answering email? Is she snooping through my house, looking for secrets to sell to *Buzz Kill?* Maybe she called her boyfriend. I didn't miss she avoided answering me when I asked if she had someone who helps her dress. Not having a roommate and not being married leaves a lot of room for other things.

I lie awake for another half an hour, one arm crooked under my head, the other holding Polly against me, and she falls asleep. I roll her off, and she curls around a pillow. I cover her with a nubby decorative throw that was folded at the end of the bed and pull my wallet out of my jeans pocket. I toss twenty one hundred dollar bills next to the phone sitting on the night-stand. I've been seeing her long enough she likely depends on the money I pay her, and I don't want her worried about next week. I brush some hair out of her face. Yeah, it would have made my life a lot easier if I could have just fallen in love, but besides an affection I have for any female I care about, it doesn't come close to how it feels to fall hopelessly, passionately in love.

On the drive home, I keep the top down. The roads are never empty, and bits and pieces of music wisp through the engine noise. I grew up here, my children live here, people I love have made their homes here, yet, sometimes I think it wouldn't be so bad to drive away and not look back.

I don't know what I'll do after the tour. Saying I'll move to a little town and hook up with the town's librarian is a lot easier than finding said town. I've been all over the world and have my choice of the California coastline, a Floridian beach, an Italian village, the French Riviera, but no matter how perfect a destination, I'd still be alone.

It's a permanent condition to need someone, with no permanent solution when no one wants you.

I park in the garage and enter the house through the mudroom rather than the foyer. I didn't show Agatha where the washer and dryer is. She might need to wash some of her things while she's here and there's no use schlepping anything to Shep's because she thinks I'm a moron who doesn't wash his clothes. I have a housekeeper scheduled a couple of times a week I should warn her about, too. I need Bobbi otherwise nothing would be clean. Not because I hate chores, but I wouldn't remember to do anything. Bobbi's also rescued things from the oven, but she's usually not as fortunate as Agatha was last night.

She's sitting by the pool, dressed in the nightgown and robe she wore to bed, and I trot up the stairs to change. She's still there when I come down wearing shorts and a t-shirt, and taking a chance she's sipping on a glass of whiskey, pour my own. This could become a very dangerous habit if I let it.

Near the pool's edge, I lower beside her, and immediately, my muscles relax. I dip my feet into the steaming water. I rarely swim unless it's to try to calm my brain. Sometimes the steady rhythm works, sometimes it doesn't.

"You're still up," I say, trying to sound casual.

"Just thinking through some bullshit, you know? How was your date?" she asks, tilting her head.

My mouth dries. "Date?"

"I can smell her perfume on you. You don't have to hide it. Just because I'm staying with you doesn't mean you have to entertain me. I have plenty going on, and now that I'm acclimated, I'll spend a lot of time with Liv."

I'm so used to Polly's scent I didn't consider it rubbed off on me while we were talking. "She's just a friend."

Agatha sips her drink, and her eyes crinkle in amusement. "A friend with benefits?"

"Sometimes," I say, infusing a little honesty into the conversation. "Is it wrong to need someone?"

"Not at all." She turns her gaze from me and stares over the water. She kicks her feet, a light purple polish a blur on her toes. "Maybe you could write a song about her."

"What about her?" Polly's pretty, and I learned quickly that the women Sharyn deals with always will be. But she doesn't make my heart beat faster. She doesn't make me think of forever.

"How long have you been friends?"

"A few years," I say reluctantly. I don't want to answer too many more questions, or Agatha will figure out what I'm doing. I'm not ashamed of it, but I don't want anyone to know I've been doing business with Sharyn, not after what Eddie found out about her.

"Then she gives you what you need. She listens when you speak, you like her company. She makes you feel special when no one else does. She laughs at your jokes. Whatever. Liv told me a lot about Sheppard and how his fame isolated him. I would imagine you're similar, even if you can shop at Whole Foods without people bothering you. Are you in love with her?"

"No. And that's probably the saddest part of the whole thing. I wish I could be." I drain my glass.

"What do you think is worse—not being able to love someone and wishing you could, or falling in love with someone you shouldn't?"

"Depends on why you shouldn't."

"Maybe they aren't available."

"There are different ways to be unavailable."

"True, but let's leave it at that for now."

"Okay. Then I think falling in love with someone who's unavailable would hurt worse. They can't be yours, and if the current circumstances held, never. But not loving someone when you wish you could . . . you can get around that. Marry anyway and hope your friendship turns into something more, or just look for the good in every day and come to terms with the fact that you will never feel like your soul is on fire whenever you're near them. That you'll never yearn to be with them when you're apart. There's something magical about falling in love, and I want that again."

"That's very romantic. I don't think you're too far off from being where you need to be, mentally. Write a song about what you have with her. I want to hear it."

I tuck a piece of hair behind her ear. "What if I want to write a song about you?"

Wrinkling her nose, she says, "What would it be about?"

"I'm not sure yet. I don't know you well enough."

"You have two weeks to unearth all my secrets." She sounds like she's teasing, but her lips tremble.

"How many do you have, Agatha Sterling?"

"Isn't one enough?"

"The bigger and dirtier it is, one is definitely enough."

We sit until she finishes her drink, and I help her to her feet. Electricity crackles around us, but I pause at the staircase's landing.

"Aren't you going to bed?" She's standing on the second step, and we're eye-level.

"No. I'm going to stay up and see if I can't write. When do you want to go to Olivia's? Did she say?"

"She has a Zoom meeting at nine that's supposed to last until ten. Any time after that."

"We can leave here at ten, then, and you'll be right on time."

"Okay. Goodnight. Um. No more late-night baking adventures," she says, but she's smiling.

I lean against the wall, relieved she's not annoyed. "I'll try. Goodnight."

She's graceful, her hand lightly skimming the railing until she reaches the top.

Her door opens then shuts.

I retreat to the sunroom and raise one of the blackout curtains. The pool's light is just enough to see by, and I sit on the floor with my guitar, a notebook, and a pen.

I want to love Polly, but I can't. I can talk to her for hours, even the sex is fine, but there's no spark. I don't miss her when I'm not around her; I don't want to consume her whenever I'm near her. She's comfortable. She would be with me, that way, if I asked. Maybe not even for the money, but she doesn't love me, either. If she did, I would feel it.

She's using me for cash and maybe companionship.

I use her for someone to talk to and getting off when I need more than my hand.

Like the song by Soul Asylum says, we're going the wrong way on a one-way track.

I don't have anywhere else to go.

Chapter Six

Agatha

Graham's called me a few more times, but I don't return his calls. I don't have anything I can give him, and he has less than that to give me. It's difficult, his rich voice sounding divine even in a voicemail message, smooth and rich, but I said what I had to say when I broke it off. If he insists on picking me up at the airport, I'll use the time to convince him he needs to leave it alone, leave *me,* alone.

I won't be his if he can't be mine. I've done it for too long and I'm tired.

I toss and turn, but I manage to drift off at some point. My alarm wakes me at eight, and groggy, I roll out of bed and stumble down to the kitchen. Brock already made coffee, and I appreciatively help myself to a mug, using the remainder of the milk. I hope he likes his black because that's how he'll be drinking it until we can go to the store later today. I want to see Brock Farris, Ghost Town's lead guitar player, push a cart in Whole Foods. I want to take pictures of that.

I'm glad I decided to throw my camera into my bag at the last minute.

Brock isn't anywhere, but he said he would be ready to drive me and I have no reason not to believe him. If something changed, I can order a car. I'll ask if he minds ferrying me around or if I should rent something while I'm here. I don't want to be an inconvenience to anyone.

I shower and dress in denim shorts and a strapless top and perch a pair of sunglasses on the top of my head. I may not be a blonde, but I want to be a California girl, too. Before I leave, I want to go shopping, eat lunch outdoors, and look for celebrities. Hanging out with Liv at the Mall of America before Michael passed away used to be something we both enjoyed when we had time.

I have a straw beach bag I pack instead of my purse, and ready for the day at Liv's, trot down the stairs. Brock's in the kitchen, and there's something that smells amazing sizzling in a frying pan on the stove.

"What are you cooking?"

"Omelets. Do you eat eggs?"

"Yeah. I'm not picky." I drop my bag on one of the chairs and sit.

"Here." He slides a plate covered in omelet and toast in front of me.

"Are you trying to stuff me so we don't go to the store later?" I ask around a mouthful of buttered toast. "Because I'm not letting you out of that. I used the last of the milk in my coffee, and that's a mandatory dietary requirement."

"No. I said I would cook, and our sandwich for dinner seems like a very long time ago."

"I won't argue. Did you write a song last night?"

He sits at the head of the table, diagonally across from me, and digs into his own omelet. "Writing doesn't work that way.

At least, not for me. I start with feelings, a vibe. Play with some notes. If Shep asks if I have anything, I can say I started. He'll know what that means."

"You guys are good friends, huh?" I ask, forking up a bite of the fluffy egg.

"We used to be better. After the tour, we'll all go our separate ways."

"Why do you say that?"

"I don't think I would have said it at all if he wouldn't have met Olivia. She's pregnant, and he'll hole up with her. By the time the tour is over, they might be thinking about trying for a second kid. I would if I were in his place."

"I suppose it's difficult for you then, with Eddie and Clarissa being engaged? Olivia told me what she went through. It must be hard to admit you're glad when someone is dead, but it sounds like Derrick deserved it."

"He did. We may never know how many women he abused." He clears his throat. "It will be a while before that happens. Things move at a snail's pace, and then it's all hurry up and you don't have time to piss."

"Sounds like publishing."

"Do you like what you do?" He sips his coffee.

I shrug. "Do you like being a rockstar?"

He lifts a corner of his mouth. "I loved it. I kissed Shep's feet every day for bringing us with him."

"What do you mean?" I ask, chewing a mouthful of cheese, spinach, and mushrooms. It's delicious, and I was starving.

"A guy like that, with his pipes, he didn't need us. He could have dumped us after the first album and did just fine on his own. You see it sometimes. But he kept the band together, treated us like family. I've got all I have because of him."

"That's sweet."

"It's dangerous. Eddie didn't want to tell Shep about

Clarissa for the exact same reason, and he gave his loyalty to Shep when he should have given it to Clarissa from day one. Nothing should be more important than the woman you love, even if it is the friendship of a man who made you rich. He's lucky she waited. Not all women would."

"She loves him, too."

"Yeah, she does."

My plate's empty and I drag my fork along the bottom, the tines screeching. I hope Liv plans to feed me lunch. I'm still hungry. "Why did you and your wife split up?"

Brock pushes away from the table. "Because I bake banana bread at 3 AM."

He doesn't talk much after that, dropping me off at Liv and Sheppard's with a brusque, "I'll see you later." I stand outside until I can't see his car anymore. I'm sorry I put him in a bad mood asking about his ex-wife. That will go on my list of topics to avoid. I've only known him for a couple of days, and already that list is longer than I'd like it to be.

I let myself inside. Scout races across the room, and I rub her head. "Hey, girl." I missed this dog.

"Hey, yourself," Liv says, stepping into the hallway, only to be interrupted by Sheppard.

"Did Liv tell you I'm going to be a dad?" He picks me up and twirls me around. "I'm going to be a dad."

I hang on, my stomach pitching. "That's great! I'm happy for both of you."

He sets me to my feet, and I stagger, dizzy. Using Sheppard's arm to steady myself, I find my equilibrium and shoot Liv an "I told you so" look. She smiles, her expression full of chagrin.

That's what happens when things feel too good to be true. You're always waiting for something to happen, and in Liv's case with Michael, it did.

He wraps her in his arms, and I bend down to pet Scout, uncomfortable with their blatant affection for each other. I love that Liv's settled and happy, but I am slowly giving up that dream for myself. I gave all my energy to the wrong man, and now I'm too drained to keep trying.

"Where are your mom and brother?" I didn't speak much to them when I was here the last time. Gina cornered me, and all I wanted to do after I talked to her was leave.

"Tony brought Mom to visit some friends who are still with us, and to the cemetery to visit some who aren't. Didn't Brock come inside with you? I wanted to run a couple of ideas by him."

"No. He dropped me off and sped away. He said he started on something and you'd know what that means."

"Yeah, I do. I'm going to keep working—the sooner we can get this album done, the sooner we can put it all behind us." He gently cradles Liv's face between his palms and kisses her.

They forget about me.

I dig around in their kitchen for something else to eat, my stomach already gnawing through Brock's omelet, and I'm pleased to find several varieties of cheese in the fridge. I could live on cheese. I'm halfway through a block of Gruyère and a sleeve of wheat crackers when he finally releases her. She staggers backward, a hand pressed to her mouth, her cheeks a delightful pink. Sheppard winks at me and says, "Have fun catching up."

When he's out of the room, I murmur, "How in the world did you think he wouldn't be happy? He had his tongue down your throat for a full fifteen minutes. You're crazy."

Tears fill her eyes, and she whispers, "He asked me to marry him."

I tug at her hand, her engagement ring glittering. "Yeah. Weeks ago."

"No, last night. After I told him. He wants to before you and his mom and brother leave. It was what I wanted."

"That's so great," I say, hugging her.

She cries on me for a few minutes, and I hold her tightly. She steps out of my embrace and swipes at her cheeks. "I'm sorry. After Michael's death, I didn't think I would find this again."

"You deserve every second. I mean it. Did you call your mom and sister?"

"Yeah. Martin's going to marry us, like you said. You'll stand up with me?"

"Of course."

"Good. I'm going to ask Clarissa and Gina to be brides-maids, too."

I widen my eyes. "This is a huge wedding for a spur-of-the-moment ceremony."

"We need an even number. Sheppard will ask Eddie, Brock, and Dalton to stand up with him." She steals a piece of cheese off the cutting board.

"Are you sure Sheppard's going to ask Dalton? From what you've told me, they don't sound like they're on good enough terms for him to do that."

Chewing, she says, "I'm going to mention it and hope he takes the hint. Years from now, when we look over the pictures, I don't want him to feel bad."

"I think he's going to feel bad Derrick turned into an abusive monster and he didn't know. You might have to compromise. Maybe you can convince him to ask Dalton to be there but not as part of the wedding party."

She sighs. "You're right, but regardless, even if we wanted to keep the ceremony small, I doubt he could choose between Brock and Eddie, and I couldn't choose among you, Gina, and Clarissa. Maybe we won't have anyone, but I wanted you up there with me."

"I'll photograph you instead. You ask Gina and Clarissa, Sheppard will have Eddie and Brock, and you'll be even and have some great pictures."

"That's the only consolation prize I'll accept."

"It's the only one I'm offering, so we both win. Let's go outside. I've been as landlocked as you and I want to see this gorgeous view up close and personal. Does Scout want to come with us?"

"No, she doesn't leave Sheppard for long. She's always with him, but I'm glad. He's struggling."

"If he's struggling to breathe, it would help if he didn't have his tongue in your mouth all the time."

She pushes at me, laughing, the old Liv coming out in her. "Brat."

"I am, and proud of it."

I retrieve my camera out of my bag and use the bathroom before we go out. The sun is shining, seagulls flying above us. "How California are you now? Do you eat at Nobu and shop at all the trendy boutiques? Go to red carpet movie premiers and rub elbows with all the celebrities?"

She scowls. "What are you talking about? When have I turned into the kind of person who would want to do that? We stay here. I'm working on EmpowerHer, Inc, and Sheppard's been writing music. If I'd wanted that kind of life, I would have started my own talk show. I don't want that. I want this," she says, covering her belly with her hand.

I bump into her. "I'm only kidding. This is just so different from Minnesota, you know?" I breathe deeply, my feet sinking in the sand. Tourists walk along the beach, snapping pictures of the houses. I snap pictures of them to the delight of some who wave. I wave, too.

"Yeah, it is, but I like it. I think I needed the change. I owe you, you know. For convincing me to come out here. If you had let me have my way, I'd still be living in that house, crying."

"I don't know, Liv. I think you would have bounced back, but helping Sheppard gave you a reason to think beyond your-self. We all need that sometimes, and you don't have to thank me. You will never know how grateful I am to see the woman you used to be before Michael's death in the woman you are right now. I was really worried about you."

"Thanks. I'm sorry I wasn't there for you, when all that happened." She pauses. "Do you think you'll talk to Gina about it? She texted me and asked me to poke you. She's on a dead-line to get her documentary done. If you're not going to help her, she needs to find someone else who will fit in with what she's trying to do."

"What *is* she trying to do?"

"Show women that no matter what life throws at you, it's important to get back up."

"I don't think I've done that."

"You didn't quit your job, you didn't lock yourself in your apartment and cry for three years."

I look through my viewfinder and snap a picture of the long expanse of beach. "No, but I wanted to."

"Talk to her. It could be cathartic."

"Oh, I'm sure it is, it's afterward that won't be fun. It's a documentary. She's going to enter it in all the award competi-tions and my splotchy face will be everywhere for months. Then I'll end up on Netflix and people will shake their heads and say, 'How could she have been so stupid?'"

"Your fate is mine, too, you know," Liv says, wading in the surf as we walk.

"Yeah, well, the difference there is you'll be married to Sheppard by then, already have your baby, and everyone will be like, 'That Olivia Bloom—' No, you'll take Sheppard's last name. '—That Olivia Carpenter, look at what a triumph she is!' and I'll be over here, doing the same shitty thing I've always done."

"It doesn't have to be that way."

"You know how my mom is. Do you think she'll let me do something else?"

"You haven't tried talking to her."

"No, I haven't. There's no point in taking her on. My mental health is already shaky, and I can't handle it now."

We walk past a grouping of rocks, and Liv points out it's where Sheppard caught her. "Sit on one. We need to memorialize these rocks."

She sits, the wind blowing at her hair, and she's laughing, happy and confident in her place.

I'll blow it up and frame it. She's beautiful, an air of American royalty about her, like the Kennedys, and I blame California and Sheppard's money for the high gloss.

It's right at that second I realize Liv and I won't be friends for the rest of our lives. She'll move on, a rockstar's wife, and I'll go home to Minnesota, a literary agent with a bad track record and the reputation of a desperate woman who can't find her own man.

We turn around, and she asks, "How's it going staying with Brock?"

"It's fine. He calls himself eccentric, but there's something else. I can't put my finger on it."

"I haven't spent that much time with him. What do you mean?"

"He's like a live wire. You can feel the energy, hear it hum, but it's dangerous. You know if you touch it you'll hurt yourself." I try to put into words how it feels to be around him. How it felt finding him at the piano, anger, fear, and hopelessness drenching his skin. How it felt to lie in his arms, like nothing could hurt me. Not Graham, not my mom. None of it would matter if he were there to protect me.

She frowns in concern. "Do you not feel safe with him? The band has a lot of secrets, and I know I don't know them all, but I trust Eddie and he would have told me if you shouldn't stay there."

I flick my fingers, irritated I can't describe what I mean. "No, it's not that. He would never hurt me. He's just so full of, I don't know. Energy, but I already said that. I don't know how to articulate it. Like, when a storm's coming, and you can smell it. Feel it in the air. Your hair stands up. You want to hide, know you should hide, but then there are the stormchasers who want to be out in the middle of it. Do you know what I mean?"

"I think so. Just be careful. You've hurt yourself enough." She looks at me out of the corners of her eyes. "Are you still seeing Graham?"

"No."

"Good. It was the right thing to do, you know," she says, the wind whipping away her words.

"I know. I just wish the right thing didn't feel so shitty."

She flops onto the sand in front of her house, and I wiggle behind her to grab her photo with the ocean as a backdrop. "Maybe you need to get out there and date. You're so pretty and smart, you can have your pick of men. Forget about him."

"That's hard to do when he's calling me every five seconds."

"Block his number."

I stare at my camera. I never considered doing that because I like it when he calls. Need it.

"Agatha."

"I know. Tell Gina I'll talk to her. If I can purge one, maybe I can purge the other."

"She'll be happy."

That's all I want to be too, but I deal with nonfiction, not fiction, and that's just the way my life is.

"There you are!"

I turn toward Clarissa's voice.

She waves from the patio, Mason anchored on her hip. She hurries down the steps and over the sand. "Hey, can I ask you something?"

She's talking to me and not Liv, and I say, "Sure?"

"Can you teach me how to be a literary agent?"

Chapter Seven

I shouldn't have been so curt with her. There was no reason to be pissed off when she asked about Bri. Facts are facts. Bri tolerated me for a long time and cut out when she couldn't anymore. She doesn't want our daughters to be around their freak of an old man, and I accepted that a long time ago.

I didn't park and go inside. That surprised her but I have something to do first, and I drive out to Sharyn's store. It's the only place she'll be. She's so fucking in love with that goddamned boutique, considers it her castle. She couldn't stop bragging when she bagged the vacant storefront next to Jennifer Meyer's. I don't know if she makes any money selling her designs, but she likes to act like she does.

I park in the self-service lot. Agatha might like to snoop around, but I don't know if she could afford anything. She dresses like she has money, acts like she has money, but I honest to God don't know how much literary agents earn. She could work for fun and live off family money like Sharyn, though she would never admit that's what she *really* does. None of this would have been possible without Derrick.

Without Shep.

It might be dangerous to never forget where the credit truly lies, but it's just as dangerous not to remember where you came from. Sharyn and Derrick did a long time ago and it twisted them into ugly, entitled people.

A little bell tinkles when I step inside, and a woman with dark skin smiles at me. "Can I help you? A gift for a girlfriend or wife?"

Sharyn steps from the back. "He's here to see me. Selma, you can take a break."

"Thanks." She pushes through the swinging doors that lead to the offices.

"What can I do for you? You're not having trouble with Polly?" Sharyn meets me on the selling floor, a pair of reading glasses in her hands, her head tilted in fake concern.

She's had more plastic surgery done, and her skin stretches across her cheekbones, her lips unnaturally plump. She's beginning to look like a cartoon, and for just one brief second, I wish Derrick were still alive to tell her. The world is full of billions of people, and the only person she ever listened to was him.

"No, but I told her I couldn't see her next week. I paid her in advance last night." I pause. "I think I'm going to stop seeing her."

Her face softens, as much as it can with all the Botox. "Why? What's wrong?"

I walk to a display case, and earrings hang from velvet umbrellas. Supposedly, she designs all the jewelry herself. They're pretty, but whenever I bought Bri, Lexi, or Layla a gift, I never bought it here. "It's getting old. She's a nice girl, but I'm not getting what I need."

She leans a hip against the sparkling glass. "You know you're never going to get that, don't you?"

I meet her eyes and they're full of sympathy. "What do you mean?"

"Brianna got rid of you, honey, and you're not going to find anyone to take her place."

"I don't want anyone to take her place." I loved Bri, but we were never right for each other. Something was always just off-center about our marriage, and I always blamed myself. Maybe I wouldn't have minded that so much—I have the self-aware-ness to know how difficult I am—but she took the girls with her and didn't look back.

"Maybe not, but you're not going to find anyone who will love you. We've heard the stories. Your insomnia, the drugs—"

I've never taken drugs. Not the kind she means. I like to drink socially, but so does everyone I know besides Shep. Olivia dried him out and he's better for it. I let her keep going.

"—your temper. You will never find a woman who will love you the way you are. The girls you pay for are going to be as good as you're going to get. Don't stop. I'll send Polly on to other men and she won't be available. You'll regret it."

She's right. I know she is. I need her until we go on tour. I need someone to listen to me in the middle of the night, someone who will pretend she cares about me until morning.

"You see her twice a week, and Anne, sometimes, if you need something extra? Bump Polly up to three times a week, and see Anne every weekend. You'll feel better. You're lonely, and you can afford it. And maybe less talking? Polly will give you whatever you want. No matter how . . . rough you want it. She's a good girl."

My mouth dries in disgust. "I'm not Derrick."

"You don't have to be to need an outlet for your frustration.

Let some of it out and it won't eat you up inside. You're hurting, Brock."

No point in denying it. "You get charged?"

She huffs a laugh. "They're trying, but they don't have anything on me, and what Derrick was doing wasn't any of my business. If I helped him, I was only being a good sister. If you need help, I'll do the same. Don't forget that."

My stomach churns. "Yeah."

"Olivia's little hick friend is staying with you, is that what the birds are singing?"

"What about her?" I ask, bristling. I don't like Sharyn talking about her.

"Be careful what you let her see. She'll run and tell her friends, and then they won't want anything to do with you."

"Shep and Eddie aren't like that."

"Maybe not before, but now Shep has Olivia and Eddie's determined to marry my dead brother's trash wife, they won't be so tolerant of your little tantrums. They're big strong men, protecting their wimpy little women," she says in a mocking whine. "How many guitars have you broken this year, hmmm?"

I press my lips together. I don't need to defend myself.

She smirks. "Right. I'll tell Polly you want her three times a week, and Anne every weekend. More fucking, less talking, and you'll feel better. I know men need it, and you're not any better. Maybe while she's here, you can bang Olivia's cute little friend. I looked her up. Got caught up in quite the scandal a couple of years ago. After you fuck each other's brains out you can talk about how pathetic your lives are. Picturing that makes me feel all warm and fuzzy inside. I need to get back to work. Anything else?"

"No," I murmur, and I don't tell her no with Polly and Anne, either. Maybe I do need to see them more, not less. Maybe I just need to fucking marry Polly, put her through school, see if maybe she'd be willing to give me a couple more kids, and call it good. It's the best I'm going to get.

I wish she wouldn't have planted that idea in my head—about Agatha. How good it would feel to hold her against me while I slide into her, how she would look at me with those pretty blue eyes, smoky with lust, her slim thighs bracketing my hips.

Then the pillow talk. Not how pathetic we are—that's Sharyn thinking everyone is below her—but sharing our fears, what we want out of the rest of our lives. We don't have to talk in bed, we could talk by the pool while we sip whiskey. I talk to Polly, too much, if I want to admit Sharyn could be right about anything, but talking to a partner, talking to a woman who's sharing your future, that's different. That's love. That's what I want.

What Agatha said has been bouncing around in my head, and when that happens, it's usually not a good thing. It's a baseball going eighty miles per hour and shattering a window. Why I let Bri force me to quit writing movie reviews for the *Times*. I loved it, and I stopped because Bri asked me to and that's how relationships work. Except, she didn't do anything with the time I had free. All it did was create a hole I had to fill because I was no longer doing that thing I liked doing.

On the way to Shep's, I call the editor of the Entertainment & Arts section. Someone new is manning the desk, and his jovial voice takes me off guard.

"This is Oliver Tatum. What can I do for you on this fine day?"

"This is Brock Farris. I was wondering if I could talk to you about reprising my movie review column."

He barks out a laugh. "No shit. That would be fantastic, man. How long has it been? Six, seven years? Christ, everyone loved it. I wasn't sitting here back then, but I remember. You really knew how to pull the intricacies out of any fucking movie we put in front of you. It was a sad day when you said you didn't have the time anymore, but we understood. You're Brock Fucking Farris, right? But, hell, yeah. Sweet. We can't make room until September, though, is that gonna be okay? Can you come up to the offices and meet with us for a hot minute? Make sure we're all on the same page?"

September.

Agatha will be gone.

"Yeah, sure. My email is the same. Shoot me off some dates, and we'll figure it out."

"Great, great. I love it. Thanks for calling."

"Yeah. I appreciate your time." I hang up, the joy of it disappearing.

It shouldn't matter Agatha won't be around to watch the movies with me or read the column over my shoulder. Bri never did any of that, either. It's another dumbass thing I signed up to do that I'll have to do alone. I shouldn't have bothered, but with as excited as that guy sounded, I would hate to call back and tell him I changed my mind.

I debate going to Shep's, but he wanted to talk about the album and I put him off yesterday to watch sharks eat people. It was fun, and that's nothing I can say about any of my days since we had to cut our tour short.

Clarissa's cute little pink convertible is sitting in Shep's drive, and I park next to it. I remember when Shep bought Olivia a new car. She kept gravitating toward the higher vehicles, like Eddie's pickup truck, wanting all-wheel drive, and finally Shep asked, aggravated, "Why do you need to be so high off the ground? I want you to drive something sporty and fun," and she said, "I need to be able to drive through the snow." I wasn't there, but I could imagine the look on Shep's face when he had to remind her there wasn't going to be any snow where she's driving. He convinced her to choose a bright blue Ford Mustang that's parked next to his vehicle in the garage. I bet after the time Melody gave him, he gets choked up over something like that.

Without knocking, I let myself into Shep's house. Scout greets me, and I rub her head. Clarissa's standing at the breakfast bar with Agatha and they're hunched over a laptop. Olivia's on the floor playing patty-cake with Mason.

"What are you doing?" I ask them, walking farther into the room.

Clarissa beams. "Agatha's teaching me how to be a literary agent."

"Is that something you can learn?"

Agatha quirks her lips. "Kind of. A lot of it is who you know. I promised her the next time I make a trip out to New York she could come with me. You can want to sell a book until the cows come home, but unless you have someone to sell it to, you're fucked. But there are things she can learn now, and I'll talk her through it." She turns to Clarissa. "Aren't you supposed to be at the Guitar Pick soon?"

Checking her cell, she says, "Oh, crap. Yeah. I need to drop Mason off with Eddie first."

"He's not here?" I was expecting a full jam session this afternoon.

"No. We had some furniture delivered earlier, and he and Abby are at the house."

"Leave Mason with us. Brock promised me a tour of Whole Foods and we can drop him off when we're done here," Agatha says.

I'm surprised she'd want to babysit Mason, and I say, "Are you sure?"

She winces. "Do you mind? I volunteered your chauffeuring services."

"No, it's fine. It won't be any trouble."

"Great! Don't forget to change his diaper soon, and he'll want a bottle in an hour or so. I'll pull his car seat out of my car and leave it by yours. I gotta get going or Ginger will wonder if I canceled. We're going over what we want done to the inside." Clarissa darts from behind the breakfast bar and kisses Mason's cheek. "See you later, sweetie. Be good."

And just like that, she's out the door.

Olivia shakes her head. "She is such a different person than when I met her."

"She didn't blink an eye leaving him with us." Agatha closes the laptop with a soft click. "She's very trusting."

"She should be. We're family," Olivia says.

"It sounds like she needed one."

"Yeah, she did."

I clear my throat. "Shep here?"

"Working on a song, like always." Olivia tilts her head toward the living room.

My guitar's in the car, but I'll ask Shep what he wants to do before I haul it in here. The piano could suffice for now.

Olivia picks up Mason, and she and Agatha follow me into Shep's hidden den.

Shep's strumming his guitar, and he can't stop the goofy grin when he sees Olivia holding Mason. "Hey," he says, standing from the armrest of the couch and nuzzling Olivia's cheek. "I love you."

"I love you, too," she murmurs against his lips.

"Knock it off, you guys. Have you ever had a woman lie on your piano, Sheppard?" Agatha asks. "Help me up," she commands me.

I wrap my hands around her waist and lift her onto the piano. She's light, and her chocolate scent tickles my nose.

Shep laughs. "I can't say that I have, though when we were

married, Melody did a giant spread that involved a piano for *Vogue*. Do you sing?"

Agatha kicks her feet. "A little. Liv and I would goof around in a karaoke bar when we had free Friday nights. It wasn't very often. I always had a networking cocktail party."

Shep scowls, but his eyes are glinting with humor. "You told me you couldn't sing," he accuses Olivia.

"What?" Agatha gasps playfully, a hand over her heart. "Liar!"

"I was *not* going to tell Sheppard Carpenter, *of Ghost Town,* I could sing. Are you nuts?"

"I must be, because I just did."

I sit on the bench and shake out my hands. "Let's hear it."

"Do you know 'Hello?'"

"Lionel or Adele?" I'd have a heart attack if she wanted to sing a Lionel Ritchie song.

She laughs. "Let's do Adele."

"Sure."

I play the somber opening chords, expecting her to start off weak or flake out, but Agatha hits every note as purely as Adele does. My fingers trip over the keys by memory, and transfixed, my eyes can't leave her face. Her husky voice sends tremors over my skin. Much too soon, the song comes near the end, and she lies over the piano's surface, letting her head hang over the keys, the last notes leaving her lips. My fingers brush her hair as I finish the song, and the intensity fades. She looks at me upside down, and I have never wanted to lean over and kiss someone as much as I want to kiss Agatha.

She laughs, breaking the silence. "I'm stuck."

Supporting her head, the strands of her hair slipping around my fingers, I help her into a sitting position.

"Jesus Christ, that was fabulous," Shep says. "You sound like that?" he asks Olivia.

She laughs. "Not on your life."

"She doesn't have my range, but she's good too, don't let her fool you," Agatha says.

Shep helps her off the piano, and I scowl. I wanted to be the one who did it. "Do you want to sing backup on our album?" he asks.

Batting her eyelashes at him, she purrs, "I would like that very much."

"Done."

Shep and I spend the rest of the afternoon working on a song's bridge he was having trouble with, and an hour before dinnertime, Agatha and I head out with Mason. He likes her, resting his head on her shoulder, his eyelids drooping. The kid must not have napped today.

We say a quick round of goodbyes, and Olivia reminds Agatha Gina wants to meet with her soon.

"Tomorrow should work," she says, flicking a quick glance my way.

I don't have any claims on her time, and I nod. I'll end up giving her a ride here.

"I'll text her. Have a good night," Olivia says.

With a hand to her back, I help Agatha out to the car. It reminds me of the times Bri and I would visit Eddie, Shelly, and Abby when the girls were babies. I miss it, having friends and shared interests, but more than that, knowing you're going home, to *a* home, with your family. Where you'll help your wife put the kids to bed and after, while they're sleeping, you'll sit up and gossip or make love. Those were my happiest, steadiest, years. Bri hadn't started hating me yet, considered my quirks and eccentricities a part of who I was as a guitar player, part of

Ghost Town. She hadn't realized that it was *me*, what she signed up to love when she married me.

I quickly buckle Mason's car seat into the back, old habits surfacing from when Lexi and Layla were babies, and Agatha nestles him in and latches the straps. He's already sleeping, and she brushes her fingers over his cheek.

"Are you really going to sing on the album?" I ask, sitting behind the wheel and putting up the top. I don't want the wind and noise to bother Mason. I pull onto the highway and we head toward Eddie's.

"Oh, no, that's just a silly thing. I won't have time. When I get home, everyone will be off their summer breaks. I have fifty calls and emails out, and once September first hits, everyone will answer in the same week. There's no way I'll be able to learn the music and fly out to record. I doubt Sheppard was serious."

I think he was. I think he'd have Agatha and Olivia sing on our album if they wanted to. "How come you didn't do anything with it?"

"Singing, you mean?"

"Yeah."

"Mostly because I never had a chance. I took choir when I could, sang in college, but I've always been on track to be a literary agent. There was no time."

"'Been on track?' Why do I get the feeling it wasn't your track?" Risking acting too familiar, I hold her hand and link our fingers.

She squeezes. "You'd be right, but as far as careers go, there could be worse. Negotiating a huge book deal is kind of glamorous, and I've met some really amazing people, like Liv."

"What would you do if you could do something different?"

Twisting in her seat to face me, she says, "I'm not sure. I don't mind being an agent, but nonfiction can be so dry. Political. It's red and blue, and I want to be mint green and pink. Women's fiction, romance. Paranormal. Romantasy. Fun books."

"Then why don't you do that?"

"The agency I'm with already has enough agents who rep that kind of thing."

"Start your own. You can do that, right? Open your own office. It sounds like you already have the connections."

She blinks. "Maybe. The connections I have now wouldn't be good for fiction, but it's easy to make new ones. That's a big risk, though, you know? I have a little saved up, but I would need money to live on until I could find new books and sell them. It's not a fast process, but not impossible. Something to think about, plan for."

There's nothing I can add to that. We're not close enough for me to offer to support her while she finds her footing setting up a new office, and even if I did, we're not close enough for her to accept it.

We sit in a lull, and we're about ten minutes from Eddie's when I say, "I followed your advice and called the Entertainment & Arts editor at the newspaper. I'm going to write my movie review column again."

She grins. "That's great! You shouldn't stop doing things you enjoy. What will your first movie be?"

"I don't know. They want to have a meeting, make sure we're on the same wavelength before I start writing anything. It'll be a bit of a juggle until the tour's done, but after that, I'll have more free time. Here we are," I say, pushing cheer into my voice and coasting to a stop in Eddie's empty driveway. The furniture people must have come and gone. "Let's get this kiddo to his dad, and we'll head to the store. Do you want to come in?"

"Sure. I'll hold Mason while you carry his things."

We walk in without knocking, and I set Mason's car seat by the door. Eddie's in the family room, hands on his hips, assessing the furniture, and Abby's lying on a new couch. He bought this house after Shelly divorced him, much like I did when I needed a place to crash and didn't care where, and filled it with whatever a decorator told him to. Now his house will feel like a home—with furniture chosen by people who will live here and create his family.

I envy him.

"What do you think?" he asks.

"It's a gorgeous color. Did you pick it out?" Agatha asks Abby.

"With Clarissa. We're doing the entire house, and I helped her paint the walls. It was a lot of work, and we were all sweaty. We jumped into the pool with our clothes on."

Watching his daughter, Eddie's eyes soften. "I helped, too, but it's easy to forget that."

"It was a family thing," Abby says casually, and he stares at the carpet for a moment, his Adam's apple bobbing.

"You all did a great job. Do you have a movie room like Brock?" Agatha asks, transferring Mason into Eddie's arms.

"No, but we have a huge TV," Abby says. "I haven't lived here very long. I used to live with my mom and her husband, but she's in Italy because they're getting a divorce."

"Oh," Agatha says, perhaps surprised to be exposed to so much family detail. "I'm sorry to hear that. Maybe before I go home we can all watch a movie at his place. Would you mind?" She rubs my arm, knowing full well she's volunteering my time again.

"No, of course not. Whenever we can make it work for everyone."

Eddie narrows his eyes. "What are you doing? Did you

want to stay and hang out? Have a drink and play some Madden? We can throw some chicken on the grill."

After the divorce, I needed invitations like this to feel human, to feel like I was worth more than a man his wife didn't want anymore, more than a faceless guitar player in a hot rock band. Maybe Eddie always knew that, or he needed validation just as much as I did, and an open invitation stood between us. Stop by if you need. Always welcome. Someone considering you a friend, valuable, is something I've never taken for granted.

At any other time, I would have settled in, opened a beer, played with Mason, chatted with Abby, and hounded Eddie until midnight when I was steeled enough to spend the rest of the evening alone. Today, I don't want to miss one second with Agatha.

"We're heading to the store. Apparently, she drank all my milk, and she doesn't believe I can walk through Whole Foods without anyone pestering me."

Abby giggles. "When Dad, Clarissa, and I were in Home Depot, an old lady was taking pictures of Dad with her flip phone. It was hysterical."

"You better look up the definition of hysterical, because that's not it," Eddie says, shifting Mason in his arms. He picks up a decorative pillow from a loveseat that matches the couch and throws it at Abby's face.

She bats it away and laughs. "Yeah, it was. People get a kick out of the weirdest stuff."

"I want to see that," Agatha says. "He promised he would feed me, and I'm holding him to it. In fact, we should go."

Eddie gives a sleeping Mason to Abby who settles him on her shoulder and walks us to the door. "Hey. I wanted to thank you for giving Clarissa time today. She called on her way to the Guitar Pick, and she couldn't stop talking. She's had it rough, and she's trying to find her way. Is being a literary agent something she can do? If she were really interested?"

"If she likes to read, is passionate about the publishing industry, and doesn't take no for an answer, it's absolutely something she can do. I'm happy to help her explore, but until she knows more about it, she won't know if it's a good fit. Thankfully, I've had more ups than downs, and I'll do my best to see to it she has the same experience." She shrugs, and her bronze skin shimmers in the sunshine wavering in from the windows.

"It's really important to me she decides what she wants to do on her own. I thought she'd work with Olivia and Gina, but that might not be what she ends up doing. I hope it doesn't hurt Olivia's feelings."

Agatha laughs. "You're forgetting Liv's a life coach. It's her job to help people figure their shit out. She's probably more qualified to help Clarissa than I am. If Clarissa doesn't want to work with EmpowerHer, Inc, the last person who would be offended is Liv. Okay?"

He blows out a breath. "Thanks. It's surreal, what she's done for the band."

"I think," Agatha says quietly, "it's a miracle what Sheppard's done for her. I love her, and she's my best friend, and there were days I thought she wouldn't be here much longer." Tears fill her eyes. "Sheppard saved her life. It's that simple. I'm happy to do anything for the band, for this family, because he saved mine."

Eddie wraps his arms around her, and he meets my gaze over her shoulder. Agatha's a good person, and I'll miss her when she leaves.

She steps out of his embrace and wipes her cheeks. "Now they're going to be parents. Sometimes there really are happy endings. For you and Clarissa, too. I'll be at Gina's tomorrow helping her with her documentary. Clarissa and I traded numbers. Have her text me when she wants to get together again. I'm not sure when Gina wants me there, but it shouldn't take all day."

"I'll let her know. I need to talk to you for a second." Eddie pulls me aside, and Agatha walks to the car, waving goodbye. "What's going on with you two?"

I frown. "Nothing. Why?"

"I don't know. You like her?"

"She's nice," I say cautiously. The last thing I need is a matchmaker. "She's got a good voice."

"That's it?"

"She's got a boyfriend. She's gorgeous, and I'm lucky she's not married." The last part slips out and I grimace.

Eddie laughs. "Neither of those situations would have stopped Shep and me. Work around him."

"No. I don't like her that way. She's funny and easygoing, and that's good enough for someone staying with me for two weeks."

"Okay, then," he says, clearly not believing me. "Come back when you're done at the store. We can still grill and I'll kick your ass playing football. Clarissa's going to be gone for a while yet."

"What would Agatha do? I can't leave her at my house by herself," I say, though I did just that to keep my date with Polly.

"She brought work with her or something, didn't she? Order her a car and she can go to Olivia's. I thought they would be spending all their time together anyway."

"No." I stare, and he smirks.

Agatha opens the car door and yells, "Are you comin' or what?"

"I guess it's 'or what,'" Eddie mumbles.

"Fuck you."

"She won't be. See you later," he says and puckers his lips.

I flip him off. As much as I envy him, I'm happy he's in a place where he can joke. The past two years sucked, and he deserves it. "I worked with Shep a bit this afternoon—he's got more than his share of songs written. Tonight I'll try to make some progress on mine. Let's plan to meet up over there tomorrow. I want to get this album done as much as he does."

"Sounds good, and I'll fuck around too, since I'll have some time later."

I hold out my hand for a handshake, and he does, but he turns it into a hug, our fists clasped between us. "Thanks."

That little word encompasses years of loyalty, emotions, and feelings. "Anytime."

I walk out to the car, my heart bursting from so many different things. I went from a poor kid growing up on the wrong side of the tracks to the lead guitar player of the most famous rock band in the world.

I'm Brock Farris of Ghost Town. I don't have anything or anybody, and I'm out of milk.

Chapter Eight

Agatha

Grocery shopping is as amusing as I thought it would be. This huge, muscular man wearing black biker boots, distressed jeans, a faded, worn-out t-shirt, the rock band logo on his chest barely recognizable (Black Sabbath), his reddish-brown beard, and his hair, severely parted and shaved on one side of his head, pushing a cart and choosing which bread to buy.

I snap pictures, and he tolerates it, ignoring me. People stare, but he was right. No one cares if he's out of coffee creamer, and we're left alone.

The whole thing jams splinters into my heart.

Brock could have been any man, in any part of the United States, or the world, for that matter. A bachelor again after a failed marriage, not a part of his kids' lives, works and goes home to an empty house where he heats up a TV dinner, flips through the channels, and finding nothing, goes to bed only to lie in the dark and try to figure out where it all went wrong.

I never did the family stint, so I don't know how it feels to go from a family of four to being alone, practically overnight.

I've always been alone. My mother's agency came before anything else, and when it was time for me to go to school, she ordered me to move out of her house and live in the dorms saying I needed to learn to take care of myself. She took so little interest in my life besides bossing me around, she didn't understand I already could.

"Is this going to be enough?" he asks.

We've covered the entire store, and what we bought could last me over a month.

The candy aisle hung me up, as did all their cheese, but I tossed in what I wanted and he didn't say a word. "I think so. We're spending the day at Liv and Sheppard's tomorrow, right? Should we bring anything?"

"I never do, but we can bring more wine if you want."

"We can do that for Sheppard's mom, but let's circle back and grab a fruit platter. Now that she's pregnant, Liv should eat healthy foods."

"I'm sure she was before, but whatever you think."

He doesn't complain when it's time to pay, sliding his debit card chip into the slot without so much as blinking at the total.

We unload, and I help him put our purchases away. His kitchen is three times the size of mine, and my bedroom's walk-in closet would fit inside his pantry—twice. He piles what belongs into my arms, and I try to shove things in the right places. He has a system, the shelves labeled, and I picture him alphabetically organizing the crackers and pasta boxes while I'm sleeping.

He shifts things around the freezer, and I sit on the island and sip a glass of wine. I like looking at him. His broad shoulders and strong thighs. Graham's sleek, designer suits and a smile he bought from the dentist. There's something earthy, appealing, *real,* about Brock's slightly crooked teeth.

"Do you want to go to Olivia's?" he asks, shutting the

freezer door. The refrigerator is a commercial-sized monstrosity. It must have come with the house, because there's no way Brock would have chosen something that huge for only himself.

"Trying to get rid of me?" I tease. When we scheduled my visit, I was all set to stay with her, and I thought I would see her more than I have. Now she's planning a wedding and maybe not feeling well if morning sickness has kicked in, and with her running EmpowerHer, Inc, staying with Brock turned into a good thing. She doesn't feel the need to entertain me all the time, and I'm not underfoot the way my mother always made me feel.

He leans his hip against the island and steals my glass. "No, but you're here to see her, not me."

"But I like seeing you," I say as he sips.

His eyes never leave my face. "Is that right?" he murmurs.

"Hmmm. You're a locked box, and the key is around here somewhere."

Rubbing his thumb over my cheek, he says, "You might not like what you find."

"One woman's junk is another woman's treasure," I say, retrieving my glass from his hand.

He chuckles. "Well, I've never heard it put quite that way before. I don't know if that's an insult or a compliment."

I brush my fingers through his beard. "I think, if you ever asked her, your ex-wife would say she made a mistake."

His golden-brown eyes flatten. "That's the last thing she would say."

He tries to step away from me, but I stop him with a hand to his shoulder. "Don't go. What would she say?"

"I can tell you what she said."

"What?" There's no sound in the room but our breathing.

He leans forward, and our lips graze. "'The money wasn't worth it.'"

I whimper, and he pushes his lips against mine, muffling the sound.

He rescues the wineglass, setting it on the island without breaking our kiss. With my hands free, I wrap my arms around his shoulders and hug him close, Brianna's words clogged in my throat.

He jerks me against his chest and angles his head, nudging my lips open with his tongue. There's nothing of Graham in the way he holds me, nothing of him in the way Brock tangles his fingers in my hair and yanks, trapping me in place. Primitive, dangerous. The electricity.

I was right, about the storm.

It's inside him, and I want to be in the middle of it.

He drags his mouth away from mine, huffing. "Agatha."

"What?" I'm breathless and I want him to kiss me again. "Why did you stop?"

"You have a boyfriend."

"No, I don't. I broke up with him before I flew out. It wasn't working." And why things weren't working can be left for another time. "We were together for three years, but it was a dead end. He wouldn't commit." That's the trouble. He did. Just not to me.

"He's a jackass."

"Yeah, he is." Brock needs affection, and I have no problem giving it. Instead of kissing him again, I pull him close with my legs around his waist and rest my head on his shoulder. "I'm sorry your wife said that to you."

He shrugs, and I understand what he doesn't say. We're taught what we know.

I whisper against his neck. "Will you feed me?"

"You're always hungry," he says, his lips against my ear.

I lift my head, and I can't stop the tear that drips down my cheek. "I'm starving."

"Angel." He wipes the tear off my cheek with his lips. "Do you still want the chop salad? Will that be enough food?"

"With the bread?" I ask, my voice small.

"With the bread."

"Then it will be enough. Can we watch a movie after?"

"Yeah."

I think he's going to step away from the island, but instead he holds me, his strong hands splayed over my back.

I lean against him, my stomach growling. He's feeding me, but in a different way, and like a plant sitting in the sun, I absorb every second.

I help him make giant bowls of chopped lettuce, tomatoes, cucumbers, ham cubes, croutons, and bleu cheese dressing. Flaky rolls accompany the salads, and by the time I work my way to the bottom, the salad is enough, for a little while. We sit at the table like we did this morning when we ate omelets, his fingers occasionally brushing the top of my hand. We don't speak, too busy inhaling our food.

There isn't much to clean up, and when we're done, he walks with me to his theatre. "What do you want to watch?"

"I'm not sure. I chose our bloodbath marathon, why don't you choose?"

"Do you like indie films?"

"Yeah. Sometimes I'll go to a showing at one of the movie theatres downtown. What do you have?"

"I helped produce a movie called *Wildflowers*. Have you heard of it?"

"You produced that? There was a write up about it in the *Star Tribune* last year, but I never saw it. Let's watch it."

We settle on the loveseat and recline, and he brings it up.

Soon we're lost in a movie about a young woman who protests to save a field of wildflowers near her home. No one understands why she's so passionate about the field, and most of the movie is of her fighting with friends and the company who wants to purchase the land from her father.

The company eventually gives up, and her father kicks her out of their house, blaming her for the loss of income.

The last scene is of her sitting in the middle of the field, and we're left with the knowledge she wasn't saving only the field, she was saving her own life. The field is where she can be herself, where she finds peace in a world that's not so peaceful.

If I had to shove this movie into a genre box, I couldn't call it a romance as there was no romance in it. It wasn't a domestic thriller or a mystery. I would call it a love story. A story about loving yourself enough to fight for what you need, even at the cost of anything else, *everything* else.

"I was going through a rough time when I decided to produce this. I could relate to her. I've always known my place, you know?" he says as the credits fade and the giant screen darkens. "Poor kid who had to go to college on a scholarship and a prayer. A member of a band that wasn't mine. Ghost Town has always belonged to Shep, and I respected that, accepted it. When I met Bri, I fell in love with her the second we were introduced, but something felt not right, and I always blamed myself. After she divorced me, if Eddie hadn't been in the same situation, I'm not sure where I'd be right now. I wanted people to know they aren't alone and being adrift doesn't have to be a death sentence. Fighting for what you need is never wrong."

"What do you need, right at this minute?" I ask, my words disappearing in the darkness. It's so black in here, I can't see his face.

"Right at this moment? If I could have anything I wanted?"

"Yeah." I want him to say me. *You, angel. Stay with me, don't go back to Minnesota.* But of course he doesn't.

"I'd want to know where I end up after the tour. We're going to split up, and I'm the only one with nowhere to go."

"I understand."

"You do?" His hand finds mine, and he links our fingers.

"Yeah. I was thinking the same thing. After my visit, I won't see Liv anymore. She'll be busy being a mom, running her organization with Gina. She'll drop me off at the airport, and I'll tell her goodbye, and that will be it." Maybe I'll cry about it later, but for now, my voice is firm, matter of fact. How I call my authors with bad news. Sorry, your book didn't get picked up. I tried my best, but we'll have to shelve it for the time being. Sorry, your proposal is strong, but there's no market for it right now. Sorry, editors loved the concept, but they want to rip it apart, something I know you don't want to do. The hard facts I tell myself. Sorry, one of your best friends won't have time for you anymore, but you can make new ones, right? Sorry, the man in which you invested three years of your life doesn't really love you. Better luck next time.

"Then you understand what I'm talking about."

"Yeah, but you live here. You can still see your friends whenever you want."

"Watch Shep become a dad for the first time, watch Eddie and Clarissa create a home with Abby and Mason. Watch Dalt and Melody do the same with their baby on the way. Why be a little kid looking through the window of a candy store when he can't go in?"

"Why can't you go in?" My eyes are adjusting to the lack of light, and I can just make out his profile.

"Why can't you? Fly out every once in a while to see Olivia? She still has family in Minnesota, doesn't she? Shep will fly up there with her whenever she wants to go. You don't know how desperately he wants her happy here. He'd do anything for her. A flight to Minnesota a few times a year would be nothing for him. Why write her off because she's pregnant?"

"Why write your friends off because they have families?"

"Because they have what I want, and it hurts to see that. You said you didn't want kids, so what's your excuse?"

"Things wouldn't be the same." It sounds lame even to my own ears. Between my job and Liv's, how often did we see each other? More than we will, yeah, but it's not like we saw each other every day. We met because of our jobs, and what it gave us it also took away.

"Life goes on, angel."

"You want more kids, huh?"

"It's more than having more children, it would be a second chance. A do-over. I haven't seen Lexi and Layla in a couple of years. The only way I know what's going on with them is if I stalk their social media. I'd choose my wife more carefully, and in the prenup, if we ever divorced, I would make sure I could keep our children. I wouldn't make the same mistake twice."

I crawl into his lap and press my chest against his. "What about falling in love?"

"I never said anything about falling in love."

Sliding my lips over his, I say, "Yes, you do. With every word you say."

He holds my face in his hands and kisses me. We make out, slow, sweet kisses in the dark.

I turn my face away and draw in a ragged breath. "I'm sorry. I should go to bed."

"Did I hurt you?" He kisses the curve of my jaw and down my neck. His beard scratches in the most delicious way.

"No, and I don't want to hurt you."

"I can be a grown up," he mumbles against my skin.

"What does that mean?"

"If you want to see where this goes, I can handle it if you can."

That doesn't sound like a good idea, but in his lap, his cock hard underneath me, I'm already close to succumbing. It would be easier to go home and face Graham if I had a fling while I was in LA. He wouldn't like it. Would likely get severely pissed off, but what do I care? I can do what I want, and if I want to sleep with Ghost Town's lead guitarist, that's none of his business.

Except, I don't have it in me to use someone like that. "You want what I won't be around to give you."

"I want what no woman in her right mind is going to give me, Agatha. The second Bri divorced me, I knew the rest of my life would be resorting to taking what I can get. If I can have twelve days with you, let me have them."

"Liv will hate me if I hurt you."

"This is between us. Please?" He covers my lips with his, gently encouraging me to open my mouth. His hand is warm against my thigh, his fingers sliding under the frayed hem of my shorts.

It will be more than a little affair between us. Liv's been here since the beginning of June, and from what she's told me, every decision ever made is about the band. What I do while I'm here will affect the band. They may have only one album left, a shortened tour, but what Brock and I do will become part of the band's history.

"Okay," I say, already regretting letting him talk me into this. "Come to bed."

"No. I told Eddie and Shep I'd have something solid tomorrow."

"Then I'm going upstairs. Thanks for the movie." I wiggle off his lap.

"Goodnight, angel."

"Goodnight."

He doesn't follow, and reluctantly, I leave him sitting in the dark.

A crash jerks me out of my light sleep, and I scrabble for my cell on the nightstand. It's 3:17AM, and knowing Brock's penchant for middle-of-the-night adventures, I pull on my robe and cautiously go downstairs. I don't hear anything, and in the kitchen, I check the oven. It isn't on.

In the living room, I peer outside, looking for Brock near the pool, but he isn't out there.

His jagged sob tears my heart in two, and I pad to the sunroom. He lifted the blackout curtains a few inches and he's sitting on the floor in the pool lights' glow, his head in his hands.

Pieces of a splintered guitar are scattered a few feet away from him.

I kneel on the hardwood floor. "Hey."

"Go away," he rasps.

"What's wrong?"

"Nothing. I said go upstairs."

"No." I wiggle between his legs and snuggle into his chest.

"Why can't you listen?"

"I am listening, but not to the stupid stuff you're saying."

"Then what am I saying if you're not listening to me speak?" His voice is nothing but an anguished growl.

Leaning away from him, I look into his eyes and say, "That you're lonely. That you're doubting your skills as a songwriter because the words won't come. That you think you aren't worth anything." With every word, more shadows fill his eyes. I didn't know how accurate my guesses would be.

If he wants the twelve days, he can have them.

I lift his hand to my breast. "Make love to me, Brock."

He gently squeezes, and my nipples harden. "Right here, on the floor, with bits of my guitar all over the place."

"No. Right here, on the floor, in this room with your demons and your wordless songs. Give me what you keep from your friend with benefits. I want it all."

He searches my eyes for one second, and then his mouth is on mine, his hot breath filling my lungs. With a strong hand between my shoulder blades, he gently guides me to the floor, and I writhe, aching to be closer.

"We need to check in, angel," he says, his lips fluttering against my cheek, his hand skimming up my thigh.

"What? Touch me."

"Do I need a condom? Do you want me to wear one? I don't have any. I wear condoms with . . . her, but I've never brought her to my house."

I pause, my hand pressed against his neck, his pulse erratic under my palm. I've always been very careful with birth control. If I decided to have children, it would be between me and my partner, planned with love, knowing we were doing something that could never, ever, be taken back.

He withdraws, lifting off the floor, thinking I'll judge him for the places he finds comfort.

"Brock."

His gaze is anywhere but my face.

"Hey." I grab his chin, needing a steady grip to force him to look at me.

Finally, his eyes meet mine.

"I'm protected, and I don't have anything. If you say you don't have anything, then I trust you."

He swallows. "I'm okay, and she is, too. I care about her, Agatha, and I pay for her checkups."

"My ex was good about his physicals, and I know he doesn't have anything." I don't let him go, my fingertips digging into his skin, and while I have his full attention, I say, "Thank you for caring about me like you care about your friend."

"I always will." He lowers his head, and I meet him halfway, pressing my lips to his, clinging to him, my arms around his neck.

His fingers find me hot and wet, and he shudders, slipping two inside me. I bear down, adding to the pressure. It hasn't been that long for me, but Graham and I lost the passion, the urgency, a long time ago. Our lovemaking turned familiar, a way to pass the time, much like I'm sure Brock and his friend with benefits share an evening in bed. That isn't wrong, finding contentment that way, but nothing can match making love with someone whose desire threatens to electrocute you with every touch.

I can't help but moan, the low rumble vibrating in the back of my throat, his control evident in the tender way he strokes me. His thumb finds my clit, and I rip my mouth away from his. "No, I want you to be inside me when I come."

"Then take your panties off," he says, and when he lets me go, I push back a cry of disappointment. I do what he says, wiggling out of the scrap of lace and tossing it toward the splintered wooden pieces of his guitar. My nightgown is bunched around my waist, the hardwood floor digging into my back, and I have never felt sexier.

"Hurry," I whimper.

He unbuttons and unzips his jeans, yanking them down just enough to free his cock. He kneels, resting his ass against his heels, and he drags me toward him, his hands gripping my hips.

I've never had sex like this before, and needing him inside me more than I have ever needed anything, I lift up, encouraging him to take what he wants.

Holding his cock, he slides into me in one smooth stroke. "You're so wet. Is this what you wanted, angel?" he asks, finding my clit.

"Yes." My fingertips dig into the floor, searching for something to hold on to, but there's nothing.

He adjusts, leaning forward, pushing inside me as far as he can go, and the tip of his cock touches the center of my body, the lips of my pussy hugging the base of his thick shaft.

"You're so beautiful, Agatha," he says softly. "Come for me. I want to watch you. I'll never forget tonight."

I close my eyes and let my senses carry me away: the feel of his fingers circling my clit, how hard he is inside me, the scent in the room, his sobs echoing in my ears as well as my heart. The orgasm builds in my belly, and my pussy clenches desperately at his cock. He can tell I'm about to come, and he slides his fingers faster and faster against my slippery skin.

"Brock," I cry, moving my hips in time with his touch.

"It's okay, angel, I've got you," he says, and even though I've heard the words before, something about the way he says them tips me over, and I come, the pleasure fizzing through my blood, my whole body sparkling.

I drift down from my high, cum leaking out of me.

He positions his body over mine without breaking our connection and brushes his lips over my cheeks. "Did you like that?"

Weakly, I laugh. "Very much."

"Good." He begins to move, and the friction starts the sparks all over again.

I gasp with every thrust, and he likes the sound, slamming

into me more forcefully with every hitch of my breath. "Harder," I urge. "Deeper."

"Fuck," he snarls, but he does what I say, ramming into me so hard I slide across the floor.

He comes, his cock jerking inside me, hot cum filling me and oozing out of my pussy. He's huge, and there's nowhere for it to go.

I'm covered in sweat, and I tremble, the perspiration cooling on my skin.

"I'm sorry if I was too rough," he murmurs, cuddling me to him, his beard scratching my cheek.

Turning my head so our lips meet, I say, "I had a feeling you needed to."

"I get frustrated, and in the moment, I never know where to put it. I don't ever want to hurt you on accident. You're going to be sore tomorrow, and it will be my fault."

"Hey," I say, and again, it's moments before he looks at me. "I asked you to, and you did. If I had asked you to stop, you would have done that, too. It won't be your fault, and I won't blame you. Do you understand what I'm saying?"

Several seconds go by before he says, "Okay, but if I ever do anything you don't want me to do, you need to tell me. I'll always be in control unless you tell me I don't have to be."

"I believe you." I tilt my hips; he's still hard. "You're a big guy."

He rests his arms on either side of my head, his fingers tangling in my hair. "I never want you scared of me."

Like Brianna was. I can hear it, even if he didn't say it.

"If she was scared of you, she didn't know you. You would never hurt me. Can you do me a favor, though?"

He freezes, expecting the worst. A learned reaction. "What?"

"I know this was my idea, but can we go to bed? You're not hurting me, but the floor is."

The tension drains out of him, and he chuckles. "That's on you. I would have been happy to carry you upstairs."

"It wouldn't have been the same. You needed me right then, and I needed you too. Sometimes you have to work with what you've got."

"Sometimes, that's true, but I will always listen to you first. I'm going to pull out. I'm sorry if it hurts."

"Kiss me," I whisper, lacing my fingers through his hair and lifting my legs over his ass. I don't want him to pull out.

He doesn't, and we end up making love all over again.

We finally go upstairs about five in the morning, the sun rising, painting the sky glorious shades of pink and orange. He undresses and climbs into his bed with me. Naked, I wrap my body around his, but I can't fall asleep.

He moves his fingers up and down my back. He knows I'm thinking about something and he asks, "Do you regret what we did?"

Resting my arms on his chest and propping my chin on the tops of my hands, I say, "I talk to Gina today."

He frowns, a slice of sunlight catching the scowl. "And you're going to tell her you regret what we did?"

"No. Stop that," I say, rubbing the tip of my nose against his. "Are your parents still alive?"

"Actually, no. They had me when they were older, and they passed away a long time ago." He smooths his hand over the back of my head, his fingers catching the snarls.

"I'm sorry. Do you have any brothers or sisters?"

"No, but my mom and dad had several between them. My

mom's youngest sister is still alive. She was a surprise, and she's several years younger than Shep's mom. I have a lot of cousins. They have families, and they invite me for the holidays but I usually turn them down. Ghost Town has always been more of a family to me, but I might have my own regrets about that now. Why?"

"Just curious. Were they proud of you?"

"My dad was too busy to do much more than work and sleep, but Mom was always worried about me. She thought I would get into drugs, but none of us did. Booze, yeah, but the other stuff, we didn't need the high. Real life was enough."

"It was easy for you, then," I say, envious his relationship with his parents was so uncomplicated.

"To make them proud of me? They loved me, but my childhood was a struggle. My mom cried when the university accepted my application, but that was mostly Eddie. He hounded me and practically wrote my cover letter. He put the stamp on the envelope himself and walked with me to the post office." He chuckles and shakes his head, caught in the memory. "They passed away while I was married to Bri, and I think that's why Mom let go. She thought Bri would take care of me for the rest of my life. I'm glad she wasn't around to see us divorce. It would have broken her heart."

"I'm sorry."

A corner of his mouth lifts. "It's okay. I've had a long time to come to terms with it. What about you? Is your mom proud of you?"

I rest my cheek against his chest and nestle into his warm body. "I don't think she's been proud of me a day in her life."

"I'm proud of you."

I scoff. "For what?"

"For caring about Olivia enough to encourage her to take Shep on as a client. For caring about Clarissa and what she wants to do with her life when she's little more than a stranger. Those might be tiny things to you, angel, but for the person on the other end, it can be life-changing."

"Those aren't anything. Any kind person would do that for someone."

"Then tell me something I can be proud of you for," he says, brushing a piece of hair out of my face. "Are you proud of yourself?"

"Are *you* proud of yourself?" I ask because I don't want to answer that.

"My life has been like pushing a boulder uphill, and I'm proud every day that I haven't let it crush me. Watching Shep flounder after Derrick's death, the appeal of it, you know?"

"The appeal of what?" I ask, my heart skittering.

He says it aloud, point blank, and the breath knocks out of me.

"Suicide."

I sit up and swallow, my mouth dry.

"You know when Shep went after her in the water, that's what Olivia was thinking about. She needed you, and for three years after her fiancé passed away, you were there for her. That's a long time to have someone's back, angel. I'm proud of you for that, even if you aren't proud of yourself." He rubs the pad of his thumb over my cheek. "You matter to people, Agatha. I care about you. Your mom might give you a hard time, and maybe you don't know why, but you grew up into a beautiful, kind, and intelligent woman." He nudges me forward and covers my mouth with his. "Who happens to be a very good kisser," he mumbles against my lips.

I laugh. "What would you have done if Sheppard hadn't recruited you into his cult?"

He sighs and rubs his face. "I don't want to think about it. I don't want to think about that at all. Go to sleep. You can have a few hours before we head over there."

I wiggle down and use his shoulder as a pillow. He wraps his arms tightly around me.

I matter to people *here*. I don't matter to anyone in Minnesota.

It would be nice if I did.

"Do you have a dress?" Brock's voice pushes through the sleepy haze.

"Do you want to borrow it?" I mumble against his chest.

"You're drooling on me, and no, I don't, funny girl. Olivia's been trying to text you and she messaged me when you didn't answer. Gina wants you to dress business casual."

"My phone's in my purse downstairs. I have something, I think. I better shower." I rouse myself and sit up. I was indeed drooling all over him, and I lick it off, gliding my tongue over his salty skin. "Hmmm."

"Keep it up, and you'll be late."

"I suppose I better not be, though spending the day in bed with you would be much more enjoyable."

"Why does she want to talk to you?"

"I got caught up in a bad book deal. It happens."

"That's it?"

I shrug uneasily. "Gina knew me. She'd obviously done some research and thought what I went through fit what she needed. It's not that I don't want to talk about it. It's that it happened a couple of years ago, and it would be nice to forget about it. I don't see the value in dragging it around, but Gina says it can help people. Whatever."

"Maybe you can. Clarissa already looks up to you. You can be a role model for other women."

A role model on how to fuck up your life, maybe. "You didn't get any sleep, did you?"

He blows out a breath. "No, and I'm not any closer to writing anything, either. Shep gets it, but the pressure's still there."

"Can I help?" I ask, crawling on top of him and sliding his cock inside me. He caresses my breasts, the pads of his thumbs skimming my nipples creating a zing that goes straight to my core.

"Do you want to be my muse?" he asks, leaning forward and kissing me.

"Yeah, but I want to be more than that." I stop when our tongues tangle together. I have to be careful what I say, what I promise.

He changes our positions and traps my hands above my head while he ravages me. I can't move, and I lie there and consume everything he pours into my body. He may not have a grasp of the words, but they're there, under the surface. He's afraid of letting them free because it will hurt, but I can't tell him it won't.

It will. It definitely will.

"Will you be okay?" Brock asks as we idle in Sheppard's driveway. Even after our lovely bout of morning lovemaking, I'm only five minutes late.

"Yeah. It won't be pleasant, but you know what will help?"

"What, angel?" he asks, holding the side of my face in his palm.

"Promise me tonight we can sit by the pool and drink."

A smile tugs at his mouth. "I like that too."

I open the car's door.

"Agatha."

"What?"

"When we go in there, they're going to know."

"Is that going to be a problem for you?" I ask, suddenly humiliated.

I'm not that great of a catch—not when someone like Brock Farris can have whomever he wants. He could go anywhere in the world, and he would have his pick of women. They would fall at his feet, and not because of the money. He's kind and good looking. I don't care if he does bake banana bread at 3 AM, any woman would be lucky to have him, and they would know it, too. Maybe there are things I don't know about his and Brianna's divorce, but if it bothered her he bashes his guitars into pieces when he's frustrated, that's her problem.

He doesn't say anything.

"I'm sorry," I mumble, staring at my feet. "We can hide—"

"I want to know if it's going to be a problem for *you*."

My gaze jerks to his. "I'm confused. Why would it be a problem for me? I just got out of a relationship, and if you think we moved too fast—"

"Because the last thing I want is for you to be ashamed you're with a fucking freak, okay? I know exactly what I am—"

"Shut up!" I yell, my voice bouncing around the inside of the car. I throw myself over the gear stick and cup holders and into his arms. I hug him, my chest heaving. "Shut up, shut up, shut up." I can't continue, sobs trapped behind my teeth, and I let out a sound that's half a moan, half a shriek, pressing my lips against his neck.

He traps me against him, burying one of his hands in my hair. "I'm sorry, Agatha. All my life I've been—"

I lift my head, tears streaming down my face. "You. You've been you, and that's perfect for me."

He kisses me hard, bruising my lips and banging my shoulder against the steering wheel. I kiss him back, ferociously, and we're lucky we're in the car and not having this out at his house. We'd be naked in five seconds having explosive sex, and we both need to cool off.

I rip my mouth away and wipe my cheeks. "I need to go inside. We were late before and we're later now. Gina might understand, but I can't be unprofessional."

"It's not a problem they know." He doesn't turn it into a question, but I treat it as one.

"No. Stop talking about it. I'm proud to be with you."

"If you keep saying it, angel, I'll believe you."

"Good. You're supposed to." I climb out of the car before we start another makeout session.

He grips my hand, maybe as a test, but I don't pull away. I'm not afraid of anything anyone inside is going to think or say. Liv will be concerned, but only because I don't live here, and yes, Brock will get hurt when I leave. He accepted that the day he suggested we have a good time while I'm here, and after I go, what he does can't be my responsibility.

The house is full, Tony and Eunice sitting in the living room with Eddie and Sheppard. Gina and Olivia are standing at the breakfast bar waiting for me. Everyone stares, and Gina's eyes widen. "You need to brush your hair, someone ate off your lipstick, and you have the worst case of beard burn I have ever seen. That's including when Shep gets a hold of Olivia. Were you crying? Your mascara's smudged up."

Liv gapes.

"Jesus Christ on a bicycle. Do I look that bad?" I mutter. "Can I borrow some concealer?"

"Yeah. Come on. You're going to look like you have a rash

on camera. You couldn't have waited until after the interview?" She's teasing, but I blush.

"Sometimes things just happen."

"Agatha."

I turn around and Brock's standing there, his eyes full of trepidation, his hands clenched into fists at his sides. I know how important this is, how much he needs the validation, and he won't get it unless I do this in front of everyone. I snake my arms around his neck and kiss him, slipping my tongue into his mouth. Tentatively, he kisses me back.

Gina yanks me away. "Your face already looks like you have measles," she chides. "You can do that after we're done."

Brock wipes the saliva off my lips with his thumb.

"Not helpful," she says, dragging me to the sliding glass door.

"Save me," I mouth to him.

My discomfort is worth everything when his eyes turn into melted Reese's Peanut Butter Cups and he smiles.

Chapter Nine

Brock

Eddie clears his throat.

Olivia opens her mouth then closes it again. She parts her lips, then thinks better of it. *I might as well use this opportunity to speak to her about Polly since I've put it off. That's not true. I forgot until something Agatha said in the car jammed it back into my head. Subjects don't have to be related for that to happen.* "Can I talk to you a minute?"

"Yeah," she says cautiously.

"Do you have a pen and something to write on? Can we go someplace private?" At this point, I'm not sure where we can go, but she grabs a notebook that always seems to be near her and tilts her head toward the patio.

We sit at the built-in picnic table, and I rest my arm along the edge of the bench. Agatha and Gina are already gone, and my lips still tingle from Agatha's goodbye kiss. She has guts. She knew I needed that and she was brave enough to give it to me.

The beach on a sunny day like this is full of tourists

gawking at the houses, and I breathe in the salty air. Agatha and I should spend the day near the water. Who knows when she'll see it again when she goes home.

"Are you all right?" Olivia asks. "Are you sleeping with her?"

I should have been prepared to defend myself—Agatha is Olivia's best friend.

"We have an agreement." I can't meet her eyes, and I stare into the distance.

"Did she tell you she broke up with someone before she came here?"

"Yeah." And I don't want to think about the bastard who wouldn't move heaven and earth to give her everything.

"Okay. What you two do is none of my business."

"That's all you have to say?" I ask. I was prepared for more of a lecture.

She lifts her hands, palms facing upward. "That's all I *can* say. She started seeing him around the time Michael passed away. I wasn't with it enough to tell her what I thought of the scumbag. She's looking for something, and I don't want her using you to find it. But we do, that's normal, and if you're going to let her, that's up to you. Maybe you'll find something you need with her, too, but you have to be prepared for that to go away. She's not going to stay here. Her mother won't let her."

"She told me her mother got pregnant with her using a sperm donor."

"Did your daughters have Barbie dolls?" she asks.

"Yeah, of course. What does that have to do with anything?"

"Little girls have dolls. Agatha's mother had her. Do you understand?"

"I think so," I say, but I don't, not really. Agatha alluded to her life not being her own, but I didn't know her mother held the puppet's strings.

"Don't fall in love with her. I don't want you getting hurt."

Sharply, I jerk my head to look at her. "I thought you would tell me not to hurt her."

"That's going to be inevitable. You're only going to add to what she's already feeling. In the time I've known her, she's never *not* hurt." She sighs. "What did you want to talk to me about? I'm going to guess it wasn't that."

"No." It's a good thing Olivia steered the conversation back to what I really needed to ask her or I would have forgotten again and Polly deserves better.

She waits.

"Eddie bought Shotgun Sally's and the Guitar Pick."

"He did. Is there a problem?"

"No, but I ah . . ." Fuck. I didn't think this through. Clarissa might even know Polly. "I know a waitress who works at one of the other bars in that area. She said it hurt when the women who worked at those places were offered a chance to go to school."

Olivia bites her lip. "I didn't consider something like that would happen, but I should have. The waitress you know, she wants to go to college?"

"Yeah. I'm willing to help her, and her friends, if that's what they want, but I have no idea how to go about something like that."

She taps her pen against her notebook. She hasn't written anything down yet. "That's a huge undertaking, and we're talking thousands of dollars."

"I can afford it. I don't have anything else to do with all that money."

"Do they need more than tuition?"

"What do you mean?"

"The waitress you know, she's working? I'm assuming you'll let her quit her job or drop down to part-time so she can focus on attending classes and homework. That means you have to supply her with a living wage while she goes to school, and if she's helping to support a family, you'll have to replace that income too. You can't just drop a load of money on people."

"Why? I trust her."

"It's not a matter of trust. Some people don't know how to manage money. You want it to last for however long this woman is in school and can find a job after she graduates. That could be years. You have to make sure she and her family are taken care of if you say she can do this. They'll be your responsibility."

"So we're looking at a trust, and a bank that will automatically deposit the money into an account they can access."

"Something like that. How many women do you want to do this for?" She winces.

"Don't you want to help them?" I ask, leaning forward. It's not like Olivia to turn away someone in need.

"Yeah, I do, but I'm not a trust fund manager. I have a life, you know." She doesn't sound angry, maybe a little put out I dropped this onto her shoulders, and I should have spoken with Pierce about it instead of her. Like Eddie, I use him whenever I need an attorney. We've known him since high school, and there's no one I trust more.

"Can't you hire someone? Someone just for this who can work for EmpowerHer, Inc?"

She scowls. "Do you want to do the job interviews? Maybe Eddie? How about Abby?"

"I'm sorry. I didn't mean to cause so much trouble."

She blows out a breath and covers my hand with hers. "You didn't. I'm worried about you and Agatha, that's all." She pauses. "Gina and I will get this sorted, and when we have something figured out, I'll let you know. Your friend wouldn't be able to enroll for Fall semester, it's too late for that, so we're looking at getting her situated for spring, though college is usually best experienced from the beginning of the school year. Next fall would be optimal if she can wait."

"She doesn't know I'm talking to you."

"Okay. I'm afraid we've taken on too much. Gina promised me EmpowerHer would stay small, but it's out of control. I'm tired all the time, and I still have to write my book, too, since Agatha already sold it, and now this wedding." Tears fill her eyes.

Agitated, I run my fingers through my hair. "Christ, Olivia, I'm sorry."

"No, I am. I like having Agatha here. I missed her." She rests her head on her hands and starts crying. Shep always knows when something is wrong, and seconds later, he's lifting her off the bench and carrying her into the house.

I didn't consider how much work it would be to arrange for Polly and her friends to go to school. I'm going to have to step up. I'm not stupid, I just need to be told what to do. Contacting Pierce would be a good start. He can work for EmpowerHer, Inc and drop some of his other clients.

"So, five hours after you told me you weren't going to sleep with her, you did." Eddie slides the glass door closed, drops into Olivia's vacant seat, and pushes a sweating beer bottle across the table.

"Twelve." Gratefully, I take a long pull, the fizzy liquid cooling the blaze in my throat.

He laughs. "You sure told me. You like her, huh?"

"She cuts through the noise somehow."

"Yeah. I know what you mean. When I'm with Clarissa, there's nothing else."

It's the same, but different. There's nothing but Agatha

when I'm with her, but Eddie doesn't have the constant static in his head I have in mine.

"Was Olivia warning you to stay away from her?"

"No, but she doesn't think we're a good idea, since Agatha will be going home in a few days."

"You never know. Olivia was only supposed to stay for the summer. Shep carried her upstairs and put her to bed. Isn't she feeling well?"

"She has a lot going on, and she's tired. Bri felt like crap through both of her pregnancies." She made sure I knew she felt like shit nonstop for two years because all I wanted was to be as close to her as possible, and sex was the only way I knew how to do it.

"Clarissa's pregnancy was hard on her, too, but while she hated me for not telling Shep about us, she still loved Mason. I'm thankful every day she went through what she did for our family. She's meeting up with Agatha later. She can't stop talking about it, and I didn't know she even liked books."

"When you have to do something, it takes time away from the things you want to do. She probably didn't have much time to read for pleasure. You should hire someone else to train Ginger and the other girls. Clarissa will want to spend as much time with Agatha as she can, and she doesn't get to see you when she's at the bar. Free up her time, Eddie."

Slowly, he nods. "I thought she was enjoying herself. You don't think she is?"

"I think she appreciates you had faith in her when you gave her the opportunity to train Ginger and the others, but now that she's been at it for a while, she doesn't want you to think she's not grateful. If she does want to be an agent, she needs time to figure it out. From what Agatha says, there's a lot that goes into it, and Clarissa can't do both."

"Okay. I'll talk to her. They're refurbishing, and it would be good timing for Clarissa to ease out of it. Thanks."

I sip my beer, content to hang out with a friend. I close my eyes and lean my head against the railing.

A few minutes later, Shep pokes his head out of the house. "You wanna jam a little? Liv's sleeping and so's Mom. Tony said he'd hang with us for a while."

"Sounds good," Eddie says, rising from the bench.

I stand up too, but I'm not as eager.

We meet in the den, and Tony's already there, strumming Shep's guitar. He was never interested in joining the band, preferred to support us by going to all our shows when we were nobodies. I sit at the piano like I always do, the phantom feeling of Agatha's hair slithering over my fingers. She wants to be my muse. Maybe I can ask her to brainstorm lyrics with me. I've never had help before, and cowriting songs that will live on forever will keep her with me after she's gone.

"Agatha says you're working on something," Shep says to me.

I lift a shoulder, my fingers resting on the keys. "I'm stuck. I can't get the words to come."

"Yeah, I got you. What about you?" he asks Eddie.

He taps out a rhythm on his legs. "I haven't made much progress there. Clarissa and I are still settling in, and having Abby with us is a change. A good change," he rushes to add, "but things are different."

Shep leans his ass against the back of the couch and crosses his arms over his chest. "We could hire out. Tell Dalt we're dry."

As much as I like the idea, I reject it quickly. "That's not our way."

"It's not, but this album won't be like the others."

"Maybe you haven't reconciled Derrick's death," Tony says from his seat on an ottoman near the fireplace.

"That was a long time ago. We can't be anything but over it," Shep says through clenched teeth.

"I don't agree," Tony says calmly. "There are still a lot of questions about who he was as a person, who you thought he was as a friend. Maybe you need to resolve those issues first. From what I know, he abused a lot of women, and none of you knew it. There has to be some guilt there."

Eddie tenses. He knew Derrick was beating on Clarissa and protected her the best he could. Maybe he does feel guilty he didn't do more—like tell Shep. I don't know what Eddie would have done if Derrick and Dalt hadn't fought on that scaffolding.

"You don't even know for sure Dalton was the one who killed Derrick." Tony strums the guitar, teasing out "Yesterday" by the Beatles.

Angrily, Shep pushes away from the couch. "Why would he take the blame for something like that? Something he could go to prison for?"

"There was no way he'd go to prison, not with how drunk Derrick was. Dalt has money to pay for the best attorney in Cali, and he did his job. The case didn't even make it to court. The judge reprimanded him, let him walk, and dismissed the whole thing. She was on the golf course half an hour later. People who get tickets for speeding are punished more harshly than that." He pauses. "Maybe he was covering up for someone. No one actually saw him push Derrick, did they? It could have been anyone."

Shep swears under his breath, but I don't know what he's reacting to. That Dalt got off, or the idea that Dalt wasn't the one to have killed Derrick after all.

I hadn't heard the court dismissed Dalt's case, and Eddie

hadn't either, his gaze meeting mine in surprise. I'm happy for him. Now he can enjoy the rest of Melody's pregnancy without that hanging over his head.

Who could have killed Derrick if it wasn't Dalt? He had motive and opportunity, but Derrick was a son of a bitch and everyone hated him. Maybe it was Melody, and Dalt took the blame. Derrick raped Shelly—maybe he tried to do the same to Melody and she paid him back. Melody isn't as soft as Eddie's ex-wife, and she wouldn't put up with that shit. Dalt's been in love with her for years. No way he would let her go to prison, especially if she killed Derrick for revenge.

I try to meet Eddie's eyes again, ask him what he thinks, but he's staring at his lap, his fingers digging into his thighs. He had motive for wanting Derrick out of the way.

Could be a lot of people did.

I did, too.

"If that's even remotely true, there's still no way to prove it, and there's no point in trying to figure it out. The only person who knows is Dalt, and if he was fine taking the blame, then he's not going to tell anyone the truth."

Tony tips his head at his brother in acknowledgement. "True. I mentioned it because I think you guys are hung up on it and it won't let you move forward. You need to start inviting Dalt to these kinds of meetings. Throw a party and tell him he and Melody are welcome to attend. You guys can't write music because you don't feel like a band."

That could be it for me. I don't feel like I'm part of a band because the end is near. I'm scared of the future, resentful Eddie and Shep have families to fall back on when the tour's over. The attitude around the final album is "get it out of the way," "let's get it done," and writing music has become a chore, not something I enjoy.

"You need to forgive him, Shep," Tony says quietly.

"Maybe Dalt had reasons for wanting Derrick dead that had absolutely nothing to do with your ex-wife. He was into some nasty stuff, and maybe Dalt was protecting the band. You guys have always been about honesty, integrity, and friendship. The band's whole brand has been built around that from the beginning. Or maybe, just maybe, Dalt really did only want to reason with him and it was an accident. Derrick was drunk, and like you said, it's over. If you're going to let it go, let the whole thing go. Olivia's pregnant and you met because no matter what the circumstances were, Dalt cares about you and has over a lifetime of that friendship. Go upstairs and be with your fiancée. She needs you now."

Without another word, Shep leaves, closing the wall behind him.

"You two have secrets," Tony says, seamlessly transitioning from "Yesterday" to "Norwegian Wood," "and keeping them is not helping Shep. It's not going to help you either, if you want to leave the past behind."

I pick up the notes, and Tony and I play until the end of the song.

I don't want to leave the past behind. It's all I have left.

Chapter Ten

Agatha

I follow Gina onto the patio, pausing to pull the pumps off my feet. "How did you know who I am?" I ask, trudging over the sand to keep up with her.

"When Olivia told me you were visiting, something niggled in the back of my brain, and I looked you up. You and Olivia act like Minnesota's in the middle of nowhere. I've actually been there several times. Some say Minneapolis is the creative hub of the Midwest."

"I don't know if I would go that far. Chicago's good for it, so is Indianapolis and Cincinnati. But, yes, we're fortunate."

Gina lets me into her house, and I brush the sand off the bottoms of my feet.

"Don't bother unless you want to put your heels back on, and you don't have to do that, either. Your feet won't be in the frame. You look nice. Thanks for humoring me."

"I just do what I'm told."

She flicks me a glance. "Yes, you do. Would you like something to drink? I usually have pastries and coffee set out, but what I would really like is to put a camera on you and catch you as naturally as possible."

Off-guard and defenseless, she means, but that sounds good to me, too. Not the natural part, but getting this over with quickly. "Can I fix my face?"

"I'll show you where my bathroom is, and you can use what you need out of my makeup bag. My foundation may be a bit too yellow for you. Perhaps dilute it with some skin cream. A clear lipgloss will smooth out the color you have left on your lips, and you can brush your hair if you don't mind using my pick. I can't drag a brush through this mess," she says, shaking her head full of kinky curls.

"Thanks."

I study myself in Gina's bathroom mirror, the white light displaying every pink blotch on my chin and cheeks. If that's the kind of affirmation he needs, I don't regret a single second. I will never let him say nasty things about himself, and he made me so angry in the car. I wish Brianna to hell and back if she let him talk that way, or worse yet, he's repeating what she told him over the years.

Gina's coloring and mine couldn't be more different, and I lightly apply her tinted moisturizer over the burn, tilting my face in the light as it disappears into my skin. That's not too bad. I take her suggestion and apply a clear coating of lipgloss over my lips, redistributing what's left of my original color. After I untangle the knots in my hair, I don't look terrible. Tired, but I always look like that, finding men crying over lost lyrics or not.

I step out of her bathroom, and she meets me in the hall-way. "You look great. I'm all set up. Your dress will look good."

My clothing was still folded in my suitcases, and the only dress I packed was a taupe sheath with a white ribbon in lieu of a belt. On the plane, I worried I should have brought more, but

Liv and I are the same size, and I thought if I needed something to wear, I could borrow something of hers. I didn't know I'd be staying with Brock, and I had to hang the dress in the bathroom to let the wrinkles fall out while I took a hot shower.

She leads me into a study decorated in white, sky blue, and hints of green. A camera sits on a tripod in front of a loveseat, and I sit my ass down, assuming it's where she wants me. She settles on an ottoman near the camera and using the viewfinder, adjusts it.

"Are you nervous?" she asks, twisting and grabbing a thin sheaf of paper from the desk behind her.

"No. I've been interviewed before on podcasts and such, though I'm not in front of a camera as much as Liv."

"Okay. I'll tell you what I told her. If I ask a question and you don't want to answer it, tell me, and I'll edit it out. Nothing is set in stone, and since you'll be here for a few more days, if I need something else, I'll let you know as soon as I can. I'd prefer not to have to finish this over Zoom. It takes away from the ambience and continuity I create filming here."

"Okay." I dry my palms on my dress. I am definitely going to need that drink by the pool later.

Gina turns the camera on. "I'm speaking with Agatha Sterling of the Sterling Literary Agency based in Minneapolis, Minnesota. Agatha, can you explain how you became a literary agent?"

I should be used to answering this. It's a natural question anyone would ask, whether they're interviewing you or not. Cocktail parties, book launches. I've been asked this several times over the course of my career, and it's never easy to lie. "My mother is a literary agent, and I liked the idea, so that's what I decided to do, too."

"Did you go to school for it?"

"I majored in publishing at the University of Minnesota."

"You were successful right from the beginning, selling your first book at auction for six figures. Why would you say that is?" Gina asks, her tone pleasant and professional.

My hands tremble in my lap. "Lucky, I guess."

"What do you tell people who say you owe your success to your mother?"

"That they're right." I never interned for an agency, was never a junior agent, never slogged through slush at midnight hoping for my big break. The second I graduated from university, I stepped into a corner office at my mom's agency complete with my own assistant. From my very first day, every editor knew who I was, and they all clamored to work with me. I never would have had that starting a career on my own. Twenty-five years old, and I was given what an agent needs years to acquire, if they do at all.

"Nepotism is a controversial subject. Where do you think you would be without your mother's influence, without her connections?"

Somewhere I wanted to be. On a path I chose for myself. "I don't know. I never had to find out, so the question is rather moot, isn't it?"

"She . . . encouraged you to follow in her footsteps. Do you resent her for that, or do you appreciate being given the opportunities you have?"

I'm irritated, and I push back. "What about you? You grew up with money, your parents are famous actors. You can't tell me you haven't used their fame and connections to get to where you are."

Gina smiles, but it's nothing the audience will see. "I would be foolish not to use them as a springboard for my own career, but I like to think that my skill as a director, my talent, is what fuels my success. Do you consider yourself talented?"

"No."

"Surely you don't credit your mother for all your accomplishments. I looked up the list of books you've sold, and it's impressive. For eleven years you've known exactly what to supply to the market, and you've had several number one bestsellers you've chosen from an overflowing inbox. How do you do that if you're not talented?"

I lift my chin. "Hard work," I say, but I boxed myself in.

"Why are you working so hard in a profession you didn't want?"

"Who said I didn't want it?"

"Did you?"

I look away from the camera and tears fill my eyes.

"If you knew the success you would have but could go back in time and choose your own career path, would you still choose to be a literary agent?"

"What good is success if no one is proud of you?" I whisper.

"Are you proud of yourself?"

Gina echoes the question Brock asked me this morning. I couldn't answer him then, and I can't answer her now.

I get up and walk out.

The second I step foot on the sand, Sheppard's on me. "Can you sit with Liv?"

"What's wrong?" I ask, surprised he sounds so worried.

"I don't know, and she won't talk to me. I'm afraid she regrets—" He chokes.

"She doesn't. I'll go talk to her. Where is she?"

"In our bedroom."

I follow him up the narrow set of steps from the sand to the patio. No one is around, not even Brock, and I'm worried he left me here until Sheppard says, "He's in the den with Eddie."

"Thanks. Am I that transparent?"

"No, but you looked like Scout when she can't find Liv."

"Hmm." I bet I did.

I've never been upstairs in their house before, not getting the tour I wanted my first day here, and Sheppard ushers me into a large bedroom, the blinds lowered. Liv's lying in bed, and she looks so much like how she would when I visited her after Michael's death that my heart leaps into my throat. I try to smile reassuringly at Sheppard, but I fail, and he quietly closes the door.

I pad across the floor and sit near her on the mattress. "Hey, Sheppard's worried about you. What's up?"

"I don't know," she says, her voice a sad rasp. "Empower-Her, Inc is taking off, and I have my book to write, my blog to maintain. I'm so busy . . ."

"And you thought if you were busy you wouldn't be homesick."

She sniffles. "Something like that."

"When are your mom, her husband, and your sister coming?"

"Two days before you leave. They're on the same flight as yours going home."

"That won't help, will it?" Seeing her family for such a short amount of time won't help at all.

"Not really."

"What can I do? I can't write your book for you, but I can email the publisher and get you an extension. I'll do it today and tell them you need an extra forty-eight to sixty-two months. I'll tell them you're pregnant and need the time. What else?"

She doesn't say anything.

"I'm going to ask Clarissa to show me how to get into your website, and I'm going to write a blogpost explaining you have a baby on the way and you jumped into getting your career back on track when you should have been focusing on your personal life. Everyone will understand. Clarissa will help me publish it, and we'll leave it up just like that until you feel like blogging again. What else?"

She still doesn't say anything.

"EmpowerHer, Inc isn't going in the direction you thought it would. When you were explaining it to me, it had nothing to do with buying bars and sending women to school. If your focus has shifted, that's one thing, but you can't keep adding what your organization will do for women without proper planning, staff, and adequate funding. You need to meet with Gina and talk to her because unfortunately, EHI isn't mine."

She remains quiet, tears leaking from her eyes.

"After I email your publisher and post that blog entry, I'm going to ask Clarissa for OB/GYN recommendations because I know you, Miss Bloom, and I bet you haven't had a checkup yet. You should be on folic acid and prenatal vitamins. You cannot be stressed out while you're pregnant. You'll get high blood pressure and that's not safe for you or the baby."

"Okay," she whispers.

"Then you need to take a cue from Clarissa and tell Sheppard you want to redecorate this house and the second Tony and Eunice leave, you want to turn one of the guest bedrooms into a nursery. I know you haven't asked Sheppard if you can make this house yours, and you need to, Liv, if you're going to think of this house as your home. And if you don't want to live here, be honest and tell him you want to choose a place together. You're homesick because you don't feel like you belong, and hun, that's not right."

She sits up and hugs me. "I missed you so much."

"I missed you, too, but I can't speak for you. Sheppard thinks you regret moving here. You need to talk to him, Liv. Just like telling him you're pregnant. He *loves* you and will do anything for you. You are not inconveniencing him telling him what you need. He wants you happy." I pause. "Regret isn't a good way to start your baby's life."

"I know. I don't. I'm just overwhelmed."

"Don't be. I took care of fifty percent of your worries. I'm going to go downstairs, fix you some lunch, and get on that fifty percent while you rest. Then later, if you feel good enough, we need to plan your wedding. You can't let that stuff go until the last minute. And you want this," I say twisting her engagement ring. "It's the only thing that matters."

She lies against the pillow, her eyelids fluttering shut. "You're right. Thank you."

"You are surrounded by people who love you. I'll send Sheppard up with a tray. He's so worried about you. You're lucky." I lean over and kiss her cheek.

Everyone looks up at me from the living room when I stand at the top of the stairs. Sheppard looks terrified, and this time I'm able to smile and ease his heart.

While I heat up soup and fill a plate full of fruit, I explain what she needs. Clarissa arrived while I was talking to Liv, and she rushes into the den for Liv's laptop.

Sheppard hugs me. "Thank you for that. I'm sorry I haven't been there for her."

"She's never been good at asking for what she needs because she's spent most of her life taking care of other people, but now that she's pregnant, you're going to have to nudge her now and then. She bit off more than she could chew, hoping to turn California into her home, but that's your job, Sheppard. You asked her to stay here, okay?"

He nods, and without another word, he carries the tray upstairs, Scout on his heels.

Clarissa and I set up in the living room while Brock and Eddie start a game of poker with Eunice and Tony. Brock's been watching me, guarded, and while Eddie shuffles, I wrap my arms around him from behind and kiss his cheek. "It's okay," I whisper into his ear.

I'm not sure why I said it or what I'm referring to, but he says, "As long as you're here, it is."

I feed Mason a bottle while Clarissa writes a blogpost informing Liv's readers why she can't blog for the foreseeable future. She's an excellent writer, professional and succinct, and she presses Publish twenty minutes later. "Can you check the comments and reply to people if necessary? I don't want Liv to worry about any part of her website," I say, pulling the empty bottle out of Mason's mouth and adjusting him on my shoulder. He fell asleep and he's dead weight in my arms.

"Yeah. Olivia's popular and there will be a lot, but I'll be able to stay on top of it. When I got here, Eddie asked if I still wanted to train Ginger and the other girls. Somehow, he knew I was getting burnt out. I want to spend as much time with you as I can before you go back to Minnesota, and I miss having evenings at home with him, Mason, and Abby. It's amazing when people know what you need and then actually take the time to give it to you. I've never had that before."

"I haven't either. It's always nice if you can find it." I snuggle Mason and inhale the sweet scent of formula and baby. "Can you go into my email and write Liv's publisher? You can pretend you're me. I would, but my hands are full."

Clarissa's fingers freeze over the keyboard. "Are you sure? I can hold Mason."

"Hey," I say, and she looks at me. "You're a good writer. I wouldn't have asked if I didn't think you could do it, and do it well."

"Thank you," she says and blushes.

"You wanna write a memoir? I could sell it for a million dollars."

Her mouth drops open. "Are you serious? What would I have to write about?"

"Are *you* serious? You went through, and survived, an abusive relationship with the bass guitarist of the most popular rock band in the world. Then you went on to marry his bandmate and have his baby, maybe not in that order, but that only adds to the appeal. You have no idea how fast people would eat that up."

She glances at Eddie, who, in that moment, looks at her, and she wiggles her shoulders. "Maybe I will."

"Don't forget us little people."

"I'll always be one of the little people."

I sigh. "I feel you there."

Clarissa writes the email to Liv's publisher, and after a little guidance from me, hits Send. Liv will have even more to write about after her baby is born, and they'll be all too happy to wait for her. After that, Clarissa and I go through some of my slush. I explain why some books have potential, why some don't, and ask her opinion on some to see where her instincts lay.

Brock pours me a glass of wine and delivers it with a beer-tinged kiss, and there's something in my heart that fizzes. It wasn't until much later when I could identify the feeling.

I was happy.

It's not long after that Liv and Sheppard come downstairs. She looks better, and she joins us in the living room. She and Clarissa talk OB/GYNs, pregnancy, and wedding dresses, and Sheppard sits in during the last few hands of poker.

We order pizza, and it's near midnight when Brock flops onto the couch and asks, "Are you ready to head back?"

"Yeah. How are you holding up?" We've been here for over twelve hours.

"I owe you a drink by the pool."

I rest my forehead against his arm. "God, that sounds perfect."

The goodbyes are spoken quickly in the driveway, especially for Clarissa and Eddie who want to put Mason to bed and check on Abby who stayed behind to sort through clothing and other things that were shipped from her room at her mother's house. Eddie buckles the baby into his car seat, but Clarissa lingers near Brock's car. "Can I see you tomorrow?" she asks tentatively, unsure if she's bothering me.

Now that I know how Liv is *really* doing, I plan to spend as much time with her as possible, and I say, "Yeah. I'll be here all day." Gina will probably corner me too, and ask to keep going with the interview.

"Thanks. I don't want to bother you."

"You're not. You're Liv's friend, which means now you're my friend. The guys will figure out times."

"Yes, we will. Come on," Eddie says, urging her toward the car with a hand to the back of her neck. "You can pick this up tomorrow."

She sighs and leans into his side. "Goodnight."

Gently, he helps her into the car, kisses her, and shuts the door with a quiet click. He backs out of the drive, and their headlights cut through the dark.

I hug Liv. "Get some sleep, and we are going to talk tomorrow, you got me?"

"Yeah." Her eyes twinkle suspiciously, some of her spark surfacing after a long day. "I have a few things to ask you, too."

"I'm sure you do, but this is about you. I love you. I never want to see you like that again."

"I know. I'm sorry."

"Goodnight, you guys."

Sheppard kisses my cheek and hugs Liv to him, her back against his chest. "Goodnight. Drive carefully."

Brock opens the car door for me, and gratefully, I sink into the seat. He climbs behind the wheel, lifting a hand to Sheppard and Liv before backing out of the drive and following Eddie and Clarissa on the highway toward their neighborhood.

We don't speak, but he holds my hand.

I doze, and he rouses me with a kiss when he parks in his driveway. "Did you want to go to bed?"

"No. I've been looking forward to this all day."

"So have I, angel."

He lets us in and walks with me up the stairs, a firm hand to my lower back. In my room, I close my suitcases and carry them across the hall to Brock's bedroom. I'm not going to pretend this isn't where I'm going to sleep for the rest of the time I'm here.

"Okay?" I ask when all he does is stare.

"Yeah." He clears his throat and changes from his jeans into shorts and a t-shirt.

He unzips my dress, and I breathe a sigh of relief when I wiggle out of it and put on my nightgown. I should have changed into something of Liv's, but with Mason in my arms most of the evening, I forgot. The satin against my skin without a bra feels divine, and my mouth waters thinking about a couple inches of whiskey and dipping my feet in the pool.

He tangles our fingers together and reluctantly lets go to pour whiskey into the glasses I like. The pool is steaming in the evening air, and I can't move across the brick and grass fast enough. He's chuckling when he catches up with me, and by the time he sits, I'm already swishing my feet back and forth, half my whiskey gone, the warmth traveling through my body.

"Did you and Gina have a good talk?" he asks, dropping next to me and dipping his feet into the water.

I stiffen. "Not really. I walked out on her."

"Angel. That doesn't sound like you. What happened?"

"More of the same conversation we had this morning. Do you know how degrading and humiliating it is when you can't say anything you have belongs to you?"

"Yeah."

Shaking my head, I say, "It's not the same. You were part of a group. You wrote songs too, contributed your musical expertise. It wasn't all Sheppard."

"Maybe not, but Ghost Town was his idea. His voice carried us through thirty years of music. He's afraid the band won't sound like us because Derrick isn't here anymore, but that's all in his head. The only way we wouldn't sound like us is if he were gone. It's humbling to be a part of something so huge, but at the same time to be such an insignificant part of it no one would miss you if you left." He brushes my hair away from my face. "If you think you don't have anything of your own, create it. Find it. You're what? Liv's age? Thirty-four, thirty-five? Do you know what you want?"

"Maybe that's part of it. I *don't* know. My mother's never let me think about what I would choose for myself."

"I think I can tell you."

"Oh, yeah? Try it, hotshot." I try to sound brave, but I'm not.

"I watched you tonight, holding Mason, talking Clarissa through what you were doing for Olivia. You want friends, and you want a man who will bring you a glass of wine because you have a baby sleeping in your lap. You want a family, angel, and when you go back to Minnesota, you should find that for yourself. You were happy tonight, and it didn't have anything to do with your job, how many books you sold, or your mother and if she's proud of you or not. The guy you broke up with sounds like he didn't want to give you those things, but there are so many men who would. You want to sing, Agatha. Go out there, stand in the spotlight, and sing."

"Maybe you're right," I say, but it doesn't sound good and I don't know why. To jump back into the dating pool after Graham, to find someone I click with, all the while trying to make my mother happy working twelve hour days searching for the perfect book that would finally erase the blight off my record. It sounds like too much for too few crumbs, and tears fill my eyes.

"You're tired. Let's go upstairs."

Wiping my cheeks, I say, "No. I want to sit down here for a little longer. Will you stay with me?"

"Yeah. This is my favorite part of the day."

I rub my lips across his. "Mine, too."

Chapter Eleven

Brock

Olivia couldn't have known she was ripping my heart out of my chest and stomping all over it when she told me not to fall in love with Agatha. I hadn't intended to go that way. Do you know how far away Mars is? That's how far away the thought of falling in love again was for me. I was simply doing what Olivia asked when I picked Agatha up at the airport, but something happened when she wanted to sit for eight hours in a dark room with a man she barely knew to watch *Jaws,* and later, when she found me surrounded by guitar shards and all she did was offer her body in hopes to soothe. Something happened in the car when she told me to shut up, and I started to think maybe she could see me and care about the man I struggle every second of my life to be.

Olivia couldn't have known my heart would end up like my guitar, broken and unable to be repaired.

I don't know what I was thinking by the pool, encouraging her to find a man when she went home. How much the words would hurt, a fork shoved into my throat. Telling her to find a life in Minnesota when I want to give her that life here.

We made love later. She was a little tipsy; I poured her too much whiskey hoping to help her relax. She was soft and pliant, spreading her legs and lifting her hips encouraging me to take her with fingertips digging into my biceps. I shouldn't have, not like that, but I needed it.

She falls asleep, and I slide out of bed.

I dress in the clothes I wore to sit by the pool and tread carefully downstairs. Agatha's a light sleeper, but maybe the booze will pull her under until morning.

I fill the Keurig and the coffeemaker grumbles, pushing the water through the pod in a hissing, whining stream. Agatha's phone chimes in her bag sitting on the island. I ignore it, but it goes off again and two more times while the coffee drips. I shouldn't look, but I don't want Agatha to sleep through an emergency. I dig for it and find her cell at the bottom of her purse.

Notifications of several unread texts fill her home screen, all from a guy named Graham.

Please call me. I miss you.

Will you text me back? Please? I miss you.

I love you, honey. Call me. We need to talk.

Honey. I need to hear your voice.

Christ, I miss you.

Along with the texts are notifications for numerous missed calls and voicemails.

This must be the guy who can't commit. It doesn't sound like he would have a problem now, and that could have been Agatha's intention. Break it off, go on vacation. Maybe she told him she started seeing someone, dangling me in front of him, the perfect ultimatum.

Her phone is unprotected by a password, and I open her

messages app, gaining easy access to all his texts. She hasn't texted him since I picked her up from the airport, but her recent calls list indicates she answered his call the day she arrived.

A new notification of a text pops up, and I swear. If she turned her read receipts on, he'll think she's looking at her messages. Fuck.

It's late. Can't you fall asleep? I can talk now and I want to hear about your vacation. How's Olivia? Call me, honey.

He knows she has trouble sleeping, and my gut burns with jealousy. How often would he get up in the middle of the night with her? Would they talk at 3 AM over glasses of wine, a fire in the fireplace on a cold winter's night? Would they make love? Would he lead her back to bed and hold her until the sun rose?

I shove her phone back into her purse. I'm going to have to confess I snooped and hope she isn't angry. I had a good reason for looking, one she may or may not believe.

The broom should be in the cleaning supplies closet, but it's not, and I find it behind the bathroom door. I don't remember putting it there, but I must have because Bobbi knows where it belongs. I sweep up the bits of guitar and throw the whole thing into the garbage bin in the garage. I don't play the ones that mean anything to me, and I store them in Dalt's office. My collection isn't as large as Shep's but I have a few I'd be sad to lose, and I don't want to risk destroying one in a fit of frustration I can't control.

I sit at the piano with my notebook and a pen.

The lyrics and notes that come to me are different than what I started on days ago. I don't think about Polly or what we could have if I could force myself to love her. The feelings materialize in words, the emotions that swamp me when Agatha smiles, or when she holds Mason, nuzzling his chubby cheek with a kiss when she thinks no one is watching. I didn't tell her earlier, but I was fucking impressed with how she took control of Olivia's life. Just like that, she knew what Olivia needed and delivered it on a silver platter. Like the last three years, Agatha was there. No wonder Olivia's shaky without Agatha in her life. They need each other.

The lyrics come, but in the end, not the happy ones I was striving for. These are stormy and dark, about losing the woman you love to another man. Shep wrote of similar worries about Liv, fearing losing her to a dead man. I didn't understand then, but now I do.

I scribble words, and in the end have different pieces of six different songs that all need more parsing out. It's a better start than I've had in months, maybe even years, but I'm nowhere near satisfied. What I'm dreading will become a reality. This Graham guy will pick her up at the airport. They'll have a romantic, teary reunion, and she'll forget all about her time in California and how for two weeks, she changed my life.

With a clank of keys, I rest my elbows on the ivory and hold my head in my hands. I don't see how I can avoid it. I can't tell her I love her. It's too soon, and I need more time. I jumped into it with Bri, and I don't regret it, but I don't need an encore of that stage of my life. She wouldn't believe it anyway—she's been here less than a week—and with that guy waiting for her to go home, she wouldn't care.

"You don't sound like you want to go at your piano with an axe," she says, padding barefoot into the sunroom, a mug in her hands and a throw off the loveseat in my bedroom dragging behind her like a dress's train.

The blackout shades are still partially lifted, the pool lights guiding her way across the floor. I'm glad I swept. I don't want her to hurt herself stepping on wooden shards.

"My process is messy. I dump the concrete, and Eddie

follows behind me and smooths it out. I'm not worried. What are you doing up?"

"I didn't feel you in bed, and I wanted to see if you needed anything. Here. I found this sitting in the Keurig when I checked the oven. I'm guessing you made it because you wanted some." She sets my mug on the piano, using a paper towel as a coaster. "I warmed it up for you."

"Thanks." I grab the mug by the handle and gulp, thinking better of it a second too late. Inwardly, I wince, preparing to burn my mouth, but she reheated it to the perfect temperature and it goes down warm.

She wanders around the room, noting the lack of furniture and the empty walls.

I expect her to ask why there's nothing in here but a sofa and my piano, but she doesn't, trailing her fingers over the blank paint. "Do you have any requests?" I ask over the silence. "What's your favorite song?"

"Do you know 'Piano in the Dark' by Brenda—"

"Russell. Yeah."

I begin to play, thinking she would sing, but she doesn't. She lets the piano have center stage as she ambles about the room, a heroine in the books she wants to rep instead of nonfiction, a lost soul hoping for a prince to sweep her off her feet and carry her away to a castle full of magic and fairy dust.

She sits on the bench, the last note fading like a shooting star into the dark room, and leans against me. "I love that song. It's beautiful."

"Why didn't you sing it? You could have."

"I didn't want to. I wanted to feel the music, not be a part of it. Thank you for playing it." The corners of her mouth lift. "I felt like I was in a music video."

I brush the backs of my fingers over her cheek. "A happy one or a sad one?"

"What do you mean?"

"It depends on the song. The happy ones are full of kissing and tender moments in front of a fire. He loves her, and she loves him, and the song is an expression of that love. The sad ones are of a lone man or woman, and that's deliberate because the songs are about being alone. They just broke up and he misses her, calls himself a jackass for doing something that made her leave, or she loves someone else." I push the blanket from her shoulders and it falls to the bench and slides onto the floor.

She shivers.

I replace my fingers on her cheek with my lips, nibbling along her jaw and down her neck. "Do you listen to the words of the songs you sing? Brenda's thinking about breaking it off with her lover. He's difficult to love, but when he plays the piano, she remembers the reasons why she's with him."

That could have been me and Bri, but she didn't care I played the piano. That's not true. She cared when I would tinker with songs at 3 AM, but I never understood why. She couldn't hear it, and I never woke the girls. After a while, I assumed it added to her dislike of how I am, but I couldn't stop songwriting. For as long as I've been a part of Ghost Town, that's been my job.

"I never thought of it that way before," she murmurs, tilting her head.

"She wants to leave him," I whisper against her skin, "but she can't. She loves him. Let me make love to you, angel."

"Where?"

"On the couch." I tug on her hand and we stand from the bench together. I lead her to the sofa, and she lies down, resting her head on the padded armrest. I resume my exploration of her neck and slide one of the straps off her shoulder. I want to take my time, but I've never been able to, always needing to be as close as possible as quickly as possible.

"Ghost Town sings sad songs, don't they?" she asks, her nails gently scraping along the back of my neck.

"Yeah. We all put a little of ourselves in our music. I don't know of anyone who hasn't been unlucky in love."

I move her nightgown away from her breast and suck her nipple into my mouth. She bucks, arching her back, and I lick the sensitive skin. She pants, her whole body trembling.

This is about as much foreplay as I can stand, and she's on the same page. "Brock, I need more."

"Me, too." I skim my fingers up her thigh and push my hand under the hem of her nightgown. She's not wearing anything underneath. "Where are your panties?" I ask, gliding two fingers into her. She's drenched, and so warm.

"I couldn't find them."

"Do you want me to get undressed?"

She scrubs at my beard, her eyes crinkling with amusement. "I want you however you want to be."

"Agatha." How does this woman always have the right answer?

"What?" She nips at my bottom lip. "Hurry up."

I yank my shorts down just enough to free my cock, and a second later, I'm inside her, my control slipping when she cries out. "Fuck, you feel good."

"You do, too," she says, urging me deeper, pressing her leg over my ass.

I try to slow down and enjoy the moment. We're cocooned in the dark, nothing to disturb us, and there isn't anything but her and her whimpers. I kiss her, long, unhurried easy licks, our tongues tangling together. "You can't come like this."

"I know, but you can. I need you," she whispers against my mouth. "Fill me up."

I do as she asks, but I don't hammer into her the way I did the first time we made love on the floor in this room. Deeply, gradually, I tease myself into an excruciating orgasm, the pressure so deep in my gut the explosion floods my body with painful pleasure. She shudders, my cock surging inside her, and I swallow back a growl. I anchor myself with a knee pressed into the cushion and it's several moments before I lower myself on top of her, giving her all my weight and blowing out a deep breath. My skin is covered in sweat, my heart racing.

She laughs a little, kissing my forehead. "You needed that. You're wired all the time."

"Since the moment I was born, from what my mother told me."

"It sounds exhausting."

"It is." I pause. "Do you want to come?"

"No. When we made love earlier, it was lovely. That's enough for me tonight."

"If you're sure."

"Yeah. This is nice." She covers my mouth with hers and pushes her hands under my t-shirt, stroking my back.

I like this too, and now that my need has been pacified for a little while, I relax and enjoy the leisurely way she kisses me, her fingertips fluttering over my skin, as if she actually likes touching me.

My dick shrinks and slips out of her, and sighing in contentment, I wedge myself between the back of the couch and her body, holding her to me with my arm over her stomach. I don't want to ruin this time with her, but I have to confess what I did or she'll check her phone in the morning and know. "When I was making coffee, your phone was going off and I looked to see if you were missing something important."

"Oh, yeah?" she asks, sounding unbothered. "Has something happened?"

"A guy named Graham was texting you. Is he the ex?"

"Hmmm." She turns her head and our lips graze.

"It sounds like he really loves you." I don't want to say it; don't want to call attention to it.

"He doesn't."

"Will you tell me about him?" I ask when it's evident she won't without prodding.

"There's not much to know. He made an appointment to talk about a memoir. He's a popular nightly news anchor for a local channel in Minneapolis, and he wanted to know if his story was interesting enough to sell. We got to talking, and our meeting turned into coffee. He asked me out for dinner. I shouldn't have, but I was drawn to him, to our easy conversations, and I said yes. We clicked, and I read into it more than I should have. This was a couple of weeks after Michael passed away, and when something like that happens, you question a lot of things, you know?"

"Yeah. You've been seeing him for a while then."

"Too long. My mother kept me on a short leash, and she still does. I've always known my place, but it's not a place I've ever wanted to be. Graham couldn't pull me out of that place, but he dressed it up with flowers and chocolate and sex. I needed that when Olivia needed me. I gave her a lot. *A lot.* I don't regret it for one second, and some of what I gave to her, Graham replaced. Then that bad book deal happened, and he was there for me—as much as he could be."

"It sounds like he cares about you, angel. Why did you break it off?" I don't want to know the answer, but I need it. It won't change things when her two weeks are over and she goes home, goes back to work and to her life, but I'll know the truth and that's important to me.

"Graham was my friend with benefits. Parts, important parts, of our relationship were missing."

"You didn't love him?"

"I thought I did, but as the months, years, dragged on, I realized he was never going to truly belong to me. Not in a way a man and woman should belong to each other. When I broke up with him, he knew it was the right thing to do. He'll get over it."

"Then you're not using this trip to show him how much he needs you?"

She laughs. "No. I wasn't thinking about him at all. I flew out because Liv didn't sound happy, didn't sound settled, and I wanted to see for myself how she was doing. Moving is an adjustment; she's never lived anywhere else. She'll be okay."

"Thank you for not being mad I looked at your phone."

She snuggles into me. "I wouldn't be mad about something like that. It could have been my mom. It could have been Liv or Sheppard, but I think after this morning, she knows to text you if she needs me. Thanks for not hiding it. You never have to hide anything from me."

That has never been true with any person I have ever known, but it's nice to think so. "Sing me the song, angel."

We lie on the couch and her soft voice drifts around us.

I'm a riddle Bri walked away from, and I don't expect Agatha to do any less, even if I can play a piano in the dark.

The sun is coming up when I coax her into bed, and having been up all night, I doze until my phone goes off with a text from Olivia asking when we're going to stop by. She includes me, but unless Shep wants to talk about the album, there's no reason for me to stay when I drop Agatha off.

That changes when Eddie texts five minutes later, asking what my plans are for the day.

Driving Agatha to Shep's. That's about it.
Can you stay? I need to talk to you.
Yeah, sure. Everything okay?
Maybe. Talk later.

I put my phone to sleep and kiss the top of Agatha's head. She's using me as a pillow, something she's started doing, but I won't complain. I like tangling my fingers in her hair, our bodies touching without any barriers. Skin to skin in the still of the morning. Just the two of us before the day's chaos starts. I even like when she drools on me, but I would never admit that. I can never turn my brain off, and lyrics to two of the incomplete songs I wrote last night and why Eddie needs to talk bounce around in a jumbled mix. I'm not concerned about what Eddie needs. He's always been intense, worried about the wrong thing, and I doubt what he has to tell me will require anything but a shrug and an, "It's okay."

"Angel," I say, thrumming my fingers down her spine.

"Hmmm."

"It's nine o'clock."

"Mmm-hmm," she mumbles.

I lower my hand and squeeze one of her butt cheeks. She's sexy as hell. "Olivia wants to know if she should make breakfast."

Her eyes flutter open. "She should be doing no such thing. Especially not for so many people. Tell her I'll fix brunch when we get there."

"She's lucky to have you."

Agatha crawls up my body, wraps her arms around my neck, and murmurs against my lips, *"I'm* lucky to have *you."*

Before I can roll her onto her back and have my way with her, she slithers out of bed. "Will you make me some coffee?" she asks before disappearing into my bathroom.

I follow her. I don't make coffee, but I give her something else to wake her up.

Agatha raids my wine closet, and we bring three bottles of champagne and three bottles of orange juice to Shep's. She carries them in a paper bag and I haul my guitar into the house. I lose her the second we step inside.

"Eunice, tell your daughter-in-law to sit down," Agatha orders, taking charge in the kitchen and nudging Olivia toward the breakfast bar . . . and a stool.

I don't see Shep or Tony, but Eunice is sitting in the living room petting Scout and feeding her treats. I kiss her cheek, tell her good morning, and hide in the den. Eddie, Clarissa, and the kids aren't here yet, and he finds me half an hour later working out the chorus to the song I like best. All six won't go on the album, but it's always better to have too many than not enough.

He paces in front of the fireplace, rubbing his neck, and I throw my pencil onto the coffee table. It's difficult enough concentrating on one thing at a time, and I won't get anywhere with him acting like the world is coming to an end when he's got the perfect life waiting for him in Shep's living room.

"Do you need a drink?" I finally ask. "Agatha brought champagne and OJ for mimosas."

"No." He blows out a breath. "We've been friends for a long time."

"Yeah, and I appreciate that." With a sick pit in my stomach, I guess where this is going. "Clarissa doesn't like me, is that what you needed to say? I would never ask you to choose between—"

His gaze shoots from the floor to my face. "What the fuck are you talking about? This has nothing to do with her. Well, it does, but not like that. She likes you fine. Doesn't know you that well, but she and Agatha were talking about a party or something. Agatha volunteered your pool."

This is the first I've heard about it, but I like the idea. I've never had anyone to the house besides Eddie popping his head in for a beer. "That's okay. Movie night at some point is still on the table, too, I think."

He forces a smile. "Is she afraid you're going to turn into a recluse?"

"I don't know. All I do know is it's going to hurt like fuck when she leaves."

He sits on the table, jiggling his leg in agitation. "Don't let her go, then. Ask her to stay here."

"Yeah, because I have so much to offer. What did you want to talk about if it's not that?"

Bouncing nervously onto his feet again, he says, "Tony wasn't wrong. About the secrets."

"Eddie." This is going nowhere good.

He glances at me sharply. "What?"

"Maybe they should stay that way."

"Not from you."

I shake my head. "He wasn't wrong, but I can't reciprocate."

"You don't have to, but I need you to know this."

"That's up to you."

"When I found out Derrick was hitting Clarissa, it tore me up inside. She wouldn't leave him, and I couldn't sit and do nothing."

Christ, I do not want to hear this. I would shut him up if I could, but he's determined to get this off his chest, and it's better me than Shep.

"That night, after I caught him slapping her, I drove straight to Dalt's. It was my idea. Pushing Derrick off that scaffolding wouldn't have been on his radar if I hadn't brought it up. I got him drunk. Drunker than he normally was. The tour was close to the end, and I needed to take a chance. Dalt beat me to it. Derrick walking in on him and Melody was a convenient excuse."

"Dalt took the blame for you." Dalt loves all of us like brothers, and I'm not surprised he went that far.

"Yeah, he did, but I would have done it myself. Derrick never would have left Clarissa alone."

"I get it." I do. Abusers like that don't stop.

"That's it?"

It's what I suspected. I set my guitar aside and lift my hands. "What do you want me to do? Send you a bouquet of flowers and a card that says, 'Sorry for your loss?' No one's sorry he's gone, and if I would have found out that son of a bitch was pounding on the woman I loved, I would have done the same thing." I wouldn't have been so meticulous, so calculating. The second I caught Derrick's hands on Agatha, it would have been game over.

"You don't hate me?"

I scowl. "No."

He sags, the tension from our confrontation, such as it was, draining out of him. "I should tell Shep."

At this, I stand from the couch and get right into his face. "Are you fucking crazy? Don't you dare. It won't do anything but hurt him more than he already is. Dalt took the blame, and by the sounds of it, happy to do it. If you tell Shep now, you'll flush what Dalt did for you right down the toilet. What you *can* do is be Dalt's friend, because he threw away Shep's friendship to get that scum off the streets. Don't let that be for nothing."

He holds his position, unconcerned my nose is half an inch away from his. "You're right. We should drive up with Clarissa and introduce Agatha to him and Melody."

"We'll try to fit it in. She said she would like to, but Olivia's struggling and Agatha's going to give her all the time she can." I scrub at my face. "You need to stop telling people this. Dalt got off because everyone thinks he was protecting his affair with Melody. Derrick was so drunk—and he would have been even without your help—I could have gassed up my car with his blood. Jesus Christ. You do not need my approval."

"We've been friends since we were kids. Of course I do."

"No, you don't. Does Clarissa know what you did?"

"Yeah, and that's why I didn't come clean to Shep about our affair. He's gonna put two and two together, eventually. I might as well confess now."

"There's no reason to think so, and if Shep finds out someone put a bug in Dalt's ear, I'll say it was me."

Eddie swallows and finally backs away, creating the space that will only grow larger when the cover hiding my dirtiest secrets is ripped away. "Why would you want Derrick dead? What did he do to you?"

I was hoping to keep this underground, but that won't happen. I'm associated with Sharyn, and everyone will know. "He was blackmailing me."

Chapter Twelve

Agatha

"Do you mind if we go for a walk before you start cooking?" Liv asks while I unload the champagne and orange juice. "Is that okay, Eunice? I'm sorry. I feel like I'm always disappearing on you. I haven't been a very good hostess, but I was hoping to talk to Agatha before the house fills up again."

Liv and I share a smile. Before Clarissa glues herself to my side, she means.

Eunice hurries in from the living room the second she spots the champagne bottles, and she rubs Liv's arm reassuringly. "No, go on ahead, as long as you don't ask me to wait to have a mimosa. These are an unexpected treat, and I can't wait. I'll have Tony or Sheppard uncork a bottle and I'll help fix the French toast when you come back."

"Have one for me. We won't be gone long. Thank you." Liv kisses Eunice's cheek.

"Where is Sheppard, anyway?" I ask.

Liv and I let ourselves out onto the patio, Scout following after us.

"He's upstairs taking a shower. Tony's on the phone with his office, consulting on a patient's symptoms, I think. Sheppard's been so happy since they came to visit. I hope Eunice is okay, but she won't be alone long."

We walk across the sand, the wind blowing my hair into my face. Using a tie around my wrist, I secure the unruly strands into a ponytail. "She'll uncork one of those bottles herself. Brock wasn't kidding when he said she was a lush," I say, laughing.

"God, I hope when we get back she doesn't have a black eye."

"That wouldn't be good for your wedding photos, but it would make for an interesting story for your kids." I pause. "You look like you're feeling better."

"I am. Thank you, seriously, for what you did for me yesterday. I never would have had the courage to do any of that for myself."

"I'm happy to do anything you need me to. You haven't been yourself since I got here. What's really wrong? Do you want to move back to Minnesota?"

"No. I love Sheppard and that will never change, but I'm surrounded by people I don't know."

My feet dig into the sand, the cool water swirling around my ankles. "So is Clarissa, if you think about it. She doesn't know you. She knows Eddie as well as you know Sheppard. She hasn't spent much time with him—not with how they met. She doesn't know Abby, but she considers Abby her daughter. From what I know, Derrick didn't let her hang around with the band, so she doesn't know Brock, either. Instead of feeling isolated, use the experience to get to know her. She could need it just as much as you do. But don't replace me, okay?" I ask, needing an absurd amount of control not to cry.

"I could never," she says, bumping into me with affection.

"Stop for a second." We approach the famous rocks, and we sit on the sand facing the water. "You've always known you wanted to be a life coach, but maybe you're trying to force yourself to be someone you're not anymore. You fell in love so quickly and now you're pregnant. Maybe that part of your life is over."

She rests her arms on her knees and props her chin on her hands. "Then what would I do?" There isn't panic in her voice, only contemplation, and I'm relieved.

I shrug. "Slow down and enjoy this new chapter of your life. Be a wife? Be a mom? Those are two completely valid options, especially while Sheppard is busy recording."

"They are, but I need more. Even if it's something small. We all need more than our families. Something that belongs to only us."

"Okay, if that's what you need and not what you think you need because someone told you to. Tell me about Empower-Her, Inc."

She explains how the organization was supposed to be an extension of her life coaching. Helping women find themselves spiritually, emotionally, after trauma, and then nurturing that growth into a lifestyle. This does sound like a natural progression of the career Liv had before she moved to California, and if she were still in Minnesota, it would have made complete sense to grow her brand that way.

"Then all of a sudden Eddie approached me and asked about buying the bars, and that was such a great idea. I've heard of that concept before, and to have the resources to implement it and be a part of something like that is wonderful. That kind of forward *motion,* movement you can see in real time. But then Clarissa backed out of training the girls, leaving us in a bind, though I would never tell her that. Her heart seems to be set on being a literary agent."

"That does sound like a clusterfuck," I admit.

Liv laughs. "It really does."

"This is in line with what you've been talking about, though. This is still life coaching, but the get-your-hands-dirty kind. Rich women won't be paying you to line up their chakras or whatever the hell. There are women, like Clarissa, who need you. You're putting food on their tables and giving them a safe place to work and a chance to go to school. You're still doing the work your dad would be proud of you for. Maybe even more so. He dedicated his life to men who were incarcerated. He would be so proud of this new direction, Liv."

She stares into the horizon. "He would, wouldn't he?"

"Yeah, I think so." I skim my fingers over her sideways cross necklace. "Pray on it. Talk to your mom."

"What would Gina say?"

"I don't think Gina will mind, hun. She wanted what we all do—to work with you because she's your friend and knows what an incredible person you are. She films women who were hurt and needed help and uses them as examples of the way they're strong enough to pick up the pieces. I think she'll be excited EHI is going in this direction. Maybe she'll make a documentary of it. That would be more pleasant than what she's forcing us to talk about now."

"Did she give you a hard time?"

"Of course she did, but that's to be expected. I don't think she's done with me either, and I'm sure she'll corner me when she finds out I'm spending the day at your house. After brunch, let's go look at the bars you keep talking so much about. I want to see them."

"To get away from Gina?" she asks, pushing back a smile.

"No, but now that you mention it . . . No. Seriously, if you think this is what EHI is going to do, I want to support you."

"You already do, just being my friend." She glances at me. "You and Brock?"

I knew she was going to want to talk about him, and I bite the inside of my cheek while I think of what to say. "He's like a little kid getting into trouble. All I want to do is protect him, keep him from chasing a ball rolling into a busy street. I can understand now why you were constantly crawling into Sheppard's bed. I want to shield him from the world. These men, they're like a pack of wounded lions."

"That's how I described Sheppard. A big, hurting bear, but God, there's nothing that can compare to him holding me and telling me he loves me. You and Brock haven't said that to each other, have you?"

"No, and I'm not sure that's what it is. I told him Graham was a friend with benefits, and he said he's in a similar situation with someone. I think what we're doing is more of that and he'll go back to seeing her when I leave." Thinking of him making love to her hurts, and I don't like it, not at all.

Liv grabs a handful of sand and lets it trickle from her fingers. "He mentioned her, but I didn't know he was sleeping with her. She works at one of the bars near the Guitar Pick and heard what we were doing for the waitresses there. She wants to go to school, too. Brock said he would pay for her tuition and give her and her family money to live on until she graduates. He asked me to help, and that's some of the reason I was having a hard time. That part of EmpowerHer exploded, and I wasn't prepared."

"How did he meet her? Aren't the bars in a bad part of LA?"

"Not terrible, but I didn't ask."

"He wasn't hanging out there with Derrick." That's not a question. I know deep in my heart Brock would never mistreat anyone or maintain a friendship with someone who would.

"No one knew what kind of man Derrick really was until Eddie found out he was hitting Clarissa."

That's true, and I have firsthand experience how well people can hide who they are underneath. I do it, too. "No matter how he met her, I'm glad he'll have her when I go."

Liv laughs. "You are not."

I laugh, too. "You're right, I'm not."

"I see the way he looks at you. He's not happy for you, either. How is it with him? Do you still feel like you're trapped in the eye of a storm?"

Choosing my words carefully, I say, "Do you remember that intern I had a few years ago? We butted heads so badly, I was close to telling the university I couldn't work with her. Finally, I said, 'Fuck it' and let her do what she wanted. It turned out all she needed was space to work her own way. I trusted her to do what I asked, and she did just fine when I wasn't micromanaging her time."

"Wait. I think I remember that, but didn't you say she had ADHD?"

"Yeah. Since you sent him to pick me up there's been something about him, and I just couldn't put my finger on it. I want to talk to Brianna."

"That's not a good idea. Sheppard said their divorce wasn't amicable."

"I know. Brock told me a little about it, but I want to know if she knew because I don't think anyone's tried to help him."

"It won't be as easy as driving to her house and ringing her doorbell. She's married to Alastair Ashford."

"Oh." Alastair Ashford is one of Hollywood's hottest directors.

"Yeah."

"Jesus Christ on a bicycle, you California people are

complicated. I suppose she lives in a castle with a moat and has a personal bodyguard."

"I'm engaged to Sheppard Carpenter, lead singer of Ghost Town, and I don't have a bodyguard," she says, teasing, her tongue poked into her cheek.

"For fuck's sake. I'm a nobody. I'll figure it out."

"What do you hope to accomplish, even if you can see her?"

"I don't know. Talk to her woman to woman, find out what she has to say? He misses his daughters. She can't be that big of a bitch. She married him—at some point, she loved him."

"You want to think that."

"Yeah, I do, because he deserves it."

"I suppose we better head back. Clarissa will need to come with us when I show you the Guitar Pick. I don't know how to get there."

"You haven't been there yet?"

"I've been too busy with the paperwork side of things. I don't go anywhere. This isn't like Minnesota."

"It's no wonder you feel out of place and lonely. Let's do a little exploring while I'm here, and you need to talk to Clarissa. Everything you're feeling, she is, too. She might have been born here, but the last thing she was doing was shopping on Rodeo Drive."

Amused, she asks, "Is that what you want to do?"

I scowl. "No. There's nothing I want there."

"What would you do if you lived here?"

We stand, and I brush the sand off my shorts. "What would I do if I lived here?" I repeat dumbly. The idea is so preposterous, my mind completely blanks out.

"Yeah. Humor me."

"Find a place to live and then set up my own agency if my mother doesn't threaten to sue me." God, I could just imagine how livid she would be if I used everything she taught me to go out on my own. "But it's the only thing I know how to do, and like you, I'd need to do something worthwhile. Ask Clarissa if she'd want to be my partner—she has good instincts for market trends. Spend time with you when you're not busy being pregnant, taking care of a newborn, buying rundown bars, or going on tour with your famous husband. Liv, you don't need me in your life to be happy. Your life is very full, you just don't understand that yet."

"I don't know what my problem is. Hormones." She trudges through the sand, her head lowered.

"We can always blame those. Come on. You're hungry and you can squeeze in a nap before we go over to the Guitar Pick. Clarissa wanted to ask me a few questions, anyway."

"How is she going to learn anything when you leave?"

"I can try to help her as much as I can from Minnesota, but eventually she's going to need to find an agent who'd be willing to mentor her. She may change her mind. I asked her to write a memoir. Maybe she'll do that instead."

"She has a lot to say."

Sheppard and Brock are waiting for us on the patio, and Scout runs off in a mad dash across the sand to reach them. Brock stares at me, and I'm caught like a deer in a pair of headlights. "We all do," I murmur. "We all do."

Chapter Thirteen

Brock

Eddie opens his mouth to ask me what in the hell I could have done for Derrick to blackmail me, but I mumble, "I need air," and hurry for the patio.

I fall onto a bench, grateful Mason's fussing keeps Eddie from following me outside and grilling me. I know he means well, but he won't be as forgiving as I was of his confession. I'd like to hold off for as long as possible, but with Eddie determined to nail Sharyn's ass to the wall, my time is limited.

The sun is buttery warm against my skin, and I breathe through my anxiety. My world is caving in, and tears burn behind my eyelids. This is all so fucked up.

Shep awkwardly slides the door open holding two glasses. "You look like you need this," he says, offering me one of the glasses filled to the brim with orange juice.

"Thanks." I sip, and the champagne bursts on my tongue. "This is all champagne."

"Yeah. Mom mixed them. She's heavy-handed with the booze. Agatha brought too much orange juice."

"She always has been, since we were kids."

Shep sits on the railing, propping a foot near my shoulder. "It's been wild, hasn't it? Going from that to this?"

Craning my neck to look at him, I squint into the sun. "There are days when I wonder if it's been worth it."

"It has. I think it has. We've made a mark on the world, in the music industry, in people's lives, and that means something. I've been thinking about after the tour."

The sweet orange juice sours in my mouth. "There's nothing after the tour."

"It doesn't have to be like that."

"Why the change of heart? You were determined this would be the last thing we do."

"Derrick's death was a shock, and I didn't handle it well. I didn't know he was hitting Clarissa. I didn't know he was abusing women and that Sharyn was covering for him. I still don't understand any of it, and maybe I never will. Eddie knew and didn't say anything, and I'm not going to pretend that doesn't piss me off. I know, it was for the band," he rushes to say when I open my mouth, "but I'm getting really tired of hearing it."

I grit my teeth. "Forget about that bullshit. Be happy with Olivia and your baby, and when the tour is done, put your time into your family. The band is gone, Shep. It doesn't have anything to do with Derrick or what he did, and everything to do with the second half of our lives. There's no reason to keep this going. I doubt Eddie would. He wants to spend time with his family, and now that he knows why Shelly was keeping Abby from him—" I clamp my mouth shut.

Shep sets his glass on the railing and tiredly rubs his face. "Is this something I should know?"

"No. Derrick's dead."

"Jesus fucking Christ," he mutters.

"I shouldn't have said anything. It's Eddie's choice to tell you or not, but nothing would change. Move on. Everyone's happy." It hurts to say it. I need what Shep was going to suggest we do after our last tour, but I'm the only one hanging on to the past. Shep, Eddie, and Dalt have futures they're looking forward to.

"You're not."

"That's not your responsibility." I gulp my champagne. There's no fucking way I'm calling it a mimosa.

"Is there anything I can do?"

I chuckle. "You've made me more money than I can ever spend in a hundred lifetimes. I think you've done enough."

"Money can't buy the things that matter most."

"No, it can't, but you can't give me those things, either—not beyond the scope of our friendship. What were you thinking about doing after the tour?" I ask out of curiosity.

"Something fun, for kicks. An album of lullabies. We never did a Christmas album. Something in the vein of what this album we're working on now will sound like . . . softer. I like the lullaby idea. Some covers, some original music. We can record it here, release it ourselves. Drop it without fanfare, without PR. For our kids."

I'm not interested. Rocking my daughters and singing to them when they were infants seems like a million years ago and not a place I want to revisit. Singing lullabies now when I don't have a baby to sing to would hurt more than I could describe. Shep will be experiencing fatherhood for the first time, and maybe Eddie would have felt the same way I do if he and Clarissa wouldn't have had Mason, but they did. They may be planning more, too, but he hasn't told me if they are.

If they want to sing lullabies, they can do it without me.

"Yeah, I'll think about it," I lie.

"It's a ways off. Now, I don't think I've seen a prettier sight," he says.

I lean around him. Olivia and Agatha are walking toward us, Scout running ahead, her tongue flopping out of her mouth. Agatha shields her eyes against the sun and lifts a hand. She's beautiful dressed in a pair of jean shorts and a dressy tank top that clings in all the right places. She pulled her hair back and it swings between her shoulder blades with every step.

"I'd worry a little less about Liv if Agatha stayed here. A piece of home, you know? I think I asked her for too much."

"Olivia wouldn't have moved here if she hadn't wanted to. She loves you, and you're her home now."

"Yeah," he says, but it doesn't sound like he quite believes it.

We all need someone, and I pull my phone out of my back pocket. I send a quick text to Sharyn asking her to set me up with Polly the day Agatha leaves. I've never been a guy to jump from one bed to the next, but Agatha's absence is going to carve a huge hole in my heart and in my life, and some booze and a night with Polly will set me back on the path I was on before I met her. I don't want to, and my stomach rolls with disgust and champagne, but I just have to hold out until the tour and then I can leave it all behind.

Agatha steps between my legs and rests her forehead against mine. "You don't look like you're feeling well. Are you okay?"

If Shep and Olivia weren't watching us, I would have sat her in my lap and kissed her, but I don't want to do that with an audience. Agatha doesn't want to hide what we're doing, and that's good enough. "Yeah. I'm hungry, I think. You didn't let me eat before we drove here."

She laughs. "I know what you wanted to eat, and we didn't have time."

That, actually, is a lie, and she knows it. I've never had a better breakfast than what I found to eat between Agatha's legs while hot water streamed over us.

"Do you need a minute?" Olivia asks, looking between Agatha and me.

"Two," Agatha says, fighting more laughter and losing.

"Funny. Here, fill your mouth before I do it for you." I offer her what's left of my champagne, and she sips and sputters.

"There's no orange juice in this drink. Eunice doesn't have a black eye, does she?"

"What?" Shep asks, confused. "Why would she have a black eye?"

I chuckle, getting the joke.

Agatha scoffs. "Never mind. I'm hungry too, let's go inside."

Shep's full house is reminiscent of the days when we were married and Eddie's and my kids were smaller, crawling around. We all got along, and the band was a huge, happy family.

I sit at the breakfast bar and watch Abby gather ingredients for the French toast. Agatha puts on a pot of coffee, and Clarissa sets a laptop near me, eager to have Agatha's attention.

Olivia, Sheppard, and Eddie sit at the kitchen table with Tony and Eunice. Someone brought a highchair for Mason, and he slams his chubby hands against the plastic, grinning while he shoves mushy oatmeal into his mouth. I catch snippets of their conversation—they're talking wedding venues.

Agatha and Abby decide how many eggs to crack, if a pound of bacon is enough for such a large group, and if they should fry another package.

I pour more champagne and orange juice into my glass and offer it to Agatha who sips and kisses my cheek with cold lips.

I wish my life could be like this, and I try to picture Polly in Agatha's place, laughing with Abby over dumping too much vanilla extract into the egg mixture. Agatha is where she belongs, and I know in that instant I would never be able to introduce Polly to my friends as my girlfriend or fiancée. It's not because she wouldn't fit in, but she doesn't belong with me because I don't belong with her. The woman I belong with is pouring coffee into a black Ghost Town mug.

She slides it to me and meets my eyes. "It's hot. Be careful."

"Thanks."

"Why did you tell him that?" Abby asks, a spatula in her hand and six pieces of drenched bread sizzling on the griddle. "He watched you pour it and he knows it's hot."

Agatha reaches for my hand and tangles our fingers. "Because when you care about someone, you want to protect them. Maybe he did know, but I wanted him to hear me say it. You know your dad and Clarissa love you, and they show you all the time, but you like to hear it, too, right? Drive safely. Text me when you get home. Call me if you need me. That's a love language everyone speaks, and it's worth saying." She nods at the griddle. "Don't burn yourself."

Abby grins. "I won't."

Agatha tries to pull her hand away and I hang on. "Angel." That's my love language and I hope she hears what I'm trying to say.

She stands with her hand clasped in mine and chats with Clarissa until it's time to eat.

After brunch, Olivia goes upstairs to nap. Shep watches her, yearning in his eyes. He wants to be with her, but he sits at the table with his mom and brother chatting about the things that have happened over the past few years, his mom's friends in the retirement community where she lives, and Tony's practice.

Mason falls asleep in Eddie's arms, and Eddie dozes in a recliner in the living room. Clarissa kisses both of them and she and Abby hide in the den, Abby on her phone texting with her friends and Clarissa with a laptop, explaining she needs to reply to several of Olivia's comments on the blog and wants to look through more of Agatha's slush.

That leaves Agatha and me free, and I use it to my advantage. "Let's take Scout outside," I say, the dog a convenient excuse to get away from everyone. It helps she plays along, lifting her head hopefully, wanting a break from the noise.

"Are you okay?" she asks, always in tune to how I'm feeling.

"Yeah. The voices, you know?" Not the voices in the room, but in my head, and being with her quiets them.

"Yeah. Let me go to the bathroom first. Too much champagne."

She meets Scout and me on the patio, and we walk in the opposite direction she and Olivia came from earlier. We sit on the sand in front of a country singer's house, but she's on tour and the windows are dark. Sitting next to her isn't close enough, and I move behind her, hugging her with my legs. Scout finds a place to pee, sniffing at the sand. Tourists walk by, but no one stops to ask for an autograph or to take my picture. I hug her to me, and with her chin on my knee, we watch the water.

I don't know how to tell her I'm starting to have feelings for her and even if I did, I don't know if I should. The chance she'll be able to see past the fact I've been paying for sex for the past few years are slim to none, and if she could, that doesn't mean she wants a relationship. So far, she's been understanding of my quirks, but she's been here less than a week. She may not want to sign up for a lifetime of me baking at 3 AM.

"Olivia told me your mom won't let you move here," I say, rubbing her back. Her hair is still pulled into a ponytail, and my fingers graze the nape of her neck.

She laughs and twists, sitting sideways and facing me. "That's a very simple summary of the thirty-six years I've been on this earth, but yes, I suppose you could say my mother would freak the fuck out if I said I wanted to move here."

"Why? I don't understand."

"I told you how I was conceived."

I nod.

"My life has been more of that. I learned early on to eat when I was told because I wouldn't get another chance until the next meal. I cleaned my room and made my bed every morning. I went to the schools she told me to go to, and there were no sick days. Earned straight As because a daughter of hers would do no less. She chose my high school classes, heavy on English, naturally, enrolled me in the U of M and told me what she wanted me to major in. I'm a literary agent because that's what she told me to be. I work at her agency. I can't rep fiction because she does. No, moving here would not fit into her plans."

"Angel, that sounds horrible."

"I've been given a lot of opportunities, and I live a privileged life because of how hard she works for me," she recites, and I swear under my breath. "I owe all of my success to her. Gina was trying to convince me that my talent made me successful even if my mother opened the door to my career, but it's her connections, her reputation, that made me what I am. Nothing I did. I can't take credit for any of it."

"Why do you let her do that to you?" I ask, my heart thudding under my ribs.

"Why not? I'm not unhappy. I have prestige, I have clout in the publishing industry. I sell books for hundreds of thousands of dollars. If you write nonfiction, you want me to rep you, full stop. I'm invited to book launches, book expos, agent panels, and author conventions. I have the perfect life. It's what I want."

I frame her beautiful face in my hands. "Angel, it's not what I want for you. I'm starting to care about you."

"Oh, Brock, that's not a good idea," she whispers, her lips trembling.

"Tell me how I can stop it."

"You have to. I'm leaving in nine days."

"Agatha—"

"No. I have to go back. I can't stay here."

She curls into herself, and I wrap my arms around her shivering body. It's not what she wants, but for thirty-six years she's done whatever she's been told, and she thinks me loving her isn't strong enough to fight that.

I have nine days to convince her she's wrong.

Chapter Fourteen

Agatha

I don't know how long we sit on the sand, his arms around me, Scout sleeping next to us. I don't keep track of the minutes he's content to hold me, his hand caressing my cheek. He cares about me, and that tiny amount of emotion, those little words, fill my heart with more than anything Graham said during our years together.

My butt's numb and I'm thirsty when I finally lean away. "I should see if Liv's awake. She's going to show me the Guitar Pick."

"Okay, but this first," he murmurs, lowering his head.

His lips touch mine in the sweetest kiss anyone has ever given me, and I whimper, urging him closer, pulling on his t-shirt.

"Brock Farris, right?" someone says, and I break our kiss.

A man older than Brock is taking our picture, not concerned at all he interrupted us or that he's invading our privacy.

"Who are you?" I ask, annoyed.

"Paparazzi, angel," Brock whispers in my ear.

"Oh, I've never had my picture taken like this before. What are you going to do with them?" I ask.

"Sell them?" he replies, confused.

"Do you get a lot of money?"

"Sometimes I do, sometimes I don't. Ghost Town's washed up, but with you in his lap, I might get a few bucks. What's your name, darlin'?"

"Ghost Town's washed up? I don't think so. You should hear the songs they're writing for their next album. They're going to blow you away."

"That so? Thanks for the tip. Are you going to give me your name for the video, or are you gonna make me look it up?"

"You're recording this? Jesus Christ on a bicycle."

"You shouldn't talk to him," Brock says. "All you'll do is stir up trouble."

"I've already had my share, but I saw Liv online. I can't let her have all the fun."

"Olivia Bloom?" The guy perks up. "You two are pals?"

"She's my best friend."

"You and Farris an item?" he asks, his camera still trained on us.

"I don't think that's any of your business."

"That's a yes, then."

"Come on, angel. You're just encouraging him." Brock stands and with a strong hand, pulls me to my feet. Now that naptime is over, Scout runs toward the house.

"Give me a name, at least?"

I dust the sand off my shorts. "Agatha Sterling."

He grins. "Thanks, Agatha. Saved me a couple of hours digging online. This turned my day around."

I scoff. "If this turned your day around, you need to rethink your life."

"I'm doing just fine. See you around, sweetheart."

Wiggling my fingers at him, I say, "Not if I see you first."

"You know he's going to get a few grand for that video?" Brock asks, holding my hand. "And you're going to be all over the gossip sites. What's your mother going to say?"

"Unless *Publisher's Weekly* prints our photo, she's not going to see it. She's very . . . focused."

"I meant what I said, you know."

We stop on the stairs that lead up to Sheppard's patio, and I stand two steps above him, making us eye-level. I brush my fingers over his forehead, down his cheek, and they linger near his jaw, his beard soft but coarse at the same time. He's so strong, yet so vulnerable, and I don't want to break his heart.

"You should stop," I say, but I don't want him to.

"I can't, and more than that, I want to hear you feel the same way."

"Brock—"

"Don't tell me you don't. What you said to Abby in there," he points toward the house, "it's like you know exactly what I need, all the time, and Jesus Christ, you have no idea how fucking *much* that means to me. That you pay attention, that you see me. Do you know how invisible I've felt, all my life? Then I pick you up at the airport, and suddenly things start to make sense, and if you leave, when you leave, things are going to go back to the way they were—" His voice cracks.

I launch myself at him and press my lips to his. "Stop it," I moan. I don't want to hear about how miserable he's going to be when my vacation's over and I have to fly home. "Please don't."

"It's only the truth, angel. It's only the truth."

I'm wet and I need him inside me, but there's nowhere we can go unless we drive to his house, and I push away the desire, the need to show him he's not alone, that he'll never be alone as long as I'm here. "I don't know what to do."

"Christ," he breathes. "Give me what you have, angel."

I want to give him all of me. "Anything. Everything."

He yanks me against him, his hands gripping my ass, and his cock is hard. He shoves his tongue into my mouth, and our teeth gnash together. I need to come, desperately, and I grind against him. He pushes me away, but grasps my hand and leads me to a concrete wall that separates Sheppard's driveway from the beach.

In too much of a hurry, he fumbles with the latch before opening the door, and he all but drags me through and to another door that lets into Sheppard's garage. It's pitch black, but Brock can see, and he lifts me onto the trunk of a vehicle. "Who's car is this?" I ask, kicking my sandals off, lying against the back windshield, and lifting my hips. "My shorts."

Brock undoes the button and yanks at the zipper. My shorts and panties are on the garage floor in seconds. "This is Olivia's car."

I widen my legs. "Touch me." I can't see him, but Brock knows exactly what I need him to do, and I gasp, two of his fingers gliding inside me.

"Fuck," he growls. "I need you."

"Yes, please."

His cock replaces his fingers, and I cry out, the tip hitting the center of my body, deliciously, painfully.

"More." It comes out in a whine, but I'm too needy to be embarrassed.

"Come," he says, his fingers finding my clit.

"Yeah." I bear down, increasing the pressure. "More."

"This is the only way I can do more," he says, nudging my ass with a finger.

I've never been touched there before, but I need it all. "Please."

He wiggles his finger inside, my muscle relaxing, letting

him in. "God, Agatha, how you feel . . ." he says between clenched teeth.

I'm full to the brim, my pussy swollen, his fingers swirling around my clit. Liv's car is hard under my back, the faint scent of gasoline in the air. There's nothing but darkness and how I feel with Brock touching me.

"Come for me," he demands, twisting his finger in my ass, frantically rubbing my clit. My pussy clenches around his cock and I come, the orgasm exploding from my belly, crashing through me.

Brock doesn't give me a second to settle down, and he thrusts, his fingers sticky with my cum digging into my knee to steady himself.

He groans and slumps onto the trunk, his cock spurting.

I hold him close, my lips against his sweaty skin.

"I'm sorry if I hurt you at the end," he murmurs. "I got a little carried away."

"No more than I did. I can't remember the last time I wanted to fuck somebody so badly."

He chuckles. "Then I'm glad it was me. I've never touched a woman here before, angel. Bri didn't like it, and other women I've been with didn't have the spark we have. I'm going to pull my finger out, okay?"

"No one's done that to me before, but I needed you touching me everywhere."

"Angel," he says softly, and he kisses me, slow, deep licks into my mouth, maybe to distract me while he gently and so tenderly slides his finger out of my ass.

I'm still swollen, and this guy, he hasn't gone down at all. He's still rock hard, and I grip around him, loving the feel of his cock inside me.

"I can't do anymore. You successfully wore me out."

"Do I get a gold star?"

"Yeah. Yeah, you do." He kisses the tip of my nose and pulls out.

"Do you think we got cum all over Liv's car? We can't tell her what we did. She would never forgive me."

"If we did, we can blame the birds."

I huff out a laugh. "She would never buy that. Can you find my panties and shorts? You men have it so easy. Just whip it out."

He slaps the side of one of my ass cheeks. "Start wearing skirts."

Giggling, I say, "Just for that, you can dress me."

"Sure." He trails kisses over my skin as he slides my panties over my feet, past my ankles, and up my calves. I raise my hips, and he positions them perfectly over my ass. He does the same with my shorts, and while I'm still lying on the trunk of Liv's car, I button them and zip the zipper.

"You're good at that."

"If we were inside, I would have cleaned you up first. You're messy. Come on. You'll have to dry off before you go anywhere or you won't be very comfortable."

I sit up, but before he can help me to the ground, I shove my hands into the back pockets of his jeans and rest my head against his chest. I didn't forget how we got here, the emotions inside his heart that led him to claim my body, but I don't know what to do. I have a life back home. A job, a place in the literary community. An apartment downtown. A man who lies and says he loves me. Everything I have ever known for thirty-six years is two thousand miles away, and my mother guards the key. Freedom doesn't belong to me.

His heart beats steady under my ear, the cotton of his t-shirt soft against my cheek. He scrapes his fingers up and down my spine.

"They're going to wonder where we are, angel. We'll spend

some time alone tonight, after you come back from the bar. We can cook dinner, drink some wine, maybe watch a movie. Sound good?"

"Yeah, it does." I sit, unwilling to move.

"Agatha."

"What?" My voice is a thin whisper in the dark.

"We're both trapped. You have to go home and that's okay."

"How are you trapped? I don't know what you mean."

"We make choices, and then there are consequences. Sometimes we don't understand what they'll be until years later, but they're there and we can't escape them. You'll be gone when I face mine, but that's the way it has to be."

"I don't want to leave you alone."

"Angel, I've been alone my whole life. I may have been surrounded by people, but very few outside of Eddie and my parents understand how I am. There is nothing lonelier than feeling like you're by yourself in your marriage. Bri and I had some happy years, we did, and I guard those with my whole heart, but I don't think, even during our happiest times, did she accept me for how I truly am. Toward the end, she hated me, and when she divorced me, she took my girls and didn't look back. I accepted that a long time ago."

I start crying, huge, gasping sobs that come from nowhere, and he hugs me in this dark garage that holds nothing but two cars and a whole lot of pain that will never fade.

"Let's go inside," he says when I calm down. "We've been gone for a long time." I wipe my face with his t-shirt, and he laughs.

We enter the house through the door in the garage, and Liv's standing in the kitchen at the breakfast bar holding Mason and eating strawberries from a gigantic fruit platter that must have been delivered while Brock and I were sitting on the beach. Her eyes widen. "Where have you been? And why were you in the garage?"

Brock clears his throat. "You don't want to know."

"There aren't any free beds here, Liv," Sheppard says from his place at the table with Eunice, Tony, and Eddie. He rubs his lips, trying to fend off a smile to no avail.

Liv's mouth pops open. "And you had to do it in my car?"

"Not in," I mumble. "Hey, are we ready to go?"

"Yes!" Clarissa rushes into the kitchen, her eyes bright and her cheeks a rosy pink. "I think I found a project in your slush that's perfect!"

My slush pile is the last thing on my mind. "Great! You can fill me in on the way."

"Wait. We're not done talking about this," Liv says, giving Mason to Clarissa who only transfers him to Eddie's lap.

"Talking about what?" Abby asks, stepping into the kitchen from the living room.

"Oh, I think we are," I say.

Abby looks between Brock and me. "If you're talking about sex, you don't have to exclude me. I know all about it."

"Excuse me," Eddie snaps, startling Mason. His big blue eyes fill with tears.

Abby rolls her eyes, a typical teen tolerating an overprotective parent. "Not like, experience, but you know. From school. We practiced putting condoms on a banana and the boys in class said that it's nothing like a real penis. Where are you going? Can I go, too?"

"We're showing Agatha the Guitar Pick, and of course you can go. In fact, you should wait outside before your dad explodes, and not in a good way," Clarissa says, covering her mouth to hide a laugh.

Abby runs for the garage door, cackling like crazy.

"You started this," Eddie says to Brock, glaring.

"Don't look at me. She's the one half-naked." Brock jabs a thumb in my direction and makes a beeline for the fridge. "Please tell me there's beer in here."

"You can't blame me. I'm in California in August. What do you want me to wear? Jeans and a turtleneck?"

"Yes."

I stick my tongue out at him. "Just for that, I hope there's no booze in the fridge. At least I'm going to a bar."

He leers. "Come back drunk, and I'll have my way with you."

"Not on my car, please," Liv says, grabbing her purse off a stool. "It's brand new. I'm going outside with Abby."

Clarissa kisses Eddie, rubbing her fingers over his scruff. "I'll check in with Ginger while we're there. Olivia's been stressed out, and we haven't talked about who's going to replace me. Ginger doesn't know everything yet, and we might have a short meeting." She brushes a kiss over Mason's cheek. "Be a good boy for Daddy."

"Hey," he says, hooking his fingers in one of her pockets when she tries to step away. "I love you very much."

"From the moment we met," she whispers, staring into his eyes. She turns to leave and he lets her, and flicking tears off her cheeks, she rushes by me.

I stand awkwardly by the breakfast bar, and scooping my straw bag off the floor that has my wallet, cell phone, and camera in it, I say, "I better not keep them waiting."

"Agatha," Brock says, and everyone looks at us.

"Yeah?"

"Be careful."

I know exactly what he's saying, and I lick my lips, my skin covered in perspiration, his cum still inside me. "You, too."

I scrabble with the doorknob and rush through the door.

Eddie asks, "What was that all about?" right before it slams shut behind me.

I'm shivering, and I drag in a deep breath of fresh air when I reach Clarissa's car. She's driving, Abby's riding shotgun, and Liv's in the backseat waiting for me. I sit next to her and shove sunglasses onto my face. I shouldn't be so flustered, but my hands tremble in my lap.

"Are you okay?" Liv asks quietly. "What's going on?"

I shake my head. I like Clarissa and Abby, but this is private.

Liv understands without me having to say anything. "Later?"

"Yeah. Thanks."

I buckle my seatbelt and listen to Clarissa chatter about the inside of the bar. "There's still a lot to do, and I'm sorry I'm not training the girls anymore, but it was just too much. I texted Ginger to meet us there. She's a little confused about what would happen now, and I had to tell her I didn't know, either."

Liv slides a notepad out of her purse. "Well, the first thing we need to do is find someone who knows how to run a bar and is willing to take on a permanent training position. I'll speak to Gina because that salary is going to come out of the money we raised at the party Dalton and Melody hosted."

Clarissa looks at her in the rearview mirror. "Is that bad?"

"No, but the sooner we get the bars up and running, the sooner they can start bringing in some income. EmpowerHer, Inc is paying the waitresses' wages, and that can't go on indefinitely. Now that Agatha cut through some of my worries, I'll be more involved."

"There are so many comments on that blogpost," Clarissa

says, confidently navigating the busy highway. "Some people want to send you a baby gift and are asking for your address."

"Oh, well, I don't think that's necessary," Liv says, surprised.

Hoping my eyes aren't bloodshot, I'm more composed and push my sunglasses to the top of my head. "I think what we should do is write another post and say a donation to the March of Dimes would be appreciated and gently remind them whom Liv is marrying. We don't want to insult anyone—their intensions are sweet—but there are a lot of women and children in need who could benefit from their generosity."

"You have the best ideas. But why not ask them to donate to EmpowerHer, Inc?" Clarissa asks, veering onto an off ramp.

"Because we have Gina," I say.

"Right. I've seen her work. She's a powerhouse."

"She's something," I mutter, and Liv nudges me with a smile.

We leave the ocean and highway behind, and soon we're driving through narrow streets crowded with strip malls, gas stations, and fast food places. The Guitar Pick sits on a corner, the front a wall of grimy windows and out-of-date posters. It looks like any crappy bar in any poor part of any town. Water-downed liquor and flat beer.

Clarissa parks in the rear lot, the concrete cracked and full of weeds. A pretty blue Rav4 is parked near the back door, and besides us, it's the only car here.

I climb out and root around in my bag for my camera. The dilapidated building makes for an interesting study, and I snap pictures of the exterior, planning to turn them black and white.

"You managed this place?" I ask Clarissa, following her into the building.

"Yep, for a few years. It could have been worse."

A pretty brunette wearing denim shorts and a white V-neck

t-shirt knotted at the waist is standing in the middle of the floor with a notebook and a pen. A smile of sincere pleasure lights up her face when she spots us. "Hi! Thanks for asking me to meet you. Vonnie and the other girls are wondering what's going on, and I haven't been able to tell them anything."

Clarissa hugs the woman, the warmth of their friendship palpable in the dim, yet surprisingly large, space. "I know. I'm sorry. An opportunity dropped into my lap, and I couldn't pass it up. Ginger, this is Olivia Bloom, she founded EmpowerHer, Inc with Gina, and this is her friend, Agatha Sterling. She's visiting from Minnesota. You remember Abby, Eddie's and my daughter. This is Ginger," she says to me and Liv. "Through the nonprofit, she owns this place and Shotgun Sally's down the street."

I hold out my hand. "It's nice to meet you."

"Likewise. Thank you so much," she says, turning her attention to Liv. "You have no idea what you've done for the waitresses who work here, and for me. It's such an honor to meet you."

"Thank you. It's nice to finally meet you too, but I can't take credit for this. Eddie made it all possible—I just filled out some paperwork. Explain what needs to be done. There hasn't been much progress made."

I wander around and snap pictures. There's a stage in the corner, microphone stands and speakers collecting dust, and I skim my hand over the surface.

"They haven't taken the picture down. Ghost Town played here when they were first starting out," Abby says, gesturing me over to a grainy black and white photo framed in cheap tarnished gold hanging with several other photos of different bands.

"Your dad looks exactly the same," I say, tapping my fingernail against the dusty glass. "Actually, they all do."

Dressed in acid-washed denim, t-shirts, leather bracelets, scruff, and messy hair, the only thing that's changed about any of them is their age.

"Dad looks funny with long hair. He's kept it short for as long as I've been born."

"It's a good look for him. Brock's sexy in his sunglasses. Wow. I want to search for more pictures. This band has so much history. I should talk to Liv about a book. No, she has too much on her plate as it is. You and I should put something together. I bet your mom has a lot of pictures, doesn't she?"

Abby squeals. "You want to work with me? That's awesome!"

The second she says that, I want to take it all back. I won't be here to work with her. Going through boxes of keepsakes isn't something I can do from Minnesota. How easily I'm opening an agency with Clarissa, putting together a huge photo history of the band with Abby, and maybe, what I want to do most, telling Brock I love him. I need to shut the fuck up because I can't stay here.

I force a smile. "We'll figure something out. Maybe I can visit again near Christmas."

Jesus Christ on a bicycle. I won't be doing that either. Why put Brock through that? Why put myself through that? Fuck.

"I'm going to text Mom and see what she has in storage." Excitedly, Abby skips away, pulling her phone out of the back pocket of her jeans.

My stomach churning with broken promises, I check out the bar, opening an ice bin that's full, noting the numerous kinds of beer on tap and what I would drink if I had to choose. Like any bar, liquor bottles sit in front of a mirror that could use a good wash. I push through the swinging door and peer into the back. There's nothing but a kitchen that has seen better days. I doubt the stove has been used in years, and I'm definitely not brave enough to look in the old refrigerator that rattles and hums. Another exit lets out into the back parking lot, and pallets of beer collect dust, the motes dancing in the sunlight streaming in from the door's crusty window.

This place definitely needs a makeover.

I let the door swing shut and rack up balls at a pool table that needs new felt. I don't know how to play, but I bet Brock and the other guys do. I fantasize for a moment, feeling Brock's hard body hug mine as he shows me how to hold a pool cue. I'm falling hard, and I'm falling fast, and leaving is going to kill me.

The bar's rear door opens, and sunlight shines into the hall, illuminating a dark figure shuffling toward us.

Ginger steps forward. "Can I help you? The bar's closed for renovations right now. You shouldn't be in here."

A grizzled old man steps into the room, floorboards creaking under his booted feet. He's dressed in dirty jeans and a worn-out t-shirt. A grey beard covers the lower half of his face, and his hair is on the longer side and greasy. This man is tired of life, and I want to offer him a beer. What stops me is the rifle in his hand.

He cocks it, a quick snap with the jerk of his arm. "I want to meet the woman responsible for stealing this bar from me."

Chapter Fifteen

Brock

Despite Agatha's nasty (and unnecessary) wish, there *is* beer in the fridge, and I gratefully uncap one. Shep hasn't lost his amused expression, unperturbed Agatha and I had a go at ruining Olivia's paint job, and I retreat to the den. I don't know how long the girls will be gone, but I want to be here when they get back.

I sit on the couch and close my eyes. The lyrics of the songs I've been working on slam into my head in a cacophony of screeching noise.

"Can you hold Mason for a sec?" Eddie asks. "I'd ask Shep, but he's going to do some cleaning and prep steaks for later. Are you and Agatha eating dinner here?"

"No. I want to be alone with her."

He sits Mason on my lap. "I have to hit the head. Give me a minute."

Mason watches his father leave and then turns his big blue eyes toward me. "You're dad's a lucky guy." He grins, drool leaking out of his mouth, and I wipe it away. "I didn't think much about having kids until I met Bri," I murmur, knowing full well I'm having a conversation with a baby. "She got pregnant, but I didn't understand how special that was, you know? When I held Layla for the first time, I couldn't believe she was a part of me. Half of me. If I would have known how things would turn out, I wouldn't have taken so much for granted."

"It's harder when you don't know," Eddie says, reappearing and holding his own beer. He closes the faux wall and sits next to me on the couch, but he doesn't reach out for his son. Mason lunges for Eddie's beer bottle and attempts to tug it out of his dad's grasp. Just in the nick of time, I keep him from landing on the floor with an arm around his stomach. "You're too young." Eddie trades the bottle for a puzzle piece out of the diaper bag sitting on the floor. Mason chews on it and settles against my chest, content to be held.

"Did you resent her for not telling you?"

"Yeah, for about five seconds, but it was my fault. The worst was thinking Mason was Derrick's. I still loved her, still loved Mason with everything I had, but I didn't experience her pregnancy the way I could have had I known he was mine. I held myself off from it, from them. I felt like an outsider, but I couldn't stay away. I'd rock him while she slept, and there were times I hated Derrick so much for giving her what I wanted to give her." He pulls from the bottle and swallows. "But I'm to blame, for all of it. You're never going to confront Brianna? Did you ask her about Derrick? If he did anything to her?"

"No. There are so many things that don't matter anymore. Even if Derrick had done something to her, what's the point? She chose not to tell me, and he's dead. Knowing would do nothing. Shelly gave you Abby back, and I'm happy for you, but she waited a whole year after his death. Do you think if she hadn't been going through her own shit with Connor she would have admitted Derrick raped her? That she wouldn't have waited until Abby turned eighteen and couldn't control what Abby did? I don't know the lies Bri's fed the girls all these years. Layla's sixteen and has her driver's license, but she never asks to stop by. Answers my texts with a word or an emoji. Blaming Derrick doesn't make that go away."

"I asked Shelly why she waited, and all she said was there was so much damage already done she didn't know how to undo it."

"You can't, and she knew it was impossible. We'll never get those years back, and all you can do is enjoy Clarissa and Mason. Enjoy having Abby back in your life, no matter how that happened. Confronting Bri won't change who I am."

He props a foot onto the coffee table and rests a wrist on his knee, his watch glinting. "I wanted more for you. After all this."

I nod. "I appreciate that. I really do. I'm going to have a good time with Agatha, and hope maybe one day I can find a woman who can care about me like she does. I wish it wouldn't have been her, at this moment. The timing's horseshit."

"I thought that too, when I met Clarissa. She was another man's wife. A *bandmate's* wife, and I gave up my integrity, my sense of honor, because I couldn't stop loving her. Whatever's keeping you two from going all the way, fix it. Find a way around it."

"It's not as simple as that. You were lucky and Clarissa forgave you for a lot of shit, but not everyone is as fortunate. I've done some things that can't be so easily passed over."

"Is this what Derrick had on you?"

"Yeah, but I'm not going to talk about it."

"I can respect that, but do you remember what you told me a long time ago? Not everything is as important as it seems. You proved that when I told you I had a hand in Derrick's death and you didn't care. Whatever it is you've done, or think you've done, maybe it's not that big of a deal. You can't know until you say something. You can always talk to me, and I will listen without judgment. It's what our lifetime of friendship is for."

I want to believe that. I want to believe I could say I've been paying Sharyn to set me up with a couple of cocktail waitresses from North Hollywood. That I've been paying for sex and companionship because I didn't know what else to do. I want to believe he would be as nonchalant as I was and say, "It's okay. I understand," but he won't because it's not okay. Derrick did terrible, terrible things, and maybe I didn't know Sharyn was covering up for him, but once I found out, I didn't stop using her. I needed Polly and that need created consequences I will never be able to escape from.

Agatha will think I'm dirty, maybe hate me for sleeping with her, even though I told her the truth and I wear a condom every time. It's that I've done it at all, and I can't take it back.

There is nothing that will hurt me more than putting Agatha on that plane, but I have to keep my secrets.

Until I can't anymore.

Eddie's cell chimes and he lifts his ass and slides his phone from the back pocket of his jeans. His hands start to tremble, and reaching for the remote on the coffee table, he knocks over his beer, the contents fizzing over a few issues of the *Los Angeles Times*.

"What is it?"

"I-I have Google Alerts set to go off if a news article mentions Clarissa."

"She's Derrick's widow and your fiancée. That should happen a lot."

"It does." He turns the TV on and bypassing all the streaming apps, navigates to a local cable channel.

An urgent news bulletin is interrupting a late afternoon talk show, and a male and female anchor sit behind a desk at their station, staring seriously into the camera. The female anchor says, "Our reporter, Shanna Wilson, is on the scene. Shanna, what can you tell us?"

The camera cuts to a slim woman with dark skin wearing a black blazer accented with a hot pink scarf. The Guitar Pick and three police vehicles, their lights flashing, are parked in the street behind her. Officers lean against their cars, their weapons drawn, waiting for any sign of trouble.

"Thanks, Cassandra. I'm standing in front of the Guitar Pick on the corner of Archwood and Beck, a bar purchased not long ago by EmpowerHer, Inc, a nonprofit founded by Olivia Bloom, fiancée to Sheppard Carpenter of Ghost Town fame, and Gina Baker, longtime partner to director Jeffrey Morgan. A paparazzo followed Clarissa Hayward, Derrick Pavleck's widow, to the bar. For those who don't know, Derrick Pavleck fell to his death last year after a Ghost Town concert in Chicago, and just recently, Dalton West, Ghost Town's manager, confessed to the crime. We think the paparazzi photos are what instigated the situation."

"And what is the situation?" Cassandra asks. "Can you explain what's happening for our viewers at home?"

"It appears to be a hostage situation, Cassandra. An unidentified white male is inside with Olivia Bloom, Clarissa Hayward, and other unidentified females. We believe one of them may be literary agent, Agatha Sterling. A reporter for *Buzz Kill* filmed her earlier today sitting with Brock Farris on the beach near Sheppard Carpenter's house. We're trying to learn more. As you can see behind me, law enforcement is taking this very seriously."

"Do you know who alerted the police?" the male news anchor asks.

"It seems the paparazzo who followed Clarissa Hayward to the Guitar Pick called 911 when he heard a gunshot."

"Jesus Christ." Eddie lurches from the couch.

I can't tear my eyes away from the screen.

"Do you know if there are any casualties?" the male news anchor asks.

"Not at this time, Alex. I'll keep you posted. This is Shanna Wilson for KNBC news. Back to you."

The camera cuts to the inside of the news station, and the video that asshole took of Agatha and me plays on the screen behind Alex and Cassandra. She's beautiful, her black hair dancing on the breeze, her tanned skin sparkling. She wriggles her fingers at the camera. "Not if I see you first," she says. We walk toward Shep's, and the fucker filmed us the entire way, zooming in when we stop on the steps of Shep's patio. The guy's far enough away that no one will be able to read my lips, but my agitation, my desperation, are on full display. So is my need for her, our need for each other, and he didn't stop filming until I dragged her into the garage.

"Abby went with them," Eddie croaks. "God, Abby went with them."

He doesn't wait for me, and I sit glued to the couch, Mason sleeping in my arms.

Chapter Sixteen

Agatha

"That would be me," Olivia says, stepping forward. "I helped with the purchase. What can I do for you, Mr. . . . ?"

"Thompson. Judd Thompson, and there's only one thing I want." He lifts the rifle, aims at the ceiling, and pulls the trigger.

I jump, my skin crawling and my ears ringing, and Ginger edges away. Olivia holds firm, her arms crossed over her chest. Clarissa, too, remains calm, hiding Abby from Thompson's cruel stare. This may not be the first time she's heard a gun go off in here. Behind me, Abby's sweaty hand finds its way into mine, and I squeeze.

His eyes land on Clarissa, and he points at her with the muzzle of his gun. "You. You managed this place for me for a few years."

"Yes, I did. Maybe you wouldn't have gone through managers so fast if you had paid us better. I worked my ass off for you."

"That's enough. Sit on the floor. I need to think."

Clarissa flings her arms into the air. "Think about what?"

"What the fuck I'm going to do with you. I have demands."

I can guess what she's going to suggest he do with his demands, but Olivia rubs her arm and Clarissa thinks better of running her mouth. We sit on the dirty floor in front of the windows that face the street. This place is a dump, and Liv could have bought a better bar. Maybe Shotgun Sally's is nicer, but I don't think we'll make it there today.

Abby's cool and watchful beside me.

"It's okay," I say, wiggling so close to her our thighs touch.

"Shut the fuck up. No talking," Judd says, and with a clatter, throws his gun onto a wobbly table sitting near an old jukebox. He shuffles behind the bar and selects a bottle of whiskey and a shot glass. Never taking his eyes off us for one second, he drops into a seat at the table and pours.

Sirens shriek outside, and Judd nods in satisfaction.

Three LAPD cop cars skid to a stop in front of the building, their lights flashing. Someone must have heard the gunshot, though in this part of the city, I don't know why that would have made anyone call the police.

"What are you going to do with us?" If I can keep him talking, maybe it will distract him. There's an exit through the swinging doors, and I need to get Abby, Olivia, and Clarissa out of here. Mason needs his mama, and I want Olivia and her baby safe. I don't know anything about Ginger, but maybe she has children, too. I can stay behind.

He props his feet onto a chair in front of him and knocks back a shot of whiskey. "Don't know yet. I've got time to figure it out."

I rest my hand on Abby's leg and try to point unobtrusively toward the bar. Leaning against the front windows, we're in the perfect position to crawl behind it and sneak out the swinging door. That's if I can keep Judd talking and Abby's cautious enough to go unnoticed. She stiffens. If she has any knowledge of this place, she knows exactly what I'm trying to tell her to do.

"Are you married? Do you have any children?" I ask, crossing my legs and leaning forward. I don't have to pretend to be interested. Like Brock, this man is all broken heart and maybe all he needs is someone who's willing to listen.

He laughs, a bitter sound, and fear skitters down my back. "A long time ago, I fell in love and married her. Wasn't many years after that she got sick. Tried to help her hang on, but money talks, and I never had any of that. Nothing you rich bitches would understand. Couldn't afford the medicine and she passed."

"I'm sorry, Judd," Ginger says, her voice quiet. "I lost my dad the same way. He had prostate cancer and we didn't have insurance. Everyone says sign up for insurance through the state, they'll help you, but no one tells you doctors don't have to accept it. What good is it if you can't find a doctor to help you? He died in hospice. They'll take your insurance for that." She pushes a hand to her mouth and tears roll down her cheeks.

"I'm sorry for your loss." Judd closes his eyes.

I push on Abby's leg, and she wastes no time getting onto her hands and knees and crawling around the corner of the bar.

Olivia's eyes widen, and I point to her.

She shakes her head viciously, and I frown. I will not let her stay for me. She nudges Clarissa's shoulder, and Clarissa, thinking Olivia's showing her affection, hugs her.

If she wants Clarissa to go first, fine, but she and I are going to need to swap places. Judd's eyes flutter open. The sirens outside stopped, and a crowd is starting to gather behind the police cruisers.

"You didn't have any children?" I want to keep the conversation going, but this line of questioning is dangerous. It's obvious Judd Thompson hasn't had a pleasant life.

"A little girl," he murmurs, "but she lived for only a few days. She was born with half a heart, and that's how I've lived the rest of my life—with half a heart." He pours another shot glass full of whiskey, downs it, and drags the gun into his lap.

Jesus Christ on a bicycle.

"I think we need a little music! Let's have a party!" he announces with a cheerfulness edged in malice, hitting the floor with the butt of his gun. Pushing away from the table, the legs of his chair squealing under his weight, he digs into his pocket and pulls out a quarter.

He stands at the jukebox, and I hope Abby uses the chance to slip out the swinging door. While his back is turned, I shove my ass between Clarissa and Olivia.

"What are you—?" Clarissa starts in a confused hiss but then notices Abby's gone.

Judd selects a song, violently jabbing at the button, and turns toward us. We're leaning against the window, casual as you please, and I try desperately to pretend he's in control and not call attention to Abby's absence or my new place on the floor.

Sheppard's rough voice fills the bar, and Olivia covers her face with her hands.

"Oh, you thought I didn't know who you are, huh? I read up on you, Olivia Bloom. A dead father, a dead fiancé. You're no better than anyone else, even if you act like it. Don't you fucking cry. You have no right to fucking cry."

Olivia drops her hands into her lap. She wasn't crying. She's worried about Sheppard and how he's dealing with this.

I try not to look toward the bar, try not to invite Judd's attention to the fact that one of us is missing.

My fingers linked with Liv's and Clarissa's, I pray Abby's able to tell her dad, Sheppard, and Brock that we're okay.

For now.

Chapter Seventeen

Brock

I drive.

My nerves are taut, my mind racing a million miles an hour, but my hands are steady as I grip the wheel. Shep sits next to me, the news turning him into a zombie. Eddie's no better, sitting in the back seat, tears wetting his cheeks, staring at nothing out the window.

It wouldn't be fair, wouldn't do my feelings for Agatha justice, to say I don't have as much to lose, but Agatha's not pregnant and a madman isn't holding Lexi and Layla at gunpoint. So my hands are steady, and I pray to any god who will listen to spare the woman I've fallen in love with.

It's a forty-minute drive of sheer hell, and I have to park in a Chinese restaurant's parking lot a couple of blocks away. Police blocked off the streets, but Shep's intent on only one thing, ignoring the barricades and jogging toward a man wearing a crisp black suit who looks to be in charge.

Eddie and I follow at a slower pace, and when we join them, the cop's scowling, annoyed with our blatant disregard of his wishes. This is LA, and he doesn't give a fuck who we are.

"My fiancée's in there," Shep says, pointing at the Guitar Pick. The front windows are filthy, and I can't see anything. Band posters, beer signs, and lottery ticket advertisements cover most of the glass. "Don't tell me to calm down. That's not going to happen."

"Look, we're doing the best we can. We don't have all the details yet."

"What *do* you know?" I ask, shielding the detective from Shep's desperate anger. I'm not going to let Shep piss this guy off. We need someone who will tell us what's going on, and if this cop pegs us as troublemakers, he won't give us one goddamned thing.

He leans tiredly against the front fender of a squad car. "A reporter for the *Hollywood Beat* spotted Clarissa Hayward's car on the highway and followed her here. Took quite a few pictures of her and her friends getting out of her vehicle and walking through the parking lot out back. You know how it is, gossip in real time, and someone was waiting for this to happen. The second Miss Hayward's location hit the internet, the guy shot his shot. The reporter took his picture before all hell broke loose. Do you know who he is?" The detective pulls a cell phone out of the pocket of his slacks and wakes it up. He shows us a picture of an old guy wearing dirty jeans and dirtier t-shirt carrying a rifle into the bar, his face partially turned away from the camera.

I don't know who he is, never saw the guy in my life.

Shep shakes his head.

Eddie pauses, considers, and finally says, "He seems familiar, but I can't tell you where I've seen him before. Maybe if I could get a better look at his face."

"This is the only photo we've got. We're working on identifying this asshole. Once we do that, we can figure out what he wants. People don't take hostages for the hell of it, and if we know what he'll want for a trade, we can strike a deal. I'm waiting for my negotiator to get here. She's damned good, and I'm not going to reach out to him without her. You want me to do this right, give me time to do my fucking job."

"Thank you," I say, holding out my hand.

"You're Brock Farris, right?" he asks, his clasp firm and dry.

"Yeah."

"I'm Detective Patterson. I'll talk to you. You two," he says, waving his hand between Eddie and Shep, "get out of my face and suck down a Valium. I mean it. Stay out of my way."

Shep's eyes harden, but Eddie thinks better of letting Shep do his "Do you know who I am?" thing and yanks him to the side of the street. The crowd gives them space, and they lean against the window of a barbershop, never once looking away from the Guitar Pick.

"Tell me who's in there," Patterson says, jerking his head toward the bar.

"Olivia Bloom, Shep's fiancée. Clarissa. She's engaged to Eddie now," I say, and Patterson nods. "Eddie's daughter, Abby."

"Fuck," Patterson mumbles. "I didn't recognize a kid in the pictures. How old is she?"

"Fourteen. She and Clarissa are the same height. Abby might have looked older than she is."

"Okay. Who else? Jesus Christ. Is there anybody else?" His thumbs fly across his phone taking notes.

"Agatha Sterling, Olivia's friend. She's visiting from Minnesota, and Ginger, Ginger something. I don't know her last name. She owns the Guitar Pick and Shotgun Sally's. Eddie bought both of them through Olivia's organization, EmpowerHer, Inc."

Patterson cuts me a sharp glance. "Details."

"Olivia's pregnant."

He blows out a breath.

"Eddie and Clarissa's son is a year old. This is hard on him."

"What about you? Do you have any skin in the game?"

I want to say I'm in love with Agatha, that I want to ask her to marry me and if some whack-job kills her, I don't know how I'll keep going, but that sounds too dramatic for a woman I just met and mumble, "No," feeling like I'm betraying her.

He's shrewd, and he waits.

Caught under the weight of his stare, I capitulate. "Agatha and I might have gotten close while she's been here."

"Don't lie to me. No matter how small or inconsequential you think it might be, tell me. Anything else?"

Mentioning Derrick and Ginger's past would be bad, as much for Ginger's anonymity as for my own relationship with Sharyn, and I say, "No."

This time he believes it. "We need to know who this guy is. It could be as simple as paying him off. If he has mental health issues, maybe he's off his meds. You guys have any enemies?"

"As a band?"

"Yeah."

"I think the only person who had an axe to grind is dead."

"Derrick Pavleck. Is that who you're talking about?"

"Yeah."

"I've been on the force for a long time, and you're smack in the middle of one of the most notorious cities in the world when it comes to secrets and death. Secrets don't die, even if the people keeping them do." He pockets his phone. "I take it you guys aren't going anywhere?"

Shep and Eddie are watching us, looking for a sign Patterson is telling me something they want to know. "No."

"If I need anything else, I'll find you. Thanks."

I join Shep and Eddie and lean against the brick wall. The barbershop's open, but they won't get any business with all this going on in the street.

"What'd he have to say?" Shep asks.

"Wanted to know who was inside. They're trying to ID the guy as quickly as possible."

Eddie's skin is grey, and Shep's not looking much better.

"They're smart, and they're strong. It's why we love them," I say around a ball of fire in my throat. "They'll be okay."

"I didn't kiss her goodbye," Shep murmurs, his eyes filling with tears.

"What?" I meet Eddie's gaze, and he frowns and shakes his head.

"I didn't kiss Liv goodbye. I didn't hug her, didn't tell her I love her. I should have told her—" His voice cracks, and he sinks to the sidewalk.

"She knows," I say, but I don't think he hears me.

Time crawls. The cops crowding the street stand around, their weapons secured in their holsters, and Patterson is nonstop on his phone, looking more and more frustrated with every passing minute. An unmarked police van parks behind Patterson's car, and a woman wearing a navy blue pantsuit joins him. The sun starts to drop, and without any action, some of the gawkers on the sidewalk drift away, needing to go back to their own troubles.

I step toward Patterson and the woman I assume is the negotiator. We've waited too long without news.

"Dad!"

Abby's voice echoes through the evening air, and Eddie stumbles away from the barbershop window. "Abby!" He runs into the street, ignoring Patterson's order to wait, and Abby jumps into his arms.

Eddie clings, crying into her neck.

Shep staggers to his feet, searching urgently beyond Eddie and Abby for Olivia, but Abby's alone.

Patterson paces, his fingers mussing his hair, eager to question Abby. Eddie's reluctant to let her go, but he wants answers too, and he sets her on the ground, keeping his arm around her.

Relaxing his stance and trying for nonchalance but failing, Patterson says, "I'm Detective Patterson. You must be Abby Conrad."

Abby nods. "Yeah."

Shep and I stand with the negotiator. The words I want to fling at Abby are like razor blades against my tongue. I need to hear Agatha is okay, but I wait as impatiently as Shep who's vibrating with fear and rage someone would be stupid enough to do something like this to the woman he loves.

"I'm going to ask you a few questions, but if you don't know the answers, it's okay. It's not your fault and you haven't done anything wrong. You're not in trouble."

Eddie's grip tightens around Abby's shoulders. "Okay."

Patterson pulls out his phone. "First of all, are you all right? Is everyone okay? We heard a gunshot. Does anyone inside need medical attention?"

"I'm fine. Agatha held my hand the entire time and I wasn't scared. Everyone's okay."

"He didn't shoot anyone?" Patterson confirms.

"No. He shot at the ceiling."

Patterson's tone is firm but kind. "Did he say who he is?"

Abby licks her lips. "His name's Judd Thompson. He used to own the Guitar Pick. He recognized Clarissa."

Patterson shoots me a dirty look. "Why would he know her?"

"She used to work here."

He sighs. "Would have been nice to know that."

Embarrassed for my oversight, I say, "I'm sorry. I would've said something if I'd thought of it."

That Clarissa managed the bar wasn't in my head, and I swear at myself for my stupidity.

"Do you know what he wants, Abby?" Patterson asks.

"He accused Clarissa and Olivia of stealing the bar from him. He said he has demands."

"Did he say what those are?"

"No."

"How did you get out?"

"He made us sit on the floor by the front door, and Agatha distracted him, asking him questions. I crawled behind the bar while they talked, and I snuck into the back room. There's an employee entrance."

"Good girl. This Agatha Sterling. She's steady?" Patterson asks.

"Yeah. She was the one who gave me the idea to sneak out. Clarissa stood in front of me when he barged in—she's going to be my stepmom—and when he asked who bought the bar, Olivia said she was the one. Ginger's in there, too, and when he first walked in, she told him to get out. Even with Judd yelling at us, I felt safe."

"It sounds like you're in with a good group. Do you think Judd Thompson's dangerous?" Patterson asks.

Abby shakes her head. "I think he's sad."

"Or desperate," Patterson mumbles. "Is there anything you think I should know?"

"I don't know." Tears fill her eyes. "Are you going to get them out?"

"I will do my best. I will do my very best."

Chapter Eighteen

Agatha

The music fades, but Judd doesn't feed the jukebox more quarters. He lights a cigarette and regards us through the smoke, the rifle laying comfortably in his lap.

"Have you lived in LA all your life?" I ask.

"For most, yeah. I did some time in the Army before I met my wife. Did a few things I'm proud of, saw a few things I still have nightmares about. Came back with a bad back, two bullet holes, and PTSD, but no one cares about us after we're done shooting the shit out of people. They throw a bottle of pills at you, tell you to be grateful you're still alive, and slam the door in your face."

"I'm sorry." The words are inadequate.

"Meeting my wife helped. Watching her die didn't." He jerks his chin at Olivia. "What about you? How'd your dad kick the bucket?"

"He was our church's pastor and he volunteered at the local prison. One of the inmates didn't appreciate that so much and when he got out, he found my dad and shot him. He was on parole for a total of three hours and fifteen minutes before he was arrested again. The time my dad gave him meant nothing."

"Can't speak for him, but I doubt he wanted to be out in the real world and did the first thing he could think of to get himself sent back. Got a taste of that after the Army cut me loose. When your life has always been one way but you're shoved into something else. There's fear and not a lot of people around to put up with it."

Liv smiles wryly. "I think I know what you're talking about, moving from Minnesota to here."

Judd scoffs and waves his gun at us. "You got your friends, your rockstar boyfriend. Who did that convict have? Gang buddies he was trying not to be like anymore. Family who was pissed he spent his life locked up when he could have been working, contributing, and raising his kids. A parole officer who didn't give a shit."

"Maybe instead of shooting my dad, he could have asked for help," Liv snaps, tired of listening to Judd make excuses for the man who shot her father in the middle of an outdoor church sermon.

"And sometimes that ain't so easy." Judd draws from his cigarette and snubs it out on the table. "Sometimes you ask and there's no answer. I don't guess any of you know how to play pool." He pushes away from the table and turns his back on us to rack the balls on the pool table I was screwing around with before this started.

Clarissa opens her mouth to reply, but I push her so hard she almost falls over. She wastes no time scurrying behind the bar, and to hide the noise of the swinging door as she pushes through it, I say too loudly, "I have no idea how to play pool, but I can play a decent hand of poker."

Judd swears, not impressed.

Olivia squeezes my arm and whispers, "Thank you."

"It's your turn," I murmur, but she shakes her head. I understand she doesn't want to leave, but she's not thinking clearly. I cover her belly with my hand. "Go."

She presses her lips together and looks away.

Kissing her cheek, I say against her skin, "It's okay. Go."

"I hear what you're planning, and I saw that little blonde take off. You're not fooling nobody. I'm keeping one of you. You can decide."

I don't give Liv or Ginger a chance to say anything. "I'll stay."

"No!" Liv scrambles to her feet, her chest heaving with fear and anger. "No."

"Sounds good to me," Judd says, and very deliberately, he picks up his gun from the table and slides the safety off. "Get out of here."

Clutching the windowsill, the cream paint chipped, Ginger stands. She's shaky, but she's not scared. She can't be if she's going to own two bars in this part of the city. This won't be the last time something like this could happen.

I stand too and grip Liv's shoulders, wishing I could knock some sense into her. "Think about what you're saying. You're pregnant, and Sheppard needs you. What you came out here for, that hasn't gone away. Go now, you and Ginger, and I'll hang out until Judd gets tired of seeing my pretty face." I choke, remembering Brock saying that to me not long ago.

Judd's finger curls around the trigger. "Listen to your friend. She's talking a lotta sense. Get out of here."

Pressing her lips into a thin line, Liv gestures for Ginger to follow her, and rather than escaping out the swinging door, they go through the customer entrance at the rear of the build-ing. She's pissed, and I'm going to catch hell later, but I don't care. She's safe, and now I can focus on the matter at hand. "Do you mind if I have a drink? Yours looks pretty good."

"You earned it."

"Thanks."

Behind the bar, I choose a bottle of José Cuervo. This place hasn't been closed for long, and there are still lemons and limes jumbled in a basket under the bar along with a paring knife. A salt shaker is already sitting near a laminated list of the types of beer the Guitar Pick serves. I quarter one of the lemons. It's overripe, but it'll work.

The phone rings, the harsh bell in an old rotary phone shattering the silence, and leaving his gun on the table, Judd carries his shot glass and the bottle of whiskey to the bar. I could run out the swinging door, but I don't think Judd will hurt me, and I stay while the telephone shrills.

"Answer it," Judd demands.

I lift it onto the bar and pick up the receiver. "Hello?"

"Agatha, this is Detective Raylene Burke with the LAPD. I'm a crisis negotiator and I'm outside, standing in front of the Guitar Pick. How are you doing?"

Judd sits on a barstool and cracks a peanut shell open from one of the bowls sitting next to a pile of cocktail napkins.

"Fine, doing fine. Are my friends okay?"

Judd pops a peanut into his mouth.

"Yes, they are. Detective Patterson and I appreciate what you did, but your safety is our main concern. May I speak with Mr. Thompson?"

"Just a moment." I hold the receiver out to Judd. He takes it and drops it into the cradle.

"You don't care what she has to say?" I ask, returning to cutting my lemon and trying to look like what he did doesn't bother me.

"Not yet. I gotta let 'em stew. My old man taught me that."

"Yeah." I'm well aware of what he's talking about. When my mother gets angry, she keeps me on pins and needles for days, sometimes weeks, until she lets me know what I did. It wasn't until I was in high school and I took an intro to Psychology class did I learn that the cold shoulder is a form of emotional abuse. Knowing that didn't change how I felt whenever she'd get pissed off and took her sweet time letting me know what I did wrong and what my punishment would be. She still does this. And it still works. "What do you want, anyway?"

I look around for a shot glass, a tiny one, because the next time I get drunk, it will be with Brock, and sigh.

"They're over there," Judd says, tilting his head toward one end of the bar.

"Thanks." I find a washtub full of clean ones under the cash register and fill one halfway. I salt my wrist, shoot, and suck on a lemon wedge. It's good. I haven't done tequila shots since college. Mom had no idea what she was doing when she kicked me out to live in the dorms. As long as I pulled straight As, she left me alone. It was the most magical time in my life. And the loneliest. I needed her attention like a smoker needs his next cigarette. She created a dependency, but over the years that dependency turned into resentment, and now I hate her because she's lived my life for me and I don't have the courage to tell her to stop.

"I'm not sure what I want," he says, cracking another peanut shell open.

"That's why you didn't talk to her. You didn't know what to say."

"Maybe."

"Hmm." I do another shot, and the booze fizzes in my blood.

"What about you?"

I lean against the bar. "What about me?"

"You were quick to stay."

"I don't have anything else going on at the moment. Tell me about your wife."

His face turns red in anger, but the fury drains from him just as fast. "She liked old movies and chocolate cake. She was a homebody, and she'd get tipsy off boxed wine. Met her here, and it's stupid, what they say, but the second I saw her, she took my breath away."

"That's nice. How long has she been gone?"

"It'll be twenty-three years next month." He leans to the side and yanks his wallet out of his back pocket. He shows me a picture of a sweet looking blonde, her hair done in pin curls wearing a pink dress. She's posing saucily against a pool table.

"Was that taken here?" I ask, surprised. The pool table looks exactly the same.

"Yeah. I've been through hell and back with this bar." He sips his whiskey. "You're not hitched."

"No. I'd like to be someday. I think it would be nice to have someone love you so much they'd want to marry you. I got a man out there," I nod toward the front doors, "who's worried about me."

"What's the holdup then?"

"Distance for one. I'm not from here."

"Minnesota."

"Yep."

Judd sips his drink.

"When did you buy this bar? *Why* did you buy this bar? Sorry, that sounded snotty."

He huffs a laugh. "Didn't. My dad left it to me when he passed away. He won it in a poker game, if you can believe it."

"That explains a lot." I wince. I'm sucking at getting on his good side, but all he does is look around at the interior that's decades old.

"It was in better shape back then. Bills pile up, too many

fights destroy the insides. Bands don't want to play anymore when gangs rule the neighborhood. That was the big draw, you know. Get those bands in here, but I had to find decent ones I could afford to pay, and that wasn't always easy. I gave her a hard time, but Clarissa did all right. She put in the work I was too tired to do. I didn't die with my wife, but she took a lot of joy with her, yeah, she did. You'd think after twenty-three years I would have gotten over her, dated, but I had my one chance." He rubs his thumb over her photo.

I cover his hand with mine and squeeze. "I'm sorry. If you love this bar so much, why did you sell it? Why didn't you say no?"

Judd pours more whiskey into his glass. "Fuck. You say that like it's so simple. I had an asshole lawyer breathing down my neck, threatening me if I didn't sign on the dotted line."

Stiffening, I say, "Liv would never do that."

He scoffs. "She might not, seems like the decent sort, but lawyers are paid to get the job done, and he did. I had no other options, and he knew it. No money coming in, my waitresses working for less than they ought to. I hired a couple of managers after Clarissa pulled her Cinderella act, but they never lasted long, fed up with the bullshit of running a place like this. Tried my best with the paperwork after the last one quit, but I'm an old man. I can only do so much."

"Then it sounds like Liv did you a favor."

He leans heavily against the bar, this old man with grey scruff and tired eyes. "Woulda been nice to have had a choice."

I stagger backward and crash into the bottles behind me.

That's it.

That's what I've been looking for my entire life. My mother robbed me of all my choices, and I never understood that, simply followed her orders like a good little soldier. She never once asked me what I wanted to eat for dinner, what kinds of clothes I wanted to wear. She never asked what classes I wanted to take, what kind of career I wanted for myself. She robbed me of my agency when she could have asked me to work with her. I grew up admiring her; my second home was at her office. I very well could have followed in her footsteps on my own.

But she didn't give me the choice.

"You don't look so hot all of a sudden," Judd says, trickling more whiskey into his glass. "Stop with the pussy stuff and have some of this. You okay?"

I nod, more times than I need to get my point across, and I down the shot of whiskey he poured me. Warmth seeps into my bones, eating at the last words my mother and I exchanged before I flew to California.

"You're only going because I'm letting you go. Don't forget that."

"Yes, ma'am. I know. Thank you," I said meekly, scurrying from her office like a scared little mouse lest she call me back, ordering me to stay and work on the next deal.

She never called to see if I landed safely, and what I told Brock is true. She'll never see what that paparazzo filmed on the beach because the only thing I'm good for is the next six-figure deal and how successful I appear to people she holds in the highest esteem. Nothing I do will ever be enough. Her approval is a bar so high I'll never reach it.

She stole my choices, but at thirty-six, I can steal them back, if I'm strong enough.

If Brock loves me, I just might be.

"What did you do with the money you got from the sale? Liv might not have known her attorney pressured you, but I know they paid you fairly. She's not a cheat, and she doesn't work with people who are."

He jerks a shoulder. "Paid some debt, paid off my house.

Bought a fresh bouquet of flowers for my wife's grave and had ten bucks left over."

"You don't have any money coming in?" I ask, concerned. Even debt-free, he still needs income.

"Could retire, I suppose," he says, blowing out a sigh. "I'd have to see if that's enough. Don't got a mortgage payment anymore, so maybe. Why? What are you cookin' up over there?"

I explain what Liv's trying to do buying the Guitar Pick and Shotgun Sally's, Clarissa's desire to learn how to be a literary agent instead of training her friends to manage a bar, and Ginger's time crunch. Eddie's heart may have been in the right place, but if Ginger wants to go to school, she doesn't have time to take classes and do homework while managing two bars. Especially since she doesn't know how. "You could still have a hand in the bar, but you wouldn't have the financial worries of owning it. Liv's organization has the money to pay you, and you'd be doing something good for the girls who worked for you."

Judd rotates his shot glass on the bar top. "You think she'd go for it?"

"I might have to put in a good word for you."

"Why would you do that?"

Smiling sympathetically, I say, "I know how it feels not to have any choices. I hadn't reached my desperation point, and maybe I never would have. I didn't know how numb I was feeling inside until I visited Liv and met Brock. I never had anything to fight for until I met him."

"Lost my fight when my wife died."

"Find it again. Live a life she would be proud of you for."

"If you can fix it, I'll do it."

"Liv's not unreasonable, but there's no doubt you pissed off Sheppard. You're going to have to go to therapy, maybe anger management. He won't let her around you until he knows he can trust you."

"Understood and long overdue."

I grab a cocktail napkin and find a pen near the cash register. "Write your number down. I'll get in touch after I speak with her, and I'll tell her you need a lawyer. Out of all the women in this city, Judd, you sure can pick 'em."

He scrawls his number on the napkin. "It seems like it was my lucky day."

"You know what?" I muse. "Mine, too."

Using the rotary phone, I dial 911. "Can you connect me to one of the cops outside? This is Agatha Sterling, and I'm inside the Guitar Pick."

"Just a moment please," the flat-toned dispatch says, and several clicks later, a brusque-sounding man snaps, "Detective Patterson."

"This is Agatha Sterling. Judd and I have reached an agreement, and we're coming out. We won't have anything in our hands, and he's not dangerous. I would appreciate it if no one shot at us. We'll use the front door."

"Are you injured? We'll be apprehending him. There's no way around that."

"I understand, but he's not a threat. Please don't use any unnecessary force. He didn't hurt any of us."

Judd tries to lift a corner of his mouth. The next twenty-four hours won't be a pleasant experience for him. With a groan, he hefts himself off the stool, and he leaves his rifle on the table. Since I said I would have empty hands, I don't grab my bag. I'll come back for it later, and everyone else's, too.

I step out ahead of Judd, hoping there aren't any trigger-happy cops anticipating us getting one off first. They have their weapons drawn, but a distinguished man wearing a sharp black suit, his dress shoes shining, holds a hand in the air to steady them.

Two officers rush to my side and cuff Judd, wasting absolutely no time taking him into custody and pushing him toward a police cruiser.

Sheppard's holding Liv, and from the sidewalk across the street, they're both anxiously watching the front door. Ginger's leaning against a building near them, doing the same.

Eddie, Abby, and Clarissa are standing in a tight huddle near Sheppard and Liv.

I stagger across the street toward Brock, my heart breaking. He looks so scared, the skin around his eyes and mouth pinched, standing away from everyone, waiting alone.

We meet near the bumper of a police cruiser, and he sweeps me off my feet, crushing me to him. I lose sight of Judd, but he can wait for a moment. I need this, and I lock my arms around Brock, his skin still smelling like the love we made earlier. He's trembling so terribly, it's a surprise he can hold on to me at all, and I murmur, "It's okay, I'm okay," over and over while everyone crowds around us, eager to ask me how I managed to convince Judd to let me go and how I am.

I'm fine now, Brock's thrumming heartbeat under my ear, his strong hands splayed over my back. I'm fine now.

He releases me without letting me go, and I inhale the warm evening air, the musty scent of the bar stuck in my nose. "I can't ever lose you, angel," he says, rubbing my cheek with the pad of his thumb, tears in his eyes. "I don't know what I'd do without you."

Resting my trembling hands on the sides of his face, I don't speak until I have his full attention. "I know, and I feel the same way. You wanted me to say it, and I do. I feel the same."

Liv can't hide her unease over our declarations of love shrouded in obscure language. She knows what kind of person my mother is, understands we don't have a mother/daughter relationship, that it's more employer/employee, but maybe what she doesn't understand is I've never been in love before, and not with a man who needs me to protect him no matter the cost. If losing my mother's approval is the currency, I'll gladly pay it and the return on investment will be more than I ever dreamed possible.

Detective Patterson questions me, and I explain Judd needs therapy. His actions were a cry for help, and we didn't have any interest in pressing charges. Sheppard and Eddie object, but Clarissa, surprisingly, defends him.

"Fine," Eddie snaps, "but only because he didn't hurt anyone."

"Look on the bright side," I say, safe with Brock's arms around me. "I found us a new trainer."

Liv's eyes widen in alarm. "Jesus Christ on a bicycle."

Adrenaline rushes from my blood, and hiding my face against Brock's chest, I laugh.

Chapter Nineteen

Brock

Ginger followed Olivia who was stomping across the street, tears filling her eyes, her cheeks flushed. She wasn't scared or unhappy, she was pissed, and the only reason she would be that angry was if Agatha volunteered to stay behind. Shep didn't give her a chance to say one word, immediately covering her lips with a kiss so full of desperation, fear, and love we all looked away, including Detective Patterson.

Shep released her, and she confirmed my suspicions when Patterson questioned her, asking the same question he asked Abby: "Do you think Thompson's dangerous?"

It didn't help my heart's erratic beat when she said no, echoing Abby's thought he was only down on his luck and needed someone to talk to.

I couldn't be around them and stood off to the side. I couldn't be exposed to the relief and love that radiated from the group. Ginger, too, felt out of place, but I couldn't wait for news with her. Using Sharyn to schedule my dates, I felt like an accomplice in what Derrick did to her, and shame kept me from approaching her to even tell her I was glad she was all right and ask if there was anything I could do.

Patterson's phone chimed, the music shattering the tense silence, and the air changed around us. Moments after he hung up, the bar's glass door slowly opened.

The second I saw Agatha was okay, that second will be seared into my memory for the rest of my life. Her tanned skin, the ends of her hair brushing past her shoulders, the tired, yet relieved expression on her face. She searched for me, and something lit her expression that hadn't been there before. A peace, maybe. A realization, and I prayed to God it didn't have anything to do with that guy waiting for her at home and everything to do with how much I love her . . . and how much I hope she loves me.

Only a few other instances can match what I felt holding her after she stumbled into my arms: making love to Bri on our wedding night when I thought I married the woman I would spend the rest of my life with, holding my daughters for the first time after they were born, and when I was able to hold my mom's hand when she passed away. I told her I loved her and that I would be okay. She died with a smile on her lips, and I'm grateful for that every day.

"I can't ever lose you, angel," I say, my throat raw, my voice quaking. I graze her cheek with my thumb, tears in my eyes. "I don't know what I'd do without you." I don't. Life isn't such a jumbled, fucked up mess when I'm with her.

In that eerie, intuitive way she has, she doesn't answer me until I can stare deep into her eyes and bat away everything else clattering in my brain for attention. She holds my face in her hands and says, "I know, and I feel the same way. You wanted me to say it and I do. I feel the same."

Eddie's flinty gaze bores into me, and Olivia inhales. Everyone knows what Agatha and I are saying to each other, and no one can piece together, least of all me, how we're going to make it work. Admitting we love each other is only slapping a bandage over a wound on a limb that will eventually need to be amputated. There's nothing to be gained by it, and all it will do is hurt me more when she has to leave. When she *chooses* to leave.

I couldn't care less who trains the waitresses, and maybe that's selfish considering we're talking about the rest of one man's life, but I'll worry about Thompson's fate another time. We hang around long enough only to answer Patterson's questions and confirm we weren't going to press charges, something both Eddie and Shep want to do. The women retrieve their bags, and I don't let Agatha out of my sight. Thompson's gun laying on one of the rickety tables is a harsh reminder of just how close an accident could have happened. Thompson may not have wanted to hurt anyone, but exploding like a pissed off bat out of hell could have had dire consequences.

Ginger hugs Agatha and thanks her for letting her leave with Olivia. She runs out the back door to the parking lot in the rear, and I wonder if this afternoon will change things or if she's familiar with the violence that comes with working in crappy bars and this was just another day of the same.

Eddie, Clarissa, and Abby drive to Shep's in Clarissa's car. She wants to see Mason as soon as possible, and we left him with Tony and Eunice, figuring he couldn't be any safer than with a mother (even if she is a lush) and a doctor. I want to drive Agatha straight to my place and carry her to bed, but that would leave Shep and Olivia without a ride and I'd look like a horny asshole.

The negotiator clicks over the cement in her heels. "You did a great job," she says, holding out her hand in Agatha's direction. "How did you know what to say?"

"It was obvious he was hurting. People get lost in the

shuffle of everyday life, and we found common ground. Sometimes it's as simple as that. Will you find him the help he needs?" she asks, and I couldn't love her any more if I tried.

"Yes. He'll be evaluated and we'll supply him with the resources to find affordable care. I spoke with him for a moment." She pauses. "Thank you for giving him something meaningful to look forward to. We all need purpose. It may be the difference between him living the rest of his life in peace or putting a gun in his mouth. Good work." Briskly, she turns and walks away.

"Thanks," Agatha murmurs to her back.

Exhausted from the emotional afternoon, we trudge down the cracked and worn sidewalk to the Chinese restaurant where I hope my car hasn't been towed. The gawkers left, leaving the streets quiet, and the last of the cop cars slowly drives away, rocks crunching under its tires.

"You shouldn't have made me leave," Olivia says as we walk through the restaurant's parking lot. The scent of fried rice wafts through the air, and my stomach gurgles with sick hunger.

"Ginger didn't need to be there any more than you did. If you want to thank me, schedule a prenatal appointment. I want you checked out after what happened."

Olivia thins her lips before she says to me, "You need to take care of her. She thinks about everyone but herself."

"She sounds like someone else I know," Shep says, opening the back door, hurrying her with a gentle nudge to her shoulder. He wants to go home just as badly as I do.

"Hmmph," she mumbles, climbing in.

I want to wait and kiss Agatha when we're alone, and I lightly brush my lips over her cheek before I open the door for her. She hugs me, and I lean against the car, stealing a moment before the drive to Shep's. "You scared me, angel."

She looks at me, and there is nothing I wouldn't do for her. In her way, knowing that at this moment what I *can* give her isn't the same as what I *want* to give her, she asks, "Will you feed me?"

"Let me guess— double order of eggrolls, two pounds of chicken fried rice, and enough chicken chow mien to feed the southern half of California?"

She grins, but it doesn't quite reach her eyes. "You know me so well."

"I'm sure the others will be on board. I'll read your fortune."

"I don't need to hear it," she says, her lips pressed against mine. "I know exactly what it will say. Let's go. I need wine, food, and your lap, in that order."

"Sounds good, angel."

We spend the evening at Shep's after all. On the way, he orders enough Chinese food to feed fifty people—not exactly the southern half of California—and a delivery person is unloading the numerous plastic bags from a car when we arrive.

True to her word, Agatha sits in my lap sipping on wine while I feed her eggrolls, and this is the happiest I've been in a while.

The fortune the cookie holds that Shep lobs at me isn't a surprise: *Nothing lasts forever.*

In my life, that's a fortune that's come and gone many times. I could open a thousand fortune cookies, but that will always be my fate.

The tighter I try to hold on to something, the faster it slips away.

I make love to her that night. I don't rush, my lips lingering on every inch of her skin. I don't say what I want to say—that I love her. That when the time is right, I want to marry her. I've known her less than a week, but my heart wants her for the rest of my life.

She falls asleep, but I can't, and I hold in my misery just long enough to dress and fumble my way down the stairs. I don't want a drink and pass the bar on the way outside. It doesn't feel right to sit out here without her, but I don't want her to hear me cry like Mason. He has an excuse, the baby's tears the only way he has to tell someone what he needs. I have words, but I can't find any, not any Agatha would accept.

I'm not sitting near the pool for long before she finds me. She's not holding a drink either, but she's wearing her night-gown. She settles next to me and dips her feet into the pool.

I try to stop crying; I don't want her angry. Brianna hated it when I cried. She said it wasn't a masculine thing to do, that she couldn't trust me to protect her or the girls if I was going to cry over every little thing. My tears are a form of expression, and to bottle them up would be like asking me to stop playing the piano, or to stop writing, or to stop producing movies, stop being who I am, which, after our divorce, I understood was the only thing Brianna wanted. She wanted me if I wasn't me.

"What's wrong?" Agatha asks, no censure or disgust in her voice, only sympathy and compassion.

I lower my head and try to get it under control. I hate this part of me as much as Brianna. Just once I'd like to shut my heart off and not feel anything. "I don't know," I say, but I do. There's plenty wrong, but I can't fix it.

She's quiet, swishing her feet back and forth, her hands in her lap. The night hums around us, the light pollution blocking out the stars. "I didn't tell you what I told you this afternoon only to leave. I can't."

It's my every wish and my darkest nightmare. That she would love me enough to stay.

"Is that okay?" she asks when I don't say anything.

"Agatha. You don't know me. You don't know anything about me."

It's not what she expected, and she swallows. "Is this about your friend with benefits?"

Somehow she knows, she always fucking knows. "Yeah, it is."

"I'm sorry. You said, and I thought—" she stumbles, getting to her feet.

"Agatha—"

"No, I get it. You said you didn't love her, but—" She runs across the grass.

I follow, frantically searching for the most truthful lie I can come up with. I grab her arm to stop her, but she struggles away, tears glinting on her face. "You don't understand. I told her I would take care of her, and I knew you wouldn't like—"

"I already know. Liv told me you're going to support her while you put her through school. Why would I care? Why would I care she's had a hard life and somehow she met you and you make it easier? She's lucky she has you, just like I am, but if you want me to go after my vacation's over, I will."

Her voice is full of false bravado, her chin quivering with sobs she's managing to somehow keep from spilling out.

The last thing I want is for her to go, and I yank her to me, twist my fingers in her hair to hold her still, and growl the stupidest thing I have ever said against her lips. "Don't leave. Marry me."

She scares the fuck out of me when she whispers back, "Yes."

Chapter Twenty

Agatha

Something's going on, and I'm going to find out what. Like the flask he kept in his car that's still in my purse, there's a story that has more to do with putting his friend through school. He wasn't crying because he thought I was going home after my vacation's over. He's worried about something else, and we better finish this poker game and lay all our cards on the table.

Both of us.

The first thing I need to do is talk to Brianna.

I'll worry about my own shit later.

He's propped up against the pillows, the sunrise highlighting the worry on his face. Proposing didn't help the situation, likely made it worse. Engagements can be broken, and it would hurt more than saying goodbye to someone you can convince yourself you had a two-week fling with. I'm not going anywhere—if we break up it's because of what I've done—but there's nothing I can do about that now. I made my choices long ago, and I didn't know how I would pay the consequences. All I knew was that in some way, I would.

I kiss his bicep, my lips trailing over his daughters' names and birthdates. I could ask if we had children if he would add their names to his skin, but instead, I say, "What's the plan for today?"

"You don't want to go to the jewelry store?"

I could be hurt he asked that like he was asking me to schedule him a root canal, but I feel the same way and force a smile showing all my teeth. "Let's put a pin in that for a moment."

"Do you regret saying yes?"

I sit up, covering my boobs with the sheet. "Do you regret asking?"

We stare at each other. I know he doesn't regret asking. He just thinks for some reason asking to altar isn't going to be possible. It may not be, but not for the reasons he thinks.

With an arm around my back, he holds me close to his chest. "I don't regret asking."

I melt into his body, happy he's not going to try to talk his way out of something he wants. "I don't regret saying yes, but I don't want to worry Liv. Let me talk to her first before we announce anything."

"You're worried about what Olivia's going to say? Shouldn't you be thinking about your mom, angel? Don't you want to call her and tell her that you're staying?"

Call me a hypocrite, but I'm not ready to burn that bridge yet. She might be the only thing I have left when Brock tells me he never wants to see me again. "I'd like to put that off for as long as possible. You don't mind, do you? I don't know if she'll want to meet you. She'll despise you for stealing me. I've never been a daughter, only a possession." I hate that tears fill my eyes. I don't want to go back to that. I don't. But what's the alternative? Stay here anyway? I couldn't do that, even if Liv likes it here and I could follow through with plans to open my own agency with Clarissa and create a photo history book of the band with Abby. I couldn't be here knowing what Brock thinks of me.

"Shh. Do whatever you need to do. Do you feel all right after yesterday? Do you want to stay in bed? Watch a movie later? Look at me, angel."

I wipe my cheeks and sit up again. I could stay in bed with him all day, make love whenever the fancy struck us, watch a movie after we cook dinner together. It's what Graham and I would do when he could get away. Those were lovely evenings, when I could pretend he was mine.

"It doesn't feel right after six days," he says, holding my hand and rubbing the finger where an engagement ring would go if he were to buy me one. "And my proposal didn't sound sincere after what happened at the Guitar Pick and our conversation about Polly. Fear shouldn't be the reason why a man asks a woman to marry him, but you've known me since I picked you up at the airport, and you know I was. Scared of what would happen if you left, scared of what will happen if you stay. They say love can fix anything, but I know it can't. I loved Bri and I love my kids, but that hasn't done a goddamned thing. When it all comes down to that pivotal moment, when we have to choose, love doesn't mean a whole helluva lot. So you remember, last night, the grass under your feet, the milky sky above us, you remember that when I asked it was because I love you, and if I would have wanted to accept less, I would have asked Polly to marry me a long time ago."

My shaky laugh is full of tears. "And you say you have trouble writing songs. I love you too. And I have something to ask you, as well. Remember that I didn't expect to meet you, didn't know my life would change visiting Liv in LA. I haven't lived a perfect life, and I made choices I regret now. They're a part of who I am, and most days, I don't know who that is. I've lived my entire life in my mother's shadow, and I'm scared to step into the light. I'm scared because you're going to see things I don't want you to see."

"If what you show me scares me away, or if you can't love me despite my mistakes, then we know we weren't meant to be together. Love can't fix everything."

I want to say that's a load of bullshit, but I know it's true. I loved my mother for a long time, still do, in my own distant way, but no matter how much I loved her when I was a little girl begging for it, she never loved me back. It was a quiet realization after school one day when I'd been allowed to go to a friend's house. I'd seen how her mom treated her before, but there was something different that day, something in the way her mother brushed her hair out of her eyes, or the way she smiled when her daughter spoke. My mother never looked at me that way, never touched just to touch. I walked home and sat on a swing in an empty park. That evening, I quietly turned my heart off, and until Graham touched my hand over coffee I shouldn't have been drinking with him, I lived in the dark. I played with matches to see the spark and feel the heat. I was too weak to tell him no.

Love can't fix everything, but I will do my best to see to it that after I go back to Minnesota, he'll be happy. That starts with visiting his ex-wife.

I lower the sheet. "Make love to me."

I don't need to ask. Since the night he had me on the floor downstairs, pieces of his broken guitar scattered around us, he hasn't done anything but love me.

"I think we should have that pool party tomorrow," I say, buckling my seatbelt. We're running a little late, but I think after last night, everyone needed the morning to say a prayer of thanks and take time to express how grateful we are things didn't head south the way a situation like that could have.

He kisses the back of my hand. "That's a good idea, angel. Who are we inviting?"

I tamp back a smile. "I don't know. Who do you want?"

"I'll talk to Eddie and Shep. See what they say. Maybe they'll want to keep it small."

Playfully, I poke out my bottom lip. "Then how is that any different than all of us sitting around at Liv's?"

"The pool, for one," he points out. "We don't swim at Shep's. Maybe you'll put more than your feet in it."

"You just want to see me in my swimming suit."

"Angel, I've seen you in your birthday suit, and I like that just fine."

I press my face against his arm and laugh.

When he parks at Sheppard's, I crawl into his lap. There's not a lot of space between his body and the wheel, but he doesn't move the seat back. I search his brown eyes, and it's there. The worry, the pain. "You wanna marry me." I say it with wonder in my voice because no matter what he thinks he's done, he could have anybody, and he said he loves me.

He brushes my cheek with his thumb. "It sounds like that Graham guy would marry you if you gave him a chance to ask."

"He can't. Come on, let's go inside." Stiffly, I move back into my seat.

Graham can't, and that's the truth.

"I'm sorry. I didn't mean to bring him up. I'm a little jealous, that's all."

I lift my purse off the floorboard and open the door. "I could be jealous of Polly, too, and it wouldn't do either of us any good. Graham is less to me than what Polly is to you. I can't claim Graham and I are even friends. He's a mistake I'm trying to leave behind."

He won't let me, either. The texts are piling up, missed calls and pleading voicemails. Today I'm going to have to find five seconds to text him, tell him I met someone, and that he needs to leave me alone and move on. It doesn't matter Brock won't be sliding a ring onto my finger.

Liv's in the kitchen sipping coffee when we barge in.

Her eyes widen.

I must not be acting like myself. She's never given me so many googly eyes before. "That better be decaf. Let's go," I say, pulling her arm, sloshing coffee onto the breakfast bar. Clarissa, Eddie, and their kids aren't here yet, and I want to scoot before she wants to talk to me about that project she found in my slush. "Crap. We parked behind your car."

"Take mine, angel," Brock says, his keys still dangling from his hand. "Where are you going?"

"Yeah, where *are* we going?" Liv asks, sucking down her coffee as quickly as she can. She must not have been up long.

"Party planning."

"Will there be wine?" Eunice asks, holding a coffee cup rather than a flute of champagne, I mean, mimosa, but God knows what she doctors her coffee with.

"Of course there will. I think we'll need a lot of alcohol to get through a party like this."

Sheppard chuckles. "I don't know if I should be curious or scared."

"Frightened anticipation always works. *Come on*," I urge Liv, and she finally sets her empty mug down and grabs her purse.

"Hey," Sheppard says, "I need a kiss before you go."

Liv steps into his embrace.

Brock rubs my shoulders. "He didn't kiss her goodbye yesterday."

I glance at them, Shep's hands trembling against her back. "Oh. He really needs her."

"I know how he feels, angel. Be careful, wherever you're going."

"I will. Later we should clean up your house and order food. I was joking, and I want tomorrow to be fun."

"And a movie alone tonight?"

"It's my turn to pick."

"That it is."

I reach onto my tip toes and whisper into his ear, "No matter what, I want you to know I will never forget how it feels when you hold me. That just for a minute someone who's worth anything thought I was worth something too."

"Angel—"

"I know. Have fun with the guys. Tell Clarissa I'm sorry we didn't wait for her. I really want a little time alone with Liv today."

"She'll understand."

"Thanks. I hope so."

Sheppard releases Liv, and she stumbles backward, two fingers pressed against her lips.

I clutch her hand and we escape before any more men and any more kisses can keep us from this important task.

"Where are we going, and it *was* decaf, thank you for asking." Wearing shorts and a dressy top in a teal that makes her eyes pop, she waits by the passenger door of Brock's car both for me to unlock the vehicle and to spill my guts.

I do one, and settling behind the wheel, do the other. "He asked me to marry him."

"Oh, Agatha," she sighs, but she's not happy. "What did you say?"

"Yes." I rest my forehead against the wheel.

"Why would you do that?" She's not mad, but her question is valid.

"It's not because of my mom," I say, turning my head to look at her. "He'll never understand Graham."

"He might understand it. From what I can tell, he and Eddie are still friends, but that doesn't mean he'll trust you to be faithful if you do get married. You never should have been with Graham. Working with him on his memoir, okay. Friends, even, if you could have ignored his charms, but you didn't, and you started sleeping with him. It wasn't right."

"You're not telling me anything I don't already know. That's why I'm going to do what I can so when he tells me he can't be with me, at least maybe he'll have a shot at being happier than he is. He's fucking miserable, and I want to help him before I leave."

"You didn't cancel your flight."

I scoff. "Of course not. I'm going to wait until the last possible second to tell him what I did, and then I'm going to get on that plane and go back to what I was doing before."

"Agatha," she says, her tone sympathetic yet tinged in disapproval. She knows why I started seeing Graham in the first place.

"Not the Graham thing. He wants to pick me up at the airport. Fine. I'll let him and explain . . ."

"Explain what?"

"Explain that I'm better than the way he makes me feel." Tears dribble from my eyes.

"At least you know that. Then find a man who's available."

My heart cracks a little more with every word she says. "You don't think Brock and I will make it?"

"I think you're forgetting about your mother. Nothing has ever made you tell her to fuck off. If anything, I would expect you to find a happy medium. Stop doing every little thing she says, but marry someone she would approve of and still work at her agency. Are you brave enough to tell her to go to hell? Would you be okay if she never spoke to you again?"

"I would be if I had Brock."

"You're going around in circles. You're not going to have him. You already think that, and you should plan for that to happen. When Sheppard told me to go home, I went into shock. All I could think about was curling up into a ball on your couch. I don't want that for you because I won't be there and I'm afraid all you'll do is run right back to Graham. He's been there for you, and I'm sorry I wasn't. I am really sorry."

She turns her head but not before I catch the shine of tears in her eyes.

I tell myself what I tell my authors. Plan for the worst and hope for the best. What's the worst that could happen? I tell Brock about the real circumstances between Graham and me, and if he thinks we can't build a relationship because of my past, then yeah, I'll go home. I'll keep going to work, meet a man who's available like Liv said. Maybe he won't set my soul on fire, but steady and dependable is okay, too. Find a happy medium. It wouldn't be the end of the world if Brock rescinded his proposal.

Maybe he wouldn't settle for his friend with benefits, but I've accepted second best all my life. No reason to think that has to change.

I don't want to sit here so long we miss our chance to do this by ourselves, and I scan the dash, all the buttons, knobs, and sticks a jumble. "Where does the key go?" I ask, dumbfounded.

Olivia leans over and presses a button. The engine hums to life. "Are you going to tell me where we're going?"

"Jesus Christ on a bicycle. I don't drive a dinosaur, but I still use a key. Yeah. You need to tell me how to get there. I want to talk to Brianna. If I can make Brock happy before I leave, then anything else that happens will be chocolate frosting."

"How did you get tangled up with Graham?" she asks as I back out of the driveway.

"He was smooth and kind, and he listened," I say, remembering our first date. I accepted, knowing it wasn't right. He convinced me he wanted to talk, and we did, over candlelight and filet mignon. He listened to my stories about work, about my relationship with my mother, about how I liked living in Minneapolis and the parts of the world I've seen, and he filled something inside me that wasn't his to fill. I should have stopped it then, but he asked me out again, this time to a bar in a hotel. I knew where we would end up and we did. He gave me as much as he could, and in the end, it wasn't very much at all. I'm tired of accepting so little, but I will, again and again, because it's all anyone wants to give me because it's all I'm good for. "And he remembered what I said."

She sighs at her phone. "You're going the wrong way."

"Where does she live?" I ask, immediately slowing and looking for a place to turn around.

"In a mansion near the ocean. Where do you think she's going to live? I don't know how you think we're going to bust our way in there. For all you know, she's in Paris."

"At least I can say I tried."

"The road to hell is paved with good intentions."

"As long as there's wine at the end."

She scoffs.

The drive's short, and we ride along the ocean. I could have enjoyed the view if I wasn't so worried about what we'd find. I tried to sound like I didn't care if Brianna wasn't home gardening or doing whatever the fuck it is rich people did, but I want this for Brock so badly. I want her to understand how much he's hurting. If I could do this one small thing, if, when I went home I knew his daughters were back in his life, then I could say goodbye and not look back.

Of course the driveway is blocked off, and a speaker is built into a stone column standing guard. I slide my window down and look at Liv. She shrugs.

"Can I help you?" a tinny voice asks, somehow knowing we're waiting.

"I'd like to speak with Brianna Ashford if she's available," I say, my voice loud and strong. I don't want to be intimidated because she has a boatload of money. Some of its Brock's. There's no way she walked away with nothing when she divorced him.

"Your name, please?"

"I'm Agatha Sterling, and Olivia Bloom is with me."

"Just a moment."

Two minutes later, to my surprise, the gate swings open, and I slowly move forward, following the curved path of pristine light brown brick. The driveway opens into what I can only call a parking lot, and a four-stall garage sits to my right. I have no idea where to park, and I stop the car where we are, hoping I won't be in anyone's way for the five minutes Brianna will give me to speak to her.

A woman dressed in beige pants and a white dress shirt meets us at the door. I'm stupid and I never looked up pictures of Brianna online, but this older woman isn't her. I don't know what she did before she married Brock, but Brianna can't be anything but beautiful, and a ball of humiliation lodges in my throat.

"My name is Marlena. I'm Mrs. Ashford's personal assistant. Follow me, please."

I glance at Liv. A personal assistant. What does she do all day she needs one of those?

We follow her through a gorgeous house. "Why don't you live in one of these? Instead of Sheppard's little beach shack?"

"I happen to love his little beach shack. Would you live here?"

Marlena stops in an elegant library and steps to the side, her hands clasped in front of her.

"I'm afraid if you have your sights set on something like this, you'll be disappointed. When we were married, we lived down the street. He hated it. I'm willing to bet he doesn't have any furniture in his house. Would I be right?" Brianna Ashford asks in a well-modulated voice that tells me only two things: she's used to being heard and getting her way.

"You've never been inside," I say dumbly. I can't get past how beautiful she is, and I can honestly say it doesn't have anything to do with surgery and everything to do with genes, sleep, nutrition, and exercise. She could be Diane Kruger's clone, and the ball of humiliation grows. How easily she would have belonged by Brock's side.

"Is there anything else you need, ma'am?" Marlena asks.

"We'll have coffee outside," Brianna says, and her assistant nods.

We follow her, Brianna's heels clicking against the hardwood floor. "I can't say that I have, though I doubt I'm missing much." She leads us through a gorgeous living room and out a set of French doors to a grouping of chairs made for the outdoors.

She gestures, inviting us to sit. I'd rather stand, but Liv sits, and so do I, setting my purse on the patio made of brick that matches the driveway and sidewalks.

Marlena used magic to brew the coffee, and we're only getting comfortable when she appears with a coffee tray, sets it on a table positioned between our chairs, and exits again, as silently and as efficiently as she came.

"I'm—" I reach my hand out to introduce myself.

"Agatha Sterling, a literary agent from Minnesota, yes, I know," Brianna says, amused. "My friends wasted no time showing me the video of you and my ex-husband making out on the beach. Classy." Her focus shifts to Liv. "I'm glad to finally meet you. I never wished the band any ill-will, and it hurt to see Sheppard suffer after Derrick's death. I'm glad you were able to help him, even if it took a little fucking to do it."

"That's not—" Liv starts.

Brianna pours coffee from an elegant silver carafe. "Please. Don't bother to deny it. All the photos of you that popped up online oozed sex. I've never been to Minnesota. I didn't realize the women there were so quick to warm up." She offers me the cup, and I accept it. She does the same for Liv while I add cream and a sugar cube in the shape of a heart to my coffee. "Now, I think that's enough idle chitchat. How can I help you?"

"I want to know why you and Brock divorced," I say, trying to be polite so she'll answer my questions. There's nothing I dislike about her, but I don't like her, either. She's not the only one who needs to thaw out.

She drops the façade. "Look, you seem like a nice woman, and it's obvious from the video you care about each other, but you don't know what you're taking on getting involved with him."

I know more than she thinks I do, but I ask, "What do you mean?"

"The constant sex for one thing. I didn't need his cock inside me every fucking second, pardon the pun. Tell me the minute you spread your legs you've kept him out."

"Did you think maybe that's his way of showing you he loves you?" I ask in his defense. I noticed it too, his need to be touching me, inside me, but I've been so starved for sincere and honest affection, I want every moment of that intimacy.

"A kiss on the cheek and a hug can suffice."

"He's hardly a rapist, Brianna. All you had to do is tell him you didn't feel like it."

"Yes, of course. Why didn't I think of that? Then he looks at you like you killed his favorite puppy, and he slinks off only for you to give in because you can't stand how guilty you feel. If you haven't been treated to the Brock Farris Guilt Trip, you haven't been together long enough."

I sip my coffee. "You didn't divorce over sex."

"No, we didn't. After years of tolerating it, I couldn't stand the energy around him, the constant sizzle. He couldn't sit still, always had to be doing something. It rubbed my nerves raw to the point I was on Xanax."

I flick a quick glance at Liv. That's exactly how I described him, too.

"You know what I'm talking about," she says, catching me.

"Yes, I do. But he has an outlet for that. His music, the movies he produces, the movie reviews he was doing for the paper. He's bursting with creativity, and maybe it is like a wildfire out of control, but you were never in the middle of it."

"You try putting up with that at 3 AM for years. Every fucking night, I'd wake up and he wouldn't be in bed, instead tinkering with his piano, or puttering around making a godddamned mess in the kitchen. Or worse yet, pacing the floor, mumbling lyrics and poetry and movie lines, and the only thing that would calm him down was sex."

"Love," I say over her, and she presses her lips together.

I lean forward, the coffee cup cradled in my hands. "Did you ever stop to think he has ADHD? That he might be on the spectrum?"

She rears back, and it's all the answer I need. She turned

his creativity into something about her, never once considered Brock's energy came from somewhere deeper. "What? I don't understand."

"It's not that difficult, Brianna. He can't turn his mind off, and when he's agitated, he can't look into your eyes. Did you think that instead of anger, he could have used a little compassion and some help? A diagnosis? Medication isn't for everyone, but there is treatment and therapy available."

"I didn't see it," she whispers.

"Because you were jealous. He told me you asked him to quit writing film reviews. Why? The music, the movies, the baking, and everything else, you were jealous because none of that was about you, but you know what? He would have gladly shared every single piece of all of that with you. He loved you very much, and he loves his daughters. Cries, because he misses them. He's so passionate, and for some strange reason, you decided to hate him for it instead of love him. Lexi and Layla are going to do the same thing. They're going to explode with creativity, and you're going to be jealous they're taking after their father instead of you and you're not going to be able to help them."

Her gaze jerks from her lap to mine.

"It's already starting, isn't it?" I set my delicate coffee cup onto the tray and stand, my own nervous energy needing a place to go. "Let me guess. Lexi can play ten different instruments with her eyes closed, and Layla can speak six languages while the Olympics court her as their star gymnast."

Brianna stands too and scoffs. "Close."

"If you don't want to lose them like you lost Brock, get them evaluated and support them. If you hide from who they are, you'll never be able to relate to them. You took them away from Brock, and that was cruel. He would never hurt his daughters, and you know that because he never hurt you. Let him see his kids."

She pauses. "I will, but you have to do something for me first."

I frown. "What can I do?"

"You're a literary agent. Layla wrote a book, and she wants to know if it's any good."

"Just one?" I ask, quirking my mouth.

She huffs a quiet laugh. "You understand more than I gave you credit for. No, not just one, but she's serious about this particular novel. Can you look at it? Let me know if it has potential?"

"I don't want to read it without her permission."

"The girls saw the clip, and they were asking about you. I told her I would reach out if I got the chance. I didn't know the chance would pop up at my door."

"Okay, but I'm not going to lie. Either it will be brilliant, or writing won't be her thing. I'm guessing it will be brilliant."

"Thank you." She taps her smart watch and a moment later, Marlena appears. "Can you run up to Layla's room and grab her memory stick? Miss Sterling said she would look at Layla's book."

Marlena disappears without a sound.

"She could get a book deal without my opinion. Who she is will open many doors."

"I know, but I don't want her given things simply because of who her father is or who her stepfather is. Success is greater appreciated if it's earned, and if her book is good, then I want someone real to tell her that."

"Thank you. I'll give you my honest opinion. I don't rep fiction, but I can put you in touch with several agents who would be happy to represent her." My mother would drool worse than Mason over a book written by Layla Farris whether it was any good or not. That's what editors are for.

"That's all we need."

Marlena hands off a bright pink memory stick to Brianna only for Brianna to pass it to me. I tuck it into the front pocket of my shorts.

"We're having a pool party tomorrow at Brock's. Stop by with the girls. Abby will be there. I assume they were close for a time?"

Brianna nods and picks up her coffee cup. "They were and still are. Shelly and I are very good friends."

"Maybe I'll get to meet her someday. Stay for a glass of wine. I'll introduce you to Clarissa, and you can visit with us. We'll talk about something more pleasant."

"He's very lucky to have you. You won't believe me, but it never occurred to me he could have something like ADHD. I'll look for signs in the girls now that I know, but I think their teachers would have mentioned if they were having problems in class. Have you spoken with him about it?"

I pick up my purse, a blatant signal I want to go. I've pressed my luck, and we can chat tomorrow with something a little stronger than coffee. "No. Things have moved fast, but they're complicated."

Brianna shakes her head. "Agatha, is it okay if I call you that? Everything Brock does will be complicated. If you love him and want a life with him, find your backbone. You have one, or you wouldn't be here. When it's time to fight, put your boxing gloves on. I didn't want to play. Decide if you do."

"All I want is for him to be happy. Being a part of Lexi's and Layla's lives again will go a long way."

Liv stands with her purse, a silent spectator, and we walk to the front door together. I could understand why Brock wouldn't want to live in a house like this. He didn't feel like he was part of a family here, rooms upon rooms of nothing but expensive furniture, when what he really wanted was for Brianna to love him and show him she did.

"I can respect that. I want my husband to be happy, too, but it's not easy."

"No, and I don't expect it to be, but I've decided at this point in my life, I'm choosing my battles more carefully."

"Then all I can say is, I hope Brock appreciates it if he's one of them. You were ballsy to come here. Thank you."

"You're welcome. And Brianna?" I ask as she opens the door for us.

"Yes?"

"His banana bread is really good."

For the first time since we arrived, her smile is genuine. "It is. Did he bake the kind with chocolate chips?"

I shake my head.

"Keep some on hand, and he will. It's all I ate when I was pregnant with Lexi. A year after her birth I had to have a tummy tuck I gained so much weight. You were right, about a lot of different things. I didn't appreciate what I had. He's a good man, albeit, mixed up."

I don't agree. If he was mixed up when they were together, it was because she made him that way. "See you tomorrow?"

"You will." She nods at me and shakes Liv's hand. "It was nice to meet you. I'm interested in speaking with you about what your organization is doing."

"Anytime. Gina will be there tomorrow, and I'm going to ask the guys to invite Dalton and Melody. It seems now is a good time to mend fences."

"I'd love to see them again. It's been a long time. Thank you for inviting me. Goodbye."

This time Brianna closes the door, and taking a chance she's not watching us, I stagger to Brock's car, bend over, and suck in a deep breath. I had no idea how that would go, and I am so thankful Brianna wasn't as bitchy as she could have been.

Liv rubs my back. "You did a good thing. Are you going to tell him you were here?"

I fish for Brock's keys in my purse and unlock his doors. "No. If she decides not to show up after all, it will hurt him more than he already is. A surprise in the other direction is better."

"That's a good idea."

Before I pull onto the street, I toss her my phone. "Can you text him and ask where they are? I need to see him."

"You're going all in, aren't you?"

"I can't help it. Was there ever a time after you met Sheppard you could have walked away?"

She sighs and opens my messages app. "You have got to block Graham's number. He's texted you twenty times already, and it's barely noon."

"It's two o'clock there, if that helps," I say, my stomach twisting.

"It doesn't. And to answer your question, you know I couldn't. He owned me before I even met him. All of this is your fault."

"Is that good or bad?"

"It turned out good for me, but I don't know how it's going to turn out for you."

"I was afraid of that."

Eddie and Brock are at Brock's, and Liv and I find them playing their guitars and testing lyrics in his sunroom.

I tug on his hand and lead him into the hallway, with an amused, "Well, then," from Eddie.

"Are you okay, angel?" he asks.

I rush him up the stairs, and I'm on him the second we step inside his bedroom. "Yes. Make love to me." I pull his t-shirt up revealing his flat abs and hard chest, and I drag my lips across his skin. I'm hot and feverish, sweat slicking down my back. If this is the way he shows the women he loves how much he loves them, then I need it.

He shoves my hand onto his cock, and I whimper. I need him inside me. To hurry him along, I unbutton his jeans, unzip the zipper, and greedily wrap my hand around him, the tip already wet.

"That's how you want it? Quick and dirty?"

"Yes, please."

"Take your shorts off."

I do, reaching for my panties, too, but he stops me, roughly turns me around, and pushes me against the bed. He lowers his jeans just enough to free his cock, and leaning his body over mine, shoves my panties aside and rams his cock into me with a low growl.

I cry out, the comforter muffling my sob. It's not of pain, but relief. I don't feel so empty when he's inside me.

He goes at me, ferociously, and I rub my clit, his hands too busy holding onto my hips, keeping me in the exact place he needs to go as deeply inside me as he can.

I come, and God, it feels so good, the tip of his cock hitting the center of my body, my pussy clenching around him. Sparks fly, and stars burst behind my eyelids. "Harder," I moan, wanting him to feel as good as I do.

His fingers dig into my skin, and he mutters a deep, "Fuck." With a hand to my stomach, he lifts me off the mattress and comes. I haven't felt him this big before, and I'll ache tomorrow.

Trembling, he holds me steady until the very last drop of cum is either inside me or leaking down the insides of my thighs. When he's done twitching, he lowers me to the bed and folds himself around my back, anchoring himself with his forearms so he doesn't crush me.

"What was that?" he asks, panting, his lips pressed against my cheek.

"I needed to be close to you."

He laughs. "I don't know if I should thank you or ask what's wrong. Where did you and Olivia go?"

"Nowhere important. Drove around, sightseeing, really, because she said she doesn't get out much. It was nice to hang out alone with her." It's not exactly a lie. "I missed you while I was gone."

"I missed you, too. This is gonna hurt, angel. I'm sorry."

"Then don't."

"We left Eddie and Olivia downstairs. I'm all for giving you what you need, especially if that's me half-naked, but we can't stay in bed when our friends are here."

"I know. Do it. I've never been with anyone as big as you before."

He gently slides out of me. It helps his cock went down, and it doesn't hurt, but I'm raw, and my skin stings. My panties are twisted in an awkward position and I should put on fresh ones.

I stand up, my legs cramped, and he turns me around with a touch to my shoulder. "I love you. Does it scare you?"

"Not that. I don't want to lose what we have."

He always looks so tired, and my heart skips a beat. All I want is to protect him for the rest of his life. Is that so much to ask? "There are no guarantees, angel. Enjoy the time we do have and the rest will work itself out."

That's the only thing we *can* do, and I say, "I need to clean up."

"So do I."

We use the bathroom together, and I change into fresh panties. "Can I do laundry soon? You have a washer and dryer, don't you?"

His cheeks redden, and I half expect him to say no. "Yeah. I keep forgetting to show you where they are."

"Later, but at this rate, if I don't do a load, I'll be going commando."

He spanks me, the delightful slap snapping through the lace. "I wouldn't complain."

I meet his eyes in the long mirror attached to the wall over his and hers sinks. "Anytime you need me, just ask. I'll give you whatever I can. Attention, love, my body. I will always be yours."

"Forgiveness?" he asks, strain pulling at his features.

"Especially that. If I can have some, too."

He forces a small smile and kisses the top of my head. "Anytime."

Soon, I'll be testing that. I can't be disappointed with the results.

Eddie and Liv are waiting downstairs, and it's like Liv to have found something in common with an aging rockstar drummer.

"Judd's been released," she says as we walk into the sunroom, Brock's hand at my waist. "Detective Patterson contacted Sheppard, and he said Judd started seeing a therapist. His first appointment was this morning and he's signed up to participate in group therapy at a community center near the Guitar Pick. Sheppard doesn't like it, but he left the decision up to me and Gina. I called her while you were upstairs. She doesn't have an opinion either way, but she said it's a convenient solution and left it up to me since I was at the Guitar Pick yesterday."

Brock sits at his piano. The longer I stay, the more I can

parse out his defense mechanisms. He feels safe behind a piano, here and at Sheppard's. I wonder where he gravitates at Eddie's. Eddie probably has a piano, too.

I stand behind him, scraping my fingernails against the nape of his neck while he plays a song I can't identify. "Is giving him a job still something you think you'll do?" I wish I were going to be here to work with Judd too, stay in contact with him and be a friend, but while Brock made forgiveness sound like a simple thing to give, I know how untrue that is.

"Since I'm not the one who will be working directly with him, I think we should leave that decision up to Ginger." She turns to Eddie. "We should invite her, Vonnie, and some of the other girls to the party tomorrow. We can talk about it, and if Ginger feels safe working with him, Agatha can give him a call and we can plan a proper meeting at the offices Gina rented. The paint's dry, and we'll start using the space more regularly. We need to decide how much he's going to earn and how long we're going to keep him on. We shouldn't assume Ginger wants this responsibility. She may be having second thoughts like Clarissa did."

Eddie winces. "You're not upset about that, are you?"

"Of course not. I've had to make my own adjustments in the past few days, and Agatha was a big help. I would never resent Clarissa a chance to follow her dreams. We should all do that whenever we can."

Liv pins me with a stare, her subliminal message not so subliminal. She's telling me I should do what I want when I get back to Minnesota, not blindly follow my mother's commands. She can so easily forget how a broken heart tears you down to the point where you don't care if you're living much less how you're paying the bills. The difference between her and me is when Michael passed away, her mother brought her homemade chicken noodle soup. My mother would tell me to stop fucking crying and get back to work. My mother has never had a broken heart. You have to have one for it to break.

"Let's talk more about that at Shep's. Clarissa's there with Abby and Mason, and she's asking where you are," Eddie says to me. "I hope you're not getting tired of her. You can tell her to back off if you are."

"Not at all," I partially lie. I did what I wanted to do today. It's not Clarissa's fault she's indirectly asking me to work during my vacation. And who knows, maybe she did find a diamond of a proposal in my slush. I can never have enough six-figure book deals. "Did you finish up here?"

"Bobbi will come by early in the morning. We can order food tonight and have it delivered. That should do it," Brock says, his fingers skittering over the keys.

"Who's Bobbi?" I ask, but what I really want to know is if she's another friend with benefits.

"My cleaning lady. I'd be lost without her."

"Oh, does she rescue banana bread at 3 AM?" I tease.

"3 PM, maybe. You're the only woman who's been in my bed in this house, angel."

"And you've already had your fun," Eddie says, rising from the couch. "I need a beer."

We spend the rest of the day at Sheppard's, and I help Liv set up a make-your-own-taco buffet on the breakfast bar. Abby can't stop talking about the band's photo history book I mentioned at the Guitar Pick, and she chatters away about the things her mother has in storage while we add fixings to our shells.

"I think we'll need to take a raincheck on that movie, angel," Brock whispers in my ear, handing me a glass of wine.

I turn my head and kiss him. "That's okay. I like this."

"I do, too."

That night, we stumble into his house, drunk on wine and

tacos. We make love on the floor in the foyer, too eager to wait, and after Brock falls into a troubled sleep, at 3 AM I text Graham. I tell him I'm in love with another man.

Exactly forty-two seconds later, he replies and says he loves me too much to let me go, he's ready to leave his wife, and if he asked me to marry him, would I say yes.

Chapter Twenty-One

Brock

"Are you good?" Shep asks, lifting one end of a patio table to help me carry it from the storage shed to the other side of the yard.

"Yeah, why wouldn't I be?" I lift my end and tilt my head in the direction I want us to go.

I'm not good. I couldn't sleep, and for once, I was the one to go downstairs and search for Agatha. She was sitting by the pool, her feet in the water, looking into space. Her eyes were dry, her skin was pale, and when I asked if she'd heard bad news, all she did was stare at me as if she had never seen me before.

I ended up carrying her inside and putting her to bed. I think she might have fallen asleep until Bobbi's puttering downstairs woke her, and she blinked her sleepy eyes, smiled, told me she loved me, and acted like nothing happened.

It was a bad idea, but I checked her phone while she was in the shower. I didn't see anything that would have upset her like that. The texts from that Graham guy were gone, and she cleaned out her recent calls list and deleted all her voicemails. It's like he never existed.

"You haven't had a party here before," he says, setting down his end in the grass near the pool.

Before we left Shep's, we invited quite a few people—everyone from Ginger and Vonnie to Dalt and Melody. Even with the short notice, all of our friends responded and accepted.

I want everyone to have a place to sit, and Shep's been helping me drag some tables and chairs out of storage. In a few minutes, a deli is going to deliver so many sandwiches and bags of chips and so much potato and macaroni salad we'll be lucky if we get through it all. Eddie's doing a liquor run, and Agatha's upstairs on her laptop. She said a project came up at work and was skimming something on a pink memory stick.

"I wouldn't have bothered if Agatha hadn't wanted to. We could have done this at Eddie and Clarissa's, but it makes no difference to me."

"It's a nice day for it," he says, his hands on his hips.

The pool water sparkles in the sunlight, there's not a cloud in the sky, and the grass is a brilliant green. It *is* a nice day for it, but like every day in my life, nothing feels right, and anxiety is a fizzing firecracker waiting to explode. "How are wedding plans?" We head toward the storage shed for chairs.

"Something came up with Liv's stepdad's church and they can't make it out like they wanted. They rescheduled their flight for next month, but that means her sister can't come. She and her husband are fostering, and the kids will be in school. Liv's disappointed, but we'll get there. She doesn't want to admit she wants us to be married before she starts showing, but I think that sums it up. We were trying, but not trying. It took her off guard it happened so fast. We should have waited a year or two, after the tour, but I'm old and selfish."

"I get it." There's nothing in this world I want more than for my relationship with Agatha to work out, for us to get married and have a baby. My children growing up with Shep's and Eddie's would be a dream come true. I had that dream once, when Lexi and Layla toddled around with Abby, and I thought my life couldn't get any more perfect than that.

"Eddie said you and Agatha are getting serious."

"It's complicated."

"It's not going to stop being complicated," he says, hauling two chairs by their backs and heading toward the pool again.

"Thanks for the pep talk," I say, doing the same.

"No use in pretending it won't. Liv says her mom's a real treat, and if Agatha does tell her to fuck off, that won't be so easy. There's a loss there, even if she can have all this." He drops the chairs and holds his arms out, encompassing, I assume, not just my house, but friends and family, and all that would come along with moving to California.

"I would never ask her to choose."

"You wouldn't be the one asking," Shep points out, and he's right. If her mother issues an ultimatum, it would be up to Agatha to decide, but I already know after the things I've done, I don't stand a snowball's chance in hell of her choosing me.

"This looks good," I say, scanning the pool area and the tables with their umbrellas scattered along the brick and grass. "I have a few coolers I can fill with ice for the beer and wine bottles. You've been drinking. You doing okay?"

"I don't need it as a crutch anymore. One of the best things about being in a relationship again is Liv always has time to listen to me. Three in the morning and she knows when I have something on my mind. She always has a realistic perspective I can appreciate. Derrick turned into someone I didn't know, and it's taken me a while to learn I'm not responsible for that. People change, and he hid it. Derrick abusing Clarissa was fucked up, but it's not for me to take the blame. I can sip a beer, appreciate the flavor, sip on a glass of wine and appreciate the notes for what they are, and when I really need something, I have Liv and Royce."

"I'm glad you have her, Shep, I really am."

"She saves my life every day."

It's like Shep to be that honest, that transparent with his emotions, and I don't doubt what he says is true. "Where is she? I thought she would come with you."

"Her stomach was feeling off, and she stayed in bed sipping ginger ale. Now that the wedding planning is tabled for the time being, maybe Agatha can get her to a doctor. I'm worried."

"It will turn out."

"Yeah," he agrees, but he doesn't sound convinced. "She'll drive over later with Mom and Tony or catch a ride with Gina and Jeff. They texted this morning and said they could swing by for a bit. You're gonna have a full house."

"It's good," I say, wishing it felt more permanent.

My cell chimes with a text, and I pull it out of the back pocket of my shorts. I half expect it to be Agatha wanting some playtime before the party starts, but it's Eddie. *A little help here?*

"Eddie's out front. He wants help hauling in the booze."

"Let's get to it."

"Did you clean the place out?" I ask when Eddie lowers his truck's tailgate. Cases of beer and wine are packed tight, and more wine bottles are in the extended cab.

"It doesn't go bad. What we don't drink now, we will later," he says, lifting a case of beer. "We have a lot of celebrating to do."

"Yeah, we do," Shep says, a slight smile on his mouth.

I wish I knew I was included in that, but when things come crashing down, and I know they will, it will destroy anything

Agatha and I could have had. I would be an asshole if I wasn't happy for my friends though, and I have to grin and bear it.

We start carrying in cases of Guinness, Heineken, and different kinds of wine. We'll need a few trips.

As I set a case of red wine onto my kitchen table, Eddie says, "Ginger called me. She said she and a couple of other girls who Sharyn paid off to keep quiet are thinking about talking to the police. She's nervous, but the incident at the Guitar Pick got her thinking. Agatha, actually, was a big help with that."

"Oh, yeah?" I hope to God I don't sound like my world is coming to an end. The second Ginger and the other girls give their statements and the cops have enough to search Sharyn's house, it's all over for me. There's no way Sharyn doesn't keep a paper trail. She says they have nothing to pin on her, and that might be true right at this moment, but that will change when Ginger and God knows how many others tell the investigating detective what she did to keep her brother out of jail.

"Yeah. She said Agatha's bravery and selflessness made her start thinking differently. Agatha stayed behind to talk to Judd, and now Ginger wants to pay that forward. Sharyn doesn't deserve to be living her best life, not when she supported Derrick and the sick things he was doing. She should pay for that."

Shep's steady, carrying a case of beer and setting it on the floor. He's listening, maybe wondering how far back this started, but he'll never know Derrick turned a decade ago. Eddie will never say anything.

I agree Sharyn should be held accountable for helping Derrick cover up what he was doing to women like Ginger, but if she hadn't set me up with Polly and Anne, I'm not sure where I would be now. Not all of Sharyn's clients would abuse their women, but that won't matter to Shep and Eddie. I should have met Polly and Anne without Sharyn as a go-between, but she made it easy booking the hotels and staying in contact with them. I didn't have to worry about scheduling our time or reserving the rooms. I could simply show up, take what I needed, pay, and go.

My anxiety grows, and I excuse myself, pretending I have to hit the head when really, I sneak out a side door and hide in the yard, leaning against the wall struggling to breathe.

With her intuition, Agatha knows I need her. She rounds the corner, her hair pulled back into a ponytail, sunglasses perched on her head, and a sheer coverup over a high-waisted bikini that makes her look like a 1950s pinup model. She tucks herself against me and presses her lips to the side of my neck. She can feel me trembling, the anxiety building in my chest threatening to crack my ribs open.

"Talk to me," she murmurs.

I shake my head. I can't tell her this. If she finds out, she'll hate me just as much as the others will.

She leans back and holds my face in her hands. "I will never stop loving you. I will always love you as much as I do now, in this very spot. Talk to me."

"Give me a few days."

She smiles, and I swear to God, I see every one of the rest of my days in her eyes.

"A few days is all we have left."

Her words haunt me. I don't know what she means and I was too scared to ask. Did she mean her flight, or did she mean something else?

She can't move here without going home first. Olivia needed to sell her house, transfer the title of her car to her sister, and she was there when her mother married the pastor of their church. Shep went with her and met her family.

I want to do the same. Help Agatha pack up her house, or her apartment, or condo, wherever she's been living, and she'll need to sell her car, and I want to meet her mother, if only for my own sake and tell her I'll take care of her daughter for as long as I'm able. But she made it sound like she knew moving here wasn't an option, that we wouldn't stay together, and I don't know what she was referring to. There's no way she could know about Polly. No one knows, and no one will find out until Ginger and the others give their statements, the police have enough for a judge to sign off on a search warrant, and they find Sharyn's books and paperwork for her other "business."

Maybe it has to do with her ex-boyfriend after all. There was a reason why she deleted all his messages. She knew I snooped before, knew I would do it again, and she erased her reply. She loves him too and can't wait to see him.

She wouldn't lie to me like that. It's my own insecurities running away with my anxiety and fear I'm going to lose the best thing that ever happened to me.

I sip my beer, praying the alcohol will smooth out my rough edges. I need to calm down or my blood pressure will give me a heart attack.

"I told him," Eddie says, holding his own beer.

"Was that a good idea?" Dalt asks, sipping from a glass of the rum and Coke he favors. He swishes his drink, the ice clinking against the sides.

My backyard has never had this many people in it before. Everyone is here—Eunice, Tony, Olivia, Clarissa, Ginger, Vonnie, a few of the other waitresses from the Guitar Pick and Shotgun Sally's, Melody looking like she could go into labor at any moment, Abby and Mason, and Gina and Jeff. No one's been swimming yet, but we're only an hour into it. The atmosphere is easy, lubed with sunshine and booze, but there's an underlying tension that no doubt has to do with Dalt's presence and Shep's reluctance to mingle with our manager. He's sitting on the grass with Mason and Jeff. Olivia keeps throwing him concerned glances. She wishes he would talk to Dalt, forgive him, and be done with it. Life would be a lot easier if he would, especially since, if we're being honest, Dalt did the world a favor.

"He's not going to say anything. Will you?" Eddie asks me.

"Will I what?" Agatha's standing in a group with Olivia, Clarissa, Ginger, and Vonnie, who turns out to be a spunky waitress with dreadlocks. Agatha can feel my eyes on her, and she looks at me from across the pool and wiggles her fingers.

I should have bought her a ring. So when she goes home she'll remember me.

"See?" Eddie says. "He doesn't even know what we're talking about."

"How's Shep doing?" Dalt asks and sips.

"Better. Olivia gave him a scare. She got in over her head with her coaching business and the organization, but Agatha stepped in."

Dalt turns and studies her over the pool. "She's a cute little thing. Didn't sound like that over the phone. I expected an old lady. You like her?" he asks me.

"What?" I ask, their conversation buzzing around my head.

"He does," Eddie says, amused. "They were banging her first day here."

"Third," I mumble.

Dalt laughs. "He's paying attention after all." He pauses. "I never wanted to hurt Shep. I'm truly glad he's getting the help he needs to get past this."

"He was talking about doing another album." I lift my bottle and finish off the dregs.

"This one, you mean?" Eddie asks.

"No. After. Lullabies or something." I try to focus, but all I can see is Agatha. I want to sit with her on my lap and talk to her for a bit.

Dalt scoffs but he's smiling. "You know what? That doesn't sound half bad. I don't have to ask what gave him that idea."

"First I've heard of it, but I'd be on board," Eddie says.

"Yeah?" I'm surprised he'd give Ghost Town more time.

"Why not? Not your thing, though." He studies me with narrowed eyes.

I'd be the only holdup, but Eddie knows I wouldn't care about something like that. Not with the way things are now. I'd have a lot more interest if Agatha looked like Melody, and I push back a spike of jealousy. "I'm going to get another drink. Do either of you want anything?"

They decline. We've been standing here for the past half an hour; they'll want to check in with their women soon.

I'm halfway across the yard when two voices scream, "Dad!"

My mind snags like a record player's needle scratching across the vinyl, and I search frantically for Abby in confusion. Does she need Eddie? No, Eunice is teaching her and a couple of Clarissa's and Ginger's friends how to play poker.

"Dad!" the voices call again, and this time my mind catches up with my heart. Lexi and Layla run across the yard dressed in swimsuits and holding towels. Lexi reaches me first and flings herself at me. I catch her, dropping my beer bottle onto the grass.

"What are you doing here?" I can barely force the words out around my shock.

Lexi steps away, and Layla hugs me. At fifteen and sixteen, they're almost as tall as I am.

"Mom said you were having a pool party and we were

invited. It's so cool. You never have people over. I see Abby. I'm gonna go talk to her." Lexi dashes off.

"I'm coming too. Wait for me," Layla says. "Thanks for the invite. Missed you." She kisses me on the cheek and runs after her sister.

"I hope you don't mind," Brianna says, floating across the brick dressed in a black swimsuit and coverup. "The girls were excited and packed overnight bags, if that's okay."

"Yeah, sure. I don't understand." My throat is so dry, I can't swallow.

Brianna blushes. "Someone who cares about you very much paid me a visit yesterday and told me a few choice things. I listened. She invited me to stay for the party, if it doesn't bother you."

"No, but why would she do that?" I search for Agatha. She's where she was before, standing with Olivia. They're both watching me, and now I know where they rushed off to yesterday morning.

"She loves you, and she defended you. I needed to hear it. The girls need you, *want* you, in their lives, and I forgot that. Can we talk later? I have some apologizing to do, but I would rather do it in private."

Agatha breaks away from Olivia and the others and approaches us. I don't waste a second, pulling her to me and covering her mouth with mine, a firm hand to the back of her head. No one besides the band and my mother ever went up to bat for me, and I will never be able to pay Agatha back for what she did when she talked to Brianna.

She breaks the kiss and nuzzles my cheek with her nose. "I'm going to show Brianna where the wine is, okay?"

"Yeah," I choke.

Agatha links her arm with my ex-wife's, and they walk toward the house, talking. I pick up the beer bottle I dropped into the grass, drinking in the sight of my daughters sitting at the edge of the pool with Abby like old times, giggling about boys and catching up. I have no idea when they last saw each other.

"Marry her," Eddie says at my elbow.

He has no idea how much I want to.

Chapter Twenty-Two

Agatha

"I'm so ashamed of myself," Brianna whispers as we step inside Brock's living room. After what she said to me, I looked at his house in a different light. He didn't try to make this house a home—blank walls, no pictures. I find my camera that's still in my straw bag and turn it on to see if it needs a charge. It's at sixty percent—I should be able to take quite a few photos to capture this afternoon.

"Someone just needed to remind you that despite him having a few roadblocks, he's still their father with feelings. Even animals miss their young when they're separated from their babies. It's ingrained. You need to encourage Lexi and Layla to see their dad whenever they can. It won't be long before they're off to college."

She stops me before we enter the kitchen. There is so much food, and we're drowning in macaroni and potato salad. "You'll treat them well, won't you?"

I frown. "I don't know what you mean."

"Lexi and Layla. Alastair's a good man, but he's indifferent.

He's never tried to get to know them. He treats them like pets and nothing more. You'll be their stepmother when you marry Brock and I want to know if you'll treat them well. Shelly was worried about that when Eddie told her he and Clarissa are getting married. Women can be so cruel."

I can't resist the jab. "Yes, they can."

She flinches. "I deserve that."

"I told you yesterday that this is complicated. He's hiding something from me. Do you know what it is? Red or white? Rosé?"

"Whatever you're having is fine. No, I wouldn't know. It could be as simple as hesitancy. I wasn't nice while we were divorcing, and he may be having trouble opening his heart to another woman. I wanted to hurt him; I resented him having such a full life without me in it. If you want to pay me back, do, but please don't use my girls to do it."

I pour two glasses of white. The light wine will complement the sandwiches if she chooses to stay long enough to eat. "I would never do that. I see how much Clarissa loves Abby, and you can pass along to Shelly Clarissa treats her like she would her own daughter. Even if Brock and I somehow manage to make this work, Lexi and Layla are busy young women and realistically, won't have time to see Brock much. That he has them back at all is something he needed, no matter how little, and I appreciate what you did. If I didn't want them in his life, I never would have gone to see you."

"Thank you for that. You have every reason to hate me, but you don't."

"There's no point in it. I have Layla's memory stick upstairs. I'll run grab it." I retrieve it off Brock's nightstand and trot down the stairs. "It's amazing, just like I knew it would be. Do you have an email or a business card? I can put you in touch with a few fiction agents who rep YA fantasy and you can reach out."

We trade contact information, and with wine, my camera, a sleeve of saltine crackers and a glass of ginger ale that I set in front of Liv, we sit with her and Gina. Brianna questions Liv about the organization, taking a sincere interest, and Gina's eyes sparkle with the possibility of a new wallet to open. I take what photos I can from my position before getting up to walk around the pool.

While I was talking to Brianna inside, Brock and Eddie set up a net over the water, and they're playing volleyball. It's Brock, Layla, and Lexi against Eddie, Clarissa, and Abby, and Brock's having so much fun. I love snapping pictures of him splashing his daughters and them spraying him back in retaliation.

In a burst of pure, masculine exuberance, Eddie jumps and hits the beach ball too hard and in the wrong direction. It flies out of the pool to the dismay and mock cries of the others.

Laughing, I catch it on camera, the colored ball flying against the blue sky and white clouds. I have no idea what I'll do with it, but I'm pleased I was quick enough to capture it.

"Shit. Sorry!" Eddie calls.

"Not a big deal. I'll get it," Brock says, already swimming to the edge.

I take pictures of him levering himself out of the pool, the water sluicing over his tight body. These can go into my private photo album. Age has done nothing to soften him up, and desire coils in my belly. He snatches the ball that rolled onto the brick, his fingers digging into the plastic in the exact same way his fingertips sink into my skin to hold me in place, and I move a little closer and kneel, hoping for a different shot. He doesn't see me, too intent on razzing Eddie. He bumps into me, and I lose my grip. With a plop, my camera drops into the pool and sinks. I don't feel like getting my hair wet, and shielding my eyes with a hand, I look up to ask Brock to swim to the bottom of the pool for me.

He freezes, and such a tortured look transforms what was his previously happy expression. "I am so sorry," he says, his voice shaking. He wipes at his face, hoping to hide the panic in his eyes. "What can I do? Buy you a new one or—"

Everyone stops talking to stare and gauge my reaction to the loss of my camera. Lexi and Layla freeze, and I wonder just how often Brianna dressed Brock down in front of them.

I stand and rest my palms against his cheeks. His gaze is anywhere but my face, his lips trembling. "Brock."

"I can't, I'm sorry," he says, and no matter how much I'll try to get along with Brianna, I will never forgive her for what she did to this poor man.

"Brock, look at me."

Finally, he does.

"I love you. Do you hear me?"

He nods.

"I love you and an accident like this won't make me stop. You didn't ruin my camera. It's waterproof. But even if you had, it's okay. It's only a camera. Right?"

He relaxes and blows out a breath. "Right. I'm sorry."

"It's okay. You can do something for me though."

"Anything."

I could demand whatever I wanted and he would try his best to do it to make up for something that was simply an accident, and my heart breaks. How he feels, the panic and shame, how much I wished for this kind of understanding from my mother, for her to say, it's okay, I still love you. "Grab it for me?" My camera is a black and red wavering blob at the bottom of his pool.

He presses a cold, wet, kiss to my mouth. "I love you."

"I love you too."

It's nothing for him to jump in and retrieve it from the bottom. He hands it to me, pausing near the side. He grips my ankle, and I tense, thinking he's going to pull me in, but he kisses my ankle bone. Shaking water out of his hair, and with another glance to ensure I'm not angry, he resumes their game.

I sit down next to Brianna, and Liv offers me a towel.

"You're so good with him," Brianna says, watching me dry off my camera.

"Because I treat him like a person?" I ask, still disgusted with the way I think she treated him during their marriage.

She tips her head. "Touché. Is it really waterproof?"

I quirk my mouth. "Yes. I wouldn't bring a camera that isn't to a pool. But even if it wasn't, it wouldn't have been a big deal. I connected it to his internet, and every picture I take is saved to the cloud. You're rich, right? You understand he could have bought me a new one like he offered?"

She sucks in a breath, and I think I've gone too far, but she laughs. "You are exactly what he needs. Exactly. I like you, Agatha Sterling, I like you very much."

"Thanks. I think."

I take more pictures of Brock and his daughters, Eddie and Abby, and Sheppard and his mom and brother. I want everyone to remember this day for years to come, and even if I'm not here and part of Ghost Town's family, I'll create photo albums and try not to hate myself for the things I've done that kept me from being a part of it.

The energy of the pool party drifts gently into evening, people settling into small groups to talk.

Brock holds me in one of the patio loungers, covering my face with kisses. "Where did I find you?" he asks in awe.

"At the airport, and you thought I was an old lady," I say, laughing, snuggling into his chest.

"I've never been so glad to be so wrong. Thank you, for what you did. I've tried for years to get her to listen to me, to talk to me. I don't know how you did it."

Brianna's still speaking with Gina, though she's giving off vibes she'll be leaving soon. I sit up and wait until I know he's listening to me. "She was jealous, and it's as simple as that. She was jealous of your talent, not just playing a guitar, but playing the piano and writing for the paper. You can bake and cook and sing, and probably draw and paint too, and after a while, if she was ever proud of you, it turned to jealousy. I don't know her. I don't know what she does when she's not standing around being pretty and rich, but I know, from experience, how difficult it is to feel like there is nothing special about you—"

"Angel—" he starts.

"No, I get it, and denying it doesn't make it any less true. There is nothing special about me, and there is nothing special about her, and when she was married to you, she let it eat her up inside. Keeping Lexi and Layla away from you was her way of punishing you for your talent. When I talked to her yesterday, she admitted your daughters are following in your footsteps, and she's going to encourage them to spend as much time with you as they can so you can nurture that."

"She hated me for how I am."

"She hated you for the way you have to express yourself." I lightly touch his temple.

"You understand me, angel."

"Yeah, I do, and she didn't. But listen to what I said. There's a chance Lexi and Layla are taking after you, that way, too. Help them, so they don't grow up like you did."

He swallows and nods. Searching my face he says, "You don't mind."

"No, I don't mind."

"Does your camera still work?"

He's so worried about it, and it breaks my heart. I smack his cheek with a loud kiss. "It's just fine."

He attacks me, covering my mouth with his and tickling my ribs.

I shriek.

Brianna clears her throat, amused. "I hate to intrude, but I need to be going. It's still okay for the girls to spend the night, isn't it? I heard Abby is going to stay as well."

No one told me Abby's staying here, but with the friendship Brock and Eddie have, Eddie probably assumed it would be fine, and it is. Brock opens his mouth to ask, and while I appreciate him checking with me, I say brightly, "Of course it is. We'll drop them home whenever you say you want them back."

Brianna reaches out to shake my hand, and I stand from the lounger. "I appreciate that," she says. "For what it's worth, I don't have any reservations leaving them here. It was nice to see you again."

I could be offended she implied there was potential for her not to trust us, but she doesn't know me, and if I were a mother, I might feel the same. "It was nice to see you, too. Thanks for staying. I hope you had a good time."

"I did. It was pleasant to see everyone again. Brock, can you walk me to the door?"

"Yeah, sure. I'll see you in a minute, angel."

"Take your time. I'm going to clean up a little."

"Thanks."

I lose all motivation to start gathering abandoned bottles and glasses and drop onto a patio loveseat with Liv. Tilting my head at Shep, who's talking with Eddie, Dalton, and Jeffrey, I say, "It looks like things are getting better there."

She nods, just as tired as I am. "Yes, and I'm so relieved." She stifles a yawn with a hand over her mouth. "My mother said they aren't going to make it after all. Something came up at their church and she and Martin can't get away. I'm so tired, I'm almost glad I don't have to plan a last minute wedding on top of everything else."

"I'm sorry, hun. Do you think you and Sheppard will make it legal soon, anyway? Just for peace of mind?"

"I'd like to, but I can't think any further than going home, brushing my teeth, and changing into my pajamas. What's up for tomorrow?"

"Nothing. Why don't you lie in bed all day and rest? Brock has his girls, and while he hangs out with them, I'll give Clarissa some time with my slush. My vacation is almost over."

"When will you tell him about Graham?"

"At the last possible moment. I want to remember how happy I was."

"I'm sorry you met him," Liv says, her voice hard and defensive.

I say, "I am too," just as Brock steps onto the patio, and I have a feeling we're talking about two entirely different people.

Chapter Twenty-Three

Brock

It's been two years since I saw Brianna in person, and she looks the same. Honey-blonde hair, slim, not a wrinkle on her face. She walks with quiet confidence, money padding her footsteps. We met at a cocktail party. She was there as a friend of a friend, and I was there because Eddie forced me to go. He was courting Shelly, and he'd heard she would be there.

I knew the second I saw her I wanted to marry her, the buzzing in my head intensifying like a swarm of angry wasps whenever she looked my way. I thought it was love. Red is for desire, but it's a sign of danger too, and the noise that filled my heart wasn't passion, it was a warning, a warning I heeded too late.

It was fast, like Eddie and Clarissa, or Shep and Olivia for that matter, but it started to crumble the first year we were married. I've picked apart every minute of our marriage, every painful second, and I reach the same conclusion I always reach. I'd do it all over again, no matter how much it hurt, because of the two girls inside who call me Dad.

She leans against her blood-red BMW. "I like her. You two are a good fit. She's patient."

I stand uncomfortably in front of her, never knowing how to act or what to say, always expecting something I'm doing to set her off. "Is there anything I could have done?"

She stares at her toes, her nails painted the same color as her car. "When we married, I thought you were exciting, all that energy directed at me. Your need to be moving, going places, doing things. Cooking, writing music, having sex. You devoured me, consumed me, and I loved it. I was a part of you, of Ghost Town, and it was a high I thought I wanted. You never needed to rest, but I did. You never slept, never sat still for one second, and I didn't know how to communicate that wasn't working for me. I didn't know how to explain I needed more. It sounds stupid. You were giving me all you had. It was too much and yet, not enough. No, there was nothing you could have done. It was all me."

I step closer and skim my thumb along the strong, yet delicate, line of her jaw. "I loved you so much. I didn't know what I did wrong. I never changed, Bri. I was always who I was. When we dated, after we married."

For just a moment, she leans into my touch, then she turns her face away. "Agatha accused me of being jealous, and I never wanted to admit I was. It wasn't that you baked banana bread in the middle of the night, it's that it was delicious. It wasn't that you played piano at 3 AM. It's that you could play anything, everything, even the songs with notes you grabbed from nowhere. It wasn't that you wrote, it was that you wrote for the *LA Times,* the editor falling all over himself to give you a half a page for your opinion. You couldn't be mediocre, could you? You excelled at everything, and I couldn't be proud of you. I hated you, and I still do." She smiles, trying to soften her words, but she fails.

"And you think Agatha's going to be different? I can't change who I am. I'm lucky I was talented, that my mom and dad supported me, that Eddie was there for me, or the system would have swallowed me, and I'd be on the streets. You've always known I'm not normal."

"No, you're not. You're extraordinary. I was your wife, and I should have supported you. Instead, I belittled you. I've never been anything but a pretty face, and all that talent crammed into one person isn't fair. I think she *will* be different. She's successful in her own right, and I never was, never tried to be, either. I could have done anything, anything at all, and I chose to hang on your arm and hate you for holding me up."

"You're still doing it. With Alastair."

"Yeah. I am, but it's easier, somehow, to tolerate him. Maybe because when I wake up at 3 AM he's in bed snoring, and I can pretend I'm half of a normal couple. When I would wake up and you'd be playing piano, I would sit in the hallway, listen, and cry. It was so beautiful, and I knew I could never compete." She reaches for my hand. "There was nothing you could have done. I would have always felt inferior. I'm sorry for the way I treated you. I've done a lot of growing up in the past few years, and I can say that to you now and mean it."

That's one of the many differences between Agatha and Bri. When Agatha hears me up at 3 AM, she doesn't sit at the top of the stairs and cry. She finds me and asks what I need. Listens, if I want to talk, lets me play, if that's what I want. When I need to cry, she's there. She isn't a fiery red, she's the calming color green, my safe place. Where I can go and know I'm loved.

"Thank you, for the girls." I loved Bri, and we would still be together if she hadn't hated me, and I will always, always, thank her for giving me two little girls.

"They were excited to come."

"No, I mean, thank you. For having my children. You might think I have everything, can have anything, but when I held them for the first time, my greatest achievement was being their dad."

She smiles, a little sad, guilty, maybe, for the things she's done in the past few years. "They missed you, and I shouldn't have kept them from you. They knew I wouldn't be happy if they contacted you behind my back, and that was wrong. Layla's a good driver, and I trust her not to be on her phone in the car. After today, I'll tell them they can see you whenever they like." She pauses. "They're smart, and it's scary."

"They're taking after me." As much as it thrills me, I push back a ball of dread. I had such a difficult childhood, and now they're going through it, too.

"They are. Agatha said, well, she said a lot of things, but I don't want what she said to come true. I don't want to feel about them the way I felt about you while we were married. Jealous, resentful. I want them to grab whatever life throws at them. Will you help? Show them life doesn't have to be over-whelming? Lexi's obsessed with the music, and Layla never sleeps, she's always writing, and I see so, so much of you in both of them."

"I'll try, but the noise—"

"Talk to Agatha. I think she's got something figured out. You may not like what she has to say, but listen. She loves you and would never hurt you. Not like I have. Are you going to marry her?"

"I don't know. I've only known her a week."

"And me less than that."

"Yeah, I know."

She scoffs. "You don't trust it, and maybe if it were any other woman, I would tell you to be careful. But after what she and I talked about yesterday and what I saw today, I think she's exactly what you need. She will never, ever, let you down. I'm glad you found her, Brock. You deserve to be happy."

"Thanks." I lean to hug her and she meets me halfway.

"Alastair's in New York filming, and I was invited out. I might go since the girls are spending the night. They don't need my permission to stay. They have plans tomorrow night, but there are a couple weeks of summer left. If they want to stay here for the rest of it, they're welcome to."

She turns to open her car's door, but I say, "When we were married, did Derrick do anything to you?"

A slight shiver runs down her back and settles at the base of her spine. "Why would you ask me something like that?" she asks, not meeting my gaze.

"Because he hurt Shelly, and Eddie wanted me to ask if he hurt you too."

"No. He never did."

She speaks to the ground, and I know she's lying. If she doesn't want to tell me, I won't try to force her. Derrick's gone, and she can keep her secrets, but I say, "You should have told me."

"What would you have done?" She's not bitter, only curious, her hair dancing in the breeze, her skin glowing in the sunset.

"I would have given up everything to protect you."

"And that's exactly what I didn't want you to do. He propositioned me right before we divorced, but that's not why I left. You know that."

I nod. I do know that. Our problems far outweighed Derrick wanting to fuck my wife.

"I wanted you to have Ghost Town after I left. You would have broken up one of the most successful bands in the world over a sneer, a lewd comment, and a couple of bruises he left behind when he grabbed my arm, and I couldn't let you do that.

You didn't need to be different for our marriage to work—I did. Agatha will never ask you to change. We all need to be loved for who we are, and she will. Have a nice evening. Thank you again for inviting me."

This time, when she turns to open her car's door, I let her, and she drives away. Beautiful and rich with nothing to show for it.

Eddie's feeding Clarissa chips when I go back inside, holding her close and kissing her between bites of sour cream and onion. Lexi, Layla, and Abby are in the living room shrieking over celebrity gossip, and I find Agatha talking to Olivia near the pool. Without hesitation, I sit beside her and wrap my arms around her. I never need to ask if it's okay, or if I'm bothering her. She doesn't stiffen the way Bri would have, the millisecond of hesitancy before she would relax and return the affection. Agatha leans into me the moment I sit, linking her fingers with mine.

It's good to see Shep talking with Dalt, Tony, and Jeff, Ginger and Vonnie playing with Mason and Scout in the grass nearby.

I let the conversation fizz around me, and my body loosens, the tension of speaking with Bri draining away.

After everyone leaves, Agatha helps me store leftover sandwiches in the fridge. She hoists herself onto the island with a glass of wine, and I step between her legs and brush my lips over hers. "This was the perfect day. Thank you."

She scratches my beard. "You hosted. I should be thanking you. Now what do you want to do?"

"I have an idea," I mumble against the side of her neck, gently cupping her breast through her bikini she's still wearing.

"Why don't we watch a movie first? Do you have something the girls would want to see?"

"Disney sent me the live adaptation of *The Little Mermaid*. What do you think?"

She tilts her head, encouraging me to nip at her skin. "I think that's perfect."

The girls are excited to have an advanced viewing of one of the most popular movies of the year, and we settle in with bowls of ice cream. Lexi, Layla, and Abby sit on one of the couches, and Agatha and I sit on the loveseat in front of them. She angles herself, lying half in my lap, and I feed her ice cream, licking the sugar from her lips.

We make love that night, slowly, carefully. I try to show her how much I love her and how devastated I'll be when it's ripped from me. All my life I've struggled to find a place where I didn't have to try so hard to fit in. I thought I found that place with Ghost Town, and I thought I found it when I slipped a wedding ring onto Bri's finger.

But it's tonight, when I can't sleep and I crawl out of bed that I know I've found my true place in this life.

At 3 AM, Lexi's at the piano tinkering with a song she's writing, and Layla's sitting on the sofa with her laptop, the keys clicking away in her haste to get the words down as quickly as possible.

Agatha followed me downstairs and she sits with Layla, a throw wrapped around her shoulders.

This is my family, this is my place, with my children, the woman I love, blank walls, and a piano.

I didn't fall asleep after we went back to bed. Agatha did, dozing on my chest, but my mind wouldn't shut off, pictures of the party flickering behind my eyelids in a blurry montage.

Having my girls sleeping down the hallway is a dream

come true, and nothing I thought would be possible, ever again. Bri would never return my calls when I tried to beg for even five minutes with my daughters, and after all these years, I never knew if she poisoned them against me. I'm grateful she didn't, but I'm still angry, still hurt she robbed me of so much time with them because she was jealous. Something else she said bothers me. That Agatha has something figured out. Unease coils in my stomach. If there's something anyone shouldn't try to do with me, it's figure me out.

"What are you thinking about?" she murmurs, rubbing her cheek over my chest.

"How did you know?"

"I can feel it. You're angry. What's wrong?"

"What did you and Bri talk about when you went to see her?"

"Mostly that you missed your daughters, and it wasn't right for her to keep them from you. Why? You thanked me for it yesterday. Are you having second thoughts? I'm sorry if I over-stepped." She sits up and rubs the sleep from her eyes. She's so beautiful, her hair tousled, her lips swollen from the love we made. If I felt between her legs, she would be full of my cum, and knowing it makes my dick hard. I want her again.

"Mostly," I say. "What else?"

She lifts her chin in that false bravado, and I wonder if that's what her mother taught her. To pretend to be brave when what she really needs is someone to show her they love her. My arms remain at my sides, my hands clenching the sheet.

"That I think you might have ADHD, that you could, maybe, be on the spectrum."

Anger rips through me along with panic and fear. I don't want something like that to be wrong with me. "Are you trying to fix me?" I demand. I wasn't good enough for her after all. She doesn't love me the way I am. "You liar."

She gasps when I grab a handful of her hair and jerk her to me. I want to punish her, need to. The last several days were nothing but lies, my future built on nothing but false hope and contingencies.

I push her down onto the mattress, her face shoved into the comforter. With a hand to her stomach, I position her ass just where I need it. She sucks in a breath, and I don't ask for permission or consent, don't ask if she wants me, too. I'll never forget her moan and my shame as I slide into her, gentleness and love mere shadows of what I feel thrusting into her. I grip her hips, holding her in place, my fingertips bruising her delicate skin. I know I'm hurting her, but I can't stop. I'm hurting too, and misery gathers in a ball in my belly along with an orgasm. Her cries spurn me on, my balls slapping against her ass.

I come, my cock shooting off deeply inside her, one of the most forceful orgasms in my life. I fall from my high, but it's not easy, like a tree leaf floating to the ground. It's all at once, a body shoved from an open window, and I hit just as hard. She lowers to the bed, trembling, and I cover her body with mine, the prison I held her in while I fucked her turning into a caress that won't make up for how I treated her.

"I'm sorry, angel. I'm so sorry," I whisper into her ear.

She curls into a ball, trying not to cry.

"You should stay with Eddie and Clarissa for the rest of your vacation."

In a blaze of fury, she rolls over and props herself onto her elbows. Startled, I rear backward. She braces a foot against my chest, keeping me away. "You think this is about sex? You fucking coward. I'm not trying to fix you. I'm trying to help you."

"What?" A freight train slams through my head, the whistle

shrieking, drowning out everything. I'm standing on the tracks, and I can't move.

The fight drains out of her, and she lowers her foot. In a cloud of chocolate body lotion, the scent of our musk, and understanding and compassion I should have known Agatha would never have discarded, she kneels and loops her arms around my neck. "Do you think I've never had rough sex before?" she murmurs against my lips. She moves my hand between her legs. "Make me come."

I push my tongue into her mouth and find her clit. She wasn't scared of me. What I did turned her on, and her clit is large and swollen, waiting for my touch. My fingers circle the nub, and she rocks her hips, tilting her head and pressing her body against mine.

I want her to come while I'm inside her, and I sit, leaning against the headboard. She eagerly lowers onto my cock, never once, even for a second, breaking our kiss. "Hmm," she hums, rocking, accepting every inch I can give her. "I'm almost there," she whispers, and I rub harder, faster, her pussy gripping my cock as the beginnings of an orgasm spark inside her.

She grinds down when she comes, our teeth gnashing together. She's gripping my head, holding me in place. Panting, she rides it out, and our cum trickles out of her, saturating my skin.

"Is that what you wanted?" I ask, pulling up the comforter and covering us.

"Yeah," she says, resting her head on my shoulder. She doesn't move to get off me, and I'm glad. I want us connected. Need us connected during the conversation we're about to have.

"Agatha, I'm sorry. When you said that, all I could think was that these past few days have been a lie, and you were trying to find a way to change me. I know I'm odd, and I know

I'm difficult to live with, though you seem to accept that. I thought Bri accepted it too when I asked her to marry me and she said yes. I don't want you to regret this like she did."

"When I asked her about it, she was genuinely surprised. If I wouldn't have had an intern with similar qualities—"

I don't miss she turned my eccentricities into something positive.

"—I might have overlooked it too, and just chalked it up to your personality like so many others have. It wouldn't hurt for a psychiatrist to evaluate you. That's all the further it has to go. But, if he thinks there's something there and you want to try medication, you can do that. I'm not trying to fix you—you're not broken. I just want you to have better quality of life, that's all. You can't tell me you've been happy."

"I'm happy with you."

She nuzzles my neck with her lips. "I'm happy with you, too. Just the way you are. I'm sorry if you don't believe that."

I sigh and bump my head against the headboard. "I want to, so much, angel."

"The only thing that will convince you is time, but I don't know how much of that we have." She lifts her head and looks into my eyes. "You have a secret you're not sharing with me. I have one, too. Neither are good, and if we were smart and brave we would have it out. Right here, right now."

As much as I want to, I can't. I *am* a coward. "No."

"Okay," she says, and I don't know if she's relieved she doesn't have to tell me hers or if she's disappointed we aren't getting it over with. "Will you ever tell me?"

"I won't have a choice, angel. It's going to come out when Ginger and the others talk to the police. Eddie's been persuading her. He wants Sharyn locked up for helping Derrick, and Ginger will give in. Yesterday, he told me she was close."

She frowns. "You weren't hurting anyone."

"Not the way Derrick was."

Shaking her head, she says, "I don't believe you were hurting anyone, in any way. I won't believe it without proof."

I brush the hair out of her face. "I hope you always have my back, angel. Gimme yours."

"I didn't tell you everything about Graham."

My heart beats dully against my ribs. "He *does* want to marry you."

"I told him I met someone, that I was in love, and he needed to leave me alone. He only proposed because of that. Otherwise, he never would have."

"I thought you told me he can't, or am I misremembering?"

"No, you're right. But he's willing to . . . rearrange some things to make it possible." She swipes tears off her face.

"Is that what you want? Do you want to go home and marry him?" The picture of her walking down the aisle and meeting a faceless man who will promise to take care of her shouldn't hurt, but it does. I knew when we met that my relationships with Polly and Anne would interfere with anything real I found with her, but I couldn't stop myself from falling in love.

"No. I love you. You're the only man I want to marry."

I help her rub the tears off her cheeks and say the first stupid thing that pops into my head. "You're so beautiful, and I love you so much. Will you introduce me to your mom?"

She laughs around a sniffle and says, "Sure. What the hell. I want to see her face when I tell her I'm abandoning her to marry a rockstar." She pauses. "Will you talk to Sheppard? Ask him for his therapist's contact information?"

Jumping from talking about her marrying her ex-boyfriend to a diagnosis I don't want to confront doesn't lessen the tension behind my eyes or the ache thumping at my skull. I don't know if labeling how I feel will do any good, but I'm not against medication. If taking a little pill helps Shep not feel like he wants to walk into the ocean and not come out again, maybe it can help me, too. "Okay. Will you go with me?"

"I wouldn't let you go alone. I'll always be here for you."

I adjust, and she sucks in a breath. I haven't gone down, and bracing her hands on my shoulders, she wiggles too.

"When's your flight?" I caress her breasts, rubbing my thumbs over her nipples.

"Saturday. Mom expects me at work on Monday."

"We'll get it figured out before then." One way or another.

"Okay," she whispers, kissing my cheek and down my neck.

"Agatha."

"Yeah?"

"I'm sorry for earlier. I didn't ask, and I was rough. Did I hurt you?"

"You didn't have to ask because I can open my mouth and say no. Your intent was quite clear. You were rough, but it didn't hurt me. What you said hurt me. No matter what happens, these past few days haven't been a lie. Maybe after all is said and done you won't believe it, but it's true. Make love to me, then I need to shower and head over to Liv's. I'll order a car and bring Abby with me. Clarissa and Eddie will be there. Spend the day with your daughters and talk."

I don't want to admit I'm scared to be alone with them, but it's what we need. "Thank you."

She leans backward, and I follow, covering her body with mine as we settle into the mattress. "You are always," she says, tilting her hips, encouraging me to sink deeper, "very welcome."

Chapter Twenty-Four

"This isn't bad," I say, skimming the proposal Clarissa found in my slush.

I'm sitting on the floor playing with Mason, helping him put together a large wooden puzzle, Scout sleeping next to him, watching over us. Liv took my advice to heart, and she's in bed, dozing. I'll bring lunch up to her in a little while. Eddie and Sheppard are in the den, working on some music. Tony and Eunice are visiting friends before they head back to Crescent City, and Abby's sitting in a recliner near us, her attention split between listening to us and her phone.

At first Clarissa was confused when she started going through my slush and was finding proposals for books that weren't yet written. I explained that sometimes nonfiction writers will write up a project proposal first hoping to find an agent to collaborate with to shape the book into something that would be sure to sell. "But what would you change to make it marketable?" I ask, testing her.

Clarissa skims the proposal about a self-help book for parents whose children are bullied. "It reads like it's all about white kids."

I nod, pleased. "Yes. If this author wants to sell her book, she needs to include all children. Being that she's white, she may want to partner with a Black author who can lend her experience and point of view. I know someone I can put her in touch with. They could have a very strong collaboration."

She widens her eyes. "You can do that?"

"Sure. That's the whole reason she sent the proposal in the first place. Also, this proposal leans toward in-person bullying. What else should she include?"

"Social media," Clarissa says right away. "But I also feel like she's talking about school bullies, and family can bully you, too."

"Exactly. You're good at this. We'll reply and start a conversation. Maybe she doesn't want to collaborate with anyone, or she has a friend she wants to co-write with."

"What if she doesn't want to take our, I mean, your, suggestions?"

Mason opens his mouth for a kiss, and I lean over and let him slobber all over me. "If she doesn't want to take *our* suggestions, we'll pass. We don't want to work with someone who's not flexible, and we don't have to take on a book that doesn't have a good chance of selling widely. She can send her proposal to other agents. She doesn't have to work with us. Me." I correct myself and swear. It would be nice if Clarissa and I were partners. We work well together.

She types the email with a little help and sends it.

I grimace. "That's enough work for me today. How are you feeling after the Guitar Pick incident?"

Abby lifts her gaze from her phone with interest.

"Oh," Clarissa says, flicking her fingers in the air. "Fine. I didn't know Judd was so attached to that place. He was kind of an asshole when I worked for him, but what he's been through explains a lot of that. I didn't know any of it. He never talked to me unless it was to bitch me out about something. Ginger said she doesn't mind working with him, and the other girls are okay with it. He's crabby and lonely, but he wasn't going to hurt anyone. He's working with Ginger tonight, in fact, and he was asking about you. Said he'd like to see you again before you go." She frowns. "But you're not leaving, are you? Only to pack up and move here?"

I rest my chin on one of my knees. "I don't know. What's Ginger going to talk to the cops about?"

"Before he married me, Derrick abused a lot of women. Sharyn paid them off to be quiet. You know that's his sister?" she asks.

I nod.

"Eddie hates she's not in jail for that, and if Ginger and some of the other girls give their statements, maybe there will be enough for a warrant to search Sharyn's house. He's hoping she kept proof."

Brock said his secret would come out when Ginger and the others stepped forward, but I don't understand how he's connected. "I know all that, but how would Brock be involved?"

She shrugs. "I have no idea. Why would you think so? The only thing he could be doing is using Sharyn to find women to sleep with."

"Would you think poorly of him if he was?" I ask out of curiosity, the blurry picture of his friend with benefits suddenly becoming clearer.

"He's Brock Farris. He could have anybody. He wouldn't

need Sharyn's help, and even if he did use her, he would never hurt anyone. Derrick was an asshole who needed violence to get hard." She glances at Abby. "Sorry, sweetie, this isn't a conversation we should be having in front of you."

Abby sits up, her phone forgotten. "Is that what he did to you?"

"He tried. Your daddy protected me the very best way he could. Derrick's gone; we don't have to worry about it anymore."

Derrick might be gone, but I don't think Sharyn dropped her little side hustle. If Brock's using her, no, he wouldn't beat on the women she set him up with. There's not a cruel bone in his body, and I believe that even after I made him angry this morning. He was doing other things with them, and tears fill my eyes. Could I be with a man who would do that?

"Why are you crying?" Clarissa asks.

To hide it, I give her a hug. "I'm glad you're okay, that's all."

She hugs me back. "I wasn't in a good place for a long time, but now I have Eddie, Abby, Mason, you and Brock, and Olivia and Sheppard. It's a good life. It's a good, good life, and I'm looking forward to every second."

Gina cups her hands around her eyes and peers into the living room through the glass door. She spots me and slides it open. "Come," she says, and it doesn't nearly as enjoyable as when Brock says it.

"Fuck," I mumble, standing up. I owe her the second half of my interview and unconsciously dressed for it in blush pink summer pants and a white and pink matching sleeveless blouse. I hope it's professional enough. At least this time my makeup's in place and Gina won't have to do damage control. "I don't know how long this is going to take. Will you be all right?"

"Yeah, sure, but if we're not here when you're done, we'll see you later. I might head back to the house so Mason can nap in his crib. There's nothing for Abby to do here, and she's still unpacking her things from her mom's house. I don't want Olivia to feel like she has to entertain us."

"I'm sorry. I owe Gina some time."

"It's okay. Good luck."

"Thanks."

Gina's waiting by the door, her arms crossed over her chest. There's no way I can escape.

"You didn't think I'd let you out of this, did you?" she asks, stepping to the side and allowing me to go out onto the patio first. Nope. No chance of escape.

"No. I'm sorry for walking out on you the first time. That wasn't polite, no matter how upset I was."

"Don't worry about it. You're not the first to leave in the middle of an interview, and it actually creates a lot of tension. I won't complain, but it would be nice if we could finish today," she says with subtle censure.

"Right. Yeah."

"Good."

I follow her into the house, coffee heating in a carafe in the spotless kitchen, and I jiggle my feet, shaking the sand out of my sandals.

"Are you another of Ghost Town's victims?" she asks, amused, leading me up the stairs to her office.

"You seem to know a lot about my life. Why don't you tell me?"

Gina's eyes sparkle with the challenge. "Let's talk about that in front of the camera."

"Yes, let's," I say, and she laughs.

I sit on the loveseat, and she takes her place on the ottoman, adjusting the camera's focus.

"We can pick up right where we left off. The viewers won't

know there were several days between interviews. No need to reintroduce you, okay?"

"That's fine. Whatever you need to do." I smooth my hair and wipe my palms on my pants.

She turns the camera on and wastes no time drilling me with the difficult questions. "You walked out when I asked if you were proud of yourself and how far you've come in your career. Why did you do that?"

"Because I'm not proud of myself. There's no reason to be."

"Can you explain why you feel that way? Is it because of your mother and how you came to be an agent?"

One day my mother might watch this documentary, but that shouldn't keep me from telling the truth. *My* truth, she would say. It wouldn't be hers.

"Of course it is. I was never given the choice to be what I wanted to be. What if I had wanted to go into medicine, or try my hand at acting. Someone who would know told me I have a good voice, but I never got a chance to do anything with that. My path was set out for me the moment I was born. While I was growing up, choices were a luxury, and sometimes they still are. I'm not proud of myself or my accomplishments. They don't belong to me."

"That's not true. Being a literary agent may not be what you chose for yourself, but you shouldn't shun your achievements. The authors you represent wouldn't. Some of them are bestsellers because of you, because of the faith you had in their work. Because of your talent. Let's discuss that, okay?"

I stiffen. I know what she's going to bring up. I don't want to talk about it, but it's the entire reason she wanted to interview me. If I hadn't wanted to talk about it, I should have said no when she approached me.

"Tell me what happened two years ago."

Her expression is full of sympathy, and I swallow back

tears and shame. I will never leave this behind. Never. I feign a nonchalant shrug. "I was looking through my queries. One of my secret passions is for memoir. It's not exactly nonfiction, but there isn't an agent at our agency who specifically reps it, and my mother *allows* me to rep them if the earning potential is there—because we don't rep midlist. At least, that's the unspoken rule at our, *her,* agency. A woman sent me a query for her memoir, and it was nothing short of magnificent. She grew up in a neglectful home, abused, and she still went on to have an amazing career as a world-renown sculptor. I requested her manuscript the second I finished reading her email."

"That sounds normal, isn't it? That kind of deal?"

"Not exactly. People live through some quite unbelievable circumstances, but they also need to have a strong grasp on how to write about it. I read her manuscript in two days. I signed her immediately and sold it within the week. She received a very handsome advance. Everyone was thrilled." Even my mother, who tried to hide it, couldn't believe the sum I sold a simple memoir for. I've relived that pause a million times.

"What happened?"

"It was all made up. We didn't find out until the book was into its second print run. The first printing sold out in days. The wait lists were miles long. She turned into a celebrity, and I was lauded in literary circles for signing her, for discovering her story. A reporter started digging around her life, talking to her family, her friends. He discovered that most of it was a lie."

"Most?" Gina asks, enthralled.

I quirk my lips. "She became a sculptor. That was the only true fact in her book. She came from a lower class family, yes, but her parents loved her. She had a younger sister who looked up to her. The reporter found out she stole her experiences from a next door neighbor, a little girl she grew up with who was abused by her parents. *She* came forward and told her story. Her father raped her every night. The author I signed left that part out. For authenticity's sake."

"How did you handle it when the truth came to light?"

"How did I handle the humiliation? The only way I could. I still went to work, still did my job. When a reporter would ask to interview me, I always told my side of it as honestly and as sincerely as possible. I would say believing in someone shouldn't have consequences, but sometimes it does, and that was one of those times."

"What did your mother say?"

"Nothing."

Gina leans back in surprise. "Nothing?"

"She didn't talk to me for months. The silent treatment has always been her way of punishing me. She would send me emails, leave voicemails when she knew I wasn't at the office to pick up my phone, but for six months, it was like working with a stranger. When we had meetings, she would look right through me."

"Did you have any support during that time?"

I can't let anyone know Graham and I were seeing each other. That for months after that happened, he would stop by my apartment when he was done filming the nightly news and hold me while I cried. He would bring me trinkets and jewelry and chocolate hoping to cheer me up, and he even treated me to a weekend away at a little lake cabin. He did everything he could, and I think without him, I would have walked out of my mother's agency and never spoke to her again.

Maybe I should have.

"I have friends who understand how something like that's possible. Social media twists things for clicks and views, but people in the industry, they know how something like that could happen. Even my mother knows, but it was that it happened to me. I smeared her agency's reputation with my mistake, and that made what I had done unforgivable."

"Did she ever forgive you, Agatha?"

"Did she forgive me?" I echo. "Did she? Six months after it happened, she started talking to me like everything was normal, but I was so shaken from that six months of silence, all I did was sit under my desk and cry. All I've done since then is try to make up for it, knowing, deep in my heart, I never will." Tears run down my face.

Graham called her every name he could think of, pissed she would treat me like that. Liv was shattered, still trying to cope with Michael's suicide. I would go to her house, take Scout for a walk, a zombie. I'd clean her house, kiss her cheek, tell her to call, but she never did. We were both barely living. I climbed out faster, with Graham's help, and it took a lot of strength to tell him I needed more. I needed more than half a man.

"When will you start living for yourself?" Gina asks, nodding to my right. There's a box of Kleenex on the side table next to the loveseat. She wouldn't pass me one—her hand in the frame would look silly. I pull a tissue from the square, white box.

"What's the point?" I'll go home after I tell Brock the truth, go to work on Monday and keep doing what I've always been doing. Listen to Graham plead and tell him to stay away from me. I'll miss Brock, what we could have had if I hadn't been so fucking weak.

"You don't think there's a point to living life on your own terms? Is that what you would tell a woman who's struggling? To give up, stop fighting? Is that what you did, Agatha? When did you stop fighting?"

"When did I ever start?"

"If that's true, then maybe it's time you did."

Instead of walking to Liv's after my interview, I trudge through the sand in the opposite direction. Brock and I aren't going to work out. I know that, deep in my bones where my darkest fears live. I expected it the first time he kissed me, prepared for it, and I'll leave with my eyes dry and my heart broken.

What I do when I go home is my choice. Brock said he wanted that for me. To find my spotlight and sing. I never cared about it because the fight seemed too intense, too hard, but so is living and working under my mother's thumb. I have enough in savings I could live without working for a couple of years. Go back to school for something I really do want to do, except, maybe that would have had some appeal before I visited Liv, but now all I can think about is opening an agency with Clarissa. That won't happen, just like marrying Brock won't happen. He can claim he'll forgive me all he wants, but even if I want to believe it, that doesn't make it true. If it worked that way, my mother would love me. Touch me just to touch me. She never has in all her life.

I need to find a life that I want to live. A man who's free to love me. Maybe I won't stay in Minnesota. I've taken a liking to the ocean. I could live in Florida, change my name and work for an agency down there. I hate my mother. I hate that agenting is the only thing I know how to do. I hate that changing my name would sink my career. I only have it because I share my last name with her.

I find the rocks that hold a special place in Liv's heart. Like the island in Brock's kitchen. I wouldn't want him to sell that house. I would live there, sit with him by the pool drinking whiskey. I sink into the sand, the sun bright, tourists roaming the beach. Time drifts, but I don't feel anything.

Liv explained once, what Sheppard felt when he stood in the water. She said he heard a siren calling him, felt her hand around his ankle. Even in my darkest days after the scandal that shamed my mother, I wasn't suicidal. It didn't occur to me that's what Liv was after Michael's death, but of course that's what she was, even without the label. She turned to skin and bones right before my eyes. I didn't tell her, but I was so scared.

When Dalton contacted me and asked me to ask Liv if she would consider hiring Sheppard as a client, I was relieved. She'd needed to get out of Minnesota and leave that god-awful house. She doesn't know, but I popped a bottle of champagne when it sold. Sending her out here could have backfired, and it almost did. I don't know how she would have made it through had Sheppard let her go back.

I'm not saying I'm stronger than she is, only that suicide was never on my mind. What would it be like? I kick my sandals off and walk toward the water, the sand smooth under my feet. I don't hear anything. Maybe a siren doesn't sing to me, or maybe my mother's voice drowns her out. I'm not good enough, I'll never be good enough. I work so hard, for nothing.

I don't care that I have pants on, and I wade into the water. The tug is there, around my ankles, what Sheppard felt, and Liv, too, when he stopped her in that photo. The grip doesn't hurt; it's comfortable in its own way.

The water laps at my thighs, my fingertips skimming the surface, and peace fills my heart. A little more, and a little more, because no one would miss me if I'm gone. Graham would stand in the back at the funeral, dressed in black, holding a single rose, tears in his eyes. He would tell himself he loved me and would mourn me for the rest of his life. My mother would preen at the reception, accepting condolences she doesn't deserve. "All that talent," her friends would say sadly, and then she would say, "I made her what she was."

And that would be true. I have no idea who I am without her.

Liv would be sad, but she has her own life to live, a man who loves her, and a baby.

Who else do I have?

That was Gina's point. I don't have anybody else, and it's up to me to fix it.

"Angel."

I don't know why he started calling me that. At first I thought it was because Agatha is such an ugly mouthful, but he says my name all the time. No, I don't know why, but I don't want to ruin the magic by asking. I don't want to ruin my heart skittering and my cheeks heating when he calls me an endearment no one else has.

I look over my shoulder. His faded jeans cling to his thighs, his t-shirt just as faded from too many washings. The setting sun brings out the red in his hair, and tension pulls at his eyes. I could have had a life with this man if I wouldn't have been so stupid. Liv would tell me I shouldn't have needed to see into the future to make better choices for myself. She'd be right. My better choices should have started a long time ago, but it's difficult, you know, when you're alone. You hold on tight to what you do have, even if that isn't much.

"Come out of the water, angel."

I think about that for a moment, but Brock wouldn't let me drown. I do what he asks, my pants soaked, and step into his arms.

Scout's panting by his side, and she presses a sand-covered paw to my leg. I rub the soft fur between her eyes.

Brock shudders and holds me, tangling his fingers in my hair. "Please don't do that."

"I wasn't going to."

He tilts my head with a finger under my chin, asking me to

look at him. "Once you start thinking about it, it's hard to stop. Don't start. For me."

"Okay."

We stand together, his steady embrace holding me in place, for a long time. Without a word, he holds my hand and we walk back to Liv and Sheppard's.

Chapter Twenty-Five

Brock

We shower together, but I can't rinse the nasty things I said out of my mouth. She doesn't hold anything against me, sinking onto her knees and giving me a blowjob. I've already come twice this morning, but that doesn't stop me from spurting, or the way my heart breaks when she looks up at me with her wide blue eyes, licking her lips after I'm done.

I'm still reeling while we dress. The girls are already downstairs puttering around the kitchen and a kind soul made coffee. I bet it was Abby—she knows how addicted Eddie is to caffeine, and she probably thinks I'm the same.

No one, not one person, ever mentioned they thought I could have ADHD. Not one person.

When I was a kid, I could understand that. Talking about mental health in the eighties and nineties was unheard of, and I was called a lot of names—by a lot of people who shouldn't have been calling me them. Disrespectful. Stupid. Unfocused. Retarded. We didn't have the compassion we do now, the understanding. I spent more time in detention than I did in class. My elementary school teachers might have thought I was stupid, but I earned passing grades after middle school, especially in music, choir, and art where so much of my grade didn't depend on assignments I had to do at home. High school was better, and Eddie watched out for me. We did our homework together, and he turned mine in with his. I didn't graduate with a 4.0 or even a 3.0 for that matter, but Mom and Dad were proud when I walked across the stage and accepted my diploma.

No one said anything in college, none of my professors, though it was evident I struggled, and Bri, well, we had a lot wrong with our marriage, but I can't blame her. She simply labeled me difficult and creatively eccentric and didn't look past it. I didn't expect anything less. That's what everyone did.

Everyone but Agatha.

Only a week in, and she turned my whole world upside down.

I don't know what to do with it. She was brave to confront me, but she scared me shitless.

For breakfast, I make crêpes and serve them with fresh strawberries and whipped cream. Agatha smears a dollop over my lips and kisses it off.

Lexi and Layla giggle. They're old enough to have boyfriends, and I have no idea if they do or not. They turned into young women during the time Bri kept them from me, grew into miniatures of their mother. They'll have access to the whole fucking world with her looks and my . . . ah. No one called me smart before. A musical genius, yes. Smart? No.

Abby scoffs. "Gross. You're just like my dad and Clarissa. Didn't you do stuff upstairs already?"

I point the spatula at her. "Yes, we did, not that it's any of your business. You better watch out. You're gonna have more than only Mason for a sibling, and you'll be on babysitting duty until you move out."

Abby puckers her lips and makes kissing noises at me, taking exactly after her old man. "I guess that goes for you guys, too," she says to Lexi and Layla. They burst out laughing, Layla covering her mouth. She was in the middle of chewing a bite of crêpe.

Agatha stills beside me.

"Easy, angel. No one's knocking you up anytime soon." I murmur and kiss the tip of her nose.

She smiles faintly.

"I'm going upstairs for my bag. When did you say we were leaving?" Abby asks her.

Sighing in relief the topic of babies is gone, she says, "Twenty minutes. Clarissa texted me. They're already there."

"Cool. I'll go up and get my stuff."

"I'm sorry about earlier," I say at the door, rubbing her bottom lip with my thumb. The car Agatha ordered is idling in the driveway, and Abby's saying goodbye to my girls. I'm grateful they enjoyed spending time together, and now that Bri has softened and Shelly and Eddie found a truce, maybe nights like that will happen more often.

"Don't worry about it. Talking about mental health can be scary, but no one is going to ask you to do anything you don't want to do. Okay?"

"Yeah." I press my lips to hers and she hums under my mouth.

"Have fun with your daughters, and I'll hang out at Liv's until you're done."

"I love you." I want to say more; my heart's full of thoughts and feelings and colors and sounds, but I can't form words.

"I love you, too. Enjoy yourself. You've wanted this for a long time."

Abby shuffles into the foyer, her backpack slung over her shoulder.

"Bye," Agatha says, brushing a kiss over my cheek.

They climb into the car, and I stand in the doorway until the vehicle disappears from my sight. I suck in a nervous breath. My daughters are strangers, but because of Agatha, I have a chance to get to know them all over again.

I didn't have to worry. Spending the day together is easy, the years I missed surprisingly melting away in laughter and deep conversation. They're into everything, and my heart swells with pride they've come this far and sadness I've missed so much. Layla's doing some modeling on the side. She said talking to Melody was awesome, an unexpected perk since she'd heard Melody and Shep divorced. Lexi can play every instrument ever made, surpassing me. She's up there with Shep who can play anything anyone puts in his hands. Layla talks about a book she wrote that Agatha supposedly read. I'll talk to her about that later, but I'm not surprised Agatha thought a book deal would be obtainable. Lexi's already been offered a place at Juilliard, but Layla doesn't know if she wants to go to college. College isn't for everyone—I only followed Eddie—and she doesn't worry me. She has plenty of time to decide.

Later that afternoon, we watch a movie, Lexi asking if we could watch a film I produced, and I queue up the film I watched with Agatha. I don't have many recent films—Bri didn't like the time it took away from her, and I lost my heart for it after the divorce.

The ending credits roll, and I shift on the couch with a sad sigh. Layla's phone chimes, and I know it's Bri asking when they're going to be home. She gave me as much time as I wanted, but until we do this more often and it feels natural, Bri will worry. I can't expect her to change in one day, and I'm grateful for this much.

"Mom reminded me we have dinner plans, and we have to go. But we can come back next week sometime. Would that be okay?" Layla asks, showing Lexi her phone.

"Sure. I'd like that. I missed you guys."

"Will Agatha still be here? You love her, don't you?"

"Yeah, I do, but she's got stuff going on in Minnesota. We'll see."

Lexi smiles, tossing her sister's phone into her lap. "Mom says Agatha has a backbone, and it's what you need. I think it will work out. Plus, we could go there. I've never been to Minnesota before."

"Thanks, sweetie. Go upstairs and get your things. I'll drive you guys home."

Backbone, huh? She certainly needs a soft heart. I could have royally fucked things up this morning if she didn't forgive so easily.

Bri's waiting, and I try not to let the resentment bubble up. I give the girls a hug and a kiss to their cheeks before they dart into the house, chattering about whatever it is they have going on tonight. She doesn't try to speak to me, lifting a hand before shutting the door, and I'm relieved I don't have to drudge up idle chitchat. I have nothing to say to her, and the girls are old enough I don't need her as a go-between if they want to see me. Their sleepover broke the ice, and it won't be so difficult to communicate with them anymore.

I have my guitar in the trunk of my car, and lyrics zip through my head on the way to Shep's. I haven't put in as much time as I should getting my songs together, but Shep's been preoccupied with his family and Olivia's pregnancy. That's given me a little room to breathe, but I don't want this album hanging over our heads forever. We've already lived in limbo while Shep mourned Derrick, and if Ghost Town is going to part ways, I want it done. Meeting Agatha and having the girls back in my life didn't change that. I need to know what's what. It's the only way I can function.

There aren't any cars sitting in Shep's driveway, and I park and go in without knocking. The kitchen's empty, and so is the living room but I don't want to jump to conclusions. Abby and Agatha left the house hours ago, and many plans could have been made between then and now. I'm skittish after the fiasco at the Guitar Pick.

Maybe no one's here. I push the faux wall aside and peer into the den.

Eddie's pacing back and forth, and his eyes are blazing with excitement. "Ginger and two others are at the police station right now giving their statements. Pierce is with them. She's letting the cops access her medical records from when she was in the hospital recovering from the whipping Derrick gave her. I don't know what he did to the other two women, but Jesus, this *has to* be enough for a search warrant. It has to be."

I nod. It will be.

Shep's leaning against the couch, a thumb pressed to his lips in contemplation. "Why didn't I see it?"

I set my guitar down and sit at the piano, my fingers playing "Piano in the Dark" without realizing it. "No one did. We knew money changed him, but we didn't know how far it went. If Sharyn goes to jail for helping him, it's time to let it go. Can you do that?" I ask over the notes.

"I don't know. I want to, Christ, I want to, but we were friends for so long. I feel like this is my fault."

Eddie frowns. "Why? If anyone's to blame, it's Sharyn. Not only did she cover up what he was doing, she chose his targets. She chose Clarissa for him to marry, and she chose the other girls who didn't have families to help them when things went bad. Ginger didn't have anyone but a couple of friends who were just as scared as she was. She has a lot of guts for finally telling her side of things."

Sharyn knows I would never hurt Polly and Anne, even when she gave me permission to do it. She divided her prostitution business into the dark side and the light side and did what she had to do to protect both. That won't save me.

"Why would she do that?" Shep's frustrated but he's not going to get the answers he wants. Not from Eddie and not from me.

"Because she loved her brother and didn't want him to go to prison. Dalt fixed it so he won't . . . but I pray to God she does. I don't care if it's only for a year. I want her to feel how Clarissa felt trapped in that fucking house."

Shep stares.

"Look, you feel guilty. I get it. I feel guilty I didn't do more for Clarissa. I did all I fucking could, and it will never be enough. I lie in bed at night, and . . ." He swallows. "You will never know everything. Tony was right about that, but you'll have to move on without the truth. I'm sorry."

"You know things."

"Yeah. I do."

Shep turns to me. "What about you? What did he do to you? Or is that another secret?"

Eddie raises his eyebrows, wanting to know, too.

I shake my head, stop playing, and scrape my fingers through my beard in agitation. "Agatha thinks I have ADHD."

Laughing so hard he can barely speak, Eddie says, "That would explain a lot."

"You think so?"

"Hell, yeah. Good on her for tagging you. I never thought of it."

"You don't think it's weird?"

Eddie sobers. "Oh, shit. You're right." He hooks an arm

around my neck and rubs his knuckles over the top of my head. He hasn't done this to me since we were kids. "Shep, we gotta take him out back and shoot him."

I jerk away, my scalp burning. I run my fingers through my hair setting it back to rights. "Fuck you. She told me to ask you about seeing Royce," I say to Shep.

"It's a good idea. We should all be in therapy anyway. I'll text you his number and you can give him a call. It's not weird. Not any weirder than my depression. You gave Agatha a hard time when she asked you about it, didn't you?" he asks, pulling out his phone.

A second later, my phone chimes.

"Yeah, I did. I accused her of trying to fix me."

Shep picks up the guitar at his feet and begins strumming one of the songs he wrote about Olivia. "I had a difficult time dealing with that when I realized I was starting to fall in love with Liv. I didn't want to be damaged. I didn't want her to be with me like that. A man not strong enough to take care of her, and sometimes I still feel like that. When she's upstairs sleeping because I kept her up all night talking about the things that keep me awake. I've come a long way, but I'll always feel less than what she needs. You accusing Agatha of that is your own insecurity, and it was mine. You had it right outside the Guitar Pick. You thought I didn't hear you, but I did. They're smart and they're strong. It's why we love them. If Agatha says she loves you, she loves you how you already are, and she only wants to help, just like Liv checking in with me. She's always asking how I'm doing, what I need, and that doesn't make me weak. I'm strong because she's on my side. Don't be ashamed— be grateful she took the time. Liv gives me everything she can, every day. Sometimes I feel like I bleed her dry, but somehow she always has more."

His speech shoves a ball of fire down my throat, a common

feeling since Agatha came into my life. "Thanks. I'll give him a call. Does Olivia go with you?"

"Yeah." He sighs. "Christ, I wish I could put this shit with Derrick away. It's what we talk about half the time in therapy. Why I didn't know what Derrick was doing, why Melody left me. Why I can't wrap my mind around Ghost Town breaking up. She never gives up, though. She never gives up."

"The Melody part is easy. She fell in love with Dalt. Can't do anything about that," Eddie says, sliding over the back of the couch to sit on a cushion. He props his foot on the coffee table. Someone cleaned up the beer he spilled when we watched the news.

Shep twists his lips. "You would know."

Eddie scowls. "I think every person in this room knows how it feels to be in love with someone you shouldn't be in love with. You try stopping it."

"No, thanks. It hurt like a son of a bitch, but I would do it over again a million times."

"And the band doesn't have to break up. We're not broken. I don't see us that way."

Eddie might not see us that way, but I do. I want us to do one last concert, one last song. One last encore, so when Agatha's gone and married to that Graham guy and Lexi and Layla are off to college or whatever they plan to do, I can leave this fucking place and not look back.

"We haven't been the same since Derrick died," Shep says.

Eddie shakes his head. "We haven't been the same since long before that. He was a drunk, and he destroyed the band's camaraderie. You felt it, so did I. Maybe no one wanted to acknowledge it, but it still happened. What Dalt did with Melody didn't help. What I did with Clarissa didn't help, either. But those things aren't anything we can't bounce back from if we want it."

"I don't," I say with just enough volume everyone can hear. "I need to move on. For my own mental health."

"And that's where it gets sticky because sometimes I feel like that too," Shep says, his hands resting on his guitar. "I need to step away and breathe."

"Then own that, but don't blame Derrick, or Dalt, or me. If we stop recording, it's because we chose it and nothing else."

Eddie's angry, and I'm not sure why. If I had all he has, anger would be the last emotion I'd feel. "Why are you mad?"

"Because what I found with Clarissa isn't going to replace what I'm losing with the band. They are two separate things, and if Ghost Town stops recording, then I get to mourn that in my own way."

"We'll always be friends."

Eddie bounces to his feet. "You can look me dead in the eyes and fucking tell me that while you're over there counting down the minutes until you can see LA in your rear view mirror? You fucking hypocrite."

"I can't stay here."

"Well, you just fucking go."

"Eddie—"

The faux wall slides open farther. I didn't close it all the way when I came in, and now Olivia's slipping through the crack. Shit.

"What's going on?"

"Band stuff. How are you feeling?" Shep asks, setting his guitar down and crossing the room to cuddle her in his arms.

"Fine. I feel like I slept all day. Why are you fighting?"

"Apparently Brock has somewhere else he'd rather be," Eddie says bitterly.

"You knew—" I start. I told him what my plans were and he didn't say anything.

"Yeah, and I thought—" He stops.

I know exactly what he thought. He thought Agatha and I were going to get married, pop out babies while I wrote film reviews and produced indie movies, and she opened a literary agency with his wife. That's what he thought. "It won't happen."

"Because of what Derrick had on you."

"Because of what Derrick had on me."

"Jesus fucking Christ."

Olivia watches us, Shep's arms wrapped around her, eyes wide.

Eddie's phone rings, and he slides it out of his pocket. He glances at the screen, preparing to dismiss the call and keep his fight with me going, but he answers it instead. "Yeah?" He listens for a few moments. "Thanks for letting me know." He disconnects. "That was Pierce. They had enough for a warrant and a judge signed off on it five seconds ago. He wasn't sure if the cops would believe Ginger. She lied to them when it happened, and they dug up the report the officer filed when he spoke with her. But her friends' stories are too much like Ginger's and they decided to try. They caught a judge out for drinks and he signed it to get them out of his face. We'll know in the morning if they find anything."

That's it then. I've got twelve, maybe eighteen hours with Agatha before it all comes out. Christ, am I going to miss her.

"Where's Clarissa?" Olivia asks. "Does she want to know?"

"She took Mason and Abby home hours ago. I told her I'd shoot her a text if we decided on dinner."

I tense. Agatha said she was going to hang out with Clarissa all day. "Then where's Agatha?"

Eddie grits his teeth and reluctantly answers me, still angry. "Clarissa said she went to Gina's to finish up their interview." He glances at his watch. "But that was about the time Clarissa went home. She should have been done by now."

Olivia sighs. "Whenever I spoke with Gina, I always needed—"

"Me. You always needed me," Shep says over her. He meets my gaze. "Go find her."

I'm standing from the piano bench before he finishes speaking. Agatha doesn't know the area well, and the only place she could go without a vehicle is the beach. "Come on, Scout," I say to the dog, and she scrambles to her feet.

We rush through the patio doors and hit the sand running. I follow Scout's lead, and the Golden Retriever knows exactly where she is. A quarter of a mile down the beach, Agatha's standing in the water, her fingertips skimming the surface, a blank look in her eyes.

"Angel." I can barely force my mouth to form the word. I want so badly to be what she needs. To protect her from her mother, give her what that asshole refused to give her. She deserves so much more than a fuckup like me.

She looks at me over her shoulder, and I've never felt so much pain hit me square in the chest. I've gone through a lot with Bri and the band, but this is something else, and nothing short of anguish rips at my heart. I love her so much.

"Come out of the water, angel."

She pauses, contemplating, licking her lips, but she finally trudges out of the water and I don't let her have a second before she's in my arms.

Scout whines, knowing Agatha's hurting, and paws at her soaking wet pants.

My chest heaves with emotions I can't release. Maybe I can't be everything she needs, not with the mistakes I've made, but I can be strong for her, right now. "Please don't do that."

"I wasn't going to."

Maybe she wasn't, maybe she just wanted to know how it feels to have the choice, the siren's hold on her ankle as real as my grip, but I still say, "Once you start thinking about it, it's hard to stop. Don't start. For me."

She presses her face against my chest, her breath warming my skin through the cotton. "Okay."

I can't let her go, too scared, my mind full of the picture of her in the water, and we stand like that for a long time, Scout keeping a watchful eye on us both.

She begins to tremble, and I know this woman in my arms. "You're hungry, and you need to eat something. Let's go find you some food and a glass of wine."

"I need you."

"I'm right here, angel. Come on."

We walk back to Shep and Olivia's, and he knows what she was doing the second we step inside the kitchen. "Agatha," he says, hugging her, a strong hand to the back of her head.

"Thank you," Olivia murmurs, watching her fiancé hug her best friend. "Talking to Gina is always so hard. I would walk away from those interviews in shock, drudging up that nasty stuff. Bring her home. She doesn't need us gawking at her all night."

"I don't know what to do."

She squeezes my arm, her eyes full of compassion, sympathy, and fatigue. "When she tells you about Graham, tell her you love her anyway."

"I can already tell her that," I say, confused. What could Agatha possibly have done?

Olivia wipes tears off her cheeks. "Don't be too sure."

I hold her hand on the way to the house, our fingers tangled together on my thigh, and the second we step inside, I send her upstairs to shower and change. I fix plates of leftover sandwiches and potato salad, not caring I already ate the same thing with the girls, and we sit outside near the pool. Dressed in shorts and a tank top, she eats slowly, her hands shaking, and I brush the back of her head, unsure how to show her I'm here, I love her, and she can ask me for anything.

She wipes her mouth and sips from a glass of white wine. Color is seeping into her cheeks, but she's missing the sparkle she's always displayed since the moment I met her.

"Ginger and her friends went to the police department while you were on the beach. They had enough for a warrant to search Sharyn's house." I want to tell her all of it, and I almost do, the confession on the tip of my tongue.

"I bet Eddie was happy," she says, twisting toward me, her glass clutched to her chest.

"Yeah. He was."

"Will you be in a lot of trouble?"

"Nothing like that."

"That's good." She sets her glass on the table near our plates and crawls into my lap. "Do you remember what I said?"

I frame her face in my hands, relieved she's looking better. "You've said a lot of things, angel."

"I told you that nothing could make me stop loving you. You remember?"

"Yeah, I do." And from the minute she told me, there's nothing I wanted to believe more.

"Okay," she says, rubbing her lips against mine. "Don't forget."

"You don't know what I've done," I mumble, her hands up my t-shirt, her nails scratching at my skin.

"It doesn't matter."

"Yeah, it will, angel. It will."

"Make love to me," she whispers.

I do, under the milky haze of light pollution, the water

lapping at the sides of the pool. I do, wishing she wasn't on birth control and that we'd had the talk, knew what we were doing, wanting children. I do, taking everything I can she's willing to give me.

I'll have no future after tonight, and I hang on to these last few hours.

I don't sleep all night, but I don't get up. I stay in bed and hold Agatha, her steady breathing fanning against my chest. I let her sleep, but at nine, Eddie sends me a text. *I need to talk to you. Now. I'm at Shep's.*

It didn't take the police long to go through Sharon's house, but I don't know how Eddie has access to what they found. Pierce must have passed along the information. I stupidly thought I would have more time, but the cops had all night to go through her paperwork, and if she's as meticulous as I think she is, every I dotted, every T crossed, it wouldn't have taken the detectives long at all to find what they needed to arrest her for prostitution, concealment, and for paying Ginger and God knows how many women hush money to keep Derrick's crimes hidden.

I don't want him to think I'll avoid this, and I reply, *We'll be there in an hour.*

Let him stew. He's pissed I did business with Sharyn, and his rage will build until it spews all over me.

I should ask Agatha to pack her suitcases and bring them with us, but I want every last second I can with her, even if that means watching her angrily throw her things into her bags to get out of here just as quickly as she can.

"Angel," I murmur, leaning over and pressing my lips to her bare shoulder. "Eddie has news and wants us at Shep's."

She blinks her big blue eyes and stifles a yawn. "Okay. Then what?"

"What do you mean?"

"Then what are we going to do with the rest of the day? When are Eunice and Tony leaving? I didn't see them yesterday at all."

"I don't know. Shep didn't say how long they were staying."

"Oh, well, maybe tonight we can do the movie thing, and you never told me how your visit went with Lexi and Layla."

I grit my teeth. The easy conversation would be normal if I wasn't like Chicken Little, waiting for the sky to fall down and crush me to death. "It was nice. I thought we would have some awkward moments, but we never did." I pause. "I'm sorry for the way I treated you yesterday. Shep explained a few things and told me instead of being resentful you interfered, I should be grateful you're on my side. I am, angel, I really am."

"Good." She nuzzles my cheek with her nose before pulling back and meeting my eyes. She always waits, always makes sure she has my full attention before she says something important, and she does this now, her hand to my shoulder. "I always will be. Let's shower."

I don't turn down another chance to show her how much I love her, and I try to bat away the resignation and bleakness that creeps in as we wash and she shaves her legs. I try to pretend like nothing is wrong while we dress, jeans and a t-shirt for me, denim shorts and a strapless top that shows off her tanned shoulders for her. Instead of drying her hair, she twists it into a low bun at the back of her head and adds hoop earrings. She's gorgeous, and the only way she could be any prettier is if she were growing my baby inside her.

"He's angry," I say, warning her in the car. This won't be unlike my fights with Bri, screamed at and demeaned for choices that weren't mine to make. Agatha's diagnosis will do little; Eddie will never understand what it's like to need someone the way I do.

"I'm sure he is," she says, squeezing my hand, and I could have sworn on a stack of Bibles she knew what this whole thing was about.

I put up the wall I haven't needed since the divorce. The wall I learned to build as a kid, when a teacher would turn her steely, disgusted eyes to me, calling me worthless before sending me to the principal's office for disrupting class. Again. I didn't need it in college, Eddie and the guys with me, and I didn't need it when I met Bri, courted her and asked her to marry me, but as we drifted apart and she grew nasty, resurrecting the wall to protect myself was second nature. When she would yell, I would hide behind it, only to come out when the storm passed—that time.

"I'm sorry." Parked in Shep's driveway near Eddie's truck, I say the only thing I can say.

She kisses the back of my hand. "It's not wrong to take comfort where we can find it, but sometimes it's the place we find it that has consequences. Come on."

I follow her into the house, my mind already retreating from the lashing Eddie's going to give me. I don't feel anything when we step inside, and I barely register where everyone's position is on the board: Olivia in the kitchen near the breakfast bar, Eddie pacing near the patio door, Shep sitting with his mom and brother at the kitchen table. Clarissa, Abby, and Mason in the living room. We're all here, and I stare at the floor.

Shep stands up as Eddie advances. Olivia freezes, a cup of coffee in her hands.

Agatha moves away, seemingly oblivious to the tension, drops her straw bag onto a stool and walks around the breakfast bar. She reaches for a mug to pour herself a cup of coffee. In my hurry to get this over with as quickly as possible, we didn't have any before we left.

"You son of a bitch," Eddie growls, and no one stops him, not even Shep who dislikes confrontation and avoids it at all costs. "Did you think we wouldn't find out?"

I catch Agatha out of the corner of my eye, and she's standing near Liv, the rim of a coffee cup resting on her lips.

"I knew it would come out, eventually," I say, the wall growing higher.

"I cannot fucking believe you were working with Sharyn. You've been using her for years to find girls to fuck. How many did you screw a week, huh? Was she covering shit up for you, too?" He clenches his hand into a fist. He wants to hit me, and that's when I completely shut down. My best friend, the guy I've depended on most of my life to have my back, wants to punch me.

Agatha slams her mug down onto the breakfast bar, sloshing the dark liquid all over the marble. "That's enough! Stop yelling at him." She runs from the kitchen and stands in front of me, reaching for my hands and wrapping my arms around her.

"This is none of your business," Eddie snaps.

"Yes, it is. You know Brock would never hurt anyone. He needed someone to talk to, someone who would listen in the middle of the night when he couldn't sleep. He's built relationships with them over the years, and these women are his friends. You make it sound like he's doing some nasty, fucked up thing, when what he was really doing was giving those women a safe place to earn money and spend the night."

Clarissa inches her way into the kitchen, listening.

"You act like he's dirty paying women for their time. Maybe he was having sex with them, but he needed the companionship more, and they needed his kindness, too. He helps them put food on the table and pay their bills. You think sex workers are despicable and filthy when they are women like Ginger and Vonnie and Clarissa. Daughters and sisters and mothers, trying to scrape by. Fuck you if you think Brock was doing anything but giving those women a safe haven when they could have been with men who weren't."

My mind is stumbling, and I can't keep up. It's several minutes before I realize that instead of agreeing with Eddie, Agatha's defending me.

"You think about Clarissa, before you met her, working at the bar, needing to find income to fill in the gaps. Now you think if you would want her with someone like Brock, who would pay her fairly, not cheat her at the end of the night, maybe buy her dinner. Who would rather talk than have sex, looking for a connection, and who would never, *ever,* put a hand on her, or someone like Derrick. She was already there, so I know which you would choose."

Clarissa moves closer to Eddie and places her hand in his.

He deflates, his shoulders drooping.

"Brock's arranging for the women he sees to go to school through Liv's organization—"

Eddie whips his gaze to Olivia who nods.

"—and he told me himself he pays for their medical care. Don't you dare try to tell me Brock is anything like Derrick. He's nowhere near it, and fuck you if you thought he could be. What kind of a friend are you?"

She turns in my arms, her face saturated with tears. Standing on the tips of her toes, she hugs me tightly and says, "It's okay."

Burying my face in the warm curve of her neck, I can't think past anything except she's not mad and doesn't hate me.

The wall crumbles, bit by bit, and the scared little boy peeks over the top. Shep's rubbing his face, Olivia's standing where she was before, watching the room. Tony and Eunice are looking on, but I think Eunice is a little tipsy—I have no idea what she's drinking at ten-thirty in the morning. Abby's holding Mason, carefully watching everything the adults are doing.

Clarissa lifts her chin. "Agatha's right. There were a few waitresses in tough spots who did that kind of thing on the side, and all of them would have been grateful to have a steady guy like Brock. I never had to, but I was one paycheck away from it —all the time. A blowjob in the parking lot, a quick fuck in the bathroom. Doing something like that when you're living that way can be the difference between food for the week and going hungry. I don't believe Brock would be cruel. You should apologize, Eddie. I tried to talk to you, but you were too pissed off to listen."

Agatha lets me go, but she doesn't leave my side. She keeps her arms secured around my waist, her head resting against my chest.

Chagrined, Eddie winces. "I'm sorry. I never thought of it like that, and I should have. You never would have hurt anyone, but I couldn't understand why you were working with Sharyn after everything we found out about her. Why didn't you stop using her then?"

"Because it was easier to let her keep handling it. The scheduling, the hotels. When Ginger told you what Sharyn did, I should have quit, but I'd already been seeing them for a few years, and the change in routine scared the fuck out of me. They gave me something I've been trying to find since Bri divorced me. I just needed something, anything, that would chase away the nightmares."

"The cops went through everything, and Pierce filled me in. You booked a date the day Agatha leaves."

Agatha looks at me, her cheeks sticky. "Oh, hun."

"I couldn't help it," I say around a ball of tears. "I thought this would end us, and I'm going to miss you so much when you go." My voice cracks.

"I'm not going anywhere unless you tell me to."

"I never will."

She smiles, but it doesn't reach her eyes.

Eddie steps toward us. "Is this what Derrick had on you?"

"Yeah, but he was the one who suggested I talk to Sharyn in the first place. When I started seeing Polly, he followed me and took pictures of us. He was always threatening to email them to *Buzz Kill* and tell them I was dating a whore—that's what he called her—but he never did. He liked fucking with me, and I never knew if he would go through with his threats. I don't know where the pictures are. Maybe the cops will find them with Sharyn's things."

Eddie drags in a deep breath through his nose. "I'm sorry I didn't listen to Clarissa. I'm sorry I thought you were capable of doing things like that. I don't want this to ruin our friendship. Please." He holds out his hand, and maybe if I didn't have Agatha, I would have let my resentment take over. She wouldn't want that, and even if I'm still stinging, I shake his hand. "Thank you," he says to Agatha, "for setting me straight. You don't take any shit, and I appreciate it."

"You protect the people you love, and I will always protect him, no matter what, no matter who it is."

Eddie narrows his eyes. "Understood."

"Good. Then we can still be friends." She squeezes me and steps away. "I need coffee. Do you want some?" she asks.

"Yeah, but I need air. I just need a minute." The pressure's building in my chest, and tamping back panic, I go out onto the beach, Scout with me. Eddie will be eager to fill us in on what's going to happen, but after this, I don't care if Sharyn is on her way to prison. A prostitution charge would have gotten her nothing but a warning and a fine she can well afford to pay. If they find evidence she paid off Ginger and the others, I don't know what will become of her. In a small way, I owe her for what she did for me, but Eddie would never accept that, and like Shep and Derrick's death, I'll have to let that part of it go.

I have Polly's and Anne's contact information, and I'll start using it. Not for more dates. I want to be the one to tell them they can go to school if they want. It's the least I can do for all they've done for me.

Agatha doesn't let me sit alone for long, and she settles in the sand and offers me a mug of coffee. "It's hot," she says, passing it to me, knowing I would gulp it down without the warning. Somehow, she always knows.

I can't believe she's with me, sipping coffee, watching the water, one hand on Scout's head when I thought after Eddie raked me over the coals she wouldn't want anything more to do with me. "You knew."

"A little."

"How?"

She lifts a shoulder. "Clarissa told me what Sharyn did and why Eddie wanted her to go to jail. When you mentioned Ginger and your secret, I kind of put two and two together. I don't think I would have if you hadn't told me about your friend with benefits when I first got here, but it made sense."

"You don't hate me for sleeping with you after having relationships with them?"

A corner of her mouth turns up. "No. You might have been paying them, but you're probably more monogamous than any guy swimming in the dating pool. I believed you when you said you don't have anything, and I still do."

"After that, what you have should be a piece of cake. Talk to me, angel."

She looks at me, tears clinging to her eyelashes. "Can you wait? I just want to enjoy the last two days I'm here."

"I'm not sending you home. I don't care what you have to say."

"I hope not. Kiss me."

I do, soft and sweet, until Eddie calls from the patio and I lift my head. It will be a while before things are right between us. I hope they will be. I hope the daydream of us living down the street from each other, our kids playing together, our wives working together, I hope that all comes true.

I let myself forget that in my life, nothing good lasts, and I didn't know I had two days before my heaven turned into hell.

Chapter Twenty-Six

Agatha

Over the next two days, I spend as much time with Liv as I can. It's difficult, when all I want is to lie in bed with Brock and memorize his features and let him tell me again and again how much he loves me and how my secret won't change the way he feels about me. He's a different person now that *his* secret is no longer an issue, and with his daughters back in his life, I've done what I wanted to do.

The day before my flight is jam packed. Tony and Eunice leave, and she hugs me, showing me more affection in a ten second goodbye hug than my mother has shown me my entire life. "Stay in touch, dear," she says, her raspy voice sad.

"I will."

She and Sheppard have an emotional goodbye, and his eyes are full of tears when they drive away. Brock shifts uncomfortably next to me, maybe picturing our own goodbye in the morning. I'll leave him before that. Since Eunice and Tony are gone, I plan to spend the night here and order a car to the airport in the morning. I would ask Liv, but I don't want the drive to tire her, and I'd rather mourn the loss of my relationship in private.

"What do you say to a beer and a jam session?" Shep says, wiping tears away with the pad of his thumb.

Standing in the driveway near Brock's car, I link my arm with Liv's and say, "That's a great idea. You men do a man thing, and us women will do a woman thing."

Clarissa perks up. I wanted to be alone with Liv today, but Clarissa's turned into a good friend, and I would feel terrible if I left her out. She leans toward Eddie, and he lifts Mason out of her arms without her having to ask.

"And what does a woman thing consist of?" Shep asks, amused and thankful to direct his attention to anywhere but his missing family.

"A prenatal appointment, lunch, and virgin cocktails," I say brightly, pleased I was able to convince Liv to schedule an appointment before I left. It will be up to Sheppard to see to it she goes regularly.

He blows out a sigh. "Good. I get so worried about you," he says, leaning over and brushing a kiss over Liv's mouth. I love how much he loves her, but once again, I think about how after I fly home, she'll move on without me.

"That could be us," Brock whispers into my ear.

It could have been. It could have been Graham and me too, only it hadn't. I won't have that with anyone. I'm thirty-six and too old to try to find someone to share my life with that way, and I would never, ever do what my mother did. Instead of trying to speak, I squeeze his hand.

"I can drive. She's seeing my OB/GYN. I like her, and I can schedule my own checkup while I'm there," Clarissa says, digging into her purse and pulling out a pair of sunglasses.

Eddie tugs on her hair. "No more babies."

She laughs, grabs Mason's chubby hand, and kisses it. "No, no more babies."

"Why?" I ask, confused. Clarissa's younger than I am.

Her gaze slides to Liv and then away. "I had a difficult delivery. Eddie said he doesn't want me going through that again." She tips her head, and he kisses her. "But I would, if he really wanted more kids."

"I want you. I'm happy with what I've got," he says, tousling Abby's hair, who scowls good-naturedly.

Clarissa sighs. "Me, too."

Abby waits, unsure if she's invited, but there's no reason not to bring her along. Catching her eye, I tilt my head toward Eddie's car. She grins, her braces flashing in the sunlight. I'll miss her too, and the project we could have created. God knows how many copies that would have sold.

"Hey," Brock says, stopping me before I climb into the backseat with Abby.

"Yeah?"

"You didn't cancel your flight, and the airline sent you a pre-check-in text. We're going to talk tonight, and when we're done, you're going to cancel it, call your mother and tell her you're getting married, and we'll fly up next week."

After Graham kind of proposed, I deleted everything he ever sent me, erased all my recent calls and voicemails, and blocked his number. With Brock's penchant for checking my phone, I'm glad I did. Lord knows what Graham's been trying to text me after he said that and I didn't respond.

Brock speaks strongly, without a hint of doubt, without any hesitation, and I want to believe it so much. "Yeah, sure."

"Agatha."

"No, we'll talk. I promise."

"Okay. I love you, and we're getting married."

"I love you too." I don't say the last part because we're not getting married.

He kisses me, nothing soft, either, possessive, and if we were alone, I would have been naked in five seconds. "Have a good time."

"Thanks. Be careful."

He rubs his thumb over my cheek, and I turn away, a little self-conscious. Our goodbye is already longer than Liv and Sheppard's and Clarissa and Eddie's combined. "Text me."

"I will."

Finally, he releases me, and I slide into the backseat next to Abby.

The guys watch Clarissa back out of the driveway and onto the highway. Three hunky rockstar men and a baby.

"What's wrong?" Abby asks, covering one of my shaking hands with hers.

"Sometimes you fuck up and it ruins your life."

She doesn't ask what, only scoots as close as she can with her seatbelt latched and snuggles into my side. Yeah, I'm gonna miss this little girl.

Liv's appointment goes smoothly, not that I know what a rocky appointment would be like. They start her chart since she's never been to a doctor in California before, and she fills out paperwork releasing her medical records from her primary care physician in Minnesota. Her Pap smear, pelvic exam, and blood draw don't take long, and she's sent on her way with another appointment scheduled in three months and a prescription for prenatal vitamins sent to a pharmacy near her house.

Next is lunch, and Clarissa drives us to a swanky little restaurant with outdoor seating. A hostess leads us to a spacious table protected by a huge white umbrella located on a patio surrounded by flowers. A couple of the tables are occupied, and conversation is a pleasant hum around us.

I skim the menu, and I squeeze Liv's hand when she does the same. I'm glad she's feeling good enough to eat.

Clarissa sets her menu aside. "Thank you, for what you said. It's so easy to forget how desperate people can be. I thought Eddie would have a little more compassion, but he was so wrapped up in making sure Sharyn gets what she deserves. Brock would never hurt anyone, and I don't think badly of him."

"At some point in our lives, we're all going to do things that need understanding and forgiveness. Brock thought once I found out it would end what we found, but honestly, I only love him more. He's got such a big heart, and it's been broken for too long. I think Brianna put him through a lot, and he'll need time to realize not every woman is going to treat him that way." I smile at a server who places water and a basket of bread at the table. It's clear we're not ready to order yet, and she hustles off to a different table. "When are you and Eddie getting married?"

"Oh, I don't know. After the tour, maybe. He promised me a big thing and a long honeymoon, and I would really, really like that."

I lean back and sigh. "That sounds lovely."

"What about you?"

I shake my head, unwilling to get into it. "We need to marry off Liv and Sheppard first. I hate that we didn't have time for that while I was here. I have no idea when my mother will let me come back."

Clarissa's mouth drops open. "What the hell do you mean, you're not coming back? Brock wants to marry you. I heard him two hours ago. He was practically on his knees."

I want to tell her to stop being a naïve fool, but I say, "Some things *don't work out*. Liv knows what I'm dealing with. Please, don't."

"You think I don't understand, but I do. I had to leave Eddie to get him to realize he was going to lose me for good if he didn't stop being a jerk. If you go home, Brock will go after you. I know it."

No, he won't, but I don't say it. Liv offers me a sympathetic smile knowing that even if, even *if*, Brock could forgive me for Graham, I still would have to confront my mother, and right now, if I do stand up to her, it's only to pack up my desk, tell her to have a nice life, and finally step away from her shadow and into my own spotlight. I don't know how I'll do that, but maybe losing Brock will push me over the edge. Or, I'll just go home and starve myself to death.

Graham wouldn't let me do that. He has a key to my apartment.

I'm so fucked.

We finally order, and I pick at my meal. For once in my life, I don't have an appetite.

Clarissa drives to Brock's and lets me off. We weren't gone long, and I'll have time to pack, check my flight information, and text Graham when he'll need to pick me up.

"This isn't the last time I'll see you?" Clarissa says alarmed, unlatching her seatbelt, prepared to leap out of the car and hug me goodbye.

"No, no. I'm going to spend the night at Liv's so I can get an early start to the airport in the morning. I'll be over later, after . . ." And I don't have the voice to continue.

Liv gets out and stands with me in front of the car. "We'll have a bonfire, and we'll stay up all night and talk. I don't want you to think you're alone, even if I'm half a country away. You're my best friend."

I will be alone, though. People drift apart, so do friends.

"Will you tell Brock I'm here?"

"Yeah."

I hug her, smacking a kiss to her cheek, and hurry into the house.

Everything is so spread out here, and it's common to need half an hour or more on the road no matter where you go. I pack, and I make his bed, plump his pillows I'll never rest my head on again. I wander his house, sadness creeping into my bones. He's lived alone for so long, and I wish with all my strength I could go back in time and when Graham asked me out, I said no. He didn't hide his wedding ring. I ignored the warning.

I skim my fingers over the books in his library, let my fingers bump over his keyboard where he'll write his movie reviews. I cry a little in the theatre room. We won't have any more movies here, no more bloody marathons.

I dig his empty flask out of my purse and set it on the island.

I searched for a place my whole life, and in fourteen days found it in a kitchen, sitting on an island, drinking wine with a man who looks like a lumberjack.

Liv texts and says Brock is on his way, and I schedule a car to pick me up in an hour. Not for a dramatic exit, but I don't want to stay here any longer than necessary.

I sit at the piano and tears drip onto the keys. He's so talented, and I'll miss all the creativity buzzing inside him. I already regret not being there when he talks to Sheppard's psychiatrist, and I'll miss reading his reviews and watching the movies he produces.

California might as well be a world away when I go home.

I feel him before he speaks. The hum of electricity, that for just a little bit, lit up my life.

"Angel."

"I'm ready to talk."

He sits on the piano bench with me and says, "Okay."

I start a story that should never have been written.

"I told you how Graham and I met. Michael had been gone for a couple of weeks by then, and I was still in shock. They were good friends of mine, and listening to her describe how she found him, the wake and then the funeral, it was like watching a movie but not being able to cover my eyes. I was there for her as much as I could be, but you have to understand my life to understand that what I gave Liv, I couldn't spare. When Graham walked in and we talked . . . I don't want to say he filled something inside me. That's too trite when you so desperately need what that person is giving you." I glance at him, and he nods.

"A meeting in my office turned into coffee and that led to dinner. A dinner I shouldn't have accepted, but stupidly, I did." I pause and press my finger on a key. I don't know what note it is, but it hangs in the air until it dissolves into wisps of nothing. "I never had a real relationship with my mother. I worked twelve, fourteen hour days, all for her to be proud of me for one second. She never was. Nothing I did was good enough, and when I met Graham, I didn't have to be anybody else. I could just be me. Until you meet someone who can give you that, you have no idea what a gift it is."

"I know, angel. You're my someone. I've never had to be anyone else around you."

I stare at the piano keys, my tears sparkling on the ivory. I stopped crying. I said I would leave California with my eyes dry, and I will.

"Talking with Judd was an eye-opening experience. He said he felt coerced into selling the bar, said he didn't have a choice because of life's circumstances. He did have a choice, though, even if not selling would have been the hardest thing he's ever done. My mother didn't give me choices, but like Judd, I had power. I just didn't use it. I could have fled, but I didn't. I stayed, did what she told me to do. From the way I held a fork to the way I fixed my hair, every choice I ever made was hers. I had nothing, With Liv mourning, I had no one, until I met Graham.

"He took me to a hotel the first night we made love. He was tender and gentle, and he made me laugh. He was perfect, but he didn't take his wedding ring off."

Brock sharply inhales and stiffens next to me.

"I knew what I was doing falling into bed with him, and for three years he told me he loved me and then went home to another woman. When I signed a book that turned out to be a fraud, I was in such a terrible place. Liv couldn't get out of bed, and every day I would stop by, take Scout for a walk, fix her a meal, do her laundry, and push her into the shower, while my mother hated me for smearing our agency's reputation and industry magazines wrote long, drawn-out articles about me and my unfortunate mistake. Graham was there for all of it, and when he would be done filming for the night, he would sit with me while I cried. He would hold me and tell me no matter what, he loved me. I don't know where I would be right now if I hadn't had him. But that's only an excuse, and a poor one. There's nothing that justifies me being with a married man."

"You broke it off before you visited Olivia."

"Yeah, I did. I wanted better. I wanted a commitment. I didn't want to be the other woman anymore. I met her once, at a bar, when I was there for a literary thing. I bumped into them, and he introduced us, cool as you please, his arm around her shoulders, her wedding ring sparkling. She was gorgeous and friendly, and when she shook my hand and said it was nice to meet me, I felt so dirty. I finally broke it off. I thought I loved him, but when I told him I didn't want to see him anymore, all I felt was relief."

I risk a glance at him, but he's staring at the keys, his face blank.

"A few nights ago, I texted him and told him I met you and had fallen in love. He told me he was ready to divorce her and asked me to marry him—that's what he had to rearrange. I don't want him to divorce her for me. The very last thing I want is to be a homewrecker. It's bad enough he gave me his time when it wasn't his to give, but I was selfish and took it because I needed it. I know you won't want a woman who would do that. Three years is a long time to do something you shouldn't be doing."

My cell laying on his piano lights up with a text, the car service letting me know my ride is waiting. I don't have much more to say.

"My car is outside. I have to go."

"What will you do?" His voice is rough.

"He wants to pick me up at the airport. I'll let him, tell him once and for all we're done, and when he drops me off, that will be it. Then I'll go to work on Monday and clean out my desk. I can't work for her anymore. I need to find something that's mine, no matter how small it is. In my whole life, I've never had one thing that's been mine alone. My career, my man. They've belonged to someone else, and I don't want to live that way anymore. I don't have a passion, don't have any skills. Maybe I'll move to New York and sing jazz in little rundown dive bars." I try to laugh, but it doesn't work. "I don't know." I turn toward him, and the pinched look is there on his face, like he has a headache ibuprofen didn't help. "You are going to be okay. Talk to Sheppard's therapist, spend time with your daughters. Find a woman who's not a fucking cheat. Marry her, and be happy."

I stand from the bench and brush a kiss over his stubbly

cheek. "Thank you, for these two weeks. I'll never forget them."

He doesn't say anything or try to stop me, but I knew he wouldn't.

The car's waiting in Brock's driveway, and the young girl with a pink and white 49ers cap helps me put my suitcases in the back of her SUV. I replay what I told him over and over, and there's nothing else I would've added. I told him everything. It's difficult hiding a secret, and it's nice to be able to breathe, even if it feels like I'm inhaling shards of glass.

Liv's waiting for me, standing near Eddie's car, her arms wrapped around herself in worry. Her shoulders slump when she sees the SUV and not Brock's car, but she knew it would turn out this way.

The girl unloads my suitcases, wishes us a goodnight, and drives away. I slide my cell out of my purse and complete our transaction, giving her a generous tip for letting me sit in silence.

"Are you okay?" she asks.

"Yeah. It went better than I thought. He listened, which was more than I hoped for, and I left. Now I just need a really big glass of wine and to cuddle on Mason for a while." I force myself to smile. Things will be all right.

"Both are inside. Come on."

I sip wine, snuggle Mason in my arms, and chat with Clarissa and Abby. Eddie stares at me with narrowed eyes, probably still angry I defended Brock and what he did.

The house feels empty with Eunice and Tony gone, and Brock's absence is palpable.

The evening melts into night, and Eddie and Sheppard start a bonfire on the beach.

Mason falls asleep, and I hold him while I sit next to the fire.

No matter how close I am, I'm still freezing.

Chapter Twenty-Seven

Brock

I don't know how long Agatha's story traps me on that bench, and for the first time in my life, I sit behind a piano and don't play a single note.

The sun sets, and with my back screaming, I stagger to my feet and into the kitchen. She returned my flask, and in the oven's dim overhead light, the metal glimmers. I go upstairs to change out of my jeans, and it's funny how quickly I got used to her things in my space. Her suitcases are gone, her makeup bag, hairbrush, and toothbrush missing from the vanity. She made the bed, and it will stay that way. I won't sleep tonight.

Wearing shorts, I go downstairs, and I feel her walking next to me, her bare feet barely touching the wood, she moved so gracefully. I pour a drink into one of the old glasses my mother used to entertain on the rare occasions she invited her friends over, and I sit at the pool alone, my feet in the water. We haven't done this for a few days, spending our evenings at Olivia and Shep's instead, but I imagine what we would talk about if she were here with me now. More about Polly and what drove me to work with Sharyn. She defended me, but there wasn't time for her to ask me why. Maybe she didn't need to. I was with Polly for the same reasons she was with Graham. I had nowhere else to go.

We would make plans for tomorrow. She and Clarissa sorting through more of her slush while Eddie, Shep, and I worked on the album. Lunch at Shep's, a quiet dinner here, a movie afterward, and a long night of making love. I could fall into a comfortable routine like that. She said she'd go with me to Royce's, but she can't do that now. I wanted her to go to the newspaper's offices with me too, and meet the editor there, but she won't do that, either. I haven't checked my email for the times he sent. Maybe I won't bother.

Tomorrow night, I see Polly. Holding her and talking about mundane things is a better alternative than spending the night by myself when I know Agatha's in Minnesota and won't be coming back. I shouldn't be alone right now.

Out of the corner of my eye, I see Eddie striding across the yard, his jaw set, and I stiffen. I'm sure he wants to bitch me out more for using Sharyn to meet Polly and Anne. He might have apologized after Agatha defended me, but that doesn't mean he agreed with her or that he's going to forgive me.

"Why aren't you at Shep's? We lit a bonfire on the beach. Agatha looks sad as fuck. What happened?" He sits next to me, the pool lights catching the hard glint in his eyes and the scruff along his jaw.

"We broke up."

"Because of her mom?"

Her mother didn't worry me. No matter how big of a battle axe she is, I could have talked to her. I would have told her I was in love with her daughter and wanted to marry her, and would with or without her blessing. Maybe it would have pissed her off, but I think eventually she would have come around. It sounded like the woman was all about appearances, and there's nothing she would have liked more than being able to say her daughter bagged a rich rockstar. That's just the way some people are.

I sip my drink and catch a flash of Agatha's feet in the water, the scent of her chocolate body lotion on the breeze, her hair dancing around her shoulders, and the quiet sympathy she was always quick to give me. "No. The ex-boyfriend she told me about was married. He wants to divorce his wife and marry her."

He frowns. "And that's what she wants?"

"She said no." I believed her when she said she would break it off with Graham for good and tell her mother to shove it.

"Then I don't know what the problem is."

I scoff. "She slept with a married man for three years. You don't see anything wrong with that?"

"I think you're a fucking hypocrite if *you* think there's something wrong with it." He steals my glass and drains it.

"Thanks a lot. If this is about Polly—"

"It's not. It's about you talking to me right now after what I admitted to you about my role in Derrick's death. It's about you fucking talking to me right now after knowing I slept with Clarissa for a year while she was Derrick's wife. It's about you, waving that aside and saying you're still my friend. So, which is it? Are you my friend or not?"

"I don't know, Eddie. You tell me. You wanted to punch me for using Sharyn, when all our lives you've protected me against bullies who wanted to do the same because I'm different. *Are* we friends?"

He springs to his feet and sets the empty glass on a patio table. All the furniture from the party is still scattered around my yard. I haven't had time to put it back into storage.

"Agatha made me see things clearly. You were only doing

what you had to do to stay sane, and I get it. After Shelly divorced me, I was fucking lonely, and dating felt so hollow. I didn't know if I would find someone who cared about me as a person, not Eddie Conrad, Ghost Town's drummer. You talk like I haven't been in your shoes, and I have, the only difference is we didn't handle things the same way. I could even say you were smarter about it than I was. I suffered alone until I met Clarissa. At least you did something. You're punishing Agatha for doing something, too. I've listened to her and Olivia talk, and for a long time Agatha was in a rough spot. Why do you get to find what you need, but she can't?"

"With a married man? How am I supposed to trust her?" I get to my feet, too, my joints creaking. I don't like him standing over me.

Eddie laughs, bitterly. "How is she supposed to trust *you?* You were the one paying for sex. She might have wrapped that up with a shiny bow, but it's not like you were keeping your dick in your pants for the past five years."

"I would never cheat on her."

"And for all you know, she would never cheat on you. What you're telling me is I shouldn't trust Clarissa because she fell into my bed so fast with another man's ring on her finger. If you're that insecure, then maybe it is better that you let her go. But at least she told you."

"What's that supposed to mean?" I grab the glass off the table and stalk toward the house. I need another drink.

Eddie follows. "She didn't have to tell you. You think that married guy is shouting it from the rooftops? You never would have known if she hadn't said something. When you let her leave, all you did was tell her the truth doesn't mean jack shit. So, good job. Next time she won't say a goddamned thing."

I open the patio door and rush to the bar. My hand trembles as I reach for the decanter. "Next time?"

"Are you a fucking idiot? You can be damned sure there's going to be a next time. You think she's going to stay single for the rest of her life? The next man she meets, she won't say anything because she's smart and she'll have learned her lesson."

I swallow. *The next man she meets . . .* Of course she'll meet someone else. Agatha is gorgeous and kind; I'm lucky I had a chance with her at all.

"I knew if I didn't tell Clarissa about Derrick it would eventually eat me alive and destroy us. I could have hated her for keeping Mason's paternity a secret—I missed out on a lot not knowing. But I forgave her for not telling me, and she forgave me for premeditated murder. Not quite even, but it is what it is. We started our relationship with a clean slate. Why can't you do the same?"

"I don't know."

"Yes, you do. Hey."

He waits until I look at him.

"What's the real reason you let her pack and walk out of here?"

The words tumble out. "I'm afraid our marriage will end up like mine and Bri's. I'm too different, too weird, and she'll grow to hate me, and if we have kids—I can't lose them. Not having Lexi and Layla in my life killed me. If I wouldn't have had Ghost Town, I don't know, Eddie. Everyone says I'm passionate, and they try to twist that into a good thing, but every ounce of pain feels more like a hundred thousand tons, and I can't live through that again." I knock back the whiskey, the burn warring with the tears in the back of my throat.

"When Agatha defended you . . . you didn't see her face. She was fierce, a mama bear protecting her cub. She loves you, but I can't promise you'll be together forever. Shit happens. But what I can say, and what I told Clarissa, is this: keep communication *open.* I said, 'If you're ever unhappy, tell me. Don't tell Ginger, or Vonnie, don't tell Olivia. Tell *me,* because I'm the only one who can do anything about it.' Shep didn't have an issue with Melody cheating, not deep down. He wanted to know if she was unhappy and why. Check in, be present. I'm not blaming you for your marriage to Bri going south, but maybe you could have stepped up. You hide when things go wrong, and you can't always do that. You're doing it now."

I glance at him in surprise. I am hiding, and when Bri turned nasty, I never stood up for myself. It was easier to run away.

"That doesn't mean it will save your marriage if it comes to that, but maybe it will." He blows out a breath. "She's miserable, and if you saw her for even just a second, you would know she regrets what she did. You both have things you're sorry for. Put it away."

"What should I do?" I want to see her, apologize and explain, but I don't know if she'll listen to me.

"Tell her the truth, and then thank her for telling hers."

Eddie drives, and I stare out the window. My mind is a messy jumble of past mistakes and a foggy future. Agatha has never not given me a chance to explain my side, and I can only hope she still will.

Olivia's standing in the kitchen, a mug of something that hints of peppermint cradled in her hands. Shadows rest under her eyes, and her face is creased with worry.

"Is she okay?" I ask urgently, the picture of Agatha standing in the water slamming into my brain.

Helplessly, she shakes her head. "She's on the beach."

"I fucked up, but I'll take care of her. I promise."

All she does is stare.

I rush onto the patio and down to the sand.

Shep's strumming his guitar near the fire, and Gina and Jeff are sitting close to him, whispering to each other. Clarissa's holding a sleeping Mason near Abby who's listening to something on her phone. There are a few others from neighboring houses, murmuring lowly and sipping beer.

I search for Agatha and find her near the water, her knees tucked under her chin. Scout's next to her, and she's absently rubbing the dog's head.

I stumble across the sand, and she looks my way.

Her eyes are dry, but they're flat. She sees me, but she doesn't.

"Angel." Jesus Christ, I love her so much.

"What are you doing here? Did I forget something at your house?"

"Yeah, yeah you did."

"I'm sorry. Whatever it is, you can throw it away."

"No, I can't. You forgot me, angel, and you forgot our life together."

She looks toward the water. "I don't know what you mean."

"Can I sit for a minute?"

She shrugs.

I sit next to her, my heart skittering, the sweat on my skin cooling to icy apprehension in the breeze coming off the water. She lets me hold her hand, and I rub her finger where I'm going to slide a ring and claim her for the rest of my life. "You know the kind of marriage I had with Bri. When we first met, it was quick, like you and me. When I tossed that flask into your lap, I knew things would be different, and they were. It scared the fuck out of me, angel."

"It scared me too, because I knew all along you wouldn't

forgive me for Graham." She tries to yank her hand away, but I hold on.

"It's not that. It's not him."

She scoffs.

"It's true. Eddie knocked some sense into me—"

Her gaze whips to mine. "He went to see you? I thought he was mad at me for sticking up for you."

"No. He's on your side, and he told me I was a fucking idiot for letting you walk away. He made me admit a lot of things. I don't want our marriage to end up like mine and Bri's. I honestly could not live through that again. It might sound melodramatic, but it's true, and I think it's true for Shep, too. The past year hasn't been easy on him, and you know how much he loves Olivia. If she were to disappear, he would be devastated, and I would be exactly like that. I lied to myself and said it was better to lose you now, for some stupid thing like your relationship with Graham, than a few years down the road when you get tired of me and how I am."

Shaking her head, she says, "I will never get tired of you, and I will never be jealous of your accomplishments. You know that. All I've done since I've met you is encourage you to be who you are."

"I know, but I've never been this lucky, and it's a difficult concept to grasp."

The bonfire reflects in her watery blue eyes. "You really don't care about Graham?" she asks.

I wrap my arm around her shoulders. "Of course I care, angel."

She stiffens and tries to pull away.

I tighten my hold. "Not the way you think. I wish he hadn't hurt you. I wish, with some sick nobility on my part, that he would have been free to marry you so you didn't have to go through that. He was there for you at a time in your life when you needed someone, and it's not my place to judge where you found support when I did the same thing. If you don't take into consideration he's married, he actually sounds like a nice guy who did what he could for you."

"Yeah, he is." She sighs. "What were you thinking?"

"Do you still love me, angel?"

She scrubs at my beard, and holy fuck, it was only a few hours, but I missed her touch so much. "You know I do."

"I love you, too, with all my heart." I pause. "We jumped into this quickly, and what would ease my mind is if we had a long engagement. I want time to get to know you. Time to set up a house, let you have space to figure out what you want to do for work, if you want to work. You don't have to. I've got a little money to support us."

Her lips twist. "What would I do if I didn't work? Stand around and look pretty?"

I brush my thumb over her cheek. "You would do it so well."

"All I know how to be is an agent."

"Then be one. Open your own agency. Tuck Clarissa under your wing where she wants to be and make it work."

She bites her lip. "What about kids?"

"When we met, you said you weren't the maternal type. If you meant that, it's okay, but if you think it would be something you'd consider down the road, we can talk. It doesn't have to be this year, or even next year. I want time, Agatha. More than anything, I just want time. I love you, and I almost let you leave." I try so hard not to, but I start crying. My emotions are such a deep well, a bottomless pit, I can never keep them at bay.

She kneels in front of me, her knees sinking into the sand, and wraps her arms around me. I sob into her neck, my fingers grasping at her hair, a lifeline.

Sniffling into my ear, she says, "My mother isn't going to like this."

I kiss the tears off her cheeks, my lips gliding over her soft skin. "Will you be okay if she cuts you off? Were you serious about that?"

She wipes away my tears, too, and I lean in, so grateful she'll never make me feel ashamed for the ways I express myself.

"While Eddie was talking to you, Scout and I had a heart to heart."

At the mention of her name, Scout lifts her head and whines.

"If she doesn't talk to me anymore, it won't be much of a change from the way things are now. I don't know what made her the way she is. Maybe someone hurt her and she couldn't recover, or she was raised how she raised me. I don't know if my childhood would have been different if I would have had a dad. Maybe he would have been just as strict and as cold as she is and I would have lived with what I did times two." She shudders out a breath. "What I'll gain marrying you and moving here can't compete with what I'll lose if my mother decides never to speak to me again. I just need to be brave until my heart catches up with my mind and what I know. Will you help me?"

I lower her to the sand, and with my lips brushing hers, I say, "Yeah. I will. Marry me, Agatha Sterling. Marry me on a night like this, with the stars shining and the moon a witness to the love we found. We'll do it all—travel, spend time with friends, build careers. We can buy a new house if you want—"

"I like your house," she interrupts. "I have fond memories of the island in your kitchen."

"Okay, we'll keep the house. I like living down the road from Eddie and Clarissa anyway. But more than anything, angel, marry me so I know when I wake up at 3 AM I'm not alone and when you have trouble falling asleep, I'll hold you until the sun comes up. We'll start every new day together."

"Yes," she whispers, and I cover her mouth with mine. Her lips are soft and sweet, hinting of salt and promises.

Our friends catcall to us, Eddie's voice rising above the rest, and Scout barks, jumping in the sand, catching the excitement in the air.

My life has been full of jagged notes and shattered guitars, but there won't be any more tears on my piano keys.

Now, when I play piano in the dark, I won't be alone, ever again. Agatha will be with me, and I'll be more than happy to give her the spotlight and let her sing.

Chapter Twenty-Eight

Brock

I could have ended our story there, but you probably want to know how things turned out with Agatha's mom.

The next day, Agatha called her, said she wouldn't be back for a few more days, and rescheduled her flight. I'm going with her. There's no way I'm letting her face her mother alone.

Clarissa, as you can imagine, was over the moon when Agatha said she was staying, but not only staying, living down the street and wanting to open a literary agency with her. Clarissa might have been ecstatic, but it was Olivia who hugged Agatha and sobbed. Maybe after a time, Olivia would have found her place in LA working with Gina and making new friends, but having Agatha near will change everything for the better. Even Shep sagged in relief, the final puzzle piece nudged into the perfect place completing the new picture of our lives.

With Agatha's unwavering support, I texted Polly and canceled my evenings with her. Her fear vibrated through my phone when she responded, *Why?*

"I don't know what to tell her," I said helplessly, but Agatha, with her kindness and compassion, knew exactly what to say.

"Tell her you met someone, and you want to meet for coffee next week."

Then it was my turn to ask why.

"She needs the money you were paying her. She'll miss you . . . you're a nice guy and she counted on you being good to her, but she'll miss the money just as much. When you meet, you can explain you'll still fill in that income and that you're arranging for her to go to school. You don't have to stop being her friend because of me. I said I'd like to meet her, and that's still true."

"Are you sure?"

Agatha framed my face in her hands and kissed my forehead. "I'm sure."

"Thank you."

She smiled. "One down."

I blew out a breath. "Yeah."

Before we flew to Minneapolis, Agatha went with me to the newspaper's office and met the editor of the Entertainment & Arts section. It meant a lot she was there supporting me, but more than that, taking an interest in the things I want to do.

I made an appointment with Royce, too, and we managed to squeeze it in before we left. She silently held my hand the entire time, letting me lead, only adding her opinion when I asked. It was terrifying, but there was something akin to relief when he agreed with Agatha's suspicions and we came up with a plan. I walked out of his office with a month of scheduled sessions and a prescription, but she stopped me in the hall.

"Fill it only if you want to. There's no pressure to do anything you don't want to do. I will stand by you with anything you choose, no matter what."

I kissed her hard, grateful she understood my hesitation. I may need time and a little push to fill it and see what medication will do for me. When we flew out of LAX, I still hadn't called the pharmacy. Agatha knew. Let me know she knew, but was leaving the decision up to me.

She fidgeted during the entire flight, and I distracted her the only way I knew how: with conversation, kisses, and whiskey.

"It's going to be okay," I say, covering her hands with mine on the drive to her mother's agency.

"I know. I've always wanted her approval. Worked for it all my life. I never earned it."

"You don't need it, angel. You don't need anyone's."

She presses her face into my shoulder and squeezes my hand.

The car lets us off in front of a highrise in downtown Minneapolis, but Agatha asks our driver to circle the block until we're done. Our suitcases are in the trunk and we don't want to bother with unloading them.

"Jesus Christ, angel. How much do literary agents make?" I ask, staring at the glass sparkling in the sun.

"Ah, it depends, but we do okay."

We enter the lobby through revolving doors, and I stop her under an elegant chandelier. "Tell me again how much you have in savings?"

She rolls her eyes. "A couple million, but I've never considered it mine."

I hook an arm around her neck and press my lips to her temple. "I think it's time."

She pauses when I try to move forward, sucks in a breath, and meets my gaze. There's something there in the deep blue, something she found in her time in LA speaking with Gina, showing Clarissa how to be an agent, and supporting Olivia, but it doesn't scare me, not like it would have. She's coming into her own, and there's nothing I want more than to be there, encourage her, and help her find what she's lived without for the past thirty-six years. "I think so, too."

"Good girl."

We ride to the fifteenth floor, and she leads me to a huge business suite. Sterling Literary Agency is written in bold font on one wall, and a receptionist sitting under the letters answers a phone. She waves at Agatha, and we walk past her.

"Can I see your office?" I ask, following her down a hallway.

"Yeah, sure," she says, forcing enthusiasm into her voice, but my angel's energy and vitality drain out of her right before my eyes. She loses her sparkle, and I want nothing more than to wrap my arms around her and protect her.

Her office is enormous and a wall of windows offers a beautiful view of downtown, but the space isn't hers. There isn't anything personal on her desk or hanging on the walls, nothing that would indicate a woman made of flesh and blood with heart and feelings worked here.

I rest my hand on the nape of her neck and ask her to look at me. "I love you. The years you spent in this office are a part of who you are, and I love everything about you. Take the good, leave the bad. No matter how your mother treated you, you are special, Agatha, and I am humbled you love me when you could have anyone."

She nuzzles my cheek with her nose. "I thought that about you, too."

"Then we both win. Let's talk to your mom. After that, we'll go to your place, open a bottle of wine, and order a meal. I know you hate traveling, and we'll decompress."

"No pool."

I chuckle. "Soon."

We walk down the carpeted hallway tastefully decorated with framed book covers, and her shoulders hunch the closer we get to her mother's office. Various office doors are open, and one woman with a sincere smile calls out as we pass, "It's nice to have you back, Agatha. We missed you."

"Is she a friend?" I ask.

"We have lunch together every once in a while, but I wouldn't call her a friend."

She stops in front of a door with a name plaque that says, *Diane Sterling*. She knocks once and waits.

"Come in," a raspy voice commands.

"Does your mom smoke?"

"No. It's from yelling at all the editors because her authors didn't get a big enough advance."

"Seriously?"

"Kind of. No. She's a big baseball fan and the Twins probably lost. Again."

Agatha doesn't let me respond. She opens the door and steps inside, and I follow her into an office even larger than hers.

A woman maybe twenty years or so older than me sits behind a massive wooden desk and doesn't look our way until she's done reading whatever it is she's reading on a giant computer monitor. This must be a common occurrence because all Agatha does is stand and wait. Several long moments later, with precision, she turns toward us, and Agatha starts to tremble. I'm not sorry for stealing this woman's daughter away from her.

"Mom, I'd like you to meet Brock Farris. Brock, my mother, Diane Sterling."

Diane rises from her chair and looks at me over the rims of her black-framed glasses. I can pick out one or two features that Agatha inherited from her, but that's it. She must take after her father. I wonder if, through the years, that hurt either of them.

Her mother shakes my hand, her grip warm, dry, and firm, but she doesn't say anything.

"Brock's—"

"I know who he is."

She doesn't say it's nice to meet me.

Agatha licks her lips and plows on, "We fell in love, and he asked me to marry him. I said yes. I'm moving to LA, and I want to open my own agency."

There isn't an ounce of anything in this woman's expression. No joy, no anger, no surprise I rushed her daughter through a two-week courtship. There's nothing. She searches Agatha's face for a moment, places her hands on Agatha's shoulders, and kisses her cheek. "Good luck."

With those two simple words, she sits behind her desk and resumes reading.

Agatha backs out of the room and once we're both standing in the hallway, she shuts the door.

Throwing herself against me, she presses her face against my neck and hugs me, her arms around my waist. I think she's crying, but she leans away, grinning.

"Was that what you expected?" I ask, confused.

She shakes her head. "No. I thought she would hate me, but she doesn't."

No one is stronger than Agatha. All she needed was for her mother not to hate her for falling in love, wanting to get married, and moving to another state. Diane Sterling may be a lot of things and I may never see her again, but I whisper a silent "Thank you" for giving Agatha something she desperately needed to move on in her life with me.

She doesn't have many things to retrieve from her office, and we exit the building just in time to flag down our car.

"Is leaving that simple?" I ask, opening the car's door for her.

She slides in and sets the paper bag of memorabilia on the floor near her feet. "No. I have established authors and deals in progress I can't abandon, like Liv and her book. Mom knows this, and she'll let me do my job, even if it is from LA. It may not have seemed like it, but she gave me permission to open my own agency, and what I do will still reflect on her, our name, and our reputation. Eventually, I'll give my authors a choice to follow me or find new representation. I don't want to rep nonfiction for the rest of my life, and over the next few years I'll slowly phase it out, unless Clarissa wants to take it over. Once we get married and I change my name, the agency will feel more like mine, but there's time for all that."

I like the part where she's going to change her name. "Then it worked out?" I'm still confused. Her mother said fewer than ten words to us, and that's generous. I included when she said we could go into her office.

She twists in her seat and beams. "It worked out. She won't come to our wedding, even if we invite her, she won't visit Clarissa's and my office once we get it set up, and she won't care when we have a baby—" she squeezes my bicep "—but it went better than I could have hoped. Now I *really* need a glass of wine. I don't have a room full of it, but I've got a couple bottles."

"I'm happy for you, angel." I pause. "Why did she have you?"

"I thought about that a lot. Even talked to Liv about it. I think she wanted to live her life again, through me. She had me just before she turned forty, and looking back, it seemed almost a response to a mid-life crisis. Maybe it was. She wanted a do-over, and she found it in me, except, she forced me to make the choices she already made, so I'm not sure if she gained anything from it. All I can be thankful for is I'm free of her control, and I'm so happy you love me."

"I do, angel. I really do."

"I know. I love you, too."

That's all the time for conversation we have. The driver glides to a stop in front of another highrise, double parking and engaging the hazard lights to give us time to unload our suitcases.

A dark-haired man wearing a suit steps out of the building as our car melts into traffic.

"Graham," Agatha says, surprised. "What are you doing here?"

"I called your mother and asked when you would be back. She gave me nothing, as you can imagine, and I went up to see if you'd come home without telling me." His gaze flicks to me. "Is this him?"

"Yes. Brock Farris, Graham Calloway. Graham, Brock."

Calloway holds out his hand, and I shake it. I don't hold any ill-will toward the guy. That's not my place.

He shoves his hands into the pockets of his dress slacks, keys and coins jingling. "You really meant it, then."

Agatha tucks herself into my side. "Yeah. I did. I appreciate all you did for me, Graham. I do, but it wasn't right and we both know it. I wish you nothing but the best." She reaches for a suitcase.

"Don't leave like that, Agatha. I know I'm a son of a bitch, but that doesn't mean I lied. I love you, I care about you, and if Farris is who you want, who you need, I'm happy for you." He holds out his arms, and tentatively, she steps into them.

It's difficult watching him hug her. He genuinely cares about her, and I know without a doubt, if he would have been free to do so, he would have married her. What their marriage would have looked like, you probably know, and some things turn out just the way they're supposed to.

He releases her and says to me, "Take care of her."

"I will. Thank you for everything you did for her." I pause. "A bit of advice?"

Calloway sets his jaw. "Yeah."

"Fix your marriage or cut her loose and let her find someone who will give her a hundred percent. It's what she deserves. Agatha's mine now. I don't share." I keep my eyes locked on his until he nods in acknowledgement and only then do I look away. I pick up both our suitcases. "Come on, angel. I have plans for you."

I say it to jab Calloway, but also to hear her laugh.

She does, her eyes sparkling. "That's two," she says, opening the glass door of her building.

"That's two." I look through the glass and Calloway's still standing there, his eyes narrowed, his shoulders stiff.

We ride the elevator to the twentieth floor, but I don't give her a second after she unlocks the door to her apartment.

I back her against the wall, my fingers desperately searching for the hem of her dress.

"What are you doing?" she asks breathlessly.

"Celebrating."

We don't stop until the sun rises.

That would be a good place to end our story, too, but honestly, I could write about us for the rest of my life and never run out of things to say.

We hire movers to pack up her things and transport them to LA. Her apartment is a reflection of her office: nothing personal, a place she lived that her mother chose, but short of a library, I don't think I've seen so many books. (I'm glad I'm not the one moving them.) I would insist on us buying a new house together if I didn't have such fond memories of my kitchen island, too, never mind my sunroom floor. I want her to have a say in all things, always.

She introduces me to Olivia's mom and stepdad who offers to marry us, too. We happily accept.

We're only in Minneapolis for a few days before we fly out, eager to begin our lives.

I think I'll end our story with us sitting by the pool, our feet gently moving back and forth, glasses of whiskey in our hands. My daughters are inside with Abby baking a cake, and we can hear shrieks of laughter from here. We're having everyone over later, an engagement party of sorts now that I finally bought Agatha a ring.

"Kinda crazy how you changed my life," I say.

She tilts her head and smiles. "Kinda crazy how you changed mine."

"You know what I think?" I ask, reaching for her glass and setting it next to mine near the edge of the pool.

"What?"

"You haven't been swimming yet."

She laughs when she realizes my intention, but she doesn't stop me.

I tug her into the water, and with my mouth fused to hers, we sink to the bottom.

I'm not scared. Her love will always lift me up.

Chapter Twenty-Nine

Dalton

I bet Tony made you stop and think, huh? Who really killed Derrick.

You know I can't carry a tune to save my life or play a musical instrument? Shep probably told you that. The guys owe him a lot. I've heard Brock and Eddie admit it, and I owe him a lot too. Bands need managers, yeah, but he could have found anybody to do my job. It was our friendship that made me a millionaire, plain and simple.

I knew some things, like Derrick turning into an absolute prick and a drunk. I knew he was hitting Clarissa, and Eddie pounding on my door desperate for revenge was a pleasant surprise as I was trying to figure out in my own way how to stop it. I didn't know others, like him beating on other women until Sharyn went to jail for covering it up. I knew Mason belonged to Eddie, but there's just some shit you don't step in, and that was one of them. That worked out. Don't you think?

I knew Brock was "dating" but that didn't concern me one

way or the other. He told me, in fact, concerned when Derrick threatened to expose his trips to North Hollywood. For the band, you know? Can't do anything to hurt the band.

My biggest regret is what it did to Shep. Not the cheating part. Derrick's death. I knew he had depression, not bad, it just made him quiet and maybe sad. Nothing like what he became after Derrick's death. Suicidal.

After a year of it, I'd had enough. He was my best friend— sleeping with his wife didn't change that. Not before he knew, anyway. I didn't know what to do. I talked to Melody, and she was the one who suggested someone move in with him. She said having someone with him twenty-four/seven would snap him out of it, if only long enough to understand he needed more serious help. I had no experience with that kind of thing, and I'm not too proud to admit I was glad she knew what he needed. Being she'd been his wife and all.

I couldn't find anyone willing to give up that much time. A whole summer. You have no idea how fucking deep I had to dig to find poor little washed up Olivia Bloom.

And that, as the cliché goes, is how history is made.

My son yawns and burrows into my chest. Melody had an easy time of it, thank Christ. No one wants to experience what Eddie and Clarissa went through. Such a fucking gamble. I brush a kiss over his head and rest my hand on his back, feeling him breathe.

Agatha drifts across the pool area holding a bottle, a spit-up cloth, and a drink that I hope is a rum and Coke. "I was sent on a mission," she says, sliding into a chair next to me. "Melody said you might be needing these soon."

"Thanks." I pick up the drink and sip. I love that woman.

Ghost Town didn't play for Shep and Olivia's wedding reception, but it doesn't stop people from dancing to the piped-in music. When they asked if they could have their wedding and reception here, I couldn't say no. I'd do anything if Shep forgives me. Maybe in time, he will. He still doesn't know everything. Doesn't know what Derrick did to Shelly and Brianna. Doesn't know Eddie's role in Derrick's death. He won't ever know. There's no reason for it. The past, I think, is finally in the past.

Shep and Olivia are dancing, his arms snug around her. I might know a lot, but when I hired her, I didn't know what I was starting. I honestly didn't know.

"Do you ever get scared thinking about what would have happened if I wouldn't have been able to convince Liv to take this job?" she asks, watching them sway.

"If I think about it long enough, I break out into a cold sweat," I joke, but it's not.

"I wanted her to take this job as much as you did. God, what a summer," she says, tipping her head back. "I think she got what she wanted."

I raise my eyebrows in question.

"Oh, the showing thing. Her dress hides it well."

"It does. Brock okay?" He started taking the medication Shep's therapist prescribed him.

"We're still getting used to it."

"That was a good call—the ADHD thing." One of the few things I didn't know.

She tips her head in acknowledgement.

"What do you think?" I ask.

"Of what?"

I wave my glass toward the party. "All of it. Do you believe I killed Derrick?"

"Do you really want to know?"

"Yeah."

"I think Brock killed Derrick that night."

The sound of blood rushes in my ears, and I need all my willpower to act naturally. "Why do you say that?"

She sits back and crosses her legs. "He was the one who had the most to lose. He knew you were having an affair with Melody and he didn't want Sheppard to find out that way. He knew Eddie was having an affair with Clarissa, and he would have done whatever he needed to do to protect his best friend. Derrick was threatening him and he needed to protect himself. That's why no one would ever suspect it was Brock. He didn't kill Derrick for the band. He did it to protect himself and his friends." She smiles and sips my drink. "Of course, that's all conjecture. I don't have proof Brock knew any of that, and I'll never ask."

"How would you feel, being engaged to a murderer?"

She plays with the ring on her left hand. "I think I would be honored to marry a man who would do whatever it took to keep me safe."

Brock approaches our table and hugs Agatha from behind. She melts into him, and even married to Brianna, I have never seen him look so peaceful and settled. "Dance with me, angel, and then let me feed you some cake."

She laughs. "Now there's an offer I can't refuse."

Before she leaves, she kisses the top of my precious boy's head and presses a kiss to my cheek as well. "Thank you for calling me."

I squeeze her hand.

Melody sits in Agatha's seat, and we watch our friends in contented silence.

It's difficult to pinpoint when this story started. When Melody and I fell in love? When Melody and Shep fell out? When Derrick turned into an asshole? It wasn't when I picked up the phone and called Agatha. Fate has a way of beginning something long before we realize it.

I'll never say if I pushed Derrick. Maybe, in the scheme of things, it doesn't matter.

But I can tell you this.

It was a pleasure watching him fall.

If you loved this trilogy, I have another available! The Lost &
Found Trilogy featuring three very stubborn, rich, and hand-
some men and the women who love them is available in Kindle,
Kindle Unlimited, and Paperback.

https://www.amazon.com/dp/B0BR88G4KJ

For news, cover reveals, bonus content, and more, sign up for my newsletter at www.vmrheault.com/subscribe. As a thank you, you'll be able to download a free full-length ugly-duckling billionaire novel, *My Biggest Mistake*.

Acknowledgments

Putting a book together is quite a task, never mind a trilogy.

I'd like to thank S.J. Cairns for helping me with the blurbs for these books. I'd also like to thank Lisa Lane for proofing the paperbacks. Your time is valuable and much appreciated.

Thank you to my online friends for your constant support and to the various Facebook groups for your time, wisdom, and resources.

And a special thanks to my sister, who contributed in no way towards this trilogy but at least she's not problematic. (This is a joke, but I told her I would include it. Her support means a lot to me!)

VM Rheault writes billionaire romance and contemporary romance under Vania Rheault.

She lives in Minnesota with her two children. When she's not writing, she's working her day job, sleeping, or enjoying the four seasons with a hot cup of coffee in hand.

Find her at vmrheault.com.

Captivated by Her (Cedar Hill Duet Book One)

Addicted to Her (Cedar Hill Duet Book Two)

Rescue Me

Give & Take (The Lost & Found Trilogy Book One)

Lost & Found (The Lost & Found Trilogy Book Two)

Safe & Sound (The Lost & Found Trilogy Book Three)

Faking Forever

Twisted Alibis (Ghost Town Trilogy Book One)

Twisted Lullabies (Ghost Town Trilogy Book Two)

Twisted Lies (Ghost Town Trilogy Book Three)

A Heartache for Christmas